Children of Tiber and Nile

Book II of
The Rise of
Caesarion's Rome

by
Deborah L. Davitt

For more information on this book and others in the *Edda-
Earth* universe, please see **www.edda-earth.com**.

ISBN-10: 0-9860916-4-2
ISBN-13: 978-0-9860916-4-3
Library of Congress Control Number: 2017915246

Foreword

No book, as I've said before, is written in a vacuum. The Caesarion books are the ones I wanted to write for ages, but didn't think I had enough background in Roman history to write, without, well, obtaining for myself that level of education. Fortunately, a long-time reader of mine, Alexander Thomas, has his master's degree in Classical Studies, with a focus on Roman military equipment and strategy. I'd like to thank him for being a good guide as I've done my research, and always being available to tell me when the source I'm reading (Suetonius, for example), might just be the tabloid journalist of ancient Rome. I'd also like to thank Anastasia Ivanova, the Russian super-fan who translated part of the first chapter of *The Valkyrie*, and Laura Ballegeer, my Canadian super-fan, for their help and support. Without the enthusiasm and encouragement of people like this, I'm not sure you'd be holding this book today; it helps to be reassured that the work is solid on days in which you feel as if you've left your talent in your other set of pants.

I started writing Book IV of the Edda Prime series, and got to a certain point with it where I wasn't sure what the characters would do next; there were new ones in the mix, and they changed many things. I started writing Caesarion as a break from that, and writing the history of the early empire has vastly clarified for me where Edda Prime will go as Sigrun allows things to unfold that will repair the damage done in the War of the Gods. Yes, that's . . . vague. I'm sorry. Wait and see how it unfolds.

As you read these books, you may be struck by how similar Roman life is to modern western life. Some of their holidays—such as Mother's Day (Matronalia), or *Compitalia* (Halloween)—might bear some haunting similarities to how you celebrate such, yourself. Other customs, traditions, values, and attitudes *may offend you*. Please understand that the characters' attitudes and beliefs reflect those of their time, place, society, and position within that society. Those attitudes do not necessarily reflect mine. Thus, if you encounter two male characters having sex, but both of them view themselves as male, comport themselves as vigorously male, and they do not consider their sexuality to be their identity? Then it's not identity for them, and has very little to do with life in the 21st century of Real-Earth.

Likewise, women married *early* in Roman times—plebeians, strikingly, less so than noblewomen—and in this highly-stratified and traditional society, everyone had a place. Caesarion breaks several cardinal rules of Roman behavior throughout these books. However, he's god-born, and half-Egyptian. He *has* to change the rules.

If you've read much on the time-period, I hope you can accept that my perspective on alternate-timeline characters in history—from a Cleopatra who's outlived her Real-Earth lifespan, to an Octavian Thurinus who was never called Augustus *or* adopted into the Julii clan, to an older, more weary and cynical Marcus Antonius, or a younger, untried Tiberius—might not be how you've seen them when you've read them in the annals of history.

If you can't suspend your disbelief, or are easily offended by characters who may not share your particular modern attitudes and sensibilities, this book might not be for you. I hope, however, that you'll give it a try anyway. Sometimes delight comes in the most unexpected of places.

Chapter I: Plots

We denounce with righteous indignation and dislike men who are so beguiled and demoralized by the charms of pleasure of the moment, so blinded by desire, that they cannot foresee the pain and trouble that are bound to ensue; and equal blame belongs to those who fail in their duty through weakness of will, which is the same as saying through shrinking from toil and pain.

– Cicero, *De Finibus Bonorum et Malorum* (*The Ends of Good and Evil*)

Ianuarius 2, 20 AC

The vast temple complexes baked under the noonday sun, crowds of people lining up outside the steps of each, waiting to be permitted inside to kneel before statues of the gods and make their offerings. Wooden scaffolds leaned here and there against the ancient red-brown buildings, and workers dozed gently in their shadow, waiting for the sun to sink past zenith before returning to the labor of painting the turquoise, white, and yellow patterns on the this wall or that set of columns. Egypt's sun leeched the color from even the brightest pigments, given just a few years' time, and a recent sandstorm had left the great temples of Thebes looking a little more pock-marked than usual.

Inside one of the temples, a man knelt before an altar, whispering prayers to Isis. "My lady, let the pharaoh return to his land soon. The Nile's floods were late this past year, and we can scarcely feed ourselves, let alone send the grain that Rome demands of us." He sighed, lowering his head. "The pharaoh is Emperor of Rome, too. He must surely see our need. He and his queen must come, and renew the land."

Hearing no reply, and expecting none, he stood, and gave way to the teeming crowds behind him. Hundreds of people, each with their own request for the goddess. *Let my pregnancy come to term easily and with a healthy child to show for it. Bring plenty to my fields. Please heal my child's sickness. Please, when the gods weigh my husband's soul against the feather, find that it is light, and grant him safe passage through the underworld.* Thousands of voices, a susurration of whispers, continually crawling along the stone walls, like the flickering light of the lamps and torches. So many appeals—little wonder that the goddess did not see fit to answer each one.

In another temple, that of Thoth, whispers of a different sort. The highest-ranked of the mage-priests gathered, under the auspices of their high priest, Padubast, and knelt in a circle in the inner sanctum on reed mats on the cool stone floor. Eleven men in total. Bare-chested, each man wore a kilt of bleached white linen, contrasting starkly with the deep tans of their desert-touched skin. All shaven-pated with kohl-ringed eyes; most wore a bracelet or two in heavy gold to denote their rank. The high priest himself wore a heavy necklace in turquoise and lapis, with an image of Thoth cast in gold at the center. An elderly man, his hand trembled as he raised a reed he'd normally have used as a pen to call for order. "We have met to discuss this subject before," he rasped. "Tahut-Nefer, you spent over six months in the barbarian lands of Rome, attempting to instruct Princess Eurydice in the use of magic—before her marriage to our pharaoh, Ptolemy, whom Romans call Caesarion." He coughed into his hand.

Tahut-Nefer was a stout man in his late forties, with a cold set to his dark eyes. "I did," he said, taking the cough as enough of a pause to speak. "I found them both to be arrogant — "

"Pharaohs are always prideful," Padubast interrupted weakly. "They are the living embodiment of the gods. I have never met one who *wasn't* arrogant."

"The princess scorned all lessons in the use of her powers," Tahut snapped. "She refused to heed my words, and experimented freely, not conforming to the set use of spells handed down to us by the ancients. We all know what can happen when someone deviates from known uses of power. They can annihilate themselves — or worse, those around them. She has no respect for power, or the consequences of its use. They cannot be allowed to rule Egypt."

Murmurs through the room. Even meeting in such secrecy, such words were dangerous.

"And yet," Padubast whispered, "they have respected our ancient ways. The Pharaoh has taken his sister, the lady Eurydice, as his wife. Word has come even so far as this, that the gods of Rome themselves blessed the union — against the customs of their people — "

"The gods of Rome have blessed them," Tahut sneered. "The gods of Egypt have remained silent. And the Nile has not brought forth its floods. Our people starve. Surely, this is a sign that our gods, the most ancient and powerful in the world, do not favor these barbarians who claim the *names* of the royal line — "

"They are the children of Cleopatra and Caesar," another priest cut in sharply. "They have the blood. They have the name. They are god-born — she of Isis, Horus, and Venus, he of Mars, Venus, Isis, and Osiris. They have the right to rule — "

"And yet they do not," another priest argued, his eyes glittering with fervor. "Who remains prefect here but Gaius Cornelius Gallus, the same man who has held that post for ten long years? Governing in the name of Queen Cleopatra and Pharaoh Ptolemy. But he is nothing but a Roman administrator. He has no more power than the armies at his back—"

Padubast coughed into his hand. "Those have always been a convincing argument before. Most of you are too young to remember the last great uprising, almost sixty years ago. When the priests of Thebes joined together to rebel against the Ptolemy of the time. It was our second rebellion inside thirty years, and the pharaoh reduced much of this great city to ash and rubble. We have rebuilt. But we have only been able to do so because Queen Cleopatra has permitted it."

"Queen Cleopatra has spent most of her reign in *Rome*." Rumbles of dissent.

Padubast shrugged. "They will pay heed when their neglect causes Rome to starve."

"But our people will starve before theirs do!"

Mutters of discontent rang back from the walls.

Tahut raised a hand imperatively. "Gaius Cornelius Gallus has been sent into the countryside to collect the shortfall in grain levies," he told them all, his eyes gleaming in the dim light. "Perhaps this is an opportunity that we should exploit to . . . garner the attention of our pharaoh, his wife, and his mother. We can defy this Roman bureaucrat, thus forcing our wandering pharaoh to turn his eyes towards us. And once he is here, you may judge his fitness to rule us for yourselves."

"What alternative do we *have?*" Padubast asked, his reedy voice stern. "All the descendants of the pharaohs have been extinguished besides the line of Cleopatra."

Tahut shrugged. "She has other children. Alexander. Selene. A babe in arms with the uncouth Roman name of

Gaius. With proper education, these younger children might be properly instilled with Egyptian values." He eyed the others in the room, clearly gauging their mood. "Of course," he added smoothly, "removing the pharaoh is always a . . . tricky business. Perhaps it will not prove necessary. Perhaps once this particular descendant of the line of the Ptolemies sees Egypt for himself, he will find a proper love for the land in which he was born to burn within his breast. A proper respect for its culture and institutions." He nodded.

"Would not sending a letter be safer than staging some sort of uprising?" another priest asked timidly. "The Roman garrison in Alexandria is well-armed. Hundreds, even thousands of our people, could be slaughtered needlessly—"

"Have any of our *letters* been heeded yet?" Tahut spat.

"A vote," Padubast said wearily. "All in favor of provoking the Roman garrison, please raise your hands. Only four? Motion denied."

The meeting adjourned shortly thereafter, and Tahut-Nefer met with like-minded priests in secret, in a separate chamber. "Fools," he muttered, glaring over his shoulder towards the inner sanctum. "They don't understand. If we do not remove the yoke of Rome from our necks, Egypt will die."

"So we provoke the garrison anyway?" one of his fellows murmured. "Without the sanction of the high priest?"

Tahut's expression turned grim. "He will be called to the afterlife soon, I think. His health daily grows worse." He met their eyes. "And when the pharaoh and his bride arrive, as we know they will. . . ."

"It cannot be traced to us," his fellow conspirators muttered.

A smirk. "Of course not. I would never use the magic of Thoth to kill them. I have . . . something quite else in mind."

The Library of Alexandria was part of a larger complex of structures known as the Musaeum of Alexandria — dozens of beautiful Hellenistic buildings, constructed in the port city since the time of the first Ptolemy. Dedicated to the nine Muses, the grounds were dotted with statues of those daughters of Mnemosyne, dancing, laughing, weeping, singing, or reading from scrolls, and towering palms cast their shadows along the many wandering paths between the structures. Philosophers sat in shady gardens, amiably arguing with their students over tiny glasses of *passum*, Carthaginian raisin wine, or heartier cups of Egyptian grain beer. In one area, musicians tuned their lyres and began to play, attracting the attention of dozens of students and researchers, who approached to listen with every evidence of enjoyment.

Inside one of the white-pillared buildings, a woman looked up from her studies, listening to the music wafting in through one of the small windows for a moment. She stood out among all the other scholars crouching over their small desks in between the racks and racks of papyrus scrolls that ran the length of this huge, dimly-lit room. All the others were male, for starters. All the rest wore Hellene chitons, Roman tunics and togas, or white Carthaginian robes. Among all those men in their simple clothing, she sparkled like a jewel in a long silk robe dyed in vivid shades of vermillion, violet, and blue, with a long vest over the top of it in a darker shade of carmine embroidered in a dusky bronze. A kind of round cap perched atop her head, in that same carmine, and translucent red veils, also of silk, cascaded from it down the back of her neck. Another veil, this one black, concealed the lower half of her face, but above it, her dark eyes were a strange shade that mixed brown and green, like a bronze statue that had just begun to verdigris.

And yet, in spite of her obvious femininity in this otherwise exclusively male enclave, not one of the other scholars came near her. Spoke to her. Or even looked at her for more than a moment. Some of that may have had to do with the man who towered over her, her perpetual shadow and guard. Tongueless, scarred, and — rumor had it — castrated, he stared at everyone around her impassively. Never seeming bored or lacking in vigilance, no matter how many hours she spent in the humid, musty confines of a nearly windowless library in a muggy port city, surrounded by sweating men.

Somehow, she never seemed to sweat, either. In spite of the heavy layers of clothing she wore, or the long hair that was — probably — concealed by the veils and the cap.

Now, she finished with the scroll she'd been copying, and took it back to the librarians, one of whom accepted it from her as if it were made of pure gold — which, in a way, it was, being so fragile and ancient. "I wonder if you might have copies of the *Ephesia Grammata* here?"

The librarian blinked rapidly. "My lady? Those are . . . nonsense words, are they not? Said to have been developed by the . . . ah. . . Magi . . ." he looked at her uneasily, "to protect those who can pronounce them correctly from demonic possession?"

"Correct." She regarded him steadily from behind her veils, and raised one hand to adjust the bracelets that jingled on her wrist.

"My lady. . ." the unfortunate librarian leaned forward to whisper, his breath carrying with it a strong smell of the anise seeds that he clearly chewed with his brown and aging teeth, "shouldn't you know those already? You are, after all . . . one of them. . . ."

She leaned forward, and her ever-present

bodyguard made a noise deep in his throat, and the librarian's eyes flicked nervously upwards towards the brute, and then, with even more agitation, back down towards her. "I do not feel the need to explain myself," she murmured softly. "Simply bring the texts to my desk. I would like to review them." She paused. "And, seeing as you know my affiliations . . . then you should know that *lady* is not my proper mode of address. You will refer to me as Magus. Magus Banit, if there is any reason for you to address me at all in the future."

Damkina Banit returned to her seat, pretending not to notice all the other scholars watching her out of the corners of their eyes. The *pock* and *scritch* of many pens, moving across papyrus or parchment, rustled like the voices of many insects. She sighed as the librarian finally found the relevant scrolls for her, and began to copy these, too, laboriously. *Yes, the Magi and the priests of Artemis of Ephesus developed these centuries ago, but scribes make mistakes all the time. Some of the rituals have been copied and miscopied so often, that they have almost no efficacy at all anymore. Thus, we compare. And, if possible, I can inlay these words, with a charge of power, into a charm that will help protect me if and when I summon spirits that are maleficent to help me hunt down those whom I have pledged to kill.*

A grunt from her guard drew her attention, as did a cooling breeze generated by one of her attendant spirits as a warning. Damkina looked up just as a hand placed a note on her desk, and then the scholar who'd set it there scuttled by, as if nothing had happened at all. She waited for a moment, then opened the note, her eyes skimming across the words there. Ah. A very boring request for an item that will restore lost potency. Who wants this one . . . ah. A Hellene philosopher in his sixties. Must have just purchased himself a new slave-boy. Ah, well, he's well-connected. Eats dinner with the Roman prefect once or twice a month. I wonder if he'll come to regret the fact that my price is information, not gold? She shrugged mentally. And of course, the item I'll provide him will indeed renew his flagging vigor. And I'll need to charge it every few weeks. Just to ensure that he keeps providing information.

But that was a concern for later. The request would keep, for now. Damkina went back to the work that she was here for, and not the work that kept her in good odor with her superiors among the Council of Magi.

Little sunlight filtered through the leaden clouds over the vast, open plain. Smoke from a fire drifted upwards, while snow fluttered down through the air, lightly feathering over the tips of the long grass, brown with winter. It fell, too, on the huge stones that marked this place as the greatest of the stone dances on this island—although there were hundreds of others. They dotted hilltops and glens from as far north as the Orkneys to places as far south as occupied Gaul—including the famous stones of Carnac, in the lands held by the Veneti tribe along the western coast of Gaul. Some marked graves thousands of years old. The men and women gathered here knew it. Could feel the graves as disruptions in the ground under their feet. Could feel how the cold soil wrapped around the softer, looser ashes, how the standing stones compressed the clay down on harder bits of bone. They all knew that here, their ancestors were with them. Ancestors who had dwelled in this land since before the Roman gods had even had names. And in testament to those gods and ancestors, further circles of wooden posts, carved and painted to represent each one, stood outside the stones. Many of which were further adorned with skulls, heads taken in battle by this noteworthy king or that, and brought here from far away. The king might have been cremated, or tucked into a barrow, but here, the worthy dead were *remembered.*

Those ancestors had chosen the sites for their stone dances for many reasons. The stones themselves, certainly, lined up with celestial occurrences—just over two weeks ago, they'd all marked the passage of the winter solstice as the stars performed their dance above the dance made of stone. But the locations, well . . . they'd been chosen because they resonated with power. The Gallic gods had been, as far as their people knew, the only ones to teach their people how to *use* the power that was in the earth, in the water, and in the sky. Flowing currents of it, leaping from line to line. The stuff, they knew, that bound the universe together. Connected those stars above to the earth below.

If other nations were aware of that power, they feared to use it. Thought that they'd tear the fabric of the universe by touching it. *That's because all they know how to do is take,* the Gauls murmured among themselves. *They don't know how to shape power gently to their need, and then let go. What they have, they need to hold, like a dog with a bone, living in fear that someone else will come and take it.*

The men and women present represented the twenty-seven greater tribes of these lands, as well as the druids who did their best to bind them together, arbitrate disputes, and pass on the old stories and learning. The druids who'd pass over the seas with the traders and sailors, to connect this island to their far-flung Celtic brethren, who dwelled in Gaul, Hispania, and even as far away as the northern reaches of Hellas. A network of similar cultures and dialects, with the Goths camped out in between. And while the Goths were cousins, and thus closer kin than the damnable Roman invaders . . . they were *not* the same. Not even by half.

"Two years ago," the chief druid said, raising his hands

for silence, "our brother Matru made it back to these shores after a year spent as a hostage to the leader of the Romans. A year in which Matru attempted to make this. . . Caesarion . . . understand the price he would pay if he came to our lands, as his father did. A year in which Matru attempted to sway this emperor's hand, as he came down upon the holdings of our cousins, the Cantabri, in Hispania." He paused. "My brother, will you not speak?"

Matru stood, moving forward into the circle of robed people, their backs a break against the wind that pushed the smoke and the snow into complex patterns in the air above them. He was a tall man, with huge shoulders; his long brown hair hung loose, but for a few braids in it. A gold torc clung to his bear-like neck, and his arms, exposed by his sleeveless wool robe, held a dense pattern of woad tattoos—as did the rest of his frame, concealed by that same soft brown wool. Yet he, like several others here, was clean-shaven, or nearly, with only a few day's worth of beard on his cheeks. And his blue eyes held a certain cold resolve, mixed with understanding. "Two of us were taken captive, two survivors of Aucissa's expedition, as you all already know," he said, in the tones of a trained storyteller. "We had the perfect ambush set up, and we would have wiped out five full legions—thirty thousand men—in heartbeats, burying them under ice and snow and rock, but for one woman. Caesarion's sister, Eurydice. She is god-born, just as he is, and a sorceress of some power. She turned aside the avalanche, sparing most of Caesarion's army."

"Aucissa nearly killed her for it, didn't she?" someone with a Silures accent asked, trying to bolster everyone's spirits. Mentioning the powerful god-born of the Morrigan might have cheered them—if only that tale hadn't ended badly.

"Threw the Roman god-born right atop a stone spire. Impaled her. And then Caesarion came down and jabbed his knife into Aucissa's throat. And used her life to bring his sister back from death," Matru said, his jaw working. He'd held to that story—the gods' own truth—for two years now. Few here believed him. No mortal man could wield that kind of power. "Then he married his sister in observance of the rites required by another kingdom. This . . . Egypt. Lands far south of Rome. Their mother comes from there."

Fascinated murmurs. They were accustomed to the notion that gods might marry their close-kin—and certainly, some heroes out of legends had lain with their sisters, too!— but it wasn't much *practiced* here. Matru cleared his throat. "As I said, two of us were captured. Docca was the other. As he was a Venicone, and Venicones are born with their mouths open, and never do learn to shut them and listen a while," a dark look at the Venicones actually present, "he made himself a nuisance and got himself executed, while I gathered information." He exhaled, seeing the steam of his own breath rise into the air. "I spent the next year with their emperor and his family. I saw their great city. Houses made of stone. Patterns and designs worked into every floor, ever so cunning. When they want to bathe, they don't go to a river or to the hot springs that the gods have made in the earth; they go to buildings where they've made hot springs of their own. Pools of water, lined in stone, and heated from below with fire." He shook his head. "Wealth so vast that they can't be counting it all."

"And yet they want more," came the condemning voices from all around him.

Matru held up his hand, stilling the others. "This Caesarion . . . think of him as a flea on the back of a large and hungry dog," he said grimly. "He's a cautious leader, for all that his own war-chiefs call him impatient. He could have gone straight into Cantabri lands. He didn't. He gave them a chance to surrender and make reparations, as I suggested. When they refused, he spent most of a year surrounding them. Taking all the tribes around them, by treaty or by force. And then, the next year, he came in force. Took the Cantabri's lands village by village, and from all sides at once. Like a snake, crushing its prey in its coils." He looked away, seeing in the smoke of this fire all the clouds that had billowed over the mountain villages of the Cantabri. "His soldiers are fine and disciplined. But they wanted spoils and wealth to bring home. He has to walk the same balance as every other war-leader, between placating his people and doing what he thinks is best. His people? Wanted the Cantabri annihilated. His generals? Told him that to leave even one village standing meant that they'd just rise up again in a generation."

"As we would," another druid muttered.

"As we *should*," came another voice.

"What did he wind up doing?" A third voice, this one from a woman standing nearby.

Matru grimaced. He'd seen the Roman war machine at its most ferocious. They'd come to this island twice before, both times under Caesar. The first had been an exploratory mission, he now realized, and had been quickly repelled. The second had been the campaign in the southeast, which they'd managed to stave off. "Any man who surrendered was captured and made a slave," he said shortly. "Men who *didn't* surrender were slaughtered. The women and girl children were allowed to go free. The boy children were taken as slaves. You can imagine their fate in Rome," he added, offhandedly. "They have a belief that slaves of both sexes can be raped by their masters. At will. And that if a boy-child is chosen for such attentions, they should be *grateful* for it, as they'll be primped and perfumed and coddled until they're adult men, instead of having to work at harder labor. Some of these concubines are even passed down from father to son as a delightful inheritance, I'm told. So that they can be used by two generations of the same family." He shrugged. "This isn't the *only* possible fate before those captives," Matru added, with scrupulous honesty, "but it explains why so many of our Cantabri brethren set fire to their own villages. Fathers killed their own wives and children before taking their own lives, rather than allow them to be sold as slaves in Rome."

"You said that he's a flea on a dog's back, though?" the woman asked, pushing closer, her expression interested.

Matru nodded. "I saw his eyes. He is, as I said, inclined towards mercy. But in this case, we'd forced his hand. Twelve thousand Roman lives were taken. He needed to retaliate in a way that his people would find acceptable." He sighed. "And he did spare the women and girls. I watched him personally execute some of his men caught raping the women." A buzz of questions, and he struggled to explain. "Once they're slaves, they're legally someone else's property, and he can't stop what will happen to them. But while they're *captives* or non-combatants . . . he can spare them. Romans are so bound up by their laws, it sometimes . . . incapacitates them." *And yet, I saw Caesarion's eyes. I saw the <u>regret</u> in them.* "Once, an entire village surrendered without a fight. He spared them. Men, women, and children." He exhaled again. "And, to a certain extent, they admire us. We interest them. They put on armor like ours to fight like us in their arenas. And I even saw a Gaul fight for and receive his freedom from slavery in one of those places where they battle to please their gods."

"But the only way to be spared their fury is to capitulate," someone with a deep southern accent shouted — from mainland Gaul, surely! "You know what they're doing in my homeland?" he said, and the crowd parted to let him be seen and heard more clearly. Long hair, still—this southern Pairisi held to Gallic norms, not Roman ones.

"They're building temples. And they put their gods inside, and say that their gods and our gods are the same—just with different names. They say that their Jupiter and Zeus are Taranis, and that we should just worship in *their* temples. When Taranis can only be venerated under the open sky!"

Matru turned his head and spat. I wouldn't have a problem with it, if they put their temples up and said "Come inside if you wish to. Worship our gods or worship your own. But saying that our gods and their gods are the <u>same beings?</u> Where is their three-faced Morrigan, then? Why is their moon a goddess and not a god? They're <u>not</u> the same. Their gods are clearly powerful, and worthy of being worshipped—but they're not ours.

"All of this, we already know," came another voice, bored and impatient. Venicone accent, and Matru stiffened on hearing it. "What are we to do about it?"

"We've been preparing for an invasion since Matru returned to warn us that this Caesarion would surely mount a retaliatory strike for our interference in the affairs of the continent," the lead druid, Minconis, replied.

"Which hasn't materialized," the Venicone replied, pushing forward. As he did, Matru recognized him—Necto, heir-apparent to the Venicone chiefdom. "A phantom invasion to go with the Caledonian love of a good tale."

"He'll come," Matru replied stolidly. "As I said, he's cautious. He had a rebellion on his eastern flank that his step-father had to crush—"

"And who would be this step-father, now? Who would follow into Caesar's bed?" Necto cracked, making the crowd laugh.

"Marcus Antonius," Matru said, clearly and distinctly, and the crowd went silent. They knew *that* name from the Roman invasion of continental Gaul. "Now married to Caesarion's mother, Cleopatra. Caesar's widow. Now that the rebellion in the east has been crushed, and the Cantabri have fallen, the only hope we have is that *something* will distract Caesarion from dealing with us, if we're not ready to present a united front against him and his armies."

Mutters from the crowd. Many of these tribes were traditional enemies. Matru personally *loathed* the Venicones; they'd taken him and his sister captive when he'd been twelve and she'd been ten. He'd survived their torture. She hadn't. But he was a druid now, and stood for *all* his people, not just his native Caledonii.

They broke into smaller groups, arguing the best course, as usual. Matru sighed and walked away; he'd done his best. His feet crunched through the cap of snow now blanketing the dead grass and he came to a halt, putting a hand on one of the stones of the great dance. Letting himself *feel* the earth here. The power humming under the upper layers of soil. *What a few of us could do here, if we made a stand . . . . would it be enough to turn the tide of Rome? Or will they push north, and north, until even my people's Forest is in flames?*

A hand touched his elbow, and he turned, startled. A woman stood there. Green eyes, red hair—from one of the eastern regions, most likely. "How did you escape?" she asked, smiling. "You left out that part of the tale."

Matru shrugged. "I gave them my word I'd not try to escape for a year and a day. On the night *after* that, we were still in the mountains of Hispania. One of their forts—what they call a *castra*. I opened the earth and let the waters below come up. They were *most* surprised by the geysers of hot water spouting everywhere. Mud and sludge and smell of sulfur, panicking animals. While they were all occupied with the flood, and under cover of darkness, I walked out the front gate and summoned a spirit. By the time they looked for me—after quite some time spent, I think, wondering how they had offended their god of the underworld—I was long gone, on a mount that needed no rest." He clenched his hands unconsciously on the knife scars that he'd made to summon the spirit with his own blood. That particular bargain to the *kelpie* of the Durius river had cost him a year of his life—but the spirit had run him the entire length of the river bed in a single night, leaving him hundreds of miles from Caesarion's camp, soaked to the skin, and deeply chilled.

She nodded, her eyes filled with deep sympathy. "I'm Sulicena," she introduced herself. "Priestess of Ceridwen. Also, daughter of Nynniaw of the Cantiaci." The name was a shock; Nynniaw supposedly had fought Julius Caesar in single combat. And not only had he survived, but he'd stripped the Roman general of his sword, which to this day, Nynniaw carried. Sulicena touched his face, now, lightly. "Tell me, did you like this Caesarion? Respect him?"

Matru closed his eyes, trying not to enjoy the sensation of her fingers on his face too much. "He has honor," he told her somberly. "And I can't help but respect a man with that much power. But if he comes here—for all that he talks of philosophy and learning and trade? His *people* will demand fire and war and blood. It's how they honor their gods. It'll be the end of everything we've built here. Our ancestors, part of this land since time began, will cry out, but there'll be none of us left to hear them."

"So what do we do? Surrender to his mercy—as much as he can offer us?" She snorted.

Matru shook his head. "No. We fight him with every last breath we have. Till the land is stained with our blood.

Make their wounds too painful for even Rome to stomach."
And pray that they break before we perish.

In Rome, Livia Drusilla, widow of Octavian and
current wife of Agrippa, sat on a couch in the *triclinium* of her
new husband's home, her face rigid as she listened to her
guests speak. Most were all of the *optimates* — the old, good
families, with whom she'd maintained such tenuous
connections after her divorce from her patrician-born first
husband and remarriage to Octavian, whose family had been
so recently ennobled at Caesar's hands. "It's disgusting," she
said flatly, drawing everyone's attention for a moment. "Even
here, in my dear Agrippa's house, I see that some of you are
wearing *kohl* around your eyes, ladies. What happened to
Roman virtue? What happened to holding the line against the
decadence of the east?"

Poppaea, one of the women so addressed, reached up
to touch her face, a little abashed, but then laughed it off. "It's
just a style, Livia, darling," she told the older woman lightly.
"Ever since Caesarion married Eurydice, Egyptian fashions
have been quite the rage. I don't see myself wearing a *kalasiris*,
and those *enormous* necklaces are simply ostentatious displays
of wealth, but a little kohl to set off my eyes? What's the harm
in that?"

Livia felt her lips harden, and felt Agrippa, her
husband, ease away from her on the couch. "What's the
harm?" Livia snapped. "It's *not Roman.* You let in one thing,
half a dozen others will crawl under the door. And by
accepting a fashion started by that incestuous harlot, you
intimate that you *accept her.*"

Another woman raised her cup, murmuring, "Actually,
the fashion started over twenty years ago, Livia, dear. When

Caesar first brought Cleopatra to Rome."

Fury can't be maintained for long. Fury exhausts. Fury dies. What's left in its wake are the banked embers of loathing and hatred, contempt and prejudice. Livia nearly choked on the black tide of her own bile at the mention of the name Cleopatra, but paused before she spoke. Pressed her fingertips to her forehead, and finally said, her voice weary and filled with a kind of sad wonder, "Has it really been so long since Caesar brought his Egyptian concubine to Rome? Has it been so long since he forced the Senate to allow his divorce, and made them recognize the house of Ptolemy as citizens for *services to Rome*—services in his bedchamber, more like." She sighed. "Has it been so long since he made a half-breed bastard his heir, and all Rome stood by and allowed it? Has it been so long since that same bastard murdered my late husband, my dear Octavian, and again, Rome stood by? Has it been so long since that same half-breed, murderous bastard married his own sister, and all Rome *applauded?*" Her voice rose with each question, reaching a crescendo by the end—a precisely calculated oratorical effect. Livia was at her best when she'd rehearsed her speeches. And this one, she'd rehearsed for several days.

Uneasy murmurs from her guests. "They're god-born," Agrippa told his wife gently, his heavy, graying eyebrows overhanging his deep-set eyes like grapevines on an arbor. "He's god-born of Mars, Venus, and others. She's god-born of Venus and Isis, too. The gods have plainly put them here for a reason. And at the moment, this isn't a good time to question the wisdom of the gods."

"Did you see what happened at the tomb of Casca Servilius?" Publius Servilius Rullus asked, shuddering. "One of my cousins from *that* branch of the Servilii family got up in front of the tomb of his ancestor, the one who tried to assassinate Caesar. Tried to call on the memory of his late, unlamented uncle, and whip the crowd into a frenzy against, as you say, the bastard-born, half-Egyptian son of Caesar. I swear, I thought I saw two or three men advancing on him through the crowd, drawing knives, but they never got there." He took a fortifying sip of his wine, and added, "Lightning struck the tomb. From out of a clear sky. The statue of Clementia—the only statue that Caesar would allow to be erected on the tomb of one of his would-be assassins—fell. Shattered. A piece struck his head, and he fell down dead. I was *there*, Livia."

"Coincidence," Livia tried to sneer, but a depressing number of her guests shook their heads vehemently.

"Coincidence that the goddess of mercy's own image was shattered in the very instant a descendant of an assassin tried to incite the mob against the son of the man his father tried to assassinate? I'd call that a very pointed sign," another man muttered. "One I don't need an augur to read, thank you. Sometimes the gods speak in whispers. That one was a shout."

"Besides," Rullus commented lightly, "it's not as if he and his sister seem to have anything more than a symbolic marriage. I doubt that they, er, well. You know." He chuckled uneasily. "Otherwise, by now, surely they'd have had a two-headed child, or at least some sort of visible pregnancy."

Agrippa—*damn him*—raised his head, and murmured, "It's amazing how often I hear about the potential for two-headed children from that pair, when not a single one of the pharaohs of Egypt for the past three thousand years has been born with that particular defect. The occasional clubfoot. The occasional cleft palate. But singularly, no double-headed infants."

"It *would* be a marvel of anatomy, but rather hard on the mother, don't you think?" a woman murmured, trying for delicacy of phrasing, and everyone tittered into their wine.

"My point remains," Rullus said placidly, "he has no heirs. Nor seems likely to have them any time soon. That will leave his brother Alexander, and he's due to marry Octavian's daughter Octavia, eh . . . sometime next year? Lad doesn't seem to be in a hurry to get her properly tied down." A hearty chuckle at that.

"He's a busy young man," came an arch comment from somewhere to her left. "Considering his social life, I wouldn't be all that eager to rush into matrimony, myself, if I were to see his age again." Considering that the patrician male saying so was heavyset and in his fifties, that would be another wonder of anatomy.

Rullus rallied. "And there's nothing that says that the office of Imperator will be hereditary. The gods seem to have decreed for Caesarion to follow Caesar. But after him? Who knows. Perhaps we'll get back to selecting the best man for the job from, well. The best of the best." He toasted those around him lightly with his cup. "But I'm in no rush to see that happen. For now, I think we can trust in the wisdom of the gods."

Fuming, Livia sat in silence for the rest of the evening. Saw her guests out. Endured Agrippa's gentle kiss on her cheek, and quiet words of, "You need to let it go, my dear. Octavian was a good man. He was my friend. He had a vision for Rome—and I'll see to it that his vision doesn't die. But you can't defy the gods themselves, my dear."

Yes, I can, Livia thought, as her personal slave helped her take down her hair for the night. Dried weld blossoms, brewed into a tisane, were brushed through her hair—officially for the herbal fragrance, but more truthfully to stave off the first traces of gray in her blond tresses. And as the Cretan slave worked, Livia brooded, staring out the window.

Poison doesn't work on Caesarion. I tried that straight away, but Lepidus, the old fool, drank from the young Emperor's cup, and nearly died for it. But those closest to him have no such immunities, do they? Well, that bitch Cleopatra has managed to dodge every dose sent her way these twenty years. Always by somehow just avoiding whatever dish had the poison in it — and usually telling Caesar which foods 'just don't look appetizing tonight, dear.' Livia's lips curled down at the corners. *Of course, if I were somehow to remove Caesarion from the game, at the moment, he has no heir. Besides Alexander. For whose life, Caesarion traded my husband's.*

And oh, how that thought burned at her. "Eritha, have there been any messages from my sons?" Livia asked.

The maid's swift brushstrokes halted. "No, *domina*."

"And the men I have placed in the Julii household? Have they seen or heard anything of importance?"

"They said that they aren't permitted near the personal chambers of the household, my lady. But they know that while Tiberius has taken a house for himself and his brother, that they still spend three nights out of every seven in the Julii house."

The girl's sweet voice irritated Livia. She tore the brush out of her hands and threw it against the wall, cracking the tortoiseshell handle. "Go! Leave me!"

The girl scuttled out, and Livia sank into her chair to brood. She had agents dotted throughout the city, who timidly reported on her eldest son's activities. How he and Alexander went to brothels and low *tavernas* together. Purchased the services of whores together. Diced together. Did everything, apparently, together. And, locked in the bottom of one of her coffers, was a report from an innkeeper in Athens, which suggested that they'd definitely tried at least a few other things, *together.*

It has been my dream for years to put my sons on a

path for greatness. The consul's chair. Then the Imperator's. Why not? They're both of the noble house of the Claudii. Each of them betrothed to the daughters of notable, wealthy, powerful plebeians — a daughter of Antony for Drusus, a daughter of Agrippa for Tiberius. She looked grimly at a stack of reports and letters piled on her dressing table. By all accounts, he'd covered himself in glory in Hispania. Entrusted with the Tenth Legion in the position of temporary legate at the tender age of fifteen. Brought back down to tribune the following campaign season, he'd led his troops into battle against the Cantabri in the worst possible terrain — and had won several notable battles. He'd become known for harsh drills under conditions as close to combat as he could make them, and as a result, his legionnaires excelled. And while the men didn't love him, they respected him. Knew he'd never send them anywhere, but that he'd be right there with them. All the things that would make him a favorable candidate for office on leaving the legion, and yet. . . he <u>sullies</u> himself. The rumors of an affair with a merchant's wife in Athens, to go along with all the rest? Where is that famous sense of honor he once possessed? She sniffed. Oh, he used to hold himself so <u>high</u> above Octavian.

A smile crossed her lips, and she nodded. "Yes," Livia murmured. "That's the way to reach him. It just needs the right words. He needs to understand that his *dear friend* is dragging him down." *And that Alexander, like all the rest of these Egyptian pretenders, must die.*

Her smile faded. Of course, if he won't see reason, I have many recourses for dealing with him. I can expose him for what he's become. Let him suffer the public condemnation and humiliation as he sees the scraps of his honor blown away from him. And if that doesn't work?

I have another son. And Tiberius — in whom I placed all

my hopes—is certain to be far less immune to poison than these upstarts who carry the noble Julii name.

Her eyes burned for a moment, and Livia settled her hand on the stack of reports, very gently. "Where did I go wrong with you?" she murmured. "You have to know how low you've sunk, my son. By now, any Roman father would be well within his rights to kill you as a shame to his house. Or at least, to disinherit you." *Of course, exercising those rights would be tantamount to confessing your immorality to the rest of the world in public. Most fathers wouldn't do that. Even Eburnus, the censor who executed his own son as a catamite, was condemned for exceeding his parental authority, and exiled.* "What would your father think of you? Not Octavian. What would *Nero* think? He'd have been proud of all those victories in Hispania, of course. But the rest?" She sighed, and patted the letters. "Perhaps thinking of him will reach you, where none of my words ever seem to. I do hope you'll listen, my son," she murmured, before leaning forward to blow out the oil lamp on her table. "Of course, children past a certain age, never do."

In quite another quarter of Rome, two young men were in bed with a whore. Each of them were eighteen, in the prime of their lives. Muscled from marching with the legions, in full kit. Riding. Fighting. Bodies sweating, straining. Muffled grunts of pleasure from the two young men, and the occasional startled sound of pleasure from the woman.

Alexander Julius Caesar paused in his work to ensure that yes, Jocasta, the startlingly beautiful Hellene attraction of this particular establishment, had closed her eyes in enjoyment of what he was doing, and then flicked his gaze over her right shoulder, meeting the gray gaze of his best friend, Tiberius, as he did so. Of all the many sexual intricacies they'd tried over the years, this act remained their favorite — both of them firmly seated in the same woman, at the same time. *The trick remains finding a woman who genuinely enjoys this.* Hazy thoughts, soon lost on the wave of his own release. And then waited, watching Tiberius' expression as he continued to work at the whore from behind. Enjoying the dazed, happy look as he, too, found his release.

Then Alexander pulled himself out of Jocasta's warm, very relaxed body, and gave her a light pat on the hip. "Thank you," he told her, smiling. "Now that we've done business, can we do *business*?" He adjusted the amulet of Sekhmet, worn on a long chain around his neck. He and Tiberius had matching ones, which had cost them a small fortune each. But the charms hawked at the temple of Asclepius didn't prevent diseases with nearly the efficacy of the talismans of Sekhmet — and talismans of Sekhmet didn't need to be 're-blessed' once a month, either, for an additional charge. His mother, Cleopatra, had strongly recommended that they purchase these items, and Alexander had seen the sense. Grimacing with burning pain every time he urinated was simply not a consequence of fun — or duty — that he particularly enjoyed.

Now, Jocasta smiled, and slid out of the bed, still naked, and crossed the small area in which she spent her nights. She opened a small chest, from which she removed a scroll, buried deep under her various garments and a variety of specialized tools of her trade. As one such fell on the floor, Alexander rolled to his stomach, pointed at it, and asked with sleepiness that was partially feigned, "Is that an extra?"

"It certainly is if you wish to put it in *me*, *dominus*. If I get to put it in one of you two, I might call that a fair trade." A saucy wink, but Alexander didn't take offense. Just held his hand out for the scroll, which he scanned now, with interest.

"Anything interesting?" Tiberius asked, already cleaning himself and getting dressed with quick, sharp, precise movements.

"Our good friend here has a new client. Rullus. Goodness. Apparently, all that public morality is really debilitating." Alexander's eyebrows rose. "Three girls *and* a boy?"

"He's the sort who likes to watch," Jocasta supplied, perching on the edge of her bed, pouting as Tiberius continued to ignore her gloriously naked state. "He had us all doing each other. Then he told the other two girls to do to him what we'd been doing to the boy. With a little something extra added, just for him."

Alexander considered himself more than a neophyte in the carnal realm these days. What he read in the description, however, sickened him. "*Excrement?*"

"Dis' teeth," Tiberius muttered. "My mother invites him to dine every time she manages to get me over to see her and Agrippa. I won't be able to *eat* the next time I see him over a dinner table."

Jocasta rolled her eyes. "Personally, I think that if everyone just would have a good solid fuck once a day, the demand for specialty acts would decline dramatically."

Alexander sat up and gave her a light kiss on the cheek. "Yes, but then where would you be?"

"Giving many more people their solid one fuck a day, instead of a smaller group their darkest desires once a month." The words were pert. Her eyes were not.

Alexander gave her another kiss, this time on the forehead. "You're one of my best information sources," he told her gently. "Rullus still seemed quite rattled about that statue, didn't he?"

"Yes. Absolutely." She sighed. "Oh, and I should mention that Livia Drusilla made me an offer last week."

Tiberius, now fully dressed and seated quite properly across the room, jerked as if he'd just been stabbed. "My *mother*?" he said, in a tone of disbelief. "She came *here*?"

"No, one of her agents. Made me the usual offer of coin for information. Largely about the two of you." Jocasta rolled her eyes again. "You should probably ask for one of the other girls next time, so that there's less of a visible pattern to your visits here. Or you, *dominus*, should come alone." She glanced at Alexander.

He nodded. "How much did she offer you?"

"A solidus."

He took out twice that, and told her, "Take her money. But I'd be obliged if you only told her what I want her to hear." He paused. "Does she know about your sister?"

Jocasta's sister was an invalid; her sister's pay at the brothel ensured that they had a slave of their own to provide care night and day, and also ensured that they could afford medications and prayers at the temples. She shook her head now. "The subject didn't come up. If she threatens Viola, I will be sure to tell you." Jocasta's eyes narrowed. "I don't like being threatened."

Alexander nodded. Threats and blackmail work on some people. Or a handle on their addictions. But not on Jocasta. She doesn't <u>care</u> if something happens to her, and a little wine at the end of the day lets her forget without recourse to poppy-blood. And try to touch her sister, and she'll try to end the person who makes the threat. But give her good money for her services, and she's loyal—to a point. "Do let me know if there's anything I can do for your sister," he murmured, putting on his own clothes.

And then Tiberius moved over, took Jocasta's hand,

and bowed over it as if she were a lady before they left, making the low-born woman smile, suddenly delighted. And that, Alexander knew, was his friend in a nutshell. Passionate in bed. Distant, reserved, and utterly polite out of it. It drove women *crazy*, and was one of the reasons Tiberius was invaluable to Alexander's work. The women that Alexander couldn't reach with smiles and light flirtation? Many of them seemed to find Tiberius' good looks and unapproachable air a challenge—or they saw the perennial melancholy in his chill eyes, and wanted to comfort him, somehow. As if each of them thought that *they* were the ones who would finally thaw and warm him.

The lowest parts of Rome were, these days, Alexander's personal office. He smiled at shopkeepers as he and Tiberius walked by, stopped in to chat with *taverna* owners, and admired new sculptures being tapped out of marble on a street full of artisans. And on every street, he checked walls for fresh graffiti that might tell him what was on the city's mind, or at least what rumbled through its troubled viscera.

About five streets from the brothel, Tiberius said, mildly, "Remember that magic powder from Qin that the ambassadors left three years ago?"

"Hmm, yes?" Alexander said, making eye-contact with another of his agents—this one a retired legionnaire who was now a *frumentarii*—a tax-collector, officially, but an information-gatherer in reality. "What about it?"

"The writings they left with it said that we should be careful with fire around it, didn't they?"

"Oh, yes. Definitely. Apparently, it's some sort of chemical compound that they use to make loud noises and drive evil spirits away." The agent walked by, and a hand brushed Alexander's, leaving a scrap of parchment in his palm.

"About how much of that," Tiberius said thoughtfully, "do you think someone would need to, say, blow up a fair-sized statue? Say, a life-sized one of Clementia?"

Alexander turned, giving his friend a scandalized look. "Ti, I'm shocked at you. You really think that I would sneak into a cemetery in the dead of night, chancing the wrath of the *manes* — "

"You don't believe in the *manes*." Clear, flat words.

" — drill a hole in the arse of a goddess — "

"Wouldn't be the first time you drilled a — "

"Shhh," Alexander said, putting a finger to his lips as they walked through a fresh crowd of people, and Tiberius fell completely silent as the jostle of limbs passed. And once they all had, Alexander leaned in and whispered, "I can neither confirm nor deny that it would take about half of the powder that the ambassadors left behind. But I *will* say that I want more of that damned stuff."

Tiberius actually laughed. "You know that they're saying the gods were responsible."

Alexander spread his hands, looking as virtuous as he could as they approached the Julii villa on the outskirts of town. "Perhaps they were! Perhaps they simply worked through me. Their humble mortal vessel." He nodded, and then laughed as Tiberius gave him a full-on shove to the shoulder, nearly hurling him into the fountain in the plaza in front of the villa.

"You, a conduit for divine will. *That* will be the day." That, as they clattered up the steps, and the servants at the door, recognizing them, opened the door.

Alexander noted that the pair of servants were Roman and new, and bit his tongue on his reply, saying merely, "Now, now, best behavior, Tiberius. My mother is here, and requires us all to attend some sort of family meeting before dinner."

Marble tiles spun underfoot in their dizzying geometric forms, while Flora and Faunus danced on the walls in a fresco opposite the more sober pair of Venus Genetrix and Mars Pater. All the symbols of home, to Alexander, for the first eighteen years of his life. But as he spoke, Tiberius paused at the stairs leading up into the family quarters on the second floor. "Then I'll see you at dinner, then," he said, nodding and turning away.

Alexander caught his friend's arm. "No, come along. You're practically family. They all know you're my brother. I've adopted you. It's settled!" Cheerful, breezy words.

Tiberius sighed and pulled him up the stairs, away from the servants' ears. Down the open-air balcony that overlooked the atrium, and which was lined with the doors that led into the various *cubiculum* that served as bedrooms and workrooms for the Julii family. Found the door to Alexander's bedroom, and stepped inside, making sure the door was locked before speaking. "Alexander, this has to stop," Tiberius said, his gray eyes serious. "*We* have to stop, soon. You're marrying Octavia inside the next year, not that you'll set a date—"

Alexander swore and kissed Tiberius, stopping the flow of words. "Octavia is a feather-brain. A very attractive feather-brain, but a feather-brain nonetheless." He swore again, irritated. "I wasn't supposed to fall in love with you. It was supposed to be *fun.*" *I was just going to keep you compromised. Make sure that you couldn't make any kind of a play for my brother's offices. Look where that got me. Eurydice would laugh if she knew how much my protestations that I didn't have <u>time</u> to be in love had turned out. Of course, damn her, she probably <u>does</u> know.*

Tiberius put his arms around his shoulders for a

moment. "Yes, well. I wasn't exactly expecting to fall in love with you, either." He shrugged, as if this weren't the first time they'd ever actually put it into words. "Everyone expects these things to pass. I'm supposed to marry Vipsania in four years or so. I expect I can endure loneliness and ardor until then."

"And I'm saying, you don't *have* to."

"Octavia, feather-brain or no, deserves a husband who only looks for passion in her bed —"

"And there's at least nine or ten months before any vows are spoken, so take your honor and shove it, Ti." Alexander turned away, fighting down any urge to beg Tiberius to understand. To reconsider. His friend had strong ideals in terms of duty, honor, and loyalty. He wouldn't so much as *look* at a married woman — unless that woman had been beaten or abused in some fashion. And while Tiberius clearly enjoyed what they did in bed, and what they did in various brothels, Alexander knew that the instant Tiberius spoke his own wedding vows, the iron curtain of duty would come down, and divide them permanently. His own feelings on the subject were that the curtain needn't be iron, but rather some form of silk. Preferably a diaphanous one. Easily raised and parted if all parties were amenable.

He tossed his various collected notes from their afternoon's outing on his desk, to be transcribed into Egyptian/Hellene demotic script for his own records, to make it more difficult for anyone who might gain access to his rooms to read. He'd burn the originals once he'd done that. Alexander exhaled, his back still to his friend. "In the meantime, you've lived in this house for three years." Alexander paused. "You're family, as far as everyone here is concerned. You and your brother. Certainly more so than Octavia." He grimaced. "My brother values you as a tribune and as a friend. Eurydice calls you friend, too. Come with me to this damned *family meeting*. Your presence will probably be the only thing that will make it endurable."

"Well, when you put it that way," Tiberius said quietly, "what choice do I have but to come along?"

Chapter II: Duty

Selene Julia Caesar knew quite well that of all her illustrious family she was the least significant. For a while, after her father's death, she'd resented it, but she thought she'd outgrown that. Certainly, it embarrassed her now to look back on how spitefully she'd behaved towards Eurydice from time to time, when Eurydice had been dropped into the position of matron of the household at the age of fourteen, when their mother had married Antony and, perforce, had left the household. While learning to ride like a man and to use all that terrifying, wonderful *magic*.

Oh, how she'd *envied* Eurydice those privileges and gifts. How she'd envied her older sister the beauty of Venus that radiated out of her, not that Eurydice ever seemed to notice it—though these days, Eurydice seemed graceful, powerful, and controlled in every movement. No longer gawky, she moved like one of her birds, always light, alert, and ready to take action.

The only way to deal with Eurydice, Selene had decided early on, was to make her happy. And the best way to do that was to take some of the work of the household off her sister's shoulders. Oh, Selene still had lessons of her own— Egyptian and Hellene, poetry and mathematics and music. But she'd made a point of visiting the kitchen every day and asking the chief cook there to teach her what each of the herbs and spices actually were. Learned how to bake bread that didn't have lumps in it. So that when Matronalia and Saturnalia came around, and the masters of the house had to serve the servants, Selene handled the bulk of the cooking, earning a grateful smile from Eurydice.

She'd always been a much better weaver than her sister, and now that Eurydice was Caesarion's declared Empress, she needed better and more elegant clothing than she had the time or inclination to make for herself. Selene therefore gave her little gifts silently through the year of silk, wool, and linen, the best products of her loom. And the sisters had fallen into a very comfortable pattern. Eurydice looked over the household account books, but Selene now kept them—Eurydice called this good practice for when Selene had a house of her own. Eurydice selected the guests for their meals, but Selene directed the menus. Eurydice handled their many visitors, including ambassadors from countries so far away that no one in Rome knew their names, and Selene might be called on to play her lyre or *kithara* at dinner . . . but Eurydice didn't push her to converse with the guests.

Which was entirely to Selene's liking.

The most Eurydice had pushed in the past three years was when she'd handed Selene dozens of scrolls on medicine, and told her to study them. Herbs. Poisons. Treatments. Surgical techniques. Selene had gaped at them, and floundered for a moment. "But why do I need to read any of this?"

"Because if someone's poisoned at a banquet, it might be helpful if someone besides me knows what the symptoms are, and which herbs in milk will help purge it," Eurydice had replied with a faint grimace. "And your stitchery is very good."

"Gods keep me from every needing to use it on human flesh," Selene had replied faintly. But she'd read the scrolls, as requested. And then had sat at her open window, playing her *kithara*, hoping she'd be able to forget some of what she'd just read.

And her other siblings? Caesarion had always been

eight full years her elder. She'd hardly seen him at all growing up—a kind enough stranger when Father had brought him back from whichever military camps they'd been visiting, but they hadn't shared the same pedagogues, or even the same meals. Eurydice might smile and say she remembered being picked up and twirled in the garden by their eldest brother. Selene had no such recollections. Already a frightening being—a person both older than she, and an occupant of the largely alien and mostly male world that existed outside the villa, when the illusions over him to conceal his strength and full power had been broken, he'd seemed like Mars Pater's personal vessel. As if the god had stepped out of the fresco on the villa's wall and stridden off for battle, with hardly a look behind.

If Selene wanted to make Eurydice happy, she wanted to make Caesarion forget she that even existed. The last thing she wanted was for those red eyes to fall on her, or a frown to cross his face. She couldn't even comprehend how Eurydice and he could love each other. Couldn't fathom the way they kissed in private, or the sounds that drifted down the corridor from their rooms at night. So she tried for invisibility around Caesarion. And most days, she succeeded in that.

Alexander? Not as terrifying as Caesarion or as frightening as Eurydice could be, when she chose. But Selene spent quite a bit of time in the kitchen around the servants. Most of whom were so accustomed to her being around—and her general invisibility—that they spoke quite freely in front of her. Whispering about Alexander. He'd acquired a cognomen of his own in the last few years, though it was one no one used to his face: Cerastes. The horned snake. The servants whispered that here was the *true* heir of Cleopatra. In charge of a shadowy network of men with long knives. A thousand eyes in the city were said to belong to him. And, every now and again, the laundry slaves would complain that they'd had to wash blood out of Master Alexander's tunics again. *Another long night questioning some Gaul. They say he keeps all the teeth he pulls out of their lying mouths, you know. In a little jar in his room.*

Don't be ridiculous. I'd have seen that in there when I go in to clean.

That's not all you'd see, if you looked. A sly insinuation to the voice. *You'd find Master Tiberius' boots under the sleeping couch, too.*

And, of course, there was *that*.

Four years ago, in a command tent outside Brundisium, there had been a fleeting mention of how perhaps there could be a marriage tie between the Julii and the Claudii—that Tiberius could be betrothed to Eurydice, or to Selene. Selene had peeked out cautiously around her sister, caught sight of Tiberius and his brother Drusus, and had rapidly tried to hide once more. Fortunately, no one had noticed that. Tiberius had been uninterested, since he'd already been betrothed to the far-younger daughter of Agrippa for several years. His gray eyes had seemed like a day in winter, cold and cheerless.

Several months later, with the brothers and Octavia Thurina, daughter of Octavian, living in the Julii villa, Selene had discovered that Tiberius knew how to smile. And that had largely been the end of it for her. The smile lightened his eyes—leaving them still melancholy, but with the precious possibility of *hope* amid all that sorrow. He remained older—a grown man, wearing a toga in the city, and armor when off at war. And thus, he, too, occupied that alien world outside the villa. In all honesty, in the past four years, Selene couldn't say that she'd said more than ten words to him. But whenever he and Drusus came back from their mother's villa, both with that peculiar mixture of anger, sorrow, and regret that visiting

Livia seemed to provoke in them, she had made it a habit to sit near them at dinner, and to play music for them quietly. Matching their mood with her music, until she gradually lifted from elegiac Hellene melodies into spritelier, happier songs. She had no idea if it helped them, but they'd never told her to leave off, either.

Selene knew it was foolish. Not only was Tiberius betrothed to Vipsania Agrippina, but . . . the Egyptian servants talked among themselves, in their native tongue, quite freely. She therefore had a fairly good idea of why Alexander and Tiberius disappeared into Alexander's rooms at night, and it didn't have much to do with drinking and dice games. *Stupid heart*, she told herself on the rare occasions when she inadvertently made eye-contact with Tiberius, or actually caught him smiling about something. *Stupid and pointless.*

And so, she made sure that she was even more invisible when Alexander and Tiberius were home from the campaigning season

Her friendship with Octavia had bloomed—and then withered. While Octavia still lived in the Julii house, waiting for her marriage to Alexander, Selene found that while she had dozens of responsibilities and tasks, Octavia never seemed to volunteer to do anything but go to the baths. And while it had been delicious, early on, to have someone *normal* to talk with—someone who wasn't god-born or brilliant or beautiful beyond compare—Selene had realized in the past two years that Octavia was flighty. While betrothed to Alexander, she'd had crushes on a half-dozen young men— most notably Jullus, Antony's second son. Which had been more than a little awkward while living in Antony and Cleopatra's house during the campaign season. Selene had watched all of Octavia's sighing and mooning over the young man, winced internally, and had carefully regulated her own behavior even more rigorously. No one was going to catch her sighing over Tiberius. The embarrassing condition of her foolish heart was *her* business. No one else's.

Of course, in and around all of that, Octavia had *also* come back from one of the Bona Dea rites a few years ago with giddy ideas. "We should practice kissing each other," Octavia had told Selene, her eyes sparkling. "So that when we finally have husbands, we'll know what we're doing!"

Selene had rather emphatically refused to participate. She had her mother's love-spell — not that the damned thing *worked* — and that was quite enough practice for her. That hadn't, however, kept Octavia from practicing with some of the maids. Selene hadn't mentioned that to Eurydice. But she didn't doubt that her elder sister knew, anyway. She took it on faith that sooner or later, Eurydice saw and heard everything.

Except, perhaps, what Selene thought or felt about anything. Silence, however, went well with invisibility.

And so, in silence, she found a wall in Caesarion's study as the rest of her family filtered in. Caesarion and Eurydice arrived together, hand-in-hand, earnestly discussing policy decisions. Caesarion took a seat behind his desk, burdened as it was with dozens of rolled-up parchment scrolls. Eurydice, as always, took a chair just to his left. Selene got a little smile of acknowledgement from her sister, and held her breath as Caesarion's eyes passed over her, exhaling once his gaze moved on. Alexander and Tiberius, never far apart, joined them moments later, taking backless chairs in front of the desk, all restless, young male energy. Unable to sit still for more than a few moments at a time, constantly shifting their legs or moving their hands.

And then Cleopatra swept into the room, bundled into a heavy cloak against the moderate Ianuarius chill. Toddling along at her side was little Gaius, now just turned three, her son with Antony. Cleopatra's hair had turned almost entirely iron-gray in the last year, but her motions still held vigor, and her dark eyes still sparked with energy. "I ask for a family meeting, and I find Tiberius here," she said with a shake of her head, as the door clicked shut behind her. "And yet, somehow, I'm not surprised."

Tiberius looked uncomfortable. "I told you I shouldn't be here," he muttered to Alexander. Looking at Caesarion, he said, "By your leave?"

"Is this just for Julii ears?" Caesarion asked wearily. "I have at least fifteen other things I need to be attending to — "

Selene dropped to a soft crouch, and held out her arms. Gaius caught sight of her, and immediately trundled over to accept a hug from her. She settled in at one of the tables behind the others now, finding a piece of parchment and a lump of charcoal with which to keep her little brother quiet and occupied. Secure in her invisibility and her general lack of importance, Selene listened to the conversation as it went on, but without paying much heed.

"These are the things that you need to be attending to," Cleopatra said sharply. ":Are you aware that the Nile's floods came so late this year that there was almost no grain crop at all?"

"I've read the reports," Caesarion replied. "The price of grain is fixed in Rome, so that the plebeians can afford to *eat*. Unfortunately, that means that the state has to pay the farmers in some other way, and prices went up. Drastically. There's a budget shortfall at the moment that you wouldn't believe."

"How bad?" Alexander asked urgently.

"Over a million solidi," Caesarion admitted tightly. "All our legionnaires, when they retire, have been promised either a piece of land, or a retirement bonus in gold. I have several thousand men asking to retire this year, and I'm going to have to ask them, if not outright beg them, to either stay in harness, or take the land and sell it on the market. Or, for the gods' sakes, farm it themselves, so we get more *grain* coming in." He rubbed at his eyes, and Selene rapidly sketched a sheaf of grain for little Gaius.

"The legions have mutinied before over lack of pay, or the perception that they are about to lose their retirement bonuses," Tiberius muttered. "I can vouch for the Fifth. You've had me with them all campaign season . . . before putting me on *sewage* issues here in Rome for the winter—" a dark look at Caesarion, who shrugged. "And the rest of the core legions love you. But the ones in the east—you've been having to recruit from the provinces where they mostly speak Hellene, not Latin. You could be looking at revolts among the troops."

"Tell me something of which I am not aware," Caesarion said, rubbing at his eyes.

Alexander shrugged. "The populace here in Rome has been sheltered from the worst of it," he put in now. "We have about a year's supply of grain in the silos. No one's going hungry at the moment. No graffiti calling for an increase in the bread dole. No mobs gathering to protest the price of food. Not yet, anyway."

Eurydice's head turned towards Cleopatra. "You're going to tell us that this is our fault, aren't you, Mother?" she asked, her voice tight, and Selene looked up at that. "We've done what the gods required of us. We married. The compact is secure—"

"You married here in Rome," Cleopatra interrupted. "You need to go to Egypt. Both of you. As quickly as you may. Seal yourselves to the gods there, renew the old spells. And *someone* needs to rule there. Not just some Roman military prefect, commanding from a *castra*. Someone needs to be in the palace of the Ptolemies." Her eyes narrowed, and her gaze met Eurydice's like a clash of blades.

Thank the gods I'm not the one meeting that stare, Selene thought. A fragment of a tune rattled through her head, and absently, she wrote it down in Hellene notation. It probably wouldn't have words, but her little musical twiddles rarely did. *And to think, it could have been Alexander and me who were consigned to Egypt. Told to marry and renew the pact of the gods. I can't even imagine that.*

Caesarion and Eurydice had both frozen in place. And then, to Selene's surprise, both of them began to protest at once.

"I can't possibly spare Eurydice. We're preparing to invade Britannia, and how do you think that will go without her eyes and magic?"

"I can't stay in Egypt, Mother. I've been setting up the school for sorcerers here in Rome, but we have all of three students at the moment, none of whom are ready for combat against the druids and their earth-magic and their spirits—"

"Aside from which, you may not have noticed, but I don't have an heir yet—"

"Then I strongly recommend that you take off the anti-conception bracelet I gave you, and *get on with it,*" Cleopatra told them tartly, silencing both of them.

Selene's head rose, and she gave her brother and sister a single wide-eyed look at that piece of plain speaking. Saw both of them—god-like creatures that they were!—flush slightly. And heard one tiny snicker from Alexander, at exactly the wrong moment—provoking an outright glare from Caesarion. Selene, not even in the direct path of that expression, withered in her seat.

Caesarion turned that glare on their mother now. "Let

me see if I understand you correctly. You want me to abandon the invasion of Britannia, take my wife on a pleasure trip to Egypt, get her with child, and . . . what, move the capital of the empire away from Rome to Alexandria?"

"No, I want you to leave her there to *rule* for a time," Cleopatra replied, this time with a hint of gentleness in her voice. "The patricians of Rome have been unthreatened for the past three years, because you've produced no heir. They have had time to get used to the idea of your marriage. They will, however, see a child that continues the line of Caesar as the deathknell of the remnants of the Republic, and the establishment of a hereditary monarchy. A monarchy in which none of them has a stake, since you did not marry any of *their* daughters." Cleopatra's mouth tightened. "I had to watch every morsel of food I ate through four pregnancies, and could barely set foot outside the villa when I had the three of you who followed Caesarion into this world," she added softly. "I don't wish for Eurydice to know that same clutching fear. Egypt will be *safer* from knives and poisons. For both Eurydice and any child you might have, my dear ones."

Eurydice sighed. "The dream has a way of coming true. I just hoped . . . that it wouldn't happen yet." She hung her head, but Selene had no idea what she meant by those words.

Silence draped over the room like a winding sheet. Finally, Alexander exhaled. "Mother's probably right on all counts. And there *has* been Parthian activity in the east. You could make a good show of shoring up the eastern borders as part of the trip to Egypt, brother. Get a good look at the loyalties of the eastern legions. Give the Eagles a good airing. And that way, it's less of a 'pleasure trip,' for you, and a very practical reason to be there, instead of preparing for Britannia."

"So, I just call off the invasion?" Caesarion muttered,

shaking his head. "It's retaliatory, for that business in Hispania. I wasn't really looking to find the northlands where the sun never sets this year, but if I don't start it soon, Rome's *vengeance* will no longer be respected and feared—"

"Send the legions into northern Gaul," Tiberius suggested. "Cicero Minor and a few others—and I volunteer as one of them—can pre-stage. Even make the crossing and get a toe-hold in the lands of the Cantiaci, or wherever you want us to land."

"You have capable legates," Cleopatra said, still standing. "Make use of them, my son. Your father didn't attend every battle his legions fought, either."

Caesarion grimaced. "I know, I know. But it's my duty to lead them. God-born of Mars. And they call me their Eagle for a reason." He caught Eurydice's hand in his own, giving her a sober look. "Mother, we can't just send Eurydice alone to rule a country she's never set foot in before."

Cleopatra nodded. "That's why I was going to suggest that you make Antony governor of Egypt—replace the current prefect and bump the title up a little. And Gaius and I will go with him, and the people there will see continuity of power, and the people of Rome will see a Roman province governed by a Roman man, and will be unthreatened by what they'll perceive as a puppet queen on a foreign throne." She shrugged.

"Gods," Alexander muttered. "How am I ever going to play the game as well as you do, Mother?"

Cleopatra smiled at him, her expression brittle. "Stay alive long enough," she replied succinctly. "It's really the only way." She turned, and now her dark eyes found Selene, startling her so much that she almost dropped the charcoal in her fingers. "And that," Cleopatra said briskly, "brings us to the vexed question of what to do with *you*."

For an instant, Selene thought she might have meant Gaius. She even looked down at the three-year-old, checking to make sure that he hadn't destroyed any priceless scrolls. "Why, ah, Gaius will be going with you and Antony, surely?" Selene offered, suddenly realizing to her horror that everyone in the room was *looking* at her.

Cleopatra looked up at the ceiling. "Four children," she muttered. "An eagle, a hawk, a snake, and a mouse."

The words might have stung, but Selene knew that they were true. But Eurydice cleared her throat. "Actually, Father used to call her his *lark*," she pointed out, her tone a little sharper than she usually used with their mother. "As a matter of fact, in his final illness, before Caesarion and Alexander came home? Selene played the lyre for him every day. And when you told her to leave off, Mother, he told you he wanted to hear his lark play. Because it cheered him to hear her. And because, I think, he knew it was the only way she could say good-bye."

"I didn't know that," Alexander said in a tone of surprise.

Selene jerked her eyes away, finding a wall to stare at, so that the tears, which had risen unbidden to her eyes, would have no reason to fall, and so that none of the others could see them.

Cleopatra sounded annoyed at the reminder. "Yes, yes, I remember. Of course, he called one of his *legions* the Larks, too, as you'll recall. And there's very little resemblance between her and them, you'll note." Tiredly now, their mother said, "Well, stand up, my girl. Let me have a look at you." A little more irritably, she added, "And look me in the eye, if you please. You're always staring off."

Oh, gods, what is this about? Selene thought frantically, and stood, slipping Gaius out of her lap. And, completely unable to meet her mother's gaze, she resorted to her oldest trick. She looked at her mother's eyebrows, instead. Giving the appearance of eye-contact, but none of the reality.

Cleopatra examined her from top to bottom, finally giving an assenting sort of sniff. "Very well. You're more than old enough to be married, my girl. Caesarion, that *must* be taken care of. Quickly. You know that Antony and I have a preference in the matter—"

Selene's mouth had fallen open, but no words came out. Her gaze skittered to Caesarion's face as he frowned a little and shook his head. "I've received several inquiries about Selene's hand, Mother." He looked past Cleopatra towards Selene now, and his voice gentled a bit as he added, kindly, "Most of them, I didn't think you'd like, sister. Lucius Domitius Ahenobarbus was one, for example."

Before Cleopatra could get a word in, Eurydice stood and crossed the room to put a hand on Selene's shoulder. "You remember who he is, right?" her sister asked gently.

Memory flickered, and Selene settled her eyes on the floor. "Lepidus' great-nephew, I think?" she murmured. "The one who talks about nothing but chariot-racing. And whipped a slave across the face last year when his Blues lost at the Circus."

"Good memory," Alexander said, his voice startled. "I'm surprised you recalled him. He's only been here to dinner once, hasn't he?"

"He's marrying Antonia Major in three months," Selene said, her eyes still tracing patterns on the tile floor. "She told me that she planned to invite all of her friends to dinner every night he spends at the races. Antonia the Elder told her that entertaining without her husband being present would damage her reputation." There were actually three Antonias: Antonia the Elder, the daughter of Antony's first disastrous marriage, and then Antonia Major and Antonia Minor, the daughters of his third wife, Octavia. It made discussing Antony's daughters—now their stepsisters—somewhat difficult in casual conversation.

Selene's words now limped out into the silence. "I don't think Antonia Major really cares, though." She doesn't like him. At all. She doesn't want to marry him. But her father, and presumably my mother, aren't giving her much choice in the matter.

Cleopatra sighed. "The match provides a second connection in Antony's family to Lepidus, even if it's only on Ahenobarbus' mother's side," she said pragmatically. "Antonia the Elder is married to Lepidus' son, Marcus Aemilius Lepidus the Younger, but a second tie makes sense. Lepidus is a patrician. Antony is a plebeian, but both were supporters of Caesar—and of your brother. But I will speak to Antonia Major about the need for discretion, at least in the first few years of marriage." Impatience entered her tone, and Selene could hear her gown rustle as she turned back towards Caesarion. "Well? What possible objection could you have to Antyllus, Antony's eldest son? A tribune who's taken the place of a legate, at least temporarily, and at a young age? I know he's mentioned the possibility of a marriage tie—"

"Excuse me?" Selene said.

"He's expressed interest off and on," Caesarion said, his tone guarded. "I haven't seen a need to rush things, however. I'm not sure they've even *spoken*—"

"Excuse me!" Selene said again, raising her head. Aware that she'd spoken so loudly that everyone's heads had snapped towards her, she fastened her eyes to a wall, and blurted out her words quickly, so that she wouldn't lose her courage. "I don't think I want to be married," she said so rapidly that the words almost blurred together. "Fabia, the lead Vestal is ill. They'll have an opening in their ranks in the next year. Mightn't it be better if I went and joined them? They handle all the wills and important documents of Rome, and it's very much an honor—" Her voice faltered. Faded. Dwindled away. *And even broaching it as a possibility might give me a year's leeway on this subject.*

"Absolutely not!" Cleopatra's voice cracked like a whip. "A daughter of mine, locked in a temple with a thirty-year vow of chastity—"

"I can see the attraction," Alexander said, having swung around in his chair to stare at Selene, just as Tiberius had. "They can own property in their own right, Mother. They can vote. Their word is considered unimpeachable—"

"But what a *waste* that would be," Tiberius muttered, his voice filtering through Alexander's. Selene glanced at him, accidentally met his eyes, and jerked her own away, rapidly, seeing a frown on his face. "It's not my business, of course," he added, mildly, "but you seem to be very good with children." He gestured at Gaius, and shrugged. "Vestals can't have families, by definition."

Selene twisted away entirely, swallowing hard. She couldn't even respond to that comment, beyond a shrug. The idea of having children wasn't unwelcome, and her heart—stupid, stupid heart—raced at the words coming from Tiberius' mouth. *Idiot,* she thought with deep self-contempt. *He means nothing at all by it.*

"Do you feel an actual calling from the gods?" Eurydice asked Selene directly. "Or is this just an escape attempt?" Sympathy in her sister's tone, rueful and true. "All I get from Isis, personally, are dreams, not words. But if you genuinely feel drawn to this service," a glance at their mother, "I don't know how I could possibly tell you no."

Caesarion cleared his throat. "Actually, there are many

reasons to say no," he put in gently, and Selene felt the world come down on her shoulders. "Selene doesn't meet the other criteria," he told them all, sitting back in his chair. "She's too old to be inducted. Both of her parents would need to be among the living, too." He looked directly at Selene, not without sympathy, though she could only see his expression from the corner of her eyes. "Mother, I just don't see the need for haste in this. If she's not ready to marry, she's not ready to marry."

Selene exhaled, a huge sensation of relief coursing through her as her shoulders, raised defensively, relaxed.

Cleopatra sighed and shook her head. "You don't see a need," she repeated slowly. "I'm going to ask a series of questions, and see which of you children sees the way through the labyrinth first. If Eurydice leaves Rome to rule in Egypt, and I am not here to take Selene into Antony's house, and all Roman women *must* live under the guiding hand of a male relative, and if Selene lives here, then who is the woman of this house?"

"Selene would be," Eurydice replied, immediately. "She'll be good at it, too. She's been handling all the domestic chores so that I could focus on dealing with magic and the ambassadors and . . . ." She hesitated, and once again, she touched Selene's shoulder. "You'd have to start speaking with people at dinner," she said gently. "You used to chatter with Octavia so much, it surprised me how silent you've been at meals with guests. And I've let you get away with shyness over dinner for years. You'll have to be brave—"

The sensation of crushing horror that filled Selene made her raise her eyes to Eurydice's. And finding nothing but pitiless hawk gold there, she turned her face away sharply.

"Think again," Cleopatra said, her voice slightly bored

now as she took a chair. "Alexander, you should see the implications quite clearly. If Caesarion married one sister, and has sent her away . . . ?"

Alexander put a hand over his face for a moment. "Yes, what will the automatic inference be, when he has his second sister sharing his couch at meals and serving as his hostess for grand events?" He pulled his hand away and looked at Caesarion. "Half of Rome will think you've traded in Eurydice for someone younger and more pliable."

"Fuck that!" Caesarion snapped, the barracks oath ringing off the walls, making Selene cringe. "I would never—"

Alexander exhaled through his teeth. "Doesn't matter what you would or wouldn't do. It's about public perceptions. Which you two have *enough* trouble with, as is." He nodded to Caesarion and Eurydice, a frown covering his face as he worked through the problem in his head.

Caesarion stood, putting his fists on his desk. "Well, it doesn't matter," he snapped. "I won't *be* here. I'll be in Egypt. Syria. *Fucking Britannia.*"

"Year-round?" Cleopatra asked mildly. "Every year?" She shrugged. "And that would, of course, leave Selene here, without a male guardian, as Rome seems to feel is so necessary for women. Which would in turn require her to travel with you on campaign—"

"Which presents the same problems," Alexander cut in, sounding dispirited.

"Not staying at least part of the year in Rome would have the same effect as moving the capital to Alexandria," Eurydice muttered, her hand falling from Selene's shoulder, her eyes flicking from side to side now, as if reading from a scroll.

Alexander's head came up. "Fine," he said, nodding to himself. "I'll move out of this villa. Selene can come and live with me. Keep *my* house. I'm not leaving Rome this campaign season. I've too much to do with my network of eyes and ears." He glanced over at Selene, smiling. "And as good as your memory is, and as adept as you seem to be at making yourself invisible, perhaps I can recruit you, eh?"

Another brief rush of hope flickered through Selene, and she nodded rapidly. She'd have agreed to *anything* at this point, short of running naked through the streets of Rome and jumping into the polluted Tiber, to escape the trap she felt closing around her.

Cleopatra sighed. "Alexander, my dear, you have a carefully-cultivated reputation for excess. If you were to move out of this villa and establish your own residence, you would either need to abandon that reputation entirely for your sister's sake, or you'd wind up tarring her with the same brush. Which of those two courses of action is more acceptable to you?" She tapped her fingers lightly on the table.

Alexander's smile faded slightly as he glanced at Tiberius, and then he drew himself up in his chair. "I don't usually bring the causes for my reputation home with me, Mother. I leave them out in the streets of Rome. Where they collect information for me."

Cleopatra nodded, her expression unsparing even for him. "Of course. Why, no one will ask her any questions about living with you at all. And in nine or ten months, or a few *more* years, or whenever you get around to marrying Octavia, I'm sure your sister will give up the keys of the house with good grace and subordinate herself to your wife peacefully."

The expression on Alexander's face was now so grim that Selene hardly recognized her brother. *He doesn't want to marry Octavia,* she thought, and she said, rapidly, "I wouldn't mind keeping Alexander's house for as long as he needed me. Months or years, it doesn't matter." *My brothers and my sister* *love me. Enough to try to pull me out of this mess. And that's enough love to last <u>anyone</u> for a lifetime.*

"She can come with *me*," Eurydice said, before Cleopatra could reply. "She can come to Egypt. Royal women are servants at court all the time. Nesa, my own wet-nurse, is Egyptian nobility, for the gods' sake. And that way, neither of us would be alone in a strange place." She lifted her chin, offering Cleopatra defiance.

Their mother sighed. "And it's very noble of both Alexander and you to offer her a place in your homes," Cleopatra murmured, shaking her head. "But it leaves out one important element. She'd never get on with her own life. Always be an adjunct to one of you. Which is why she really must marry. And before you leave for Egypt."

"Mother, you treat your daughters in such a fashion as you would *never* permit someone to treat you," Eurydice snapped.

But Selene just shook her head rapidly, and without asking for permission to leave, turned and ran out of the room. Leaving Gaius, who'd just grabbed her arm to get her to look at what he'd been drawing, to wail indignantly in her wake. *No,* Selene thought, reaching her own tiny *cubicula,* and throwing herself down on the sleeping couch there. *I won't. I <u>won't</u>. She can't make me.*

———————

Eurydice watched her sister leave, but couldn't go after her immediately. Not with a full-fledged argument now broiling between all the remaining adult siblings and their mother. Cleopatra picked up Gaius, bouncing him on her hip as she glared at Eurydice now. "I treat you in exactly the ways that your behavior merits and reality dictates, daughter."

"There is no reason to push her into a marriage when

she's not ready," Eurydice returned flatly. "She can come with me to Egypt. And when she decides she's ready —"

"And when will that be?" Cleopatra returned acidly. "When you've given in to her fears and protected and sheltered her for the next five years? The next ten? When you've allowed her to wish her entire youth away, dreaming of the *perfect* man, I'm sure. One who'll never actually ask her to do more than play her damned lyre." Cleopatra's lips thinned.

And for a blistering instant, Eurydice *understood* her mother. Saw right down to the core of her. "Good gods," she muttered, putting a hand on a scroll rack to steady herself at the insight.

"Antyllus is on your guest list for dinner tonight," Cleopatra reminded Eurydice, as her daughter stood there, dazed. "Do seat them beside each other. Selene must grow up at some point, and continuously allowing her to wallow in whatever sea of self-pity she's sunk herself in, does no one any good." A glance of asperity at Alexander. "Also, I'm sure you'll have Octavia seated beside her betrothed, as usual."

"I know my duties to Octavia," Alexander growled, his face still dark. "I'm reminded of them *daily*."

Cleopatra nodded, still bouncing Gaius on her hip. And then swept out of the room, still regal as a queen.

In her wake, Tiberius shook his head. "She's less draining than my mother, but *gods*, she's demanding," he muttered. "I don't envy any of you."

"She's jealous," Eurydice said, still shaken, which got all the men's heads to turn towards her. "She's *jealous*. And of Selene, of all people." She sat down on one of the chairs, feeling Caesarion move up behind her, his warm hand caressing the nape of her neck.

"How do you mean?" he asked quietly.

"Selene's . . . protected." Eurydice replied, shaking her head. "The way no one *ever* protected our mother. By the time she was Selene's age. . ." They all knew the grim reality of Cleopatra's youth. She'd been taken to Rome as a refugee by her father, during a rebellion by her sisters. When her sisters had been overthrown with Rome's aid, she had, when a year younger than Selene was now, watched her own sisters executed, and then, as her father's queen, had been raped nightly for three years until his death. Then another civil war, between her and her last remaining siblings, resulting in her alliance with Caesar . . . which had led to the births of her first four children. All before the age of twenty. Eurydice swallowed, and added, quietly, "Each of us was protected, yes, but . . . Caesarion and I are both god-born. Alexander protects himself. Selene *can't* protect herself—she's never been forced to. She's skilled in all the things Mother has no talent for." She shrugged a little now, and added, "And I wonder if the push to have her marry Antyllus might be an urge to . . . rewrite history a little, on Mother's part." *Wed the son of the man she could have loved in her youth, but didn't, to her own daughter.*

"Well, she and Antony would get a grandchild together out of it, without having to wait for Gaius to grow up," Caesarion muttered, clearly seeing the pattern as she did. "I'll talk to Antyllus before dinner. And make it clear that no matter what Mother and Antony think, I won't let Selene be forced into anything that she doesn't want. *She* has to give consent in this before I will." Eurydice looked up at him, seeing the grim lines on his face. "And I don't care if Mother thinks we're overprotecting her."

"Just don't let her become a damned Vestal," Tiberius said with a surprising scowl. "They *do* make exceptions for older girls now and again. A thirty-year vow of marriage to the whole of Rome shouldn't be taken just because she's frightened of marriage to a man."

"I don't think she's frightened," Alexander said slowly. "I don't know what she is. She does like men, yes?" He glanced at Eurydice.

"She hasn't confided in me since, well. . . ." Eurydice tapped beside one eyelid. "You'd be better off asking Octavia. They used to giggle together incessantly, mostly about men, I think." Eurydice thought about that. If she had to put a date to it, the giggling had diminished sharply after the Bona Dea rites of three years ago. *They had a falling out of some sort, perhaps? I thought it was just a question of Selene growing up more quickly than Octavia, but . . . .*

"Why is *everyone* telling me to talk to my betrothed today?" Alexander complained.

"You're due. Every man should speak to his wife or betrothed at least once a week," Caesarion replied, dead-pan, his hand still on the back of Eurydice's neck. And then he looked down at her and smiled. "Or more often, in some cases."

Tiberius stood. "I'll go get cleaned up before dinner," he added, asking Caesarion, "By your leave? I'd offer to go talk to your sister, but. . ." he shrugged, "I doubt there's anything I could say that would comfort her at the moment."

Caesarion flipped a hand at him in dismissal. "Go on. Eurydice can deal with her later. For the moment, can we get back on the topic of the representatives from the Gallic provinces and their complaints about the temples before dinner?"

And Eurydice, Caesarion, and Alexander sat back down to discuss the thorny issues that the policies that they'd inherited now presented.

———————

Marcus Antonius Antyllus had spent the afternoon, not at the baths, where his brother Jullus had invited him to join him and his friends, but rather at a series of archery butts located behind his father's villa. He stepped on the end of the Scythian recurved bow he'd purchased years ago during his service in Illyria — now the incorporated province of Illyricum, which his father had finished pacifying last year — and slipped a fresh string into place.

The peculiar double curve of the bow's design meant that the limbs only required a very slight deflection to string it, and it always retained its curvature, even when unstrung. . . but the draw-weight of this weapon was like nothing else he'd ever seen. Over a hundred and sixty *librae*. Archery demanded exceptional muscular strength in the arms, chest, and back — anyone could fire off a quick trick shot from a mostly slack bow, at ten or twenty feet. War archery, however, the kind that punched arrows through armor at a hundred feet, required far more skill and strength. He'd already been an exceptional archer before finding this bow, but he'd needed to develop even more strength and control to use it, and use it well.

The peculiar double curve of the laminated wood and horn intensified as the string slipped home, and Antyllus chuckled to himself; it had always looked to him like the outline of half of a smiling female mouth. Thus, in his mind, his bow was the Scythian maiden, and he definitely liked to see her smile. The hum of the string, as he plucked it lightly, was the maiden's laughter. And he went over his arrows with the same methodical care he'd applied to the bow itself. Strong arrows with heavier pine shafts and murderous narrow points, for penetrating shields and cuirasses, had their place. Lighter arrows, made of reed, with points shaped like fishtails, for taking birds on the wing. The lighter the arrow, the more likely that it needed extra weight—stone or metal—at the tip to give it penetrating force when it reached its target. A light arrow couldn't carry the *force* of this kind of bow. It would just flutter at the end of its trajectory, uselessly.

And each of these arrows had been fletched to measure. The length of his arm. The strength of his draw. The power of this particular bow. He selected medium-weight arrows, and got to work, finding the calm center of his spirit and exhaling partially as he fired. Steady hands. Even flow of motion. Using a bow too strong for the arm tended to make a man's hands and arms shake with the strain, but he'd been making this particular maiden smile for over three years. They knew each other very well. Accuracy shots, first. Then, once he'd warmed up, he aimed for *speed*. Between twelve and twenty shots, taken in a minute. Not thinking, and not particularly aiming. Just telling the maiden where he wanted the arrows to go, and letting her smile.

After a half hour, he took a break to let his arms rest, and stretched, wishing that Ianuarius would hasten past, bringing warmer weather to Rome. "Not bad," he heard his father's voice, and turned, catching Mark Antony's quirked glance at the targets. Most of which had a dozen fletchings decorating their centers.

"Eh, I'll never be able to sail one arrow through the holes at the back of twelve axeheads, all lined up," Antyllus said, remembering the part of the *Odyssey* he'd loved best as a child. "But the Cretans I usually command have told me that I shouldn't have been born a Roman. There's word that they might want to adopt me." He nodded soberly, watching his father's grizzled eyebrows rise.

"I trust you've no desire to accept?"

"No, no, I was born right here in Rome. I'd say that if

you cut me, I'd bleed water from the Tiber, except that then you'd ask me if I were full of shit, too." Antyllus grinned at his father, winning a hearty guffaw from his elder, and a slap on the back. "To what do I owe the pleasure of company during my practice session?" he asked over his shoulder, heading to the targets to retrieve his arrows.

"You'll be going to dinner with the Julii tonight." It wasn't quite a question.

Antyllus nodded, frowning slightly in puzzlement. "I visit once or twice a month outside the campaign season," he said simply, returning his arrows to his quiver. "Caesarion asked me this winter to help assess some land for an additional port—something to supplement Ostia." He paused. "Is something amiss?" Antony hadn't asked about Antyllus' comings and goings since he was eighteen. *Much in contrast to Father's own earliest years, where he apparently wandered the streets of Rome at will from about the age of twelve on. He didn't have a strong father at hand. I did. Even if we spent the first eight years of my life going from battlefield to battlefield during Caesar's civil wars, he was always there.*

"Nothing's amiss," Antony returned. "In fact, something might even go right for once. My wife went over earlier to discuss her youngest daughter's marriage prospects with her son."

Antyllus blinked. "I thought that was off the table till Selene was older."

"She *is* older. Fifteen. Perfectly suitable age for marriage." Antony patted his son on the shoulder. "Give her some of the family charm. I'd like to have grandchildren at some point."

Antyllus drew, aimed, and loosed at the furthest target. "I don't see you trying to marry off Jullus."

"Your brother is a *cinaedus*." Antony grimaced.

"Apparently writes some decent poetry, but . . . ."

"Women still seem to flock to him." It was true. Jullus had the same faintly androgynous facial qualities of a statue of Cupid. The sort of face that women *swooned* over, and Jullus, by all accounts, took full advantage of that fact. When he wasn't spending time with other men, anyway. Antyllus made a point of not asking his brother how many lovers he had—or of which gender they were. There were strong rumors about both Jullus and Gaius Cornelius Dolabella, one of Cicero's grandsons by his daughter Tullia. Son of the same Dolabella who'd slept with Antony's first wife, whom he'd divorced after producing the eldest of Antyllus' three sisters, Antonia the Elder.

Of course, the difference between a *cinaedus* and any other man with male lovers was subtle. The word suggested not only that he was on the receiving end on occasion, but that he lacked the essential qualities of a man—*virtue*. Excellence in war, courage, integrity, honor. A man's worth was known by these things, and could only be truly measured in combat. And after demonstrating that worth in battle, a man could continue to demonstrate it in public life, through a political career. The military, political, and social were therefore inextricably entwined. A man who demonstrated *virtue* could be excused any number of lovers of the same sex. Assuming he never allowed himself to be penetrated, of course. That way led to *infamio*.

All of which constituted Antyllus' reasons for turning down Jullus' perfectly cordial suggestion that they go to the baths together today to meet his friends. If the elder brother did that, he suspected that he might find out more than he really wanted to know, and would be obliged to say something pungent along the lines of family honor and *dignitas*. It was therefore better if he did *not* know. "Marry him off, and I'm fairly sure you'll get grandchildren," he said now, loosing another arrow.

"Yes, but will they be *mine?*" Antony asked dryly.

"The first one or two, I assure you." Antyllus' voice was light. "Then he'll get bored of his wife and find another bed. And she'll probably get bored, too, and find affection elsewhere, and in and around a divorce, there might be a bastard or two that slips in."

"I definitely understand *boredom*, but I'd like to avoid some of the drama," Antony replied, his tone still dry. Antyllus shot his father a wry glance; Antony's love-life had been full of exactly that, for decades. Now, the older man ran a hand over his curly, graying hair. "I blame myself. I was rather busy trying to fit myself inside an amphora of wine when you two were boys. I missed your mother. There was an . . . incident with Cleopatra that resulted in my banishment from Caesar's inner circle. And then I married Octavia. The wine jar became even more appealing from that moment on." He grimaced. "It was unmanly of me. And Jullus pays the price of my failings."

"You were there for us, Father," Antyllus replied, lowering his bow and regarding his father for a moment. "Jullus just reacted to Octavia's moralism differently than I did. That's all. He might someday decide that he doesn't have to throw it in her face anymore. Now that she's been dead five years or so." He shrugged. *Moralism and coldness. Moralism for us. Coldness for Father. Then again, I got away from the house two years before Jullus did, and I had Tincomarus, our Gallic hostage, for company many days. Three years older or not, he was still almost as good as another brother. Then my fourteenth birthday came, and I joined the legions the instant I could.*

Lifting his bow again, and aiming to distract his father, he added now, lightly, "And on the subject of grandchildren .

. . given the number of half-brothers and half-sisters I have running around," a sly note entered Antyllus' voice as he gave his father a look, "aren't the odds of there being grandchildren already in the mix pretty good?" Another shot. His father's reputation as the world's greatest lover was sometimes a burden, but it was often also highly amusing. Or at least it had been, when prune-faced Octavia had been alive to be shocked when yet another woman had turned up with a ten-year-old bastard, petitioning Antony for apprenticeship fees, or whatever else.

Antony gave his first-born son a look. "Yes, but those don't carry my *name*. Mind your tongue, son."

"Oh, I do. But taking the safest course never brought anyone victory . . . or adventure." Antyllus grinned outright, and loosed another arrow. He had his rhythm now.

"But we were speaking of you. As I was saying, apply the family charm. Your brother can't have inherited *all* of mine. Cleopatra told me that Caesarion's still reluctant, mostly because the girl says she doesn't want to marry at all."

Antyllus blinked, relaxing his hold on the string without loosing the arrow, and turned to stare at his father. "Just so we're clear, are you ordering me to seduce the sister of the Emperor—who is, by the way, my friend?"

Antony grunted. "Not in any *physical* sense, though it wouldn't hurt my feelings if you got her into bed." He shrugged. "Talk her around before we lose the only opportunity this generation for forging a lasting alliance with the Julii. Gaius is the light of my old age, but he's the son of an Egyptian queen. Not of a daughter of the Julii."

Another arrow aimed, then loosed. "I'll do my best, but every time I've so much as smiled at that girl, she vanishes." *Not that I have quite my father's way with women—no one on earth could possibly live up to <u>that</u>—but I've rarely had them flee my* *presence outright.*

A snicker from his father. "I thought you were a better hunter than that."

"Some prey doesn't come to the stream or the salt lick, Father, and takes flight at the faintest sound in the underbrush. After a certain point, you stop hunting for unicorns when you get tired and hungry, and there are deer in plenty all around." His fingers released the next arrow.

"Well, the unicorn will be brought to bay tonight. Do *try* to catch her."

"As my father commands." He brought his fist to his chest in an ironic salute, and got a light cuff across the back of his neck for his impudence—which only made him grin. *Well, looks as if I have to try to get a different maiden to smile,* he told his bow silently. *Don't be jealous.* And unstrung it to carry it and his arrows back into the house.

At the Julii villa, Alexander had been released from the policy conversation with Caesarion and Eurydice—and as he strode back towards his rooms to copy the reports he'd received and evaluate them, his mind drifted. He'd found himself deeply dismayed by the look of . . . not quite *fear* . . . in Selene's face and eyes. *Somehow, she's slipped between all our fingers,* Alexander thought, frowning as he ran up the stairs. *Here I call myself a spymaster, and pride myself on being able to read the thoughts and emotions of those around me, and I have no idea what's actually bothering one of my own sisters. I mean, I've had more important things on my mind . . . tracking the progress of the Octavianite faction, assessing threats in the city. . . . but how can I not know what's going on under my own nose?*

He paused at the balcony, considering the problem as he stared out over the atrium. And in a flash, it seemed as if all his current problems might have one singular and very neat solution.

Fact: As soon as I marry Octavia, Tiberius will quietly step out of my life. I don't want that. Even if there's no more sex . . . and I can accept that. . . I don't want him out of my life entirely.

Fact: His betrothal to Agrippa's daughter serves no current useful political need. In fact, it's a hindrance to him, since it saddles him with Octavianite connections, when he's solidly in the Julii camp.

Fact: Breaking that betrothal would be a matter of a conversation with and a possible apology to Agrippa, followed by a wrist-clasp between men, and it would be over.

Fact: My sister needs a husband who will take excellent care of her.

Fact: Tiberius is probably the most honorable person I know. He'd never cheat on her. Never beat her. She'd be treated with respect and kindness throughout her entire life — the respect and kindness that she really deserves.

Fact: I'd be welcome to visit them at any time. And while that might sound self-serving, even if I have to give up everything else, I do not *want to lose the friendship.*

Alexander set his hands on the railing of the balcony and exhaled. "Now, if I can only convince him to make the offer, convince Caesarion to consider it, and convince *her* not to reject Ti out of hand. . . ." *First thing's first. Talk to Tiberius.*

His friend was in the bath house behind the main villa, taking a quick swim in spite of the Ianuarius chill — mostly, Alexander suspected, to clean the sweat off from their earlier exertions. Tiberius popped out from under the water of the *frigidarium* area, looking surprised to see Alexander here — fully clothed — and gave him a rare half-smile. "You're overdressed for a bath."

"I'll bathe in a bit." Alexander took off his sandals and

sat on the edge, watching as, in the distance, the servants set up oil, towels, and strigils. "I need to talk to you about something first. I think you should marry Selene." Quick, blunt, and to the point. Circumlocutions and subtlety didn't work with Tiberius.

His friend stood rooted in the shallow end of the pool, staring at him. "What?" His voice echoed back off the tiled walls, causing several servants to look over in interest. Then Tiberius planted his elbows on the tiled edge and hissed, more cautiously, "*What* did you just say?"

"It's not a state secret. I think you should marry my sister. You've said many times that if Caesarion ever made noises about adopting you, you'd accept. Gods know, you've suggested taking the Julii name as if you were a manumitted slave," Alexander added that last in a very quiet voice, mindful of how his words might bounce off the *frigidarium's* walls. "Marry her. Be my brother in truth." He exhaled. "I think I'll find it easier to . . . give you up, if it's to someone I love." Alexander grimaced, looking away. *Why does the truth always have to hurt to speak? Lies are so much easier to say.*

Tiberius looked away himself, and for a long moment, neither of them spoke. "There's the matter of my being betrothed to Vipsania—"

"Tell Agrippa that political realities have changed, which is true, and that while you still respect him, you'd like to align yourself more fully with a cause with which you find yourself in full accord." Alexander shrugged. "The most you might have to deal with is your mother's affront at marrying a hated half-Egyptian Julii—"

"I'm not sure you could have spoken words more likely to make me agree to this insane proposition," Tiberius muttered, running a hand over his hair, darkened almost to brown by the water. "Alexander . . . she doesn't want to marry *anyone*. And I'm . . . cold by nature. Not particularly the loveable *type* – "

Alexander gave him a sidelong look. "You say that to *me?" When I have substantial proof that you're capable of quite a bit of passion?*

"She's not going to accept me. She never looks straight at me – "

"I haven't seen her look straight at *anyone* in years, other than Octavia. Not since Father died, anyway." Alexander sighed internally. "I think we all thought that someone else was looking after her, and it turns out that we all were neglecting her. Time to do something about that."

Tiberius turned towards him. No physical contact at all. "And your solution is *me?* Alexander, desperate times call for desperate measures and all, but . . ." He darted a glance over his shoulder at the various servants, whispering, "Not two hours ago, we were in bed with one of your better informants, and you want me to propose marriage to your sister with a whore's sweat – and yours! – still on me?" Incredulity in his voice.

"You're taking a bath right now. Ti, I think she's scared of the unknown, more than anything. You're a known quantity. You've lived in this house for years. She knows you're . . . safe."

"Oh, thank you *very* much." Tiberius snorted loudly.

Alexander looked at the ceiling. "More or less. I'm just saying that it would scarcely be a change for her at all. And I know you'd take care of her." His throat ached for a moment. "She'd be a damned idiot not to love you eventually . . . and I don't think she's an idiot. And I think she'd make you happy, and I'd have the chance to see that in your eyes every time I saw the two of you."

Tiberius put his head down on the edge of the pool, his

shoulders rigid. "An hour ago, you said things didn't have to end right away," he muttered.

"An hour ago, my brother and his wife didn't think they were going to have to separate for a year or more. An hour ago, I didn't know my younger sister needs to be taken out of this house, or that the thought of leaving it sends her into a catalepsy." Alexander reached out and put a hand lightly on Tiberius shoulder. Felt the warmth of his friend's skin, and hated himself for his next words. "Please, Ti. Talk to Caesarion. Ask to be considered as a suitor."

He felt Tiberius' shoulder tighten under his grip. "He's going to *love* that," his friend muttered. "I can already hear the comments about how we're giving up wrestling."

"He won't put it that way to *you*. He's too well-mannered, and he likes you," Alexander predicted. "As soon as he gets me in private, however, I'm in for more jokes at my expense than anyone in the city who calls me *Cerastes* would ever imagine."

Tiberius lifted his head. "Well, eagles do tend to win over snakes."

Alexander looked at the ceiling again. "I know. Gods, how I know."

Caesarion stared at the pair of young men in his study. There was an hour left before dinner, and both had bathed, oiled, shaved, and dressed in their best tunics. "Which of you came up with *this* idea?" he asked tiredly, standing from his desk to go warm his hands at the brazier that kept his tile-walled study warm, in spite of the breezes coming in through the slatted wooden walls that separated the room from both the open atrium and the *peristylium* garden.

Tiberius' glance at Alexander spoke volumes.

Caesarion shook his head. "Do you *want* to marry her?" he asked Tiberius bluntly. "Or is this a matter of maximum convenience to the most people?"

Tiberius sighed. "I've had all of an hour to think about this," he said, moving closer. "The fact is, she needs a home. I have a villa that's . . . largely empty, other than the rooms that my brother and I occupy. And I'll admit, I *hated* the thought of seeing her waste away as a Vestal. It burned."

"That's not going to happen," Caesarion replied shortly. *I didn't particularly like the thought, myself. Yes, it's a position of enormous prestige for the women who take the oath, and for their families, too. But . . . Selene? No.*

Tiberius nodded. "Anyone seeing her with Gaius? Has to know that she likes children. She'll be a wonderful mother. And it would be rather pleasant not to have to wait another six years before I can actually get married," he added, dryly. "I realize it's more usual for men of our class to wait till they've finished their first ten years of service, but . . . apparently, there's something of a hurry."

Caesarion grimaced. "Our mother is renowned for her subtlety outside of this house," he said shortly. "With her immediate family, she doesn't feel the need to employ it."

"More of a sledgehammer," Alexander agreed, his voice empty for the moment.

Caesarion gave them both a long look. "Can I expect that Selene would be treated with loyalty and devotion?" he asked.

Tiberius nodded, once. "And absolute fidelity," he replied, his voice flat.

I believe him. But I also know exactly how persuasive Alexander can be. Caesarion flicked a glance in his brother's direction, and was both interested and disturbed by the darkness in Alexander's stare. *If Selene accepts Tiberius,*

Alexander loses him. And he . . . not only knows this. He <u>proposed</u> it.

"Then you have my permission to address her on the subject tonight. Please be aware that Antyllus will be making his own address at the same time. And I'm leaving the decision in *her* hands, since both of you are . . . eminently worthy. I trust both of you. And, annoyingly, you're both my friends." Caesarion grimaced. "I can't make this particular choice for her. Just . . . abide by it, and don't let it get in the way of the work we all need to do, either in Britannia, or here in Rome."

Tiberius shook his head, his gray eyes remote. "Of course not, *dominus*."

Caesarion flipped a hand at them both. "Off you go, then."

And as the door to the atrium clicked shut behind them, the door to the *peristylium* opened behind Caesarion, and Eurydice slipped in. "Did you catch any of that?" he asked his beloved.

"Most of it. I didn't want to eavesdrop, but on the other hand, I'd rather have been dragged apart by bulls than interrupt *that* conversation," she admitted, approaching and putting a hand on his back.

"Want to put coin on which of them she'll accept—if either?" he asked. *Not really what I want to be thinking about today, but it beats dwelling on the sure and certain knowledge that I'm about to lose you for a year. Or two. Or <u>five</u>, if your earliest dreams hold true.*

"No bet," Eurydice said, putting her head against his shoulder lightly. "I checked on her a little while ago. She'd stopped crying, at least, but she's going to be red-eyed at dinner, and if she eats, I'll be surprised." A pause, and she added, her voice strained, "I spent the last hour trying to work out travel arrangements for Egypt. It would be nice to be able to set out without a full flotilla around us—"

"I don't want to talk about that." Caesarion pulled her to him, tightly. "I have no idea how I'm going to fight in Britannia without you. Every gain Father ever made on that island, the inhabitants took back within a handful of years. And they've had time to prepare."

Her arms slipped around his waist. "I've been saying for years that I might need to spend time at the Library of Alexandria," Eurydice murmured. "Maybe I'll find something incredible inside its hoard of scrolls. Perhaps I'll find a way to counter the earth-magic of the druids, or a way to convince their spirits to return to whatever realm they come from."

"And sail all the way from Egypt to Britannia and save the rest of us." It wasn't quite a joke.

"Hopefully, you won't need saving."

Caesarion prided himself on being a rationalist. He might be the high priest of Mars, among his many other titles. He might be god-born. But he wasn't prone to superstition. Except in one respect. At the very bottom of his soul, riding into battle without her, without his hawk, without the woman who could call eagles from the sky and fire from the air, seemed like leaving all his luck and half his weapons behind.

And he knew that she knew it, so it didn't bear repeating. They just stood, leaning into each other. Trying to keep time from passing for at least a little while.

Chapter III: Proposals

Antyllus was prepared for a certain amount of awkwardness at dinner with the Julii tonight. He arrived punctually, opting not to overdress. A simple red tunic without embroidery or stripes, and a heavy white toga. The lack of stripes was important. He wasn't an *equite*, and while his father had served as Consul, and thus had entered the senatorial class, Antyllus himself was not a serving senator, for all his family's considerable wealth and power. He did, however, bring a gift for his host and hostess, as thoughtful guests should—cherries and other fruits preserved in wine. A taste of summer in the midst of winter. He liked the imagery, at least.

And he did enjoy visiting the Julii villa, though as guests crowded into the *triclinium*, Caesarion greeted Antyllus with a rueful, "Until today, I was thinking I needed to build a larger villa. Possibly on the Palatine. I suppose that necessity can be put off, however."

Surprised, Antyllus replied, "I'd thought that the need to entertain ambassadors from all over the world had decided you in favor of new construction half a year ago. What changed?"

Caesarion waved him to one of the dining couches with a sigh. "The need to take Eurydice to Egypt for a while. They need to see one of us there and ruling, not just a Roman governor. And without her here, I'll meet with ambassadors, to be sure, but I have no idea how I'll entertain them. I'll practically need to appoint an extra *aedile*, just to cover all the work Eurydice's been doing." He paused, catching Antyllus by the shoulder before the other man could sit down. "You can address Selene tonight. She has another potential suitor, just so you're aware—not even she knows that part, yet. I'm letting her make the decision."

Antyllus' eyebrows rose. "Unusual. Most of the time, fathers decide for children, and you stand in the place of a father to her right now."

Caesarion grimaced, his hand still on Antyllus' shoulder. "I don't want her blaming me for ruining her life if I make the *wrong* choice. I like watching Hellene tragedies on stage. I don't need my life to become even more of one."

Antyllus chuckled, taking his seat, and called over as Caesarion moved away, "Then take care not to develop any fatal flaws of character! *Superbia's* always a favorite for the powerful, in tragedy."

Caesarion took his own seat beside Eurydice, calling back dryly, "With you and Alexander around to puncture my self-love at every turn, I fail to see how I can ever develop that particular vice." He rubbed a hand lightly over his wife's shoulders, and she turned slightly to smile at him. As they always did, they reclined on their couch both facing the same direction, with her back tucked against him. A little closer to each other than sticklers for propriety might find strictly correct, but still with visible space between them. No guest of honor tonight would join them.

Antyllus had been waved to the middle couch, the seat of honor. And to his pleasure, as Selene entered, habitually moving towards the high couch, the least favorable seats in the room, Caesarion waved her over to join Antyllus. Which she did, her steps suggesting the hesitance of someone facing execution.

Well, Father. One unicorn, driven towards the hunter like a rabbit chased by beaters in the brush. Unfortunately, I don't think arrows or spears are the correct choices here. Antyllus stood from the couch as Selene approached, and quickly made sure she was comfortable before taking his seat once more. And then raised his eyebrows as Tiberius, too, was shuttled to their couch—quite a deviation from the normal seating arrangements in this room. A quick glance told him that yes, Alexander was on the high couch tonight—with Octavia, as usual, but this time, with the poetess Servia Sulpicia joining them.

Noticing Selene's red-rimmed eyes, and wanting to give her a moment to recover herself, Antyllus turned back towards the host's table. "This room alone shows why you really do need to build a bigger villa, *dominus,*" he told Caesarion. Friendly tone, but still respectful. "You can manage nine people at dinner in here. It makes your dinner invitations exclusive and much sought-after, of course, but invariably, someone's left out, so you have to dine more often with people, just to avoid offense!" A quick grin. "If you had twice the seats, you'd only have to invite people half as often."

Eurydice sat up a little straighter. "You wait until *today* to offer that very pertinent argument, Antyllus? We'd have had the new house finished inside of a year if *that* had been given as a reason—"

Chuckling, Caesarion replied, "It's a good theory, but in application, wouldn't someone inevitably be seated further away, in a second ring of seats? And thus feel just as slighted that they weren't in the first row, at my left hand, able to converse with the most favored guests?"

"Perhaps," Sulpicia called from her seat beside Alexander and Octavia, delicately dipping a fragment of bread in *moretum*, a spread of garlic, cheese and herbs, here at the start of the meal. "But I believe, *dominus*, that most will simply be happy, when someone asks, 'Did you hear about when Virgil fell asleep in the middle of his declaiming own verse?' to be able to answer, 'I didn't just hear about it, my dear; I was there!'"

General laughter around the tables. "He's not *that* bad," Eurydice said, smothering her smile. "Nor that old!"

"No, he's just a lickarse of the worst sort," Alexander muttered. "And his vison of Venus, always appearing in disguises to her own son, never a straight word between them."

Antyllus swallowed. He'd been one of the handful present when Mars and Venus had appeared, personally, in Hispania to bless Caesarion and Eurydice's wedding. That moment had affected him, deeply. "He's indebted to Homer for that," Caesarion replied, shrugging. "He wasn't in Hispania, Alexander. He didn't see their faces directly, as we did."

"I'll never forget seeing Mars' face," Tiberius remarked from just to the right of Selene, looking down into his cup now. "As I said then, it . . . made all the battles seem worthwhile. Not just for the sake of *gloria*, for the chance to add to the *dignitas* of my family. To match my ancestors' deeds. But for the men beside me in battle."

"It's strange," Antyllus offered, into the silence that followed. "But I've noticed that of those of us who were there that day, some of us seemed to see Mars' face more clearly, and some of us saw Venus more strongly." He chuckled into his cup.

"And which did you see more clearly?" Tiberius asked, over Selene's hair. Her head kept swinging back and forth between them as they spoke, and if she'd eaten, Antyllus had yet to see it.

"Venus. I'm not sure if my father, who's *clearly* honored both in his long life, would be pleased by that fact or not," Antyllus replied with cheerful aplomb, once again garnering the laughter of those around him.

Tiberius regarded him, still over Selene's head. "You've been in the legions and with the auxiliaries for nine years," the young man said, sounding surprised. "And you *didn't* see Mars Gravidus more clearly?"

"One more year till I can stand for legate in my own right," Antyllus agreed calmly. "Not just take over in an emergency." He nodded towards Caesarion in respect for having appointed both him and Tiberius as legates in Hispania, if temporarily. "I suppose it's because while the military is the best road to a public life—and what *use* is a man if he's not involved in the life of the Empire?—it's not the only road I see ahead of me."

At this point, the servants brought out the next course—this time meat, after the light bread and cheese offered first—settling a whole baked swan on the main table, with a choice of coriander-encrusted fish and steamed mussels, and an egg-and-asparagus dish called a *patina*, made with liquamen fish sauce and enough herbs to make Antyllus' mouth water even at a distance. Enough to sate all nine guests, but as always at Eurydice's table, while the food was superb, it wasn't presented fussily. The swan hadn't been dressed in its own feathers. The fish wasn't alive when brought to the table to demonstrate its freshness, or killed before the guests and cooked there, too. And quickly sitting up to take a little of everything for his own trencher, Antyllus settled back down, frowning when he saw that Selene still hadn't taken anything to eat. He offered her one of the mussels from his own plate, cooked as it had been with liquamen and sweet raisin-wine. He held it temptingly before her lips, murmuring, "You haven't had so much as a bite. Try something, won't you?"

Her dark eyes flicked up towards his, and for a

moment, he saw so much misery there that he was deeply taken aback. Then her shoulders slumped and, rather than allowing him to slide the morsel between her lips, she reached out and took it from him with her fingers, eating it silently.

Well, as banquets intended for people to get to know each other go, this one's going _swimmingly_, isn't it?

In spite of everything, Antyllus liked what he saw when he looked at Selene. She was slightly taller than her mother, being just past five feet in height—perfectly average for a Roman woman. He was slightly above average in that regard himself, being eight inches past five feet in height. If she ever let him lean down to kiss her lips, he wouldn't have to strain his neck overly. Unlike Octavia or Sulpicia, her hair hadn't been dyed or bleached to a fashionable Hellene red-gold, but rather retained its natural black hue. Only a trace of kohl around her eyes, which accentuated the red-rimmed state. And while Eurydice wore deep scarlet tonight, Selene had opted for a *stola* in undyed wool—as if trying for invisibility among the brighter tones worn by everyone around the tables.

From the right, as everyone ate, Caesarion cleared his throat, and asked, mildly, "If you don't see the military as the only road before you, what else is there, Antyllus? Magistrate? Offering cases before the courts, like Cicero?"

Antyllus chuckled. "Oh, gods no. I've given three speeches before the Senate, and prayed to the gods each time that I wouldn't embarrass myself or my family. No. I have, eh, six years before I can be considered as a *quaestor*." Inside of Rome, a *quaestor* oversaw public games and financial issues; outside the city, they were paymasters for the legions, or adjuncts to provincial governors. "I've thought of traveling. I would very much like to see more of the provinces, other than when we're actively pacifying them."

Caesarion's eyebrows rose. "You'd like to be a *propraetor peregrinus*, then?" A judge or magistrate who dealt with foreigners who committed crimes inside Rome was a *praetor peregrinus*; a propraetor had similar powers, but outside the city itself.

"If I should live so long," Antyllus said, looking at the ceiling. "I'd have to be thirty-nine to qualify as a candidate for *praetor*, though." He shrugged. "An ambassador. A governor — not one who's just there to milk taxes into his own coffers, mind you, and not just someone who's there not just to enforce the peace with the threat of bloody reprisal. Someone who's there to . . . ." He struggled for the words. "Promote understanding between people," he finally offered. Then a wry note entered his voice. "I already speak one dialect of Gallic, and grew up with a Gallic king's son as a hostage in my father's house. I learned a lot from the retainer who'd accompanied Tincomarus to Rome to ensure that he'd actually speak Gallic when he went home to rule." He paused. "Quite a few people of this city turn up their noses at the *barbarians*, but I think there are things we could learn from them."

"Such as?" Sulpicia asked, smiling.

Antyllus noticed Tiberius offering Selene a little of the asparagus dish, coaxing her to eat much in the same way he had. With slightly more success. He shrugged, taking a bite of his own food now. "My bow," he said, once his mouth had been cleared. "It's Scythian. I say that to any other group of people in Rome, and the first thing I'm apt to hear is how the Scythians are illiterate, dirty herdsmen. Illiterate, dirty herdsmen who build warbows with a draw-weight of over a hundred and sixty *librae*." He popped a mussel in his mouth, chewing for a moment. "It's shorter than the bows used by the Cretans, which is what allows those dirty, illiterate herdsman to use those bows on horseback. And the arrows I fire from it penetrate our best armor. I want to see those bows in *Roman* hands, or at least, in the hands of our auxiliaries."

Caesarion's head lifted. "How are your men feeling about that citizenship laws?" he asked Antyllus directly.

Antyllus grinned. "What, serve for twenty years, the way they would have anyway, and on retirement, they become full Roman citizens? *Dominus*, they love you for it. They see it as the best way forward for their sons. Something to work towards that *can't* be taken away from them, the way land or a pension can be."

"There are those in this city who hate that law," Tiberius said tightly. "Who fear what will happen when many people who weren't born Roman, may suddenly call themselves that." He lifted his eyes, his gray eyes cool and distant. "I'm not one of them."

Antyllus smiled back, toasting the patrician man with his cup. "And we all thank the gods for it," he told Tiberius lightly, then glanced down at Selene again. *I have never met anyone better at being invisible in public,* he thought, and made an effort to get out of the main conversation, pointedly asking her, "So, will you be going with your sister to Egypt, then?" as if he weren't here to court her at all.

A startled look, and Selene made her first reply of the meal. "She's offered to take me there, yes."

"Hark, you do have a voice," Antyllus told her with gentle mock-astonishment. "And a pleasant one, too." He smiled, sighing internally as she looked away rapidly. *If I did not know better, I would be asking Caesarion who it was who has <u>beaten</u> his sister.* "So, do you want to go?" he pressed lightly. "I've dreamed of going there since my father told me of it when I was a child."

She shook her head faintly. "I've . . . rarely thought

about it," Selene admitted softly. "I've only left Rome once before. For the camps outside Brundisium."

"A very deft way you have of dodging questions," Antyllus scolded lightly. "I asked if you *wanted* to go, not if you've ever thought about it before."

Her eyes flicked up, met his for an instant, and then flickered across the room, as if looking for someone to provide the answer for her. No help in sight, Selene finally, haltingly, managed to reply on her own, "My mother and your father will be making the trip as well. I would . . . prefer not to accompany—I mean, I love my mother, of course—"

A distinct snort from Tiberius, and Antyllus did his best not to laugh, as well, as Selene's cheeks flamed. "Your mother is not the easiest of women," Tiberius noted dryly. "There's no shame in admitting that. Neither is mine, you'll recall."

"Oh, but I didn't—I wouldn't—"

Antyllus chuckled. "You're both fortunate, in that you've only had *one* mother each," he told them cheerfully. "My father's married four times. The first, well, she wasn't my mother. And everyone knows the sorry tale of how Dolabella seduced her." That fact had made his father intemperate in his response when Dolabella had tried to have a debt forgiveness law enacted by force. In a fit of injured pride and anger, Antony had unleashed troops on the crowds who'd risen in support of a law that Caesar wouldn't have supported *as written*—but which would have benefitted thousands of Caesar's veterans.

That incident had been one of the underlying reasons for the ongoing strain between Caesar and Antony over the years, though they'd patched the relationship later. "Then, of course there was my mother." He shook his head. "She died when I was seven, but the thing I remember most about her?

You could hear her halfway across a *castra* when she was in a temper."

"And what did you do to provoke that temper?" Alexander asked from across the tables.

"Brought her a gift of several frogs from a stream outside the *castra* once," Antyllus replied promptly. "I think we were bogged down in Hellas at the time. I wasn't supposed to go outside the walls, but one of my father's centurions saw how bored I was, and took me fishing. I caught nothing but the frogs. As she demanded, in full voice, where I had been the whole afternoon and why my tunic was covered in mud, I presented her with her tribute." He nodded sagely, and then turned to Selene, adding, "They knocked over several priceless bottles of perfume with their hopping. I was all of five at the time, mind. I think they could hear her in *Sparta* by the time she was done shouting."

Everyone at the tables around him convulsed with laughter. Even Tiberius and Selene were forced to cover their faces. After a moment or two, Eurydice recovered enough to ask, "And Octavia?"

Antyllus' smile faded. "Father married her just after my mother died." He sighed. "If my mother was strident, Octavia was . . . chilly." He shrugged. *Not chilly. Cold. Rigid. Obsessed with observing the manners of the patrician class to which her father had been raised, and to which my father, by right of his political ascent, was entitled, but has never really aped.*

"That characteristic ran in the family," Tiberius commented tightly.

"So I hear," Antyllus returned, and both men drank from their cups at the same moment. After a moment, Antyllus added, "Not to speak ill of the dead, but there are reasons I haven't been in a rush to find myself a wife." *My father's repeated injunctions to mention it to Caesarion aside.*

Which, each time, I have passed along like a dutiful son. Flirting with Eurydice a few years ago was mostly in fun. Watching her bewildered expression made dinner go by that much more quickly. He turned back towards Selene now, adding more quietly, "I'm actually rather grateful to your mother, you know. My father's in better health and humor since he married her, than he was for years before."

Selene looked down and away, but said nothing in reply. *Damnation. Her mother is a sore spot, it would appear.*

At that point, Tiberius leaned in, and asked Selene, quite politely, "I heard you practicing your *kithara* the other day when I visited. It's considered the virtuoso's instrument, isn't it? Anyone can play the lyre, but it takes someone with real talent to play the *kithara*."

"Oh, I wouldn't. . . I mean, it is more difficult, and I don't think I've mastered it," she replied hastily, looking down.

"Do you like it better than the lyre?" Tiberius asked, and Antyllus just listened for the moment, watching the way she tilted her head towards Tiberius, while keeping her eyes fixed . . . anywhere but on him, apparently.

"The lyre's much easier," Selene replied softly after a moment. "But you can do so many more things with the *kithara*. I like it very much."

"Sometimes Eurydice has you play for guests. Do you feel like favoring us with a song or two?" Tiberius asked, his tone surprisingly gentle.

Her eyes actually flicked up to meet Tiberius' for a moment. "Not if my sister has other entertainment planned—" her head swiveled towards Eurydice, who was laughing at something Caesarion had just whispered in her ear. But Selene didn't interrupt. Didn't call out for her sister's attention. Just bit her lip and waited.

At which point Tiberius called over, "*Domina!* Do you mind if Selene plays for us tonight? While the conversation's lovely, we're lacking in music. And hearing her fingers on the strings is always the best end to a long day."

Selene flushed red, as Eurydice shook her head. "Of course I don't mind. Let me send someone for your *kithara*, Selene —"

"No, no, I'll fetch it myself," Selene said hastily, scrabbling off the couch before the second course could be cleared. "I'll be right back." And off she went.

In the wake of her passage, Antyllus glanced over at Tiberius, and then leaned across the warm spot left by Selene's now-absent form. "So, you're the other suitor, then?"

Tiberius sighed. "So much for my subtlety."

Antyllus deftly caught a pitcher of wine from the table, not allowing the servants to pour it, and refilled his cup and Tiberius', his gaze flicking across the room to where Alexander sat with Octavia and Sulpicia, laughing at something the poetess had just said. "You've known her a long time. Lived in the same house." A shrug. "You have the clear advantage over me."

"You say that, but as of today, I'm not sure I know her at all." Tiberius shook his head, a shadow flickering through his eyes, then toasted Antyllus lightly with the cup that Antony's son had just filled. "Friends?"

"You ask this, when the Tenth saved my Cretans' *asses* last year? Of course we're friends."

"If memory serves, you and your damned Cretans saved *our* asses the year before that."

Antyllus chuckled. "Doesn't do to brag. That's why you buy the services of a poet to do it for you." He glanced back across at Alexander once more; Octavia looked aggrieved as Sulpicia and Alexander once more laughed at some mutual joke. *Well, that's a thing of interest.*

Selene tumbled back into the room, her *kithara* clutched in her hands. It was impossible to recline while playing, but the seating in the triclinium was limited, so she still had to perch on the edge of the same couch as Antyllus and Tiberius. She wished she dared say something sharp to Eurydice for placing her right in between the two men; Antyllus was an archer, and as such, had arms almost as wide as Selene's legs—and while it was winter, he'd opted for a sleeveless tunic, probably because of the weight of the woolen toga he wore to this formal dinner. While he surely hadn't meant to be intrusive, he simply took up so much space on his side of the couch that his arms constantly brushed against her, making her jump every time he did.

And Tiberius who had spent just as much time carrying a sword, shield, and armor, was just as solidly built, which meant that in order to avoid touching either of them inadvertently, Selene had been forced to hold as still as . . . *as still as the mouse my mother called me,* she thought, looking down as she took to the very edge of the couch. She caught flashes of what looked like genuine enjoyment on both men's faces as she settled in, touching her fingers to the strings.

But the humiliation of the discussion earlier in the day still hung over her. The anger that had prompted her tears had burned out, leaving nothing but a hollow, ashy pit in her midsection, and a constant feeling of coldness through her whole body. Her eyes burned as if she hadn't slept in a week, and she felt no impetus to play at all. Her fingers drifted aimlessly, and then she stumbled into the darker-toned notes of a piece she'd been practicing, in an elegiac Hellene mode. She didn't merely strum the instrument using a plectrum, as poets did in between their recited passages; she plucked and strummed the strings from both sides of the instrument. Stilled the strings, dampening the sound with her fingertips.

And as she played, the music became her whole world, as it always did. Let her forget that there were people listening, or watching. The intricacies were what fascinated her, extending some notes into tremulous sighs, like wind whispering through tree limbs, while the steady progression of notes through the main harmony, to her, sounded like rain weeping from the leaves of those same trees.

She was startled when that first song finished, to hear the others clapping lightly; it had happened before at her sister's dinners, but it broke her out of the almost meditative state, and forced her to remember where she was—and that there were others present. "Beautiful as always," Tiberius told her, giving her that rare half-smile.

"Thank you," she said, looking away. "Does anyone wish to hear anything else before I put it away?"

"Something cheerful!" Sulpicia interposed, smiling. "It will go better with the fruits and honey."

"Life isn't a tragedy," Alexander said, nodding.

"I wouldn't call it a comedy," Tiberius countered, his voice dark.

"Of course not," Antyllus told them all. "It's an *adventure*. An epic, grand one, if you're willing to make it one. Selene, I don't suppose you know anything that would make the journeys we all must set off on soon sound that much more exciting?"

Life isn't an epic, Selene thought, her eyes still burning. *It's not even an ode.* But she picked out a spritely enough tune, one that reminded her of flowing water and birdsong. And the music carried her with it for once. Did its work, and lightened her mood, not just that of her audience. She smiled with it, carrying on into a third song, and a fourth, and then looked up, realizing that the servants were clearing away the remains of stewed apricots and the last of the wine. And that a room full of people was smiling at her.

Caesarion called over, "It's good to see you smile, sister. I'd like to see that expression more often."

Of course, his words made her expression fade, and wide-eyed, she lowered her head and prepared to scuttle away. But Tiberius sat up and lightly took her hand in his, startling her. "You've played that second one before," he said, his eyes bright. "It always lightens my spirits. Thank you." He paused. "Could I have a word with you before you retire for the evening?" he asked.

Such a request was so unprecedented that Selene actually looked up in confusion before nodding, her brows crinkling slightly in apprehension. Thereby missing the glance that Antyllus sent in Caesarion's direction, and her brother's nod in response. "I must go shortly, too," Antyllus put in, standing and offering Selene his hand in turn. "Before I go, I'd like to discuss something with you, myself."

She wasn't really sure why Antyllus and Tiberius exchanged a look, Tiberius' dark, and Antyllus' a rather fierce grin. But she suspected she knew what the subject Antyllus had in mind would be, and sighed. *Might as well get it over with,* Selene thought, with most of the enthusiasm she'd have reserved for attending a public execution. The expectant gazes of her siblings felt like spiders crawling over her skin—the stares tickled, with an attendant mortal dread of being bitten.

So she allowed herself to be drawn out of the room and out into the chilly atrium, where the fountains burbled, even in Ianuarius, and oil lamps flickered on the pillars, adding a hint of amber light to the scene. Set her *kithara* down on one of the benches, and wrapped her arms around herself, trying to ward off the cold, after the warmth and light of the *triclinium*. Miserably aware that anyone could be watching them even now. "Here, you're shivering," Antyllus said in a tone of surprise, and rubbed his hands up and down her exposed arms lightly. "I don't have your sister's gift for fire, unfortunately. And I can't really take you into one of the other rooms, warmer though that would be," he added dryly. "A woman's reputation is a delicate thing in Rome. We have to stay in sight of others while I'm talking with you."

She nodded uneasily, looking at his hands as they came to rest for a moment on her elbows. Surprisingly warm, really. And then he lifted one of his hands and caught her chin lightly, lifting her face. "I'd enjoy being able to see your eyes and expression as we talk," Antyllus told her, smiling. "Lets a man know where he stands."

Selene swallowed, then nodded again. Nothing he'd done yet felt threatening. But she knew what was coming and couldn't stop the words that were sure to come from his lips soon.

"Do you know why I'm here tonight?"

She closed her eyes, since she couldn't look down with her chin so gently held. And the words tumbled out of her own lips, without conscious volition, and as rapidly as possible: "Because my mother and your father have it in their heads that they want a grandchild and because your marrying me would be politically advantageous to your family and because I've become inconvenient to my family so they have to get rid of me."

She knew that last was unfair even as she said it. Her siblings were going out of their way to show their support. But unfair or not, there was a bit of truth in it. She *was* an inconvenience.

Antyllus bit off half a truncated barracks oath, and her

eyes snapped open in surprise. She'd never seen that much anger cross his face before. "Selene," he said, taking her by the arm and pulling her down onto a bench beside him, before shifting his grip to her hands instead. "First . . . I'll admit that my father's pressed for a match over the years. First with Eurydice, which I didn't take all that seriously—I could see that her heart was taken, though not by *whom*." Half amused, half sour, that. "And then, yes, with you. I passed on mentions of it to your brother when my father pressed, and nothing more. What kind of a man do you think I am, that I'd blindly follow my father's orders in marriage, if I didn't think there was at least a chance of my own happiness in it?" He snorted, but it wasn't an angry sound. "Then again, while you've lived in my father's house during the campaign season on and off for the last several years, the *instant* Caesarion and Eurydice return, you've already packed and left. That hasn't really given you a chance to know me at all, let alone the sort of man I am, has it?"

Selene swallowed again, and shook her head minutely. Antyllus looked at her, shaking his head. "And you've left as early as possible each time *specifically* because your mother's mentioned this possibility?"

Oh, gods, how do I answer that without offending him? "Ah, well, not *specifically*," Selene mumbled, trying to look away at the same time as giving him the eye contact he'd requested.

He sighed. "Can I make one small request of you? Would it be possible for you to forget that your mother has ever even mentioned my name? I hate to think that you think I'm a monster solely because Cleopatra handles you like a queen handles her subjects, and not at all as a mother should treat her daughter."

Struck, Selene looked up at him. "Oh, it's not. . . I mean, yes, that probably—" she sighed. "I don't think you're a monster. I don't. . . I don't hate you." She shook her head slightly, rattled. "You've been . . . very kind."

"Ah, good." His tone was wry. "When you come to ask a pretty girl to marry you, it's a relief to hear that she doesn't hate you."

She winced, going completely still. Her hands still clasped loosely in his, she tried to edge away slightly. Antyllus looked down at their hands, and asked, gently, "So if you don't hate me, why does the thought distress you so much?"

Selene's eyes burned once more. *This day simply won't end,* she thought, despairingly. *He's actually very kind. He makes everyone laugh. Even me, when I didn't think I could laugh tonight. He'd be a perfectly nice person to marry if I weren't already in love, and if Mother wasn't pushing it so. What will it take to make this stop?*

Nothing but the truth would do it. And once spoken, that truth would absolutely ensure that Antyllus would never come back again. He'd remove the warmth of his hands from hers, and there would be an end.

That thought left her feeling emptier than it should have.

"It wouldn't be proper to marry you," Selene said, dully, and once she started, she went on with a sort of dogged determination. "I've had feelings for someone else for . . . almost three years."

Antyllus' eyebrows shot up, and he sat up a little straighter, taking his hands back from hers, as she'd known he would. "Caesarion and Eurydice never said a word of that to me—"

"They don't know," Selene told him, shrugging. "I've never told anyone."

He stared at her for a long moment. "Why *not*? They're

not monsters, you know. If you have a preference, why haven't you told them? They could make arrangements — "

"He's betrothed already — "

"Betrothals can be broken."

"And in love with someone else. So it doesn't matter." She looked away.

There was a distinct pause. "He's betrothed *and* in love with someone other than his betrothed?" Antyllus asked, his voice sharp and a little angry. "He doesn't sound like a man of honor."

"He's one of the most honorable people I know," Selene replied indignantly, and then put a hand over her face. *He is. That's just the problem.*

"And you've never even told him how you feel?" Antyllus asked. She could hear the frown in his voice.

"Of course not. What good would *that* do?" Her voice was wretched, and then she shook her head, feeling the tears burn in her eyes once more. "It doesn't matter."

To her great surprise, she felt him take her free hand in his once more. "If it doesn't matter, then. . . does it matter?" he asked her, his voice suddenly both gentle and pragmatic at once, and she let her fingers slide from her face to look up at him in confusion. "If you don't think you can ever marry him, why *not* marry me?"

"Because it wouldn't be fair to you," Selene replied, baffled by his reaction. In fact, she thought he might even be smiling a little, his dark eyes amused. "It's not right to marry someone if you can't give them your heart. If I'm in love with someone else, it's . . . how could I ever love you?" That last came out as a rush. "And you'd be . . . jealous and suspicious and . . . that usually leads to bad things." *Usually tragedy,* she thought, her heart beating rapidly under her ribs.

He picked up one of her hands lightly in his, and kissed

the palm, shocking her. Then placed her hand directly over his heart, holding it there lightly, almost companionably. "This heart, right here," Antyllus told her lightly, "is currently unused. Unoccupied. Has only had one owner—me. It's yours if you want it, because I think that I could grow very fond of you, given the opportunity. You're honest, kind, and would bring music to my life, which I could definitely use more of." He smiled faintly. "And given a chance? I would do my best to ensure that within a year of marrying you, you wouldn't even remember the *name* of this paltry fellow that you think you're in love with." A wicked smile, lighting up his eyes, gentling immediately as she stiffened a little in alarm. "If you haven't even spoken with him about your feelings, I doubt you've kissed him or held his hand, either. I don't think I'd have much cause for jealousy."

Selene felt as if she were about to swallow her own tongue. "Poets say women are very inconstant," she said, almost accusingly. "If I suddenly turned around and fell out of love with him, and into love with you, you'd always wonder if I were fickle and disloyal at heart—"

Antyllus laughed outright at that. "Not at all. I'd think that you were young when you first felt an admiration for someone. Were amazingly loyal to someone patently undeserving of your regard. And that, if you *did* love me, that Fortuna had smiled on me, and I'd been lucky enough to grab her by the forelock before she scarpered off." He leaned forward, still holding her hand to his heart, and to her great surprise, kissed her. Light. Undemanding. Faint roughness of incipient beard against her lips and cheeks. But all the warmth in the world, seeping through her

"You can't *do* that," she whispered in shock as he pulled back. "We're *not* betrothed—"

A quick, wicked grin. "I wanted you to know what it

felt like," he told her, raising his eyebrows. "It's a lot better in reality than in dreams."

Stung, Selene bit her lip, looking away. And he caught her face lightly, turning her back towards him. "That wasn't meant to hurt," Antyllus told her, frowning. "I'm sorry." He sighed. "You don't have to say yes or no immediately," he added, his eyes searching her face. "In fact, I'd be willing to go with you and Eurydice and Caesarion to Egypt. To give you a chance to know *me*, instead of this . . . shadow your mother has turned me into, in your mind. I was being truthful earlier—I've always wanted to go there."

"And if I tell you no, you'll have traveled all the way to Egypt for nothing," Selene said, swallowing. Trying to make her mind stop racing in circles.

He chuckled. "Ah, but from Egypt, it's just a skip to Syria, really. A little further north, and I'm practically in Scythia, and I can try to find bowyers willing to bring their art to Rome. Or at least, to sell me every bow they have in their possession. So even if you tell me no, it won't be a wasted trip. Hardly out of my way at all, when you think about it." He nodded to himself in blatantly feigned cheerful pragmatism.

And to Selene's great surprise, she felt a smile creep across her face, and a laugh to her lips.

He left after that, and she picked up her *kithara*, thinking hard as she headed back into the warmer rooms of the house, looking forward to finding her room, undressing, and being able to close her eyes on this wretched, horrible day. But a shadow detached itself from one of the pillars alongside the atrium, and Tiberius fell in step beside her, and she almost dropped her instrument in shock. He reached out, catching it as it slipped from her hands. "Oh, gods," she whispered. "How long have you been standing there?" *Oh, no. He had to have seen Antyllus kiss me, and now he'll think I'm a* _whore_.

"Long enough," Tiberius said, his voice sounding odd. "Come inside—it's far too cold out. I have no idea what Antyllus was thinking, keeping you out here." He tucked the _kithara_ under one arm, and offered her his other, guiding her back into the now-deserted _triclinium_, still warm from the meal and the body-heat of the others. One lone brazier still burned here, staving off the chill that threatened to permeate the room as winter air stole in through the shuttered window to the _peristylium_. He settled the _kithara_ on one of the couches, and looked at her in concern. "Are you tired?" Tiberius asked, his voice tentative. "I wanted to speak with you, but it . . . can wait."

Selene blinked, rapidly. He'd occasionally teased her gently over the years. Had clearly enjoyed it when she played for him and Drusus, but had never specifically asked her to play for them. But seeking her out in this way? Never. "I . . . always have time to speak with you," Selene said, her eyes flicking up and then down again. Wondering if the tight pain in her chest whenever she looked at him really was an illusion, the way Antyllus clearly thought it was. _It feels real. It feels very real. Of course, I could just be a stupid girl with a foolish, useless heart._

Tiberius exhaled and gestured towards the couch, and she settled down beside him, still wondering what he'd seen and heard in the atrium. _Maybe he's about to tell me what horrible, unladylike behavior that was, not pulling away from Antyllus. Not slapping him for his forwardness. Maybe he's about to tell me how ashamed he is of Alexander's sister—_

"I didn't mean to eavesdrop," Tiberius said quietly. "I was going to go to one of the guest rooms to wait until he'd finished speaking with you, but the stairs are on the other side of the atrium, and by the time I realized that he'd taken you out there in the cold, I couldn't really sneak back inside without being seen and making everything that much more uncomfortable." His cool gray eyes caught hers, and for once, she couldn't look away at all.

He sighed, looking down at her. He'd seen over the years how her face changed when she played her music, but never more strikingly than tonight, when she'd *glowed* from within while striking notes from the *kithara's* strings. "I should have asked you to play more often," he murmured, lifting her hands in his. Lightly stroking his fingertips along the string callouses on her own. "I love listening to you play. It's lightened my heart many times. But I never wanted to ask, because I didn't want you to feel like a servant."

"Oh, but I wouldn't," she said, her face and eyes suddenly shining. "I've always liked playing for you." She looked down, feeling abashed at the admission, and doubt caught at her again. *What's infatuation, and what's real love? Can they ever be the same thing?*

He exhaled. "Alexander suggested this," Tiberius told her, taking her hand in his and studying her face. She shared many of the same facial features as her brother, of course. The same dark hair, dark eyes, and skin like amber spread over ivory. But on her, the features were softened. Gentled. She had none of Alexander's buried anger at the world, and didn't share his gifts in war or spycraft. But as had become obvious in the course of the past twelve hours, none of them really knew what gifts Selene really had. The music, yes. The memory, the gentility, the kindness. *But what could she be, if someone actually allowed her to bloom?* "But regardless of the source, it's a good idea." Tiberius paused. "I've no gift for pretty words, Selene. You know that. But . . . marry me. Antyllus is a good man, and a good friend of mine. But I already hold you in affection. You don't have to wait for that to grow in my heart."

Selene felt as if she'd just turned to stone. *"What* did you just say?" she asked, her hands shaking. *I didn't just hear that. This is a dream.*

"I said, marry *me,"* Tiberius repeated patiently. "I don't know who this idiot is who holds your heart, though I'd love to know his name just so I could go beat the honorless knave—" he saw her raise her hands to try to stop his words, but continued, doggedly, "But you know that I'd never harm you. Never beat you. Never betray you." He caught her eyes and held them, so she'd feel the sincerity of his words. "I'd do my best to make you happy, though the gods know they didn't form me with a gift for giving others joy." He smiled faintly, and then realized that tears had just overflowed her eyes. "Selene, what's the matter?" He reached out and brushed the tears away with his thumbs, holding her face lightly, unsure of what to do or say to make whatever hurt it was, feel less.

Selene closed her eyes, unable to meet that bright gray stare. "It's you," she managed to choke out, her heart aching inside of her, and opened her eyes to see the flicker of shock cross his face. "It's always been you." Saying the words didn't make her feel any better, strangely. She turned away, covering her eyes with her hands. *This horrible day can just end now.*

Tiberius caught her hands in his, pulling them away from her face, a knot forming in his chest. *Oh, gods. I didn't know. I didn't know.* "You're . . . you have feelings for me?" he said, his voice sounding slightly dazed to his own ears. *I'm the honorless piece of shit.*

"I do. I did. I don't *know,* and my head's in a muddle," she said, her voice so tight he barely recognized it.

"Why in the name of all the gods didn't you *say* something?" he whispered. *The last three years of my life might have gone very differently if you had. Alexander and I might still have had fun . . . but it might not have gone as far.*

Selene twisted away, shaking her head. "Because I *know*," she told him, looking back over her shoulder. "You and Alexander—and I'd never come between you, and . . . if you feel that way about him, you can never feel that way about—nevermind. It doesn't matter!"

"For Dis' sake, yes it does!" That rang back off the walls, and Tiberius spun away himself for a moment, trying to sort out a half-dozen new realities all at once. Realities in which his friend's younger sister knew more than she'd ever let on, and felt a good deal more than that.

When he turned back, she was staring at him, wide-eyed, and Tiberius took a deep breath. Calmed himself. And wrapped his arms around her for a moment. "It *does* matter, because you matter," he told her tightly. "I like you. I've always liked you. And what I feel for Alexander doesn't matter, because while it's wonderful now, it has *no future*. We've both always known that. No matter how stubbornly he tries to pretend otherwise." He sighed. "You, on the other hand, are a future I think is worth pursuing." *The family is everything. And for a family to be a family, it has to continue forward. One more step in the great chain of being. Future connected to past, ancestors connected to descendants. If you don't have heirs, what was the point of all the blood and sweat of your ancestors? Or your own? We live, not just for ourselves, but for others.*

She'd gone very still against him. "Is this why you were so upset at the idea of marrying anyone earlier?" he asked against her hair. It shook him, to think that he, of all people, had that kind of power over someone's life and heart.

A single nod. "Antyllus said it was probably just . . . infatuation." Her voice was small.

That cut on several levels at once. Tiberius hadn't even

allowed himself to think about her in this fashion before a few hours ago. His ideals told him that monogamy in marriage and love was the only correct path. He'd only allowed himself to love Alexander on that condition; that it would *only* be Alexander, until such time as it came to marry, and then, it would only be his wife.

But Alexander had strong notions about fun, and since they both enjoyed women, it had been easy enough to fall in with Alexander's tastes and mores in that regard, because that was just sex, and not love. So long as it wasn't *love*, it didn't matter. And therefore, no other love could be allowed to whisper into his heart, like the fingers of wind pressing in from the garden outside, through the shutters. Tiberius hadn't even known how much he wanted to be loved, until he'd realized that Selene had feelings for him, moments ago. Nascent, delicate, easily-trampled feelings. "It could just be that, yes," he told her, with scrupulous honesty, feeling empty inside as realizations washed over him. *Oh, gods, have I wasted the last several years of my life entirely? I love Alexander. But right now, I want to punch him in the teeth.*

He exhaled. "Selene . . . all I want, at the moment, is to know that you're going to be happy. To *Tartarus* with your mother's insistence that everything be taken care of before Caesarion and Eurydice go to Egypt. Take your time. Make the decision in your own way." He closed his eyes for a moment. "And if Antyllus is more apt to make you happy?" He opened his eyes and looked down at her somberly. "I'll attend your wedding, and wish you nothing but joy." He leaned down and kissed her hair before standing, nothing but a raw ache in his chest. *If I'd asked her yesterday, she'd have said yes. But yesterday, I knew nothing, and was a fool.*

Alexander had had a busy evening so far. What had promised to be a deadly series of hours spent listening to Octavia talk, had given way, instead, to a lively discussion with Sulpicia, beginning with, of all things, with her question to him if he'd ever read Herodotus. Of course, he had. "Then, now that our friend Antyllus has mentioned the Scythians, do you believe Herodotus when he says that the Scythians once had a city named Gelona, hundreds of times bigger than Troy-that-burned?" she'd asked, playing with her Egyptian-style necklace.

He'd had to scramble to remember what she meant. "They're wandering herdsmen—no, wait. The bulk of them are, with red hair and blue eyes. But the Budini were part Hellene, and part Scythian, and had a great city. And when the Persians came to conquer the Scythians, the Buduni burned their own city, rather than fall to Persia. And retreated, free as the wind, burning their own grasslands before the Persian advance. Darius made no conquests there." He considered it. "I don't know if it was larger than *Troy*, however." For him, as for many others, Troy was an enormous city in his mind. At least as big as Rome.

"Ah, so you doubt the veracity of ancient authority!" Sulpicia had said, laughing. "Next, you'll say he was quite mad when he reported that the Phoenicians, back before they started calling themselves Carthaginians, actually circumnavigated Africa."

Octavia had looked between them crossly, obviously looking for a way to jump into the conversation, but quite unable to answer. Alexander had thought about his reply carefully before answering, "I doubt everything on principle, dear lady, until it's proven true. In this case, the Carthaginians were always great seafarers. But there are no maps that show just how far the lands of Africa go on. You'd think that if they ever wanted to return that way again, they'd have taken some soundings. Recorded how many days at what rate of speed, what the beaches looked like, and the names of any towns they passed . . . if any." He shrugged.

"You think there are towns?" Sulpicia asked, raising her eyebrows. "Most people think it's a trackless, burning wasteland."

"But it is!" Octavia said, finally finding a point she could latch onto. "There's nothing but sand there. Totally worthless in every respect. A waste of time to send traders that direction."

"Where there are people, there are usually towns," Alexander had replied, bypassing Octavia's comment lightly.

"Man is a social animal," Sulpicia quoted, smiling.

"And you've read your Aristotle, too," he returned, enjoying himself now.

"Naturally."

"There must be more than sand there. Because the Nile floods, and all that water must be born somewhere. Herodotus suggests snowmelt, though he can't quite fathom where it could possibly snow in the middle of all that heat."

"And you think you know?" Sulpicia had asked, popping a mussel in her mouth.

Alexander raised his eyebrows. "Hispania's a blazing hot place in summer, but it has mountains. Covered in ice year-round, some of them. And water has a tendency to run downhill, as any engineer of our aqueducts will tell you. I think there might be a southern range of Alps to match our northern ones. Somewhere. If the gods truly like balance and symmetry as much as they're said to."

"Of course they do," Octavia had objected, frowning slightly at him. "That's why we have two eyes and not just one, like the ugly cyclopses." She shuddered. "You know, if one of those could be found, it would make a wonderful beast-fight in the games," she added, brightly. "Did you see any of them while you were in Hellas, Alexander?"

He'd wanted to close his eyes for a moment at the thought of a lifetime of exactly those kinds of brightly-chirped questions. Octavia was pleasant, cheerful, kind, and utterly inane. She could hold her own in any conversation that had as its topic the conversation she'd had with someone else, last week. But she didn't read, in spite of Eurydice's frequent suggestions that she at least pick up a book of poetry now and again. And it showed in her sometimes staggering lack of understanding of the world.

Sulpicia had stepped in, smiling. "They're extinct, darling. Odysseus killed Polyphemus, and Apollo slew all the rest in revenge for the death of Asclepius. Euripides tells us so."

"But then Zeus brought them and Asclepius back," Alexander corrected mildly, pouring more wine for Sulpicia. "Because the cyclopses built most of the Olympians' weapons, and were the basis of their power."

Octavia's head swiveled between them. "So do they exist, or don't they?" she demanded.

"They're said to dwell in Aetna's heart now, toiling for Vulcan," Sulpicia returned quickly. "So, as you can see, Alexander wouldn't have seen any in Hellas. Our gods of Rome *conscripted* them!"

Alexander had laughed outright at that, ignoring the irritated frown on his betrothed's face. It was simply so *refreshing* to be able to talk to a woman to whom he wasn't related as an equal. The way he'd talk to Tiberius, Caesarion, Antyllus, or Eurydice. "Come now," he'd told Sulpicia then. "Tell the truth. In your poems, you always complain about your lover, Cerinthus. Confess." He raised his eyebrows at her. "There's no such man, is there?"

"My dear late husband certainly believed me when I said there wasn't," Sulpicia replied, a wicked sparkle in her eyes.

Octavia's head twisted towards her. "I hadn't heard that he'd *died*," she cried, sounding appalled. "Why, you're not even in mourning!"

"My father applied for my divorce about six weeks before the old sot died," Sulpicia replied without charity. "Since I was back to living in my father's house, he told me there was no need to put on a false show of mourning. I told him I admired his lack of hypocrisy, and wore white for the next three months." Since her *stola* tonight was a pale shade of green that set off her dyed red-gold hair, this had obviously been some time ago.

Alexander checked through his mental catalogue of information, and came up with the name of her now-late, previously-aging husband. "Lucius Caesennius Lento?" he asked, blinking for a moment. "One of Antony's staunchest allies, back in the day." *Also, considering the fact that the family goes back to the Etruscans, something of a scandal. He used to write plays in his youth. And owned a theater troupe, if memory serves — the basis for Cicero's allegations in the Senate that he was an* actor *himself. Then again, Cicero sometimes had a hazy relationship with the truth when he was mid-oration, gods know. He once accused Antony of being another man's wife,* stola *and all. He's lucky he had any damned teeth left after* that *speech.* "Whatever happened?"

Sulpicia smirked over her next bite of food. "He told several guests one night, deep in his cups, that he wasn't sure that he approved of all this Egyptian nonsense permeating Rome. Why, some people had Egyptian furniture these days! And the young women who went around wearing Egyptian kohl and jewelry — he quite disapproved of mine, and forbade me to wear it, which made me wear it all the more, you must understand. Which . . . quite limited the social circles I was allowed out into for the duration of the marriage." Alexander laughed at her words, as he was clearly meant to, and she went on, lightly, " — and why, some fools were marrying Egyptian women. Which of course meant that their children couldn't be citizens. And the next thing you know, that young Imperator would surely be extending the rights of citizenship to Egyptians, and not just Cretans and Hellenes who happened to put in their twenty years in the legions. Why, even Antony had an Egyptian wife — leftover and used up after Caesar had had her, of course." Sulpicia rolled her eyes.

"You heard all this?" Alexander asked, half-closing his eyes.

"I couldn't help but hear it. I was at the table with him. I made it a point to call on my uncle Corvinus the next day." She popped another mussel in her mouth.

Marcus Valerius Messalla Corvinus, Alexander had thought. *Father used to call him a political weathervane. Whichever way his loyalties inclined today, indicated perfectly from which quarter the wind in Rome happened to be blowing.* "And your uncle proved of assistance in the matter?"

"He went to my father and arranged my divorce the next day," Sulpicia replied, smiling. "It was the happiest day of my life, moving out of that house. And watching the old actor chew the scenery, calling me an ungrateful bitch of a wife, and how I'd be *sorry* someday, and that he wouldn't accept me back even if I came crawling to him on hands and knees? Fah."

"Oh, my goodness," Octavia put in, for lack of anything better to say. "You poor thing."

"It was quite entertaining. Perhaps the best performance of his life. Six weeks later, he was dead. Some sort of a splitting of the heart. The will was contested, of course. I said I didn't want any of his money, but he hadn't gotten around to changing it between the separation and his death." She shook her head. "So now, I am part-owner of a vineyard and a theater troupe. My father bought a manager for me to take care of it all. I'd love to say that the coin flows in, but the theater? It's a losing proposition."

Alexander chuckled into his cup. "So," he pressed delicately, "*Was* there a Cerinthus?"

Sulpicia snickered. "Ask me again some other day, and I might be inclined to give you an answer," she told him archly, and there the subject had lain.

Seeing that Tiberius and Antyllus were about to make their various offers to Selene, Alexander had walked Sulpicia politely to the door. Where she'd quickly whispered in his ear, "I believe you're the person to whom I should speak, if I happen to hear other unusual sentiments in Rome?"

Could be bait, Alexander thought, deep behind his own eyes. *She's never been affiliated with the Octavianites, however. She dropped out of sight, much to my sister's dismay, after to her marriage to Lento.* "I'm always interested in hearing other people's opinions," he'd murmured in return. "The more varied, the more interesting." He'd smiled as he helped her drape her *palla* over her shoulders to keep her warm on her litter-ride back to her father's house. "Do you know the *taverna* near Pompey's theater? *Merges?*"

"I do."

"The owner's a friend of mine. Former member of the Tenth. If you ever happen to pass by, ask him for a drop of Falnerian, and give him my name. If I'm in the neighborhood, I tend to stop in. We might be able to have another lovely conversation about Herodotus."

"Or Euripides?" Her eyebrows arched. "Or do you

mean about Cerinthus?"

"I'll leave it to the lady's discretion."

He'd then returned and dutifully walked Octavia back to her room. Bowed over her hand, and ignored her agitated remarks about how Sulpicia *certainly* thought she knew something about everything, and wasn't she just a horrible person, not mourning the death of her husband, and everything else. Then he'd walked back to his own rooms, and stood on the balcony outside, smiling to himself and rolling his head around on his neck.

Which was where Tiberius found him. Alexander greeted him with a smile, noting that Tiberius didn't give him an answering one. "Ti, you missed a delicious conversation at dinner."

No verbal response. Just a dark look before Tiberius put his head down on the railing, and then interlaced his hands over his head. *Well, this doesn't bode well for his proposal.* Alexander debated asking directly, but when Tiberius was deeply angry about something, he sometimes snapped if approached about it first-thing. "I wish I'd been able to spend more time with Sulpicia before this," Alexander therefore murmured. "I think I might want to fuck her mind." A hint of affected dreaminess in his voice, to cover the actual hunger there. "Slowly. And then come somewhere between the epic and the ode."

Tiberius turned his head to the side for that one. "Exactly which orifice do you have to use to get there?" His voice was muffled.

"I thought I'd start at the top, work my way down, and if and when I figure it out, I'll tell you." A snort from Tiberius, and Alexander went on, still with a little mock-dreaminess in his voice, "It may take repeated investigations and experimentation." He lowered his voice. "More seriously, either she's sniffing for information, in which case, she's a damned attractive spy for someone else, or she's *offering* information. In which case, she's connected in places I haven't had access to before." He leaned his own elbows on the railing now, looking down into the atrium as the servants scurried around, pinching the wicks of the oil lamps. "So, how did it go with my sister?"

"I don't know," Tiberius muttered.

Alexander turned slightly. "How can you not *know*?"

"Because, you idiot, she told me that she'd been in love with me for three years. That *I* am the reason she actually defied your mother today," Tiberius said, his voice harsh.

Alexander froze for a moment, and then thawed. Jealousy of his siblings simply wasn't part of the formula for the cement that made up his foundations. "Ti, that's wonderful," he murmured, putting a hand on Tiberius' shoulder. *If she feels strongly enough about him to stand up to our mother? That bodes very well for our lark.* "You two are going to be very happy—"

"She *cried*, gods damn it," Tiberius snapped, raising his head. Even so, he kept his voice down. "She cried because she's not an idiot, and she knows *just* enough about the two of us to be convinced that because I love you, I can *never* love her."

"Oh, *shit*," Alexander said, suddenly feeling numb. "*Fuck*."

"If I'd have asked yesterday, she'd probably have said yes, but Antyllus got in first, and while he has no idea *who* the dishonorable bastard is that she's in love with, he *did* plant the suggestion that she's probably just infatuated, and not actually in love with the worthless piece of shit," Tiberius went on, his voice barely audible. "Which is, let's face it, probably the truth." He moved away, and Alexander let his hand fall back to the railing.

"Ti, you're *not* dishonorable." Alexander put as much firmness as he could into his voice. "She didn't tell anyone. We were doing . . . everything . . . probably before she developed those feelings. There is no need to feel guilty." He cast about for words that would help *fix* this. "Her heart's about as fragile as glass, but I refuse to feel badly about anything we did, when she never said a word."

"Say that while looking into her eyes," Tiberius told him shortly. "Right after she's told you she'd *never get in the way*, and that's why she never said anything."

Ah, fuck, Alexander thought, feeling as if someone had punched him in the liver. He hunched over the railing himself now, most of his good mood having evaporated completely. "I'll . . . fix it," he muttered after a moment. "I'll explain to her. . ." *Shit. Shit. How do I explain it to her in a way that she can understand?* "That the kind of love I feel for you, and you for me, isn't the same," he finally muttered, grateful for the babbling of the fountains below. "That it's about fighting together. Overcoming together. Surviving together." He gave Tiberius a sidelong glance. "And fun." He paused.

Tiberius stood up now. Shook his head. "If you can make her understand that, you've got a better career ahead of you than *Cicero*," he told Alexander tiredly. "I already told her that I see a future in her. I don't know if that meant anything to her. She's tired. And so am I." He looked away. "I'm going to visit Agrippa tomorrow and terminate my betrothal to Vipsania," he went on tersely. "No matter if your sister accepts me or not, it's the honorable thing to do. And something I should have done years ago." His voice was taut over those last few words.

No one expects a man stuck in a betrothal for ten damned years before his prospective wife is old enough to wed to be faithful!

Alexander wanted to shout. *There are ideals, yes, and then there is <u>reality</u>, and you hold yourself to impossibly high expectations — half of which were fostered by <u>fucking Octavian</u>, the world's biggest hypocrite!* "And then?" Alexander said warily.

"I have the very difficult task of convincing your sister that I am capable of loving her for who she is, and not just as a shadow of you. Which I hope is true, because she damned well deserves someone who does." Tiberius turned away. "Right now, I'm going to go home, find a jar of wine, and hope it takes me to Hypnos' realm. Because I have no idea how I'm going to sleep tonight."

Alexander covered his eyes for a moment. *Was it only ten hours ago that we used the word <u>love</u> to each other for the first time? This is my fault. If I hadn't said anything about Selene, thinking it would solve all our problems none of this would have happened. Antyllus would have come, made his address, and Tiberius and I would have . . . well, kept on doing what we'd been doing. Until I married Octavia, and then there'd be <u>nothing</u>.*

When Tiberius' self-loathing was at its zenith, Alexander usually told his friend to stay the night. It usually didn't even involve sex on nights like these. It meant playing dice, sparring, drinking — anything that could, would, and did get Ti's mind off of honor and duty and his perceived failures in both. And if they fell asleep in the same bed, it meant that Ti had actually *fallen asleep*. The worst of the self-loathing spells had faded years ago, but this one looked bad. "Do I need to take your knife away from you?" Alexander asked, not joking.

"I'm not going to fall on it," Tiberius told him quietly, his back still turned. "Not tonight, anyway. Perhaps there's a reason I saw Mars' face so clearly, and Antyllus saw Venus'. Perhaps that was the message I should have taken to heart years ago. I'm for war, not for love."

"She hasn't said no yet," Alexander pointed out sharply. *And damn it, I love you, too.*

"Good night, Alexander. I'll see you tomorrow."

Shit. Shit. Shit. Alexander watched his friend descend the stairs, and heard the front door of the villa open, and then shut behind him. *How in Dis' name do I make any of this right?*

Chapter IV: Changing Tides

<u>Ianuarius 3, 20 AC</u>

Eurydice told the servants to let Selene sleep in the next morning, inwardly raging at their mother for the interference, necessary or not, in all their lives. She and Caesarion had retired very late themselves. She'd slipped the Magi bracelet off her wrist for the first time in close to three years, and placed it on the table beside the bed. And they'd simply lain there, neither of them able to get in the mood for love. They'd been so careful, for so long, to avoid conception, that even starting the process now seemed terrifying.

"Don't tell anyone about this," Caesarion had muttered, rolling to his back and putting a forearm over his eyes. "It would destroy all confidence the Roman people have in my manhood and vigor."

"And who would I tell?" Eurydice had asked, curling into his side, staring at the wall and watching the flickering light of the oil lamp beside the bed cast shadows there. "The sister who wept herself to sleep down the hall, or the brother who's probably still awake and reading over the reports of his agents?"

A little light humor to try to cover their mutual deep unease. He'd rolled to his side then, pulling her tightly into him. "The dream still says an eagle first?" Caesarion asked, his voice uneasy.

"Always," she replied, closing her eyes as her throat ached. "At least we know that since we're god-born, our children won't have any physical curses."

He'd sighed. "Small comfort."

"And we need to go to Egypt *anyway*. There's no more

putting it off."

"I know."

And still they'd lain there, unmoving, and finally found sleep only just before dawn.

At dawn, with the servants busily baking bread, Eurydice stepped out the front door of the villa, holding in her hands several offerings. Today was the first day of the festival of the *Compitalia*, the days on which the *lares* of every household were honored, as well as the *manes*. At every crossroad in Rome, offerings were made by neighborhood elders. Bread and cakes and other good things. And outside every Roman house in the sprawling empire, owners and slaves alike placed offerings just outside their doors.

Lengths of braided rope hung down from the roof of the portico, and Eurydice carefully looped them into nooses, wrapping each around a little poppet. She'd made them by hand to resemble each of the patrician residents currently in the villa. This one had Caesarion's red eyes embroidered on the cloth face, and his short-cropped dark hair. A little purple toga swathed its body. This one had her own golden eyes and longer hair . . . and a red *stola*, as she usually chose to wear these days. This one for Alexander. That one for Selene. And even one for Octavia.

The servants and slaves left their own offerings, usually cruder ones made of wadded cotton. All would be left here for several days, so that Mania, goddess of the underworld's spirits—not to be confused with Proserpina—properly propitiated, would accept the poppets in place of the mortal residents.

You know that she isn't particularly interested in your spirits, Flaminia, one of the household *lares*, told Eurydice, swarming up one of the marble pillars like a cat climbing a tree. Her tail lashed, and she hissed a little at a passing breeze.

"I'm aware," Eurydice replied, smiling faintly. "But I'm sure she likes having her name remembered just as much as *you* do."

The tiny house-spirit dropped to the ground and raced after some insect that had *dared* to threaten the doorway of the villa. *You will be leaving us soon?* Flaminia asked, her voice sad. Eurydice took it as a matter of faith that the house-spirits knew *everything*. She'd once suggested to Alexander that people who neglected their *lares*, might therefore have bribable, disloyal spirits who might be willing to turn over information for the cost of a loaf of saffron-tinged bread.

The look on her brother's face had been indescribable. And after he stopped laughing, Alexander had asked her, merrily, how that would work, since to his knowledge, she and Caesarion were the only people who could *see* the *lares* in Rome.

Eurydice was working on that part of the problem. As best she could, anyway. For the moment, she inclined her head to Flaminia gravely. "Probably   for   some   time," Eurydice said, watching as the butler opened the shutters of the front rooms, giving her a glance askance for talking to what, for him, looked like empty air. "I don't suppose I could take some of you with me to Egypt."

Oh no. We're bound to this place. I could never travel so far away. Besides, the spirits of Egypt would be cross if I went to their lands and took away from their sacrifices. Flaminia pouted. *I'd like to, but I'm just not strong enough to fight off all of them when they come around to scratch at my eyes.*

"When Caesarion builds the larger villa on the Palatine, could you be bound *there*? I would quite miss all of you, if you weren't the spirits of whatever house we happened to live in." Eurydice held out her hand, and a different spirit landed in it—this one a bright yellow spark of light that buzzed like a bee, but had no actual shape that she'd ever seen.

Now that we could manage, Flaminia replied more positively. *We like you. You always remember our cake at dinner, and the little sacrifices through the week. When you and your Eagle go off to war, the servants usually forget.* That, with a pout. *Your sister remembers, but she won't be here soon, either.*

"I'll remind the servants why it's important." Eurydice ran a hand along the hanging 'corpses' of the household, setting them to swinging, and glanced across the plaza, where the matron of another house was in the middle of the self-same task. "I promise."

Thank you. We're most grateful.

At that point, her tasks complete, Eurydice called for a horse; she was currently the only Roman woman alive who was permitted to ride one, and could leave her house more or less at will, though she always left word where she was going.

Caesarion's work in the Senate on the subject of women and their freedoms had run into opposition from the Octavianites, who wanted to hold to Octavian's requirement that a woman needed to have borne three children to a marriage enacted in a temple to be able to own property and travel without a male escort at all times—or, if a widow, to live in a household of her own. The entire affair had bogged down over the requirement of children.

Caesarion and the Julii faction had demanded to know what the difference between a woman of forty with two children and a girl who'd borne twins and then a single child between the ages of fifteen and eighteen was. Or for that matter, a woman of sixty who'd taken the oath of a Vestal, been permitted to own property in that time, but who'd outlived her oath, and now, after thirty years of perfect probity, now once more required a male 'guardian' just to manage the property that she'd previously managed for thirty years. And the Octavianites had countered that non-citizen men who joined the ranks of the legion to earn the rights of citizenship did so for sixteen and twenty year terms, per Caesarion's own laws. And that a woman couldn't just be *given* those rights; they had to *earn* them, just as the non-citizen men did. Through providing more Romans citizens.

The fact that a Roman woman could *produce* more Roman citizens — male children, anyway — but not have all the rights of a Roman citizen didn't appear to be a contradiction to the Octavianite faction's collective mind. And to the question of "and if a woman *does* 'earn her rights by having three children, do her rights automatically pass on to her girl children?" their answer was a resounding *no*.

Eurydice did her best to smile at the various Octavianite leaders when social gatherings made contact with them unavoidable. Unaccountably, they all seemed to have enormous difficulty meeting her hawk-gold stare. Particularly when she decided not to blink for a while. She also pointedly wore the *parazonium* knife Caesarion had given her on all public occasions. Women couldn't bear military arms, by tradition, and the *parazonium* in particular was a symbol of authority over armed men. Not quite *imperium*, which was the right to levy armies, but the right to *command*. Caesarion had put his own knife in her hand as a symbol of her ability to command the Sixteenth Legion, the *Accipitris*. They'd taken their name from her own unique nickname — *Accipitra*. The hawk. Women weren't usually accorded cognomens of their own, but she'd paid for hers in her own blood.

Anyone who wanted to debate whether or not she should wear that knife, Caesarion usually directed to look at every monument to Roma. On which the goddess who embodied Rome's spirit — and whom Eurydice suspected was a veiled version of Venus — wore the same exact *parazonium*, belted at her hip, in spite of the flowing lines of her *stola*.

The core of the Sixteenth remained the two thousand legionnaires formerly in the service of the Tillii family, whose lives she'd saved in Hispania. The additional four thousand men and auxiliaries, she'd recruited herself in the past three years, at her own expense, though their salaries were paid out of the state budget, as all legionnaire's pay now came. The hike in taxes to pay for a state-run army, instead of an army paid for by this patrician or that one had occasioned quite a bit of grumbling when their father had instituted it some eighteen years ago, but it was now a simple fact of life.

The Sixteenth still had a formal legate—Lucius Cornelius Balbus, a man past fifty, who'd won renown in her father's civil wars, and then had gone off to be proconsul in Africa for a number of years. He handled all day-to-day affairs, tactics, and military decisions. But the legionnaires were *hers*. Much to his initial disgruntlement. He was, after all, the only non-Roman ever accorded a triumph, and for his pains, he'd been placed in command of a legion, mostly manned by former traitors, which answered to a *woman*. He'd considered it all quite humiliating at first. Then he'd listened to the stories of the survivors, and gotten quite a bit more intrigued.

Surrounded by ten Praetorians on horseback—former members of the Tenth Legion, who'd been moved to permanent body-guard and household guard status after twenty years of service, and who hadn't elected to retire— Eurydice rode out of Rome, towards the winter encampment of the Sixteenth. Her men were all already in the practice yards when she arrived, despite the early hour, and she heard a few of them shout, *"Accipitra!"* as she passed—something that still had the power to daze her. Not only was it her cognomen, a name that she'd earned in blood, but it was also her *Name*. The name that the gods themselves knew her by. And now, all of Rome knew it, too.

She waved, acknowledging the occasional cheers of greeting, but didn't slow her pace through the camp, until she reached the headquarters building. Which had another building beside it, which was considered so secret that on joining the Sixteenth, every man took an oath before the Eagle of the Legion, and swore by Dis and the Styx not to reveal its presence or purpose.

This building was her goal. For inside, was a small library and a series of classrooms and studies. All with tile walls and stone floors — the better for preventing the spread of fire. "Good morning, *domina*," Ianthe said as Eurydice entered, leaving her escort outside with the chill air that had stung her cheeks on the ride over. The Hellene woman turned from the hearth at which she was stirring some sort of herbal brew in a cauldron. Even after three years in Rome, this priestess of Hecate still preferred an undyed *peplos* to a tunic and *stola*, though she'd draped a shawl around her shoulders as a concession to the chill. "Here to inspect our progress?"

"That, among other things," Eurydice said, smiling. "Is that tea, or something I really shouldn't sample?"

"I don't recommend it," Ianthe murmured, her dark eyes wide. "*Silphium*. The most valuable plant in the world. The Carthaginians knew of its efficacy, but believed that it could not be cultivated outside of Africa. It has nearly been driven to extinction, *domina*. But a few devotees of my lady have kept caches of its seeds, and have managed to cultivate it carefully and slowly, in fields where no men tread."

Eurydice's eyebrows rose. "What does it do?" she asked, cautiously sniffing at the brew. "Is it a poison?"

Ianthe shook her head. "No. Like the greens of wild carrots, or catmint brewed in wine, it . . . brings the menstrual flow." She paused. "Even if you happen to be with child, very shortly, you will *not* be. That is the reason why it was so highly valued in trade from Cyrenaica. Too many people find themselves with infants they can't feed. Better to prevent them from being born, than watch them scream with hunger, and die of it." She stirred the brew again. "Remember the smell, my lady," Ianthe enjoined her. "It's highly distinctive, because the most efficacious part of the plant is its resin. Little can cover its odor, but few people recognize the scent anymore. And though it is rare and costly, hands with the right amount of coin can still purchase it. And people threatened by the birth of a child to, say, an Empress?" Ianthe's smile was chill. "Might pay dearly to have such a thing added to your cup."

"Wouldn't the protective spirits bound to me recognize it?" Eurydice asked, glancing down at one of the rings she wore.

"It won't harm *you* at all. A spirit could miss its presence quite easily." Ianthe gestured. "Call them. Let them taste of it, so that they can recognize its essence."

After Eurydice had done precisely that, several others joined them in the main room with its warm hearth. She recognized them all, of course. Seleukos, a physician formerly with the Fifth Legion, had been included in this small organization at Caesarion's request, for his medical knowledge was exceptional. He was, in fact, writing an encyclopedia of medical terms, illnesses, current wound treatments, and herbal remedies—assisted ably by Ianthe in the area of curatives, poisons, and antidotes. As such, when he'd been transferred to the Sixteenth, another man of the Fifth had come with him, a very senior centurion who was his particular friend . . . who'd suffered a severe head wound some five years ago, which Caesarion had cured.

Everything comes around, Eurydice thought, nodding

now to Kheiron, a sorcerer-philosopher from Crete, and Zaracas, a Carthaginian who spent most of his time thinking about *atoms*, and having arguments in his head with long-dead Aristotle. "How goes our census?" Eurydice asked, warming her hands around a cup of safer mint tea, this one poured by Seleukos. "Do we have any new recruits?"

About two years ago, she'd gone to Caesarion with a simple theory: *We can't be the only two people like ourselves in the whole Empire, beloved. There are too many stories about house-spirits and there's too much fear of witches for it all to be merely hysteria. Some of those who claim to see spirits are probably mad. Some of them wind up entering this priesthood or that, even if just as lay-brothers and lay-sisters. And some of them are driven out of their homes and into the woods, and have real power. We saw first-hand what the druids of Britannia can do. . . . and that was just twelve men on a mountain. One, when Matru clearly . . . called on a god, or whatever it was that he did, that brought the ground to life under our feet, and then escaped in the confusion. How can we fight that kind of magic, without magic of our own?*

And thus, in proper Roman fashion, they'd started by collecting information. Systematically. Region by region. They sent some of Alexander's *frumentarii* out into the countryside, not just looking for missing taxes and disloyalty, but also searching for credible evidence of witches and sorcerers. These people were notably wary. Sulla's antique *Lex Cornelia de sicariis et veneficis* had criminalized several things—women seeking abortion, and the practice of magic among them. Even owning a book *about* magic had been a criminal act. Ianthe, as a priestess of Hecate, worker of magic, and herbalist? Would have been a felon under the old laws, and might have been executed for it.

Having been driven to the outskirts of society over the years anyway, Rome's secret sorcerers weren't inclined to volunteer information about themselves. Disappointingly, many of them turned out to be little more than herbalists. A few were plainly madmen. Others were simply cruel individuals who delighted in tormenting their fellow men by harnessing the power of superstition, leaving dead cats and toads in their homes as curses — things that Ianthe sniffed at. "If you want an *effective* curse, you need to make proper sacrifices to the correct spirits, or to the correct god," she'd murmured after meeting a woman who'd sworn that she, too, was a priestess of Hecate, living deep in the rural heart of Campagna. Her lips had curled into a sneer. "A spirit might ask for a cat's life-essence, yes, but leaving it in the house of the victim just leaves a bad smell and some fear." She'd put her head to the side, consideringly. "The right *kind* of spirit finds that sort of fear as tasty as wine," Ianthe had added, her tone musing. "But still. Sloppy. Best not to leave any evidence at all. And I see no evidence that this latest 'witch' can call the attention of so much as a mouse, even when armed with a block of cheese, let alone a spirit. I would, however, like to have a *chat* with her, if you'll permit me, *domina*. My lady does not appreciate having her Name invoked by someone who has never undergone the proper initiations."

In public, Ianthe tended to put on a show of being even meeker than Selene, scarcely speaking above a whisper. The pose deflected attention from her. Which made it all the more startling when the supposed priestess from Campagna had left their private discussion white-faced and shaking so much that she hadn't been able to walk to the door without assistance. Eurydice had never asked what Ianthe had told the woman, but she suspected that there would be no more rural curses in Campagna. Not for some time, anyway.

"Three more who can definitely see *lares*," Ianthe replied now, taking a seat at the table.

"Two more who passed the test of the candle and feather," Kheiron added, pouring himself a cup of hippocras—wine spiced with costly cinnamon and honey, in spite of the early hour. "Neither of them are noble."

"The gift does *not* seem to pass solely among patrician families," Zaracas put in, his voice louder than all the others, rich and hearty. "If magic is a gift from the gods, it seems a most democratic one. There is some evidence that the gift is passed down in family lineages, however. You would think that if magic was truly useful, people would use it to rise above their fellows. Establish great kingdoms and accrue much wealth, and set up families that endure in power for generations."

"Perhaps because those who have the gift who do not seek to placate the gods," Kheiron returned sharply, "are inevitably driven out of whatever society in which they lived—"

"Magic *comes from* the gods," Ianthe hissed under her breath. "It is sacrilege to say otherwise. The greatest heroes of Hellas all possessed it in some measure, but all of them gave correct obeisance to the gods in gratitude for the gifts they were given—"

And yet, today, Hellas is a province of Rome, Eurydice thought. *And so is Egypt, land of magic.* She held up a hand. "That particular conversation can wait," she informed them, cutting the trio off before they could completely distract themselves. "We're still seeing childhood headaches as one of the signs? Followed usually by a traumatic experience that they tried to prevent in any manner that they could?"

Nods around the room. "That is usually the pattern," Ianthe acknowledged. "Unless there's a reason to suspect at birth that a child has been marked out for greatness. Signs. Portents."

Both of which were lacking at my birth, Eurydice thought. *For whatever reason, the gods decided to let my gifts bloom unseen at first. Perhaps because the rest of Rome would have been even more threatened by two god-born in the house of Julii than they were by just one. This gave us both time to grow up.*

"We really do need to go district by district and tribe by tribe in Rome itself," Zaracas said in his usual cheerful rumble. His light brown skin and pale gold eyes shone in the morning light streaming in the window. "It's the largest city on earth. There *must* be hundreds of potential candidates among its streets."

Eurydice sighed. "That takes away somewhat from our attempts to keep our efforts here secret," she told them all, shaking her head. "Our current total is what, fifteen students, not counting me?"

A room of dispirited nods. Eurydice exhaled. "Given the spells that I've developed, based on the *limited* access I've had to the Book of Thoth and through experimentation on my own, and what Kheiron and Ianthe have brought with them, how far are the rest of our students along?"

Kheiron grimaced. "Most of them seem to be breaking along clear lines of affinity to this element or that. Fire, water, air. None of them show your ladyship's ability to harness all of the elements at once, or principles of inertia. I have some of them reading Titus Lucretius Carus' *On the Nature of Things* in an effort to make them think about how the natural state of matter is motion, not stasis, but they seem to find it hard going."

Ianthe snorted. "That *Epicurean*," she said with a frown, "wrote seven thousand lines of verse in which he claimed to explain the nature of the universe, for the purpose of teaching humanity not to fear the gods. To tell everyone that things happen because of *chance*, not because the gods will it—"

"And there *are* natural laws," Kheiron shot back sharply. "Lucretius fully acknowledges that the gods exist. He simply does not think that they meddle in the world as much as you priests would have us believe. That there is no augury in the flight of a sparrow—"

"He claims to understand everything, but he can't fit the *stars* into his grand explanation—"

Normally, Eurydice would have enjoyed this conversation, and even joined in. For she had personal evidence that yes, sometimes the gods did indeed meddle—why else would there be god-born such as herself? But on the other hand, the gods also seemed to stand apart. Content to give advice or commands, and let humans go about the business of living in the world. "Venus and Mars did specifically say that they *came* to this world," she murmured softly. "Not that they made it. And that they *met* our people. Not that they created us." She gave them all a faint smile as they quieted for a moment. "Can we agree that the universe seems to be governed by laws? And that, if they feel like it, the gods can break those laws . . . but that they don't seem to be responsible for, hmm. Overseeing them."

Kheiron and Ianthe gave each other grim glances. Seleukos coughed into his hand gently. "Far above my head," the physician murmured. "I generally content myself with 'what does this rash mean?' and my best augury is reading what Hippocrates and other *medici* have observed and written down before me."

"Precisely why we need to record everything we say here," Kheiron jumped in with enthusiasm. "Even a passing thought might actually reveal truth to us later."

Zaracas stretched, rolling his shoulders. "So, you have our candidates reading Lucretius' seven thousand lines on the nature of reality. But they're having problems with it. Is it the fact that it's couched in poetry, or is it the concepts?"

"Both. *Domina*, most of these people are . . . not well-educated," Kheiron told Eurydice, rubbing at his thick golden beard. "Half of them came to us completely illiterate. The other half *can* read, but only . . . functionally. Enough to understand a letter from their cousins. They're mostly highly intelligent, so they learn quickly, but they've never had to think about why things work. They either work, or they don't work."

"They are the sort for whom the spells as written and passed down are entirely the correct route," Ianthe put in quietly, and Eurydice covered her face with her hands. "I myself learned in that way, and most of my spells are curses. They require sacrifices. Negotiations with spirits—which I certainly can try to effect in lands not my own, but the spirits I meet outside of Hellas tend to be hostile towards me. We have yet to find a second person close to your power, *domina*."

"Or to your curiosity." Kheiron's voice quieted now, too. "With a few more years of training, however, they might become quite something else."

Eurydice kept her hands over her face, concentrating on her breathing for a long moment. "We don't have years," she finally said, taking her hands away. "The druids of Britannia have been training their people for thousands of years. The Magi of Chaldea have done the same. We lag them in almost every way." She sighed. "You will all be staying here to continue the census. Expand it to Rome itself, on my authority. If asked, direct people up the line to Alexander. He'll handle all inquiries in his usual . . . inimitable fashion." She stared at her tea for a moment. "The top half of our recruits—pick them by their ability to work beside the legionnaires—will be going to Gaul with the Tenth."

"Our top two recruits are women," Ianthe cautioned.

"Keep them here," Eurydice said, hating herself for the words. "The men of the Tenth are used to me, but I also have quite a bit more power than our recruits. They don't see me as a liability or an experiment, and I have enough personal resources in the way of horses and tents and servants that I can keep up with them on the march. Our recruits need to be able to march right alongside the legionnaires, carry the same kit, and blend into formation—until they're needed to add flame to a ballista stone, heating it until it explodes in a rain of hot fragments wherever it lands. Preferably without damaging the ballista itself." She rubbed at her eyes. "Also, Kheiron will be in charge here during my absence. Report regularly to me and to Alexander. I will be gone for . . . an unknown amount of time."

"The campaign season doesn't start for two months, *domina*," Seleukos said, frowning. His close-cropped dark beard shadowed most of his features. "If I may ask where—"

"Egypt," Eurydice said emptily. "The only good thing about that statement is that I will have unlimited access to the Library of Alexandria for quite some time. And perhaps access to priests of Thoth better equipped to teach than Tahut-Nefer was." *Perhaps someone, at some point, can explain to me why earth and metal are so damnably difficult to work with, when air and water and even fire are my good friends these days.* "Most of the Sixteenth will be coming with me," she added quietly. "We'll move a different legion into this camp, most likely the Fourth. They were in Hispania. They lost half their men there. They'll take the oaths, and they'll *understand* the value and need for what we're doing here, as few others can."

Seleukos' head came up. "May I come with you, *domina*?" he inquired. "Tahut-Nefer was an intolerable snob, but not every Egyptian physician will be quite so, ah, disdainful of others' learning, I would think. And I would like a chance to catalogue their medicaments and any alternate techniques they might have. Their knowledge of anatomy alone is worth the trip."

Eurydice nodded immediately. "Absolutely," she agreed, standing. "And now I must be off again, unfortunately. I don't have time today to train with the recruits."

The others all rose when she did, and Kheiron and Zaracas walked her to the exit. "I think you'd find Lucretius of great interest, *domina*," Kheiron told her mildly, opening the door for her.

"I've read him," she acknowledged. "Personally, I found what he had to say about free will to be most intriguing. He thinks that atoms dance by chance. And because they can move in ways that deviate from the set path of determinism, that we poor mortals can, too." She looked up at the tall Carthaginian, Zaracas. "Some days, that thought is all that gets me out of bed in the morning."

Back at the villa by mid-morning, Eurydice started going over the travel necessities once more. Decamping the entire Sixteenth to go with her to Egypt had long been planned, but that still meant that they needed close to forty-eight ships, and that *wasn't* counting the full complement of the Praetorians, clerks, scribes, and other such people as followed Caesarion and Eurydice these days. She had two personal scribes, one Egyptian, who could handle the demotic writing needed for correspondence with the nobles of Alexandria, and one Roman, who helped with communication with the current Roman prefect there. *Cornelius Gallus. Who will not be best pleased to be replaced by Marcus Antonius, who will take the grander title of governor when there. Married to Cleopatra though he may be.*

Scanning through her usual sheaf of communiques

from Alexandria, Eurydice spotted one that stated that there had been 'unrest' in Thebes, and that Gallus had taken the garrison and ridden south to investigate and put it down. Frowning, Eurydice stared at those words for several moments, as her scribes worked assiduously in her office, preparing letters of instruction for ships, provisions, and other such necessities.

Thebes. The temple of Thoth is there — well, any number of temples are at Thebes. It was the capital, on and off, for several dynasties. The Ptolemies brought the capital down to the sea, because they were Hellenes, and couldn't be parted from Poseidon's realm. Where trade in goods and trade in knowledge was available. Where in the desert, far from the sea, there are no new ideas. Just old ones.

Struck by the thought, she stood, catching that piece of parchment, and told her scribes, "Keep at it. I'll read all the copies and put my seal on them when you're done. But for the moment, I need to talk to Caesarion." And down the stairs she went, thinking, *Whenever we build the new villa, my study and library really need to be beside his. I spend all day running up and down the stairs, but there just isn't enough room in his office for all my books, and Alexander needs his own workspace* — and then the thought cut off abruptly, as she again realized, frantically, that very shortly, she wasn't going to be anywhere near Caesarion. Let alone needing to be concerned about making space available for all their scribes and clerks and everything else.

Eurydice put a hand to the wall outside Caesarion's study and steadied herself. *Don't cry. The moment of separation isn't here yet, and you've had three years to prepare for it. Three years of genuine happiness is more than some people get in a lifetime. So take a breath. Straighten up. And knock.* Her hand found the wood of the door, and she tapped there firmly.

"Come in, Eurydice!" Caesarion called from the other

side, and the door opened in front of her, without her touching the latch, and one of the *lares* scampered away, giggling.

Inside, she saw that he stood at his desk, and that Tiberius and Antyllus were both with him, leaning over the desks and tables, an assortment of maps and charts scattered on every available surface. Most of which looked to be of what little Roman cartographers currently knew about Britannia. "I can come back," Eurydice said immediately. "This isn't urgent."

Caesarion waved her in, however, and she crossed the room and let him take her hand lightly in his. "I was just telling Tiberius that he should come with us to Egypt. Britannia can wait a month or two for all of us."

Tiberius shook his head slightly. "My brother's joining the Tenth. It's his first campaign. I should be there for him."

"He'll be in the command tent, fetching, carrying, and writing letters for the first year," Caesarion told Tiberius dryly. "You and Antyllus both put your names forward with interest for Selene. Selene's coming with us to Egypt. You're not jumping at the chance to go with us?" His eyebrows rose, and Tiberius looked even more uncomfortable for a moment.

Antyllus shook his head. "Honestly, after last night, I'm not sure either of us have a shot with her," he said, his tone a little more dispirited than Eurydice had expected of the usually cheerful man. "She told me that she's in love with someone. Someone betrothed, apparently, and in love with someone other than his betrothed, to boot. I'm willing to give her time to leave fantasy for reality, and I told her so—and that I hoped I might be the reality she'd pick." He shook his head. "If I knew what man she had her eye on, I'd tell you," he added to Caesarion. "I don't think he's been leading her on; she said he doesn't even know she's alive."

Eurydice's eyebrows had risen towards her hairline, and she turned to stare at Caesarion, who looked at her in turn. "Did you know about this?" he asked her, immediately.

"No! I'll admit, she and I haven't been close since . . . everything. . ." Eurydice gestured at her own eyes ruefully. "She's never particularly confided in me, and when I asked her a few years ago if she was practicing Mother's love-spell for anyone, she immediately replied no." Eurydice frowned. *Then again, I did suspect she was lying at the time.*

"Love-spell?" Antyllus asked, in tones of intrigue. "What's this?"

"It doesn't work—" Eurydice began dismissively.

"Oh, yes, it does," Caesarion contradicted, not looking up from his maps. "At least on me. Every time. Without fail."

It was the deadpan delivery that did it. Eurydice felt her own face turn lambent with heat. Antyllus' eyebrows went up, and stayed there. "And now I really want to know," he said, grinning.

"She won't tell," Tiberius said tiredly, taking a seat near one of the desks. "Alexander did worm the secret out of Selene years ago, but he wouldn't tell me. On that note," he added, his voice so dry and distant that he could have been making a report on troop movements, "the dishonorable sot is no longer engaged to his erstwhile betrothed. I visited Agrippa this morning and terminated my engagement to Vipsania. My mother was highly displeased about the whole thing, which I have to say made it much sweeter than it might otherwise have been." His gray eyes were remote and cold as he added, looking directly at Caesarion, "You have my word on the Styx that I had no idea of your sister's attachment to me before last night."

Eurydice's mouth dropped open, her embarrassment forgotten. *Wait, she's been mooning over __Tiberius__ all this time—*

but he and Alexander . . . oh. She <u>knows</u>. She hears and sees everything in the villa, and <u>that's</u> why she never said anything. She was too embarrassed.

Antyllus was the first to recover, running a hand over his curly hair and saying, "Well . . . shit. I had no idea, Tiberius. You're hardly dishonorable—gods know, you're one of my friends. I'll bow out—"

"No," Tiberius replied, grim-faced, before Caesarion could get a word in edgewise. "Don't withdraw your suit. She needs to make a clear decision between us, on her own. Without that, there might always be a question in her mind as to whether or not she made the correct decision." A muscle worked in his jaw momentarily. "It doesn't matter which of us she picks," he added, shrugging. "So long as the decision is unambiguous, and doesn't get in the way of what we need to do." He picked up one of the maps. "Your father's troops landed every time in the western part of the island," Tiberius went on, using the exact same tone. "Perhaps there are other landing areas that might be less well-defended, and without the towering white cliffs of Dubris."

There was a long moment of silence as the other three people in the room tried to shift course with Tiberius, firmly back into the realm of war, and not that of love. Antyllus cleared his throat. "No matter where we land," he said slowly, "Caesar's ships were damaged by the tides each time he made the crossing. The seas of the north are fierce and rough. We'll need to pick a landing area wide enough to bring the ships in without risking them running up against each other."

"We have some information from the Gauls of the mainland about the southern coasts of the island. They do trade back and forth across that channel," Caesarion said thoughtfully. "There are chalk cliffs along quite a lot of the south. But here," he tapped on the southeast corner, but further west of where Tiberius had been indicating, "among the lands held by the Regini. I was along for the last invasion, though I was only ten. Spent most of the time in the command tent, honestly, but I remember my father arguing with his legates, because they wanted to land among the Regini, and not in Cantiaci territory again."

"Did he explain why he wanted to repeat the mistakes of the past?" Antyllus asked mildly.

Caesarion shook his head. "The only thing he ever said to me on the subject was that he'd lost something important in that region during the first invasion. And that it was important enough to go back for. Whatever it was, we didn't find it before having to withdraw to go deal with a rebellion in Illyrica. He was annoyed." He shook his head. "At any rate, the Regini are tributaries of the Artebates, and the Atrebates' king, Commius, remains a . . . nominal ally of Rome,"

"Reluctantly. Very reluctantly," Antyllus said, mildly. "His son Tincomarus grew up in my father's house. He was an *obses*, a hostage, for Commius' good behavior. I understand there were a few betrayals and broken oaths of fealty back during the Gallic Wars, until Commius finally brokered a peace agreement with my father. He swore he'd leave continental Gaul, if only he never had to look at another Roman again."

That got heads to turn. Caesarion blinked. "All right then. Perhaps the Regini and Atrebates are our way in. Saves trying to cut through the Cantiaci for the . . . fourth time, overall." Caesarion shrugged. "Of course, we have little reconnaissance about that area." He looked at Eurydice, his expression tensing. "And we won't have your eyes, beloved."

"Tincomarus was practically an older brother," Antyllus said, shrugging. "He went back to help his father rule five years ago. His very Roman wife and his infant son are, er, hostages now, for his good behavior. They were moved to my uncle Lucius' house for, ah, safe-keeping, when my father closed the villa down for the move here." He shrugged again when the others all looked at him. "What I mean to say is, Tincomarus should be willing to give us more information. If asked the right way."

Eurydice had closed her eyes at Caesarion's earlier words. "About my not being there," she said unsteadily, "I wanted to talk to you about the fact that Cornelius Gallus decamped the entire garrison in Alexandria—six thousand men!—and headed south to Thebes because 'unrest' had been reported." She grimaced, opening her eyes. "While Mother only asked us yesterday about making Antony governor. . . I have a feeling Gallus might be trying to show his worth as prefect. He might have had intimations about his upcoming replacement."

"And you think he might be overzealous about it," Caesarion interpreted rapidly.

"Too heavy a hand there right now, and 'unrest' might become 'rebellion,'" she murmured. "Especially with the mage-priests. Who . . . probably have ample reason to dislike us. Well, me." She grimaced, remembering the way in which she'd dismissed the insufferable Tahut-Nefer from this house. "You're going to tell me that you told me so, aren't you?"

Caesarion had already picked up a stylus and a wax tablet to jot down some rapid notes for a scribe to turn into a more polished order. "I don't need to, when you've already come to the conclusion yourself," he told her briskly. "When was that report dated?"

"Two weeks ago. He admits that it's more of a rumor than anything at the moment, but that it . . . 'doesn't do to let the soldiers get fat in winter.'" She grimaced. "That's tidied up and couched in language a bureaucrat would approve, mind.

Not that there's much of a winter in Egypt."

"By the time my order to desist gets there, whatever's going to happen, will already have happened," Caesarion muttered, but finished writing on the tablet anyway. "Might as well get it in the record that we tried to stop the avalanche." He sighed and looked at Tiberius and Antyllus. "Let's break for our midday meal, gentlemen."

They nodded, both heading for the door. And as Tiberius turned to duck out, Caesarion called after him, "You will be coming to Egypt with us." No compromise in his voice. "You said yourself that you want an unambiguous choice. And I've never seen you retreat before. Get in the damned fight already."

Tiberius' back stiffened, and his expression tightened. "Yes, *dominus*."

In the atrium of the Julii house, Antyllus caught Tiberius' arm, still looking apologetic. "I'm sorry," the older man told him, sincerity in his voice and eyes. "When she told me, I was mostly relieved that the issue wasn't just some version of a virgin's aversion. If I'd known it was you, I'd have shut my damned mouth."

Tiberius shrugged. "It doesn't matter," he told Antyllus simply. He couldn't dislike Antony's son, much as he wished he could. They'd been through too many battles together, and while that was no guarantee of friendship, since there were plenty of outright bastards in the legions, it had created a matrix of trust and fidelity among the cadre of older advisors and younger leaders with whom Caesarion had surrounded himself. "Whatever happens, happens. And as you said last night . . . friends." He offered his hand, and Antyllus clasped his wrist, looking relieved. "Do me a favor, though? Make my excuses to Caesarion about joining the family for lunch."

Antyllus' eyebrows rose. "Selene will be there. You're going to let me steal a march on you? Bad tactics."

Tiberius shook his head. "I need to talk to my brother about a number of things. And he needs to hear them from me, not from our mother or Agrippa."

Antyllus nodded. "Understood." He hesitated. "I wish my relationship with my own brother was as good as yours with Drusus. Of course, it's my own fault, really. I should reach out to Jullus more." His voice was wistful.

Tiberius blinked. "Drusus always reminds me when I've been forgetful of him. It's a street on which we can pass both ways. Not a river, always flowing from mountains to sea."

Another nod, and then a flicker of something crossed Antyllus' face. "I keep trying to tell my brother something, but he just won't hear me when I say it," he told Tiberius. "I remind him that our step-mother Octavia's dead. And that all her disapproval died with her."

That sounds remarkably like what Alexander keeps telling me about Octavian. What is it about that brother and sister, that lingers so in the lives of those they controlled? Tiberius met Antyllus' eyes for a long moment. "She might be as dead as Octavian," he told his friend quietly. "But for so long as their voices live in our heads, their ghosts stay with us. And no matter how often you hang up poppets on the doorstep or make offerings at graves, the voices never seem to go away."

As he made his way to his own small villa, this one on the Palatine, befitting the Claudii name that he and his brother bore, Tiberius reflected not on Octavian's voice in his head, but that of Livia. He hadn't been joking when he'd told Caesarion that she'd been angry. Though breaking his betrothal to Vipsania hadn't, surprisingly, been the source of her ire. No, it was the reason *for* it that had made her voice rise in fury. "All these years," she'd said, her face livid, "I have held off trying to arrange a better match for you than Vipsania, because I couldn't imagine you putting her aside. And now you do—but for a half-Egyptian *trull*?"

"Watch your tongue," he'd snapped. "Selene is probably the most innocent person I've ever met."

"If you're going to break your betrothal, why not for someone of *real* value?" she'd returned, spots of color burning on her cheekbones, and her mouth a grim slash. "Why not marry Octavia instead? A true daughter of Rome—"

"She's betrothed to Alexander—"

"Betrothals can be broken, as you've just proved," she'd almost purred. "And breaking this one wouldn't take much effort at all."

"And I wouldn't marry *Octavian's daughter* on a bet," he'd returned, trying to still the nausea that the thought provoked. *Alexander once wondered, in my presence, if he had some traces of Octavian's life or spirit in him, due to the way in which Caesarion brought him back from death. I couldn't kiss him until the unease passed. Octavian's own flesh-and-blood daughter? I'd throw up on her every time I tried to consummate the marriage. Nothing to do with her. Everything to do with <u>him</u>.*

He'd tried. Gods, how he'd tried. "Mother, you do realize that they're more than just Cleopatra's children, yes? They're also Caesar's. I'd have thought you'd be pleased, at least on some level. As political marriages go, it would be highly advantageous, assuming she agrees to it—"

And she'd just stared at him for a long moment, before hissing, "My goal has never been to see my grandchildren, if you ever get around to providing me with some, to be some cadet branch of the Julii. My goal has been to see one or both of my sons occupy the consul's chair. If not a higher one.

Getting in bed with the Julii—sons or daughters—doesn't move you towards that goal. It only cheapens you. Makes you their servant. Their slave. How many times have you been used as such, I wonder? And what would your father, to whose memory you've been *so* devoted, have thought of all this?"

The words had burned. Like vinegar poured into a wound. *Sons or daughters. She knows, or thinks she knows something.* And yet, like vinegar poured so, oddly cleansing. Tiberius had exhaled, meeting her eyes solidly. "A slave? Never. Octavian was the one who enslaved me. Had his slaves use and abuse me. Everything I've done since his death has been of my own choice. I owe my life, my sanity, my sense of self, to the Julii. I'm sorry you can't see that, Mother. Send me no more letters when I'm on campaign. If I'm fortunate enough to marry, you won't be invited to attend. Until and if you come to a better understanding of the world as it is, one more in agreement with my own, we're done, you and I."

He'd left then, with her screaming after him that he'd regret the way he'd spoken to her, with such arrant lack of respect. That the Julii, too, would regret everything that they'd done. It had sounded like raving, and he'd discounted it as such. Not even worth mentioning to Alexander or the rest of the Julii. But his brother Drusus needed to be forewarned. He might want to be a bridge between Livia and Tiberius. Or his younger brother might finally decide to cut Livia out of his life, as well.

———————

At Agrippa's house, Livia still burned inside. But the path before her now was clear. Tiberius had unintentionally given her one important piece of information. In two weeks' time, the hated Caesarion and Eurydice would be leaving for

Egypt, along with Cleopatra and Selene. Leaving *one* member of the Julii family utterly alone here in Rome. Alexander. Who, without his brother present to protect him—or bring him back to life again!—was just a mortal man, like any other.

His eyes and ears in the city were impressive, and certainly owed a debt to Cleopatra's original network of informants—but he was young, and hadn't been at the game for nearly as long as Livia herself had been. *They call him Cerastes,* she thought, sitting down at her loom to weave. *The snake. But a snake can be trapped in the right net. And the only reason men don't call me the spider? Is because I've never been foolish enough to be <u>seen</u> spinning my web.* She considered the matter dispassionately. *This is the first time that any member of that cursed family has been alone in Rome in decades. And that it's Alexander? The reason for which my Octavian died? All the better. It will sting Tiberius to the core. Make him reconsider, perhaps, all his decisions and conceptions of the world. One by one, I'll take them all.*

She called for a servant and said, simply, "That young whore you made contact with a few weeks ago? Jocasta? Bring her sister to me. We must see if she can be cured of her ailments. After all, our lives must be formed of service to others. Kindness. True *pietas*."

An hour later, and young Viola had been collected, along with the slave who looked after her. An easy matter, really. The invalid sister was paralyzed from the waist down, her legs thin and wasted under her plain white *stola*. And the slave, the best the two women could afford, was a eunuch boy of eighteen, purchased on the cheap once he'd grown too old to be a proper *puer* for some noble master or another. He had a man's height, but a life spent first as a sexual slave, and then as a servant to two women, one an invalid, hadn't trained him as a protector. The slave hovered uselessly near his invalid mistress in Livia's house, anxiety in his eyes.

"And how did you lose the use of your legs, my dear?" Livia asked the Hellene woman kindly.

"A fever, my lady," Viola whispered, shaking. "Sent by the gods when I was ten, and my sister twelve. Both our parents died of it. Jocasta was ill for a few days, but recovered. But I lost all feeling below my waist. The temple of Asclepius said the gods did not receive our sacrifices with favor." She looked down at her withered legs. "Jocasta brought me to Rome three years ago. Hoping that the gods of Rome would be kinder than the gods of Hellas. Since then, Ianos here has been my legs."

"Well, then, boy," Livia addressed the Hellene slave, "don't just stand there. Pick her up and carry her. We'll see if my physicians can do anything for you, my dear."

Incredulity in the woman's eyes. Livia personally doubted anything *could* be done for the woman. *In fact, considering the burden she is to her sister, the most merciful thing would have been for her to die of the fever, like their parents. But the gods aren't much in the business of mercy. However, when her sister arrives, she'll find Viola a very well-kept, even pampered pet. A seamstress to a good mistress.* Livia smiled faintly. *And then young Jocasta and I will talk of the future. And her place in it.*

Ianuarius 16, 20 AC

Alexander had awoken early, to see his friends and siblings off at Ostia, where they'd arrived late the previous evening. Two weeks was a short amount of time to make the arrangements for such a trip, but everything needed to be as settled as possible before the campaign season.

Frustration seethed in him, however, as he stood on the quay, the rising sun behind his back. Caesarion had given him the Imperial seal for the duration of his journey to Egypt; he still wore his signet ring, of course, for certifying formal documents and letters written during the journey. But for the next several months, Alexander would carry the weight of borrowed *imperium*. But for all that implicit power, there was nothing Alexander could do to help any of them, for the moment. *I can't control the tides to give them a safe journey*, he thought, giving his mother a kiss before she and Antony boarded their ship, young Gaius in her arms.

The next quay down, he gave Eurydice a quick, light hug, and exchanged wrist-clasps with Caesarion. His sister's eyes were haunted, and he understood why. This was an exile, of sorts. Three years as Empress, in Rome, at the heart of the world. Only to be sent to Egypt, far from her beloved. "Cheer up," he murmured in her ear. "It won't be forever. No matter how much like an eternity it might feel." *At least you have that assurance. That your exile will mean something, and will end. I'm not leaving Rome. But I'm exiled, too, after a fashion.*

Eurydice nodded against his shoulder. "Be safe," she told him, and disappeared up the ramp.

Selene tried to scurry past with just a little bob, but Alexander caught her by the arm, and insisted on a hug. "Sea voyages are dangerous," he reminded her. "Don't leave farewells unsaid."

He'd done his best to catch her alone at some point in the past two weeks, but for all that mice were a favorite prey of snakes, it had proven damned near impossible. Once he had, he'd done his best to explain, gently, that he'd feel nothing other than joy if she decided that she and Tiberius would make a good match. "I'd see you happy," he told her. "I'd see him happy. I'd see nieces and nephews born, and I'd love them for both of your sakes." All he'd gotten for his efforts were averted eyes and a series of uncomfortable nods.

Eurydice adapted. She said she'd try to see the man and not the boy. And she was as good as her word. Selene's obviously known for a long time. I'm not even sure if she's uncomfortable with me, precisely. I think it all boils down to . . . people seeing her. Being aware of what she thinks and feels, when she's been keeping it all in for so long.

In the here and now, reminded of the need for farewells, she flushed and gave him a quick hug and kiss, whispering, "Be safe and well, brother," and then scurrying away.

A quick wrist-clasp with Antyllus. And then the same for Tiberius. Alexander had gone to the Claudii brothers' villa for dinner the night before they'd all left Rome. And while Drusus had gone up to bed, his head swimming with unaccustomed wine, he and Tiberius had sat up long into the night, playing at dice. And somewhere near midnight, he'd asked Tiberius, very quietly, "Is there going to be any *us* left?"

"Depends on your sister's decision. And on if you get around to marrying Octavia." Tiberius had sighed. "There's no future in us, Alexander. You know that."

"I've never really thought much about the future. The present's far more interesting." Alexander smiled faintly. "Futures mean endings. I'd rather stay in the middle of everything. In perpetuity. Nothing but *now*." He'd rattled the dice in his cup, and tossed them. Not even a single six.

A shake of Tiberius' head. "You changed everything the moment you asked me to court her. You can't take back the words now."

"Then tonight's good-bye, then." A tightening of Alexander's throat as he glanced up across the table. "Want to make it a proper farewell?"

Tiberius had smiled faintly himself, then. "Alexander, it's not that I don't want to. It's that . . . I can't court her and keep fucking with you. It . . . doesn't work in my head." A single calm, melancholy look. "Things change. *We* change. You're not riding to the campaign this year. By the time I get back, you'll be different. And so will I. One or both of us will be married. Or not." A slight shrug, then a pointed look. "Don't let the inactivity make you get soft."

"No chance," Alexander returned, putting on a smile he didn't feel. And there the matter had ended.

So now, on the quay, nothing more than a wrist-clasp. No other words than, "Neptune protect you, and Mars watch over you." Just the tightness of fingers, trying to convey more than words. *Good-bye.*

And then watching the ships push off from the docks, oars moving in unison through the dark waters. Bumping into the occasional floating barrel, lost overboard during unloading. And then the wind caught their sails at the harbor's mouth, and Alexander stayed where he was, straining his eyes for a last glimpse, before finally turning away to mount his horse. *Exiled here in the heart of Rome or not, I have work to do. Reports to read, once I make my hour and a half ride back to the city and clean up. A speech to give before the Senate, noting that in my brother's absence, I hold his seal, and that official inquiries will come to me first, and that I will decide what gets passed along. Ably assisted by Lepidus and other counselors, of course.*

And today's work turned out to be surprisingly pleasant. For in the late evening, as he made his rounds, first to the baths, and then to an assortment of different *tavernas*, accompanied by a single discreet Praetorian, a runner caught up with him, and whispered that Hostus Titius at *Merges* had a package for him. And changing the direction of his steps, Alexander headed more or less for *Merges*, though by an indirect route.

At the *taverna* now owned by a former member of the Tenth, and a current *frumentarii*, he accepted a cup of watered wine from Titius. Listened to conversation in the common room for almost a half an hour—mostly a buzz of gossip about the Emperor's departure for Egypt, Lydia, Syria, and other such parts. And then, once he'd faded from the notice of the others there, he slipped behind a curtain and upstairs. Used the key that Titius had slipped into his hand with the cup of wine, and unlocked the door there. And found Servia Sulpicia, lying on her stomach on the bed, her feet in the air, her red-gold hair shining in the lamplight. Reading a scroll and drinking a cup of wine. "There you are," she said, her eyes flicking up, wary at first, but lightening at the sight of him. "I was just beginning to get bored."

Alexander closed the door behind him. Locked it. And tossed the key to her, watching it bounce on the sleeping couch. For some reason, his heart pounded in his ears, and he had to take a deep breath to control his voice before he told her, smiling, "My lady, seeing you tonight makes the rest of the day worth having lived through." He approached, taking one of her hands in his and kissing it lightly, but not releasing it as he straightened once more. "Before I proceed too much further," he added, still smiling, "is this visit business? Or did you come in search of pleasure?"

Her eyebrows rose. "You *are* direct," Sulpicia chided softly.

"It saves time and misunderstandings. I'm none too fond of having my face slapped." He rubbed his thumb against her palm, looking into her eyes.

"A little of both, then, if you find that you can be accommodating," she murmured, a secret smile stealing across her face.

Alexander nodded. "I can be *very* accommodating.

Business first, however." He released her hand and stepped away, taking one of the room's two chairs and sitting some five feet away.

Sulpicia nodded, sitting up straight on the bed now. "I asked some time ago if you were the one to whom I should report interesting opinions. You're aware of my uncle's reputation for . . . agile loyalties."

Alexander nodded. "Yet he removed you from your marriage to Lento on hearing of his decidedly, hmm. Anti-Egyptian sympathies."

"Anti-Egyptian, anti-Julii." She nodded. "My uncle's social circle is quite wide. I happened to overhear last night, quite by chance, a conversation about how you've been given too much authority for someone who hasn't stood election. How your brother should have left his seal with one of the consuls."

Alexander nodded. That wasn't entirely unexpected. "And here we have as consul this year Rullus and Licinus. I can't quite see my brother putting the seal into the hands of Rullus, one of his political enemies, and Licinus hasn't made his affiliations clearly known. He shifts between the Julii and the Octavianites as the wind blows." He eyed Sulpicia. "This doesn't seem to require an urgent meeting."

Little more than a half-smile at his words. "Not that, no," she murmured. "It was more the suggestion that it would be *unfortunate* should anything happen to you. What with your brother not here to enforce his decree that his family should be . . . off-limits . . . in such matters."

Alexander's hand moved under his toga, and he rubbed absently at the scar just over his heart. "Did you happen to see the faces of those who spoke those words?"

She nodded. "It was carefully said. No overt treason," Sulpicia told him. "Rullus made the comment in tones of great concern for your well-being. Livia laughed and replied that she would be surprised if a young man didn't occasionally take risks, but that on the whole, you seemed to be in wonderful health." She grimaced. "It's not much, I realize. But when I drew it to my uncle's attention, he asked me to bring it directly to you."

"He couldn't bring it to me himself?" Alexander asked mildly.

"If he visited the Julii villa, it would be noticed," Sulpicia replied, leaning back against the pillows. "His agile loyalties give him access to many people that you can't always hear from inside the Julii walls. People like Licinus. The consul who wavers with the wind."

Alexander nodded slowly. "So you're here with your uncle's approval?"

"At his specific request." Sulpicia smiled slightly. "But I think I'd have come here anyway. Have you *really* read my poems?"

"Every one of them," Alexander told her, standing and approaching the bed. "I liked the one in which you begged your uncle not to banish you to the countryside. And complained that there was no such thing as free will, because he controlled everything." He ran his fingers lightly up her leg from her ankle to her knee. Then higher, watching the expressions on her face carefully. "Do you always carry a knife under your *stola*?"

She reached down and pulled up her skirts. Unbuckled the sheath there, and handed it to him. "Only when I'm about to meet with someone in a room in a *taverna* that's completely under his control," Sulpicia replied. "My uncle suggested I bring it. However, I don't think I'll be needing it." She ran her own fingers lightly over his shoulders now, before interlacing them behind his neck.

Alexander tossed the knife across the room and lowered himself to the bed. Kissed her deeply, and murmured in her ear, "Talk to me," before nibbling his way down her throat.

"About . . . what?"

"*Anything.*" That came out in a hungrier tone than he'd ever intended her to hear.

She closed her eyes and, as he kissed lower, and still lower, began to quote, "So it is more useful to watch a man in times of peril, and in adversity to discern what kind of man he is—"

"Only in adversity?" Alexander asked, pulling her skirts up higher, and applying lips and tongue to her sweetest place. Felt her hips, in his hands, buck in surprise.

"So . . . Lucretius. . . says. That truth's then drawn—oh my *gods*—from his heart . . . and reality . . . shines through . . ." Her fingers locked in his hair, and for a moment, Alexander thought she couldn't decide if she wanted him to stop, or to keep him precisely where he was.

"Does he say anything about being able to tell who a man is, in moments of extreme pleasure?" he asked mildly, kissing the inside of her thigh.

"I can't seem to remember right now," she admitted, her eyes sparkling.

"I think I'm finding out quite a bit about you at the moment," he murmured. "You can quote accurately from memory even under . . . duress." At her laugh, he added, "Of course, I must remember, that what a woman says to her lover in passion, should be written in the wind, or in swift-running water."

And as he lowered himself to her, he was rewarded with a gasp and a light slap on his arm. "Catullus? You quote *Catullus* to me?"

"Can you write better?" he taunted in her ear, and found his neck bitten for his pains—but lightly, oh, so lightly.

"I'd like to try," she murmured. "I haven't set stylus to wax in three years, thanks to my wretched old husband."

"Will you write about *us?*" He rocked his hips against hers, letting her feel his desire.

"Only . . . after. . . I change . . . your name. . . ." Her eyes closed, and he could feel her relaxing against him. Yielding.

"What do you want me to call you when I love you?" he whispered. He wanted, quite badly, to join their bodies, but a lingering voice of caution warned him that this would be a bad idea. Not least because he could get her pregnant. "Servia is a severe name. And Sulpicia," her family name, ". . . seems . . . very *formal*. . . at the moment." Each set of words punctuated with a little more pressure. Edging closer and closer to union.

He felt her fingers slide down to lift his face up, so that her hazel eyes could meet his. "No Roman woman has her own name," she whispered, a hint of bitterness in her voice, even in this moment of deep intimacy. "I hate the sound of my own."

He'd rarely encountered such breathtaking honesty. "Choose one for yourself," Alexander told her. "I'll call you by nothing else."

Her lips curled up. "Then you'll have to wait a while, for I wouldn't wish to choose a name in haste, only to hear something I grow to detest, ever on your lips." She leaned up and kissed him. "Love me."

Alexander wrapped his arms around her, and did precisely that. Heard her shocked gasp as he joined their bodies. A voice at the back of his mind hissed that this was not the best of ideas, but he ignored it for the moment, driving himself as deeply into her as he could. Finding, if not peace precisely, at least forgetfulness, for a time. Though he made very certain to pull himself free of her delightful embrace when his release hit. And in the bright wake of it, he swore repeatedly and silently to himself at having allowed himself to have explored her so completely. *You know better. There's a dozen ways you could have found pleasure, all less risky.* And yet, rolling over, to her side, he felt surprisingly . . . content. An odd sensation, to be sure. He forced himself to sit up.

"Ah, you don't fall asleep immediately," Sulpicia murmured stretching. "Refreshing."

"I never *sleep* anywhere but in my own bed," Alexander told her lightly. "I'm sure I'll live longer for it." He caught her hand, kissing it lightly, and changed the subject. "You know, in and around all the distractions I just found myself . . . distracted by. . ." he grinned. "I didn't get around to asking. *Was* there a Cerinthus?"

She laughed, peals of it echoing through the room, and threw herself back into the pillows with the abandon of her own mirth. "You *are* persistent."

"Utterly." That, with more seriousness than he'd intended.

She sat up, meeting his eyes, her amusement fading. "There was," Sulpicia told him frankly, but her eyes, for the first time, looked a little ashamed. "Marcus Claudius Marcellus."

Alexander felt as if she'd jabbed him with a red-hot poker. "One of my friend Tiberius' distant cousins," he said, blinking rapidly to cover his confusion. The Claudii family was large and extensive; he'd met Marcellus at a dinner at Tiberius' villa just a few months ago. The man was younger than Caesarion, but older than Alexander himself by four years. Pleasant-faced, with a constant, rather braying laugh. Memory's scroll unfurled, and his eyebrows shot up. "The son of Octavia, by her first husband. Before she was pawned off on Antony." *A step-brother of Antyllus, too — and half-brother to some of Antyllus' half-sisters. Not quite an in-law, thank the gods. This . . . well, it's unexpected, but all the noble families are densely intermarried.* He slid back down into the sheets, lying on his side to take her hand and play with her fingers. "Why on earth didn't your family marry you off to him? He sounds perfectly suitable. Not that I'm complaining about your availability," Alexander added, fervently.

"He was betrothed when he was three to Sextia Pompeia, daughter of your father's sworn enemy, Sextus Pompey Magnus Pius. Youngest son of Pompey the Great himself," Sulpicia reminded him dryly. "His family didn't annul the betrothal when Pompey was defeated and his daughter disappeared in the east somewhere. So Marcellus and I found all *sorts* of occasions on which to meet. And he introduced me to practically everything two people could do that *wouldn't* break my all-important maidenhead." She sighed.

"Oh?" Alexander said, with more enthusiasm, sitting up. "*Do* tell—" She pushed at his supporting elbow, making him laugh. "What happened?" he asked, more gently.

"Sextia Pompeia and her guardians re-appeared three years ago, once your brother took power. Her father was dead. But they all reminded the noble Claudii of their arrangement. Worse, she's also a distant cousin of mine on her mother's side, so my father couldn't fight it. Marcellus married her, and my family rapidly found someone for me. Just in case I had been lying about having kept my so-called virtue intact." Brittle humor. A smile, but one that covered years of unhappiness.

"Do you still love him?" No emphasis on the question.

She snorted. "You quoted Catullus at me not long ago.

Do you remember this one? 'It is difficult suddenly to lay aside a long-cherished love.'"

Alexander went still at the words. Forgetfulness faded away. "It is," he said, looking away. *Gods. She's so* _warm_. *So* _open_. *All the hurts in her have formed her differently than Tiberius. Instead of folding in, to protect herself, she blazes out. And yet, if he were here with us . . . I wonder if she'd like him. Us. Not that it matters now. And perhaps it won't ever matter. Don't think about it. There is no future. There's only now.*

"It's far less difficult to do so when that love tells you that he'd appreciate it if the poems you wrote for him never saw further circulation." Her tone remained brittle. "As they might prove embarrassing to his new wife." Sulpicia shrugged. "He told me that he burned his copies. I was fortunate to have kept my own, and my uncle had tucked a few in with Tibullus' in a manuscript that's been passed around. I never even used his real name. He could have returned my pages to me," she added, emptily. "Instead, he burned them. As if they didn't matter at all." She sighed, and Alexander wrapped his arms around her tightly. "In the end, it's an old story, but not as bad as it could have been. I didn't present Lento with any children that he could have used to shore up his reputation for virility even in old age." She nuzzled Alexander's shoulder. "I did appreciate your, ah . . . discretion." She glanced down between them, meaningfully.

"Mmm." *Never had to worry about pregnancy with Ti. Exposure, yes. Pregnancy, no.*

She had an independent enough mind that he suspected she'd be a resource even without her uncle's 'permission' to tell the Julii what she heard in his household. She was an asset. And she made his heart *race*. "I'd like a chance to be discreet with you again, *domina*." He kissed her fingers. "As often as you're willing to meet with me. Bring your poems. I want to read all the ones I haven't seen publically circulated." He stroked her hair back from her face. "Bring your books, too. If you ever just want a quiet place to work . . . I can provide that, my lady." He gestured at the room, encompassing the desk, chairs, and bed.

Her eyes went wide. "How did you know that it's impossible to write in my father's house?" Sulpicia demanded. "Do you really have eyes everywhere?" She looked around them, as if looking for eyes glistening in the walls.

Alexander snorted. "Many eyes, yes, but in this case . . . . my sister frequently complains that her own studies are constantly disrupted by servants asking her how well-done she wants the meat tonight, how the tables should be decorated before meeting with the Parthian ambassador, and other such trifling matters. You keep your father's house now that your mother has passed away. Peace, quiet, and time for your writing is doubtless at a minimum." He kissed her hand again, and then reluctantly sat up to reach for his clothing.

Only to see her kick his tunic as far from the bed as she could manage, and then she rolled on top of *him*. Kissing. Touching. Stroking her fingers along the scar over his heart, her eyes intent. Lightly touching the amulet of Sekhmet around his neck—sacred to him, not just for its protective qualities, but for the fact that Tiberius wore its mate.

No poetry. And yet, he felt as if she'd set his soul on fire with words, when all she gave him was silence and bliss.

Chapter V: The Delta of the Nile

<u>Februarius 4, 20 AC</u>

A sea journey of twenty-five days took Caesarion's flotilla from Rome to Alexandria. It would have been faster by a good ten days, if they'd only had the one ship, but keeping eighty ships together in formation added to the length of any voyage.

Twenty-five days at sea—close to a month of being completely out of contact with the Empire. Caesarion was at this point in his life so accustomed to waking before dawn to read whatever urgent dispatches had come in by courier overnight that he'd snapped awake on every one of the last twenty-four days, wondering how in the gods' names he'd slept in so late, and which servant had been derelict enough not to bring him his morning cup of vinegar-touched water and his sheaf of reports.

And then the slow rocking of the ship impinged on his consciousness. The smell of brine in the air. The feel of Eurydice's body against his on the sleeping couch. For once, they weren't aboard a troop transport, and therefore had an actual cabin to themselves, with four walls, on the uppermost deck. Selene had one beside theirs, but Tiberius and Antyllus were belowdecks, bunking with their Praetorians. Caesarion lifted his head slightly, muzzily registering that their surroundings were, if not palatial, substantially more pleasant than the ships they'd taken to Hispania and Illyria in the past three years.

His mother had *insisted* on this, for this journey. She had no intention of making the long journey in anything other than comfort, and that included the prospect of regularly washing her hair, if not bathing in asses' milk. And she'd pointedly mentioned that Caesarion's quarters on his ship should be rather more *kingly* than was his normal wont.

He hadn't been sure what that comprised, honestly. *Golden basins to throw up into when we catch bad weather, Mother?* he'd asked, receiving an irritable snort in reply. Occasionally, he asked servants at home, or even in a *castra,* to fan the still, unmoving, sweltering air in Sextilis, but it was *Februarius.* Even now, as far south as they were, their cabin held a slight, pleasant edge of chill. The coverlet draped over their bodies wasn't military-issue wool, but had silk atop a warmer core. That was, as far as Caesarion could tell, the most *kingly* he could be on a ship, subject as it was to salt water and harsh weather.

Eurydice stirred against him, and all his vaguely irritated thoughts vanished as he leaned down to kiss her lightly into wakefulness. While so much enforced relaxation had agitated him, he had to admit that he'd enjoyed every night of the last month. No dinner parties to attend at other villas. No dinners of their own to host, beyond simply eating with Selene, Antyllus, and Tiberius each evening. Then retiring to their quarters. Eurydice reading out loud from this philosophical tract or that poem. And then, as night fell with the utter darkness possible at sea, moving together under that silken coverlet. Over and over again. Both of them trying to deny, fiercely, the passage of time. And the inevitability of endings.

Golden eyes opened, meeting his, and just as he moved into position to pick up where they'd left off the night before, a lookout shouted overhead, "Land! Land in sight!"

Caesarion stayed precisely where he was. "They won't need us for hours," he muttered, and heard his beloved's soft laugh in reply.

A bit later, she managed to slip out of the bed, saying, lightly, "You were so busy making Antyllus and Tiberius spar with you yesterday afternoon, that you entirely missed Nesa opening the chest that has what Mother considers our investiture clothing in it." She wrapped a *palla* over her otherwise bare shoulders, looking back at him as she did.

Caesarion wasn't so busy admiring the line of her spine, still visible through the translucent silk, that he lost track of the words. "*Our* investiture garb?" he repeated, raising his eyebrows. "I was invested with the title of pharaoh when I was three. I . . . vaguely remember the ceremony."

Eurydice sighed, taking one of the chairs, bolted to the deck as it was. "That's the thing. You have to crown me as your queen. Which means full regalia for you, too. She said before we left that it wouldn't be a bad thing to let the priests marry us there. Again. So that the Egyptians can see it."

Caesarion rolled to his stomach on the bed, suspicion coursing through him. "Somehow, I don't think that my purple *toga picta* is what she has in mind." He hated the damned thing. Nearly half again as heavy as a normal toga, it bled violet dye onto anything he wore under it, including his skin, and it was freighted with gold embroidery as well.

She shook her head mutely. Caesarion sighed. "All right, let's see what she picked out. While we're still twenty miles from shore, and only the sailors and the birds will hear me shouting." He paused. "You, first, however."

Eurydice looked up at the ceiling for a moment, then stood and stepped behind the wooden screen that concealed the dressing area from the rest of the cabin. She tossed her *palla* over the top, and he could hear shuffling for a moment. "This is fairly difficult to get into without Nesa's help," she called, sounding uncomfortable. And then she stepped around the screen, flicking her hands down at herself.

Caesarion's eyebrows rose. "No," he told her, uncompromisingly.

"I know."

"No!" His voice rose.

"I'm not arguing! I don't feel comfortable in it at all!" Another helpless gesture down at the *kalasiris* encompassed all the reasons why a Roman woman might not be comfortable wearing it. Eurydice had worn such garments on and off for most of her life, though she clearly usually preferred the flowing layers and lines of a *stola* and tunic. A *kalasiris* clung tightly to the body, leaving little to the imagination. It was typically made of thin, almost translucent cotton, to stave off the heat of an Egyptian day, though this one was made of pure white silk. But it wasn't the thinness of the silk or the tightness of the dress that left little to the imagination this time. It was the fact that her breasts had been left completely exposed, the straps that usually concealed and supported them being narrower and thinner, and much further to the sides. "In Mother's defense," Eurydice said hastily, "Egyptians don't think of the breasts as sensual. They view them as a measure of a woman's fertility and fitness for motherhood. Nothing more."

Caesarion sat up on the bed, riding on an enormous surge of anger mingled with a disconcerting hint of desire. Even though he should have been *quite* sated by their morning activities thus far, it took an effort of will to raise his eyes to his sister's own. "*They* might not find them sensual, but I do," he said between his teeth. "Sensual, and private. Something for *us*, not for everyone in the palace. Or the mob outside, when we go to greet the people together."

"I know," Eurydice said, shifting her shoulders uncomfortably.

"Not to mention that the ceremonies will be attended

by quite a few non-Egyptians! Hellenes, Romans, Syrians, Parthians, a handful of Judeans — "

"I know," she said, taking a seat once more, fidgeting.

Caesarion paused in mid-rant and gave her a long look. "You hate it. You're uncomfortable in it. You agree with me. And yet, I sense that a 'but' is about to enter this conversation."

Eurydice winced. "I'm going to be living there for . . . the gods only know how long." Her eyes looked haunted, and he felt it too, like a kick in the stomach. "I have to appease the people there who will surely say that I'm too Roman to be their queen." She closed her eyes. "I *hate* it. I hate the dress. I hate the jewelry and the wig she sent with them. I hate every single thing about it. But it's . . . probably necessary. This one day." She sounded nauseated. Uncomfortable. And Caesarion hated that she felt that way, yet remained compelled to follow their mother's advice.

"Fuck that," he told her sharply, the barracks oath vivid in the air around them. "Dress in some combination of Roman and Egyptian styles, just like back home — "

"On every other day, I will," Eurydice told him, still not opening her eyes. "One day of humiliation to appease thousands of people. It's . . . not so much to ask, I suppose."

That's the problem. Mother isn't asking. As usual. She's compelling. Good reasons or not, it's getting damned annoying. Caesarion stood, moving to his wife's side. And knelt, taking both her hands in his. "I don't like it," he told her simply. "I don't like that *you* don't like it. And surely, there will be some people in the crowd who will say 'Look, there goes a Roman woman, dressed like one of us, but with no right to it.'"

She nodded, her expression tight. "But I need to do *something* to make up for how . . . stridently . . . I dismissed Tahut-Nefer, years ago," Eurydice whispered, opening her eyes. "And whatever enmity he's sowed against us, since then." She looked at him, her lips compressed into a taut line. "You won't be living there," she added, her eyes fixed on his. "You don't have to . . . wear what she's picked out for you. Which I'm sure you will find as demeaning as I find this." Another self-conscious gesture down.

Caesarion kissed her hand, and stood. Stepped behind the screen. And *stared* for a long moment at what he found there. "Is this where I ask 'where's the rest of it?'" he asked tiredly, picking up the *shendyt* kilt. Multiple folds of bleached linen cloth, asymmetrical in cut, it was a poor substitute, in his mind, for a set of leather *pteruges*. He wrapped it in place and grimaced, finding a belt with which to keep it all more or less together.

He was perfectly accustomed to going about sparring practice in nothing more than a loincloth. Naked at the baths, or when wrestling. That was fine. But Roman custom dictated that only defeated enemies and slaves went naked outside of a gymnasium or practice yard. The thought of going half-naked, without armor, in front of thousands of eyes made him uncomfortable. Not out of shame over his body, which was an odd concept held by certain nomadic desert tribes and the Judeans, but because he wouldn't be an unconquered Roman citizen if he didn't *dress* like one. *Thank the gods there's no mirror made of polished bronze in this cabin, to go with the golden vomit basins I wouldn't allow here, either. I'd have to look myself in the eye if there were.*

Eurydice peered around the edge of the screen. "You look marvelous," she told him.

Caesarion grimaced. "I feel like an idiot. Every Praetorian we have will be biting their lips bloody, trying not to laugh." He rolled his shoulders uncomfortably, not sure where to put his hands if he didn't have the heavy leather belt of his armor to hook his thumbs into, or the folds of a toga to manage. "I assume there is jewelry and other such shit to go with these . . . *costumes*?"

She nodded, trying not to look dispirited. "There's even a crown for you," she added.

"Now *that* I remember from when I was three," Caesarion admitted. "Mostly, that it was heavy and *hot*." He sighed and looked down at her, pulling her into his side for a moment. "If you have to suffer through it for one day, I will, too," he told her, his voice grim. "But under *no* circumstances will I put *kohl* around my eyes."

Her lips quirked. "But it would look so good on you," Eurydice teased, very softly, playing with the pleats of his kilt. "And given what the *rest* of you looks like in this, no one would ever mistake you for being anything but a man—"

"No!"

She exploded into laughter, and Caesarion gradually let his sour expression fade. "Let's get *properly* dressed before anyone comes in here and sees us," he muttered. "And when we go from the palace to the Temple of Isis, or wherever the investiture will be held, we'll ride, too. No damned litters. Let the people of Alexandria see who we *really* are, as well as who they want us to be."

Eurydice managed a half-smile. "Normally, I'd cheer," she said. "You know how much I hate litters."

Caesarion frowned down at her. "Please don't say that it's better for the look of things. The pharaohs *used* to be warrior kings. Their people should be used to seeing them on horseback or in chariots. Or would be, if the last ten or so hadn't been grossly overweight. Quite a step down from the warlords who used to follow Alexander the Great over half the world—" He paused. She still looked worried. "Accipitra, what's wrong?" He caught her face in his hands, and tears rolled free of her eyes, slipping down to splash his hands. "Are you sick?"

"No," Eurydice told him, her voice holding an ache he'd never heard in it before. "But I think I'm with child. I haven't had a moon-flow since I took the bracelet off. Six weeks." She closed her eyes. "Too early to be sure, but . . . best that I not ride, perhaps."

Caesarion's knees suddenly felt unaccountably weak. More so than at any point since Germania, when he'd suffered blood-loss from a dragon's savage claws, and had been debilitated by some manner of attack by a northern goddess. His head swam a little, and he pulled her into his arms, wrapping her there. They'd tried to hold this moment off for so long, but now, it was here. And he had to see it for what it was. *Creating a family. Establishing* our *line. Continuing the lines of the Julii and the Ptolemies. Except I can't be here with her through it. In September, I'll probably still be in* Britannia. *And if I left all the men there, in winter camp, and raced across the world, the fastest I'd be able to get to her side would be . . . December. If that. I can't bring her home to Rome, both for her safety, and the safety of the child — too many threats of poison and knives, as Mother said. I can't take her with me into a war-zone; other men can take their wives and children, but an Imperator? And there's the issue of governing Egypt. Alexandria's the second most powerful city in the Empire. And the source of half our grain.*

"Your dreams always used to suggest I wouldn't see our child till it was three. Or even five," he finally said against her ear, his throat tight.

"That was before the gods changed everything," she whispered, her head planted against his shoulder. "I don't want to do this alone." Her voice shook for a moment.

"If I can be here with you, I will," he told her, simply. "I will write to you. Every single day. It might not be more than a paragraph, added to a longer letter. The dispatches might take time to reach you. But you will be in my thoughts every night. And I *will* return to you. I promise that." He cleared his throat. "You won't have to do it all by yourself." *Somehow.*

She nodded against his shoulder, and looked up, her eyes red-rimmed. "Should we get out of these ridiculous clothes?" Eurydice asked.

Caesarion swallowed. "Come high summer here, and they'll probably feel much more comfortable, and far less ridiculous," he allowed. "But . . . yes." He looked down at her, at the waist that still looked impossibly slender, and felt his mouth go dry with fear. *Venus and Juno, I can't be with her when her time comes. Please, let her pass through this safely. We have all the assurance of her dreams. But . . . prophetic dreams have a way of hiding the truth sometimes. They're cloaked in allusion and metaphor. Let her be safe. Let the child be born gently.*

Two hours later, their ship was the first to touch the quays of the Royal Harbor at the center of the port, Antony and Cleopatra's gliding in beside theirs a few moments later. And to Caesarion's considerable surprise, the prefect of Egypt, Cornelius Gallus, was nowhere at hand to greet them. In fact, the honor guard that might have been expected to welcome the Imperator of Rome to the second-largest city in the Empire was a scant fifty legionnaires, behind which the Egyptian and Hellene palace staff stood, looking uneasy. *I'm not usually one for ceremony, but this is practically an insult. The question is, is it an intentional one?*

Caesarion waited for the centurion in charge of the welcoming squads of legionnaires to hasten up the ramp of his ship, and thump his chest in salute. "*Dominus,*" the man said, looking deeply uncomfortable. "Gaius Hosidia," the centurion introduced himself. "I regret to inform you that Prefect Gallus left the city six weeks ago for Thebes, and has been bogged down there ever since. He sent word for me to greet you in his name, however."

Caesarion, wearing his scaled armor now, and seated in a curule chair on the deck, under the cover of the roof that sheltered the upper decks, found his hands curling on the arms of the chair, and forced himself to relax his grip. "His last dispatch spoke of *unrest*," he said carefully, keeping a leash on his temper. "Six weeks in a city with a full legion should have quelled *unrest*." *Exactly how badly has this situation been mishandled, and what are we walking into?*

The centurion's face tightened. Embarrassment. Awareness. But Caesarion hadn't asked him a direct question, so he couldn't actually respond. "Yes, *dominus*."

"What form has this *unrest* taken?" Caesarion asked, feeling Eurydice slide a hand to his shoulder, lightly. "Are we looking at food riots?"

Hosidia grimaced. "The locals were already upset about the failure of the crops. The prefect announced that there would be additional tax-collectors sent, to ensure that everyone had paid their due. Several of the tax-collectors went, ah, missing."

Tax-collectors? Or were they <u>frumentarii</u>*? Alexander hasn't spread his net this far yet, I thought. Either way, no, that can't be tolerated.* "And Gallus mobilized the entire legion to look for a handful of men?" Caesarion asked sharply.

The unfortunate centurion shook his head rapidly. "No, *dominus*. He sent a century to investigate. They were . . . set upon, outside Thebes. Eighty men set out. *Five* came back, babbling about the desert rising up against them. Swarms of scorpions. The wind carrying sand that hit them with such force that their armor was pitted, and buried their companions where they stood. Frankly, the *medici* would have called it heat delirium, if it hadn't been so cold." Hosidia chewed on his lower lip uneasily.

Caesarion turned towards Eurydice, and murmured quietly, not in Egyptian, but in Hellene, *"Either some spirit is indeed angry because of the loss of the royal magics, or the mage-priests took a hand in events."*

"Why would the mage-priests take such a risk?" she replied softly. *"They can't hold out against Rome's entire might, if it's turned against them. Why provoke a response?"*

Caesarion looked back at the centurion now. "And since then, your commander's been in Thebes. Trying to quell sand that buries men eighty at a time?"

Another look of acute discomfort. "He believed that the guides led our men into a trap. Poisoned the survivors, making them hallucinate. And, as prefect, he said he had the obligation to demonstrate Rome's power to the locals, and punish them. There was talk of crucifixions, my lord. One man out of every ten in Thebes, unless they gave up whoever the ringleaders were, and turned over any surviving tax-collectors and legionnaires. Or at least their bodies."

Caesarion exhaled, and looked over his shoulder, first at Eurydice and Selene, standing side by side to his right, and then at Antyllus and Tiberius on his left, both of whom had gone grim-faced. "That will be all, centurion," Caesarion said, his voice tight. "Have your men form up for escort detail. My Praetorians will provide the bulk of our security, both moving through the city and in the palace."

And once the man moved away, Caesarion swore, rapidly and virulently. "Gods *damn* it," he finally concluded, exhaling.

"I can't say that I mightn't have done the same thing as the commander, at least to start with," Tiberius said, his eyes remote.

"You wouldn't have," Caesarion told him sharply. "I

know you. You wouldn't have sent eighty men to poke around. You'd either have sent a handful for inquiries, or a full cohort. No half measures."

Antyllus smiled, but for once, no humor touched his eyes. "If you're going to make a show of force, there had better be *actual* force behind it."

"And now that he's committed his entire legion to the cause of putting down *minor unrest,* he's turned the entirety of Rome's forces in Egypt into a sideshow," Tiberius finished, sounding tired. "He's swung a hammer at a gnat."

"And has just kept swinging. For six gods-be-damned-weeks. He's making us look like idiots who can't fix a simple problem, and antagonizing all of the locals. Just in time for the Roman pharaoh and his Roman queen to show up." Caesarion put a tight smile on his face that he didn't feel, and offered Eurydice his hand, looking up at the Royal Palace on the promontory high above the docks. "Shall we, Accipitra?"

"I am somewhat eager to be off this swaying ship," she admitted. "I haven't been seasick since that storm on the way to Hispania, but I do feel rather nauseous right now." She raised her other hand, and the eagle that she'd found in Hispania and nursed back to health, which had been perching on the wooden stand that they usually provided for it, launched itself and landed on her slender, bare arm. Somehow, the bird never even nicked her skin. And she even managed a smile for Caesarion as they walked down the ramp, flanked by Malleolus and the rest of their Praetorians, and followed by Selene, Tiberius, and Antyllus.

The Roman legionnaires parted ranks and backed up, allowing them easy access to the stairs leading up to the palace; Caesarion could already see that several litters had been prepared, and he grimaced, gesturing for his men to get his horse unloaded. *The litter's necessary for Eurydice right now, though she'd be just as safe if she rode with me. My mother and Selene have never ridden. But I'll be damned if anyone* carries *me up the stairs. Several hundred of them or not. Though if the litter-bearers drop Eurydice right now, I will have their heads.* That last thought came out unbidden, surprising him with its vehemence.

On the smooth stone of the quay, Antony and Cleopatra met them. The contrast between mother and daughter was striking, even today. Cleopatra wore a wig of dark hair, braided into thousands of cords, each tipped with beaten foil gold, a heavy diadem atop the wig, and weighty gold earrings that fell to her shoulders, along with a thick turquoise and lapis collar that, as usual, spanned her skin from collarbone to sternum. Caesarion had no idea how his mother could move her head, let alone keep it all balanced. Eurydice, however, was the picture of simplicity. A white *kalasiris,* her gold betrothal ring, a signet ring that held a tie to one of her bound-spirits, and a diadem made of pearls atop her natural hair—his gift to her on Matronalia this past year.

As Cleopatra stepped off the ramp, she raised her hands to the assembled servants, as if in benediction. And every one of them suddenly knelt before her in profound obeisance, making Caesarion deeply uncomfortable. "I have not stood before you in seven years," Cleopatra called to her servants, a kind of affection in her voice. "I have been too long from my home, and I thank you for your welcome. This is my son, your pharaoh, Ptolemy Julius Caesarion Philopator Philomator. Born of Isis and Osiris, born of the long line of kings going back to the dawn of time. Welcome him, and his bride, my daughter, Eurydice Julia, shortly to be your queen."

She paused. "Also, welcome my youngest daughter, Selene, and my new son, Gaius Antony." She gestured as one of the servants from her ship brought young Gaius down the ramp to his parents now. Antony hadn't moved yet, himself, his lined face completely still, as if he were a statue carved from basalt.

Caesarion did his best to keep his face impassive, but his skin crawled at the introduction. Most days, he managed to forget he had any other names besides Caesarion or Aquilus. The *Julius* was important. But hearing his *praenomen* of Ptolemy inevitably made him uncomfortable. He hadn't even realized that his right hand, covering Eurydice's as it lay atop his left arm, had tightened, till she made a sound of mild protest. "Sorry," he apologized under his breath.

And then he grimly acknowledged the various servants—some of whom, he knew, had to be Egyptian nobles by birth, distant kin of the pharaohs, just as Nesa herself was. And told them, twitching internally, "Please rise. I have no need of obeisances." Then he handed Eurydice into her litter, and waited for his horse to be saddled. After four weeks at sea, the creature was as restless as he was, himself, snorting and straining at the reins as a Praetorian brought the stallion to him. *All right. Let's get on with this. Maybe we can actually look as if we belong here. In a city so accustomed to the blend of Hellas and Egypt, you'd think they could manage stirring some Roman culture into the mix, too. Perhaps by standing on their damned feet, to start with.*

Antyllus did his best not to gape like a yokel as they disembarked in Alexandria's port. *You were born in <u>Rome</u>,* he scolded himself mentally. *The heart of the world. Rome was founded centuries before Alexandria . . . probably.* That last thought snuck in a little shamefacedly. Romans believed their city to have been founded some seven hundred years ago; Alexandria's establishment a little over three hundred and fifty years ago by Alexander the Great was a matter of historical fact. *But he didn't plant a city in the middle of an open beach. There was a port here before he imported Hellene architecture and ideals, too.*

Still, that architecture and those ideals were on display everywhere he looked, but somehow, beautifully commingled with Egyptian ones. They'd landed in the central area of the port, at the Royal Docks, while the rest of the flotilla was making for the naval docks on the western side, near the island of Pharos—where the huge Lighthouse of Alexandria towered above their heads.

Antyllus had never seen anything so tall in his life before, barring mountains. It hardly seemed like it could be the work of human hands, and yet, there it stood. Blocky at the base, it cut in after a hundred feet or so, rising in a second, cylindrical tier, followed by a third tier, again, cylindrical. The great beacon wasn't lit at the moment, of course; it was daylight. But from his angle, he thought he could see the metal mirrors that helped send light out over the waves. *I'll find a window when the sun sets. I want to see this great eye, peering out into the darkness, calling all the ships home to shore.*

Beside the Lighthouse, he could see a huge, Egyptian-style temple, blocky and bold, presumably dedicated to Isis, judging by what he could see of the statues outside it. Behind it? One of several temples to Poseidon, all within easy viewing distance, that dotted this bustling port.

A long, man-made causeway connected that island to the mainland on the western side of the harbor. Tons and tons of soil and stone had been moved there, filling in the depths, and then capped with a road of perfectly fitted stones, leading into the smooth, curving embrace of the half-circle beach— lined with hundreds of piers and quays, and a confusion of masts all jutting up, blocking the view. In the center, where they were now, there was a huge promontory, on which the Royal Palace of the Ptolemies looked down over the bustling harbor, directly across from the Lighthouse, but all the ships kept a respectful distance from the royal docks and the waters surrounding the palace itself.

At first, Antyllus found it jarring; a palace meant for kings and queens, positioned at the heart of commerce? *Then again, they get sea breezes up on that headland. They're positioned right where they can, on a whim, take a leisurely cruise on a barge or a sailing ship. And they're no more than a stone's throw from all the ships of their navy. That's the* Hellene *in the Ptolemies. Never far from the sea, from the nets, from the oars.*

And that alone made the city jarringly unRoman for him — but also, delightfully different in aspect.

Several other fingers of land reached out into the waters of the port, and Antyllus could see, even from here, that the streets of this area of the city had been laid out in a neat grid, reflecting the Hellene qualities of organization, harmony, and unity. Along the sides of the wide streets, buildings rose, smiling behind their colonnades of fluted white marble, and their faces brightly painted in red and blue patterns, almost seeming to glow under the warm sun. A Hellene-style theater — where Caesar and his troops had once defended themselves against a mob — stood beside Egyptian obelisks, which pointed up into the sky like needles. And beside that, still near enough the harbor to benefit from its breezes? The Tomb of Alexander himself, and west of it, the Great Library and its sprawling grounds.

He and Tiberius hadn't brought their own horses; there would be plenty here in Egypt, but Caesarion preferred his own mount. So they walked up the hundreds of stairs from the royal docks to the palace, sweat starting to form under their armor. One to each side of Selene's litter, and surrounded by Praetorians in their white-crested helmets, taking in the view of the gleaming waters of the harbor as each twist in the stairs led them higher and higher.

Finally, at the top, the bearers set her down, and Antyllus took another look, inhaling at the huge palace complex, which seemed to be made up of dozens of buildings, linked to each other by roofed, shady paths. The pillars were Hellene on the outside, but the statues scattered around the grounds? Purely Egyptian.

The servants opened the doors, admitting them into the cool, dim depths of the main building, and they followed the others inside. Gold-embossed images on the doors, of the jackal-god, Anubis, and hawk-headed Horus, and dozens of others. And in the grand entryway, Selene half-laughed, slapping her hand over her face, trying to stifle the noise on this solemn occasion. "What is it?" Antyllus whispered from her right, while Tiberius' head swung over from the left.

Still biting her lip in amusement, Selene pointed at a black, highly-polished statue of a naked woman against the far right wall. A woman wearing the headdress of a pharaoh, but with the smooth, balanced proportions of Hellene sculpture, one foot slightly in front of the other, hip angled, as if ready to step off her pedestal. And for a moment, Antyllus stared at it, trying to understand why her face looked so familiar. *Except smoother, perhaps? Younger — oh, shit.*

"That's your mother, depicted as a goddess?" Antyllus whispered, snapping his eyes back to the front, lest it be said that he was ogling his step-mother's naked form. *Not to mention the former Empress. On the other hand, it's right here in the entryway. Presumably, it's meant to be ogled.*

"Oh, gods," Tiberius muttered, and his head jerked away, too.

"Yes," Selene managed, laughter welling up in her

voice, but she kept it tightly under control, at least for the moment. A good thing, too; the various Praetorians around them had just swung their heads over to see what the fuss was about—and then *their* heads snapped to the front, as well.

An hour or so later, they'd settled into large, private rooms that were startlingly bare of furniture, for all the opulence of the paintings and carvings on the walls, and the genuine lapis and turquoise inlaid into the floors. The few furnishings were odd; chairs and stools so low that even his young, healthy back protested as he lowered himself into them. And a bed, inclined slightly so that the feet were lower than the head, which lacked a pillow entirely. Instead, at its head was an object that looked like a very small stool, made of jade. Antyllus hesitantly lowered himself onto the bed, still dressed, and attempted to rest his head on this . . . pedestal. *How in the name of the gods do they expect someone to sleep, let alone do the other things one might conceivably do in a bed?* He carefully picked up the priceless jade . . . artifact . . . and settled it under the bed, instead. *I can ask the servants if they have anything else. If Cleopatra's hospitality doesn't extend to Roman pillows, then I can roll up my cloak and use that.* His lips quirked as he stared up at the ceiling. *Or I can apply to Caesarion and Eurydice. I do not see them enjoying a bed like this one. In fact, I would be greatly surprised if there isn't hasty redecoration going on this very moment in the chambers of the pharaoh and his queen.*

Sitting up and laughing to himself, Antyllus left his room, plagued by restlessness. Four weeks at sea, and now, finding himself in one of the greatest cities in the world, he wanted to see it. Wandering the palace halls in sandals—the various legionnaires had been required to leave off their nail-shod boots, for the sake of the costly floors—Antyllus finally found Selene and Tiberius sitting on a bench under a palm tree in one of the many cool, shady gardens around which the palace complex sprawled. Gardeners labored in the sun, pulling unwelcome weeds and cutting back old, yellowing fronds from the palm trees, chatting idly as they worked.

"There you are!" Antyllus told them cheerfully enough, though at the back of his mind, he wondered if Tiberius had finally stolen a day's march on him, while he'd been investigating the palace's rooms. Probably not. *There are too many servants around, doing their work.* "You've never been to Alexandria before, correct?" he asked Selene. *Four weeks at sea, and I have no idea if either Tiberius or I are making any headway with her. Of course, that four weeks was also spent under the – ha! – eagle eye of her brother. That accounts for much.*

She shook her head quickly. "Father never allowed any of us to go. He felt that we needed to be as Roman as possible."

"Well, then, what do you want to see first?" Antyllus asked her, gesturing at the sprawling city just barely visible through the garden's gate.

Selene blinked. "I . . . oh!" She paused, then admitted, sheepishly, "I thought I'd be staying in the palace for the month of the celebrations and whatever."

Again, Antyllus had to stop and make himself remember exactly how sheltered her life had been. *She's been as far as the baths in Rome, always under escort. Never allowed out of the Julii villa, except under guard. One siege camp near Brundisium, where again, she wouldn't have been allowed out, except under escort. Is it any wonder that by this point in her life, she doesn't even think about where she might go? The answer has always been no. Of course, I contrast this with my sisters. Antonia the Elder always trying to sneak out of the house while Octavia was our step-mother. . . .*

"Personally," Tiberius put in quietly, cautiously leaning

back against the palm's trunk, and then sitting back up again as a monkey leaped from a nearby roof and into the tree, chattering wildly, "I'd like to visit the Tomb of Alexander. Probably make an offering."

Selene sat up a little, looking surprised. "You consider him a god?"

"Some people here have declared him one. I think it's closer to the old Hellene concept of declaring someone a hero after their death. Not quite a god. Not quite human." Tiberius' head turned until he was looking more or less towards the building that housed the pharaoh's private chambers.

Antyllus caught his meaning immediately. "Well, we are in the service of one such, yes." A quick smile. "I somehow don't see Caesarion trying to conquer the world, however."

Tiberius shrugged. "Son of a war-god. Son of Caesar."

"Yes, but for better or worse, the man has no ambition. His father did. Octavian did. My father? Absolutely." *For all that he's a divinely-inspired fighter and tactician, who loves living among his men, and is happier in a* castra *where the walls are so green that sap drips from them, than in a palace? Caesarion would be just as pleased to stay in Rome, putting up new buildings. Listening to philosophers. He'd deny it if I said it to him, of course.*

"And you?" Selene asked, the first direct question she'd ever asked them both. "Do the two of you have ambition?"

Antyllus paused, struck by the question. He honestly didn't know how to answer it. "My father's been a consul. There's only one chair higher than that, and it's occupied by someone I feel personal loyalty towards," he answered, shrugging a little. "Do I want to add *dignitas* to my family's name? Of course I do! But there's ambition, and there's reality. Your brother's god-born. Anyone whose ambitions flare up so high that they feel they must become Imperator while he holds that title? Deserves to be burned by the flames." He gave Tiberius a quick glance. "You're very silent on the subject."

Tiberius snorted. "My mother has put me off the topic of ambition, honestly. I'll stick to *gloria*."

"Some would say that *gloria* is worthless if you don't put it to use," Antyllus pointed out, wanting to poke Tiberius. "What's the point of covering yourself in fame, if you don't live a public life?" *First gloria, victory in battle, demonstrating that you're a man of courage and virtue. Then public service in which you get to change things that need changing. Ideally, anyway. Though quite a lot of that public service winds up as a naked power grab, and large sums of money change hands to ensure that some things never change at all.*

"I'm still working on that part," Tiberius admitted, shrugging. "Maybe the point of *gloria* is just that, for some people. Maybe winning is enough, and maybe virtue is enough, on its own merits. Without trying to turn it into coin or power."

"Easy to say for someone who has both," Antyllus pointed out, grinning, perfectly aware of how much money and influence his own family possessed. "And of course, that money and power goes to improve the position of your family. So that the next generation can improve, and the next, and the next." *In theory. And that's the dignitas of the family, all over again.*

Selene swung her head towards him now, confusion written in her expression. "But I thought you wanted to avoid the usual career path of politics. And be an . . . ambassador. A governor. Something like that."

Antyllus chuckled, taking a seat on the bench beside her. "I do. I'm just pointing out that Tiberius here can cover himself in *gloria* all he wants. But fame is power. And sooner or later, someone will expect him to *use* that power—or they'll find him useless, and try to remove him." *After all, we can't have someone sucking up all the fame like water through a hollow reed. There will be none left for everyone else.* He laughed outright at Tiberius' dark look. "So, Selene, where do *you* want to go in this vast city? Surely, after the investiture ceremony tomorrow, you could get your brother's permission to explore. At least a little." *Under heavy guard, if the people in this city have become agitated due to the mess at Thebes.*

"I don't think that's necessarily a good idea," Tiberius said sharply, clearly thinking along the same lines. "It would be better to get an idea of the locals' mood first, before running around to see the sights."

Antyllus glanced at Selene, and felt a tinge of hope as she said, hesitantly, "I *would* like to see more than just the roofs of the buildings. I can ask my sister to ask Caesarion. When she's less busy."

She won't ask Caesarion directly. But she also didn't curl up into a ball of fear, either. That's progress.

Chapter VI: Shadows

Damkina heard the tap at the front door, but continued working in her study, knowing that her servants would attend to whoever it was. Here, in the privacy of the unassuming house she'd purchased in the Hellene district of Alexandria, she did not wear the concealing veil across her face or the heavy hat to cover her long, dark hair as she crouched over a bench. Her fingers twisted gold wire with just enough magical power to melt the gold as she dripped it, drop by drop, into the script she'd already cut into an amulet made of cold, hard iron, wrapped around a cabochon ruby.

The words and symbols on the amulet were protective in nature, designed to keep out the intrusive tendrils of a spirit's thoughts. But it was the crystalline matrix of the ruby that would hold the charge of power she'd place in it. Every time a minor spirit tried to touch a human who wore this talisman, a little of that power would dissipate, unfortunately, requiring the device to be recharged at some later date. A powerful spirit might be able to overcome the device's effect entirely. But it was a layer of protection that most people didn't have, and given what a spirit *could* do? People aware of the danger would pay dearly for such a relic.

Of course, Damkina had no intention of asking coin for this item. She'd wear it herself, the next time she opened her grimoire to entreat a spirit capable of hunting humans to do so for her.

A tap at her study door now, and as she acknowledged it, it swung open. Ehsan, her guard, loomed there, and then raised his hand, making a series of gestures. "Visitors? Unless they're my existing contacts, send them away. I'm busy."

Another gesture or three as a scowl crossed his scarred

face. Her expression tightened, and then she set her work aside, covering it with a cloth. Put her hat back on her head, and covered her face with her veil. "Very well. If they're so insistent, I'll see what they have to say." The finger-language Ehsan used was very limited, unfortunately. She frequently wished that she'd found him before . . . everything. But that was a foolish wish, and she knew it.

Ehsan escorted the visitors into her study, and stood there, looming once more by the door. She sat in her chair, as regal as any queen, not rising as the two Egyptian men entered. Studying them. Listening to her spirits as they, too, investigated the men. "Lady Damkina—" the stout one began in Hellene.

"Magus," she corrected, raising a finger. "You have come to my house for assistance in some matter. You will address me as Magus Banit." This demand usually had the additional benefit of throwing people off-balance.

He paused, looking irritated, but concealed it rapidly. "Magus, we are merchants. Of enough means to make it worth your while if you were to assist us in an endeavor of some . . . sensitivity."

Educated inflections to his Hellene. Upper Egypt accent, not Lower. He doesn't spent much time speaking this language, but speaks it well. Damkina's eyebrows arched slightly. "And what would this matter of such sensitivity be?" she asked quietly.

They exchanged glances, and the thinner of the pair replied, hesitantly, "We have a former . . . business associate . . . who has cheated us of substantial sums of money."

"Are there not courts to handle such matters?" Damkina asked. If she'd thought for an instant that they were telling the truth, she'd have already been bored and sent them out the door dismissively. Of course, they weren't. She could see ink-stains under their well-manicured nails, not dirt. The smell of incense clung to their skins, not spices or tanning agents. And her spirits whispered to her, *They are both bound in service to some greater spirit or god. Their souls are hidden from our sight.*

An awkward glance between the two men, and then the stout one offered, "He has bribed the courts to rule in his favor."

"Of course he did," Damkina murmured, and one of her bound spirits whispered, *Lie!* in her ear. "Gentlemen, my time is valuable. Please, reach the culmination of your argument." A tiny, dismissive flick of her left hand, and she watched the ire rise in two sets of eyes. *They don't like my tone. They're either unused to women in authority, or are of sufficient rank that they're unused to anyone treating them cavalierly.*

"To be blunt, then," the stout one said, running a hand over his shaved head—*no wig. A merchant of such supposed wealth would wear one. His hand has lighter bands of skin on his fingers, showing he recently wore rings, which he stripped off before entering my house* – "we seek vengeance, Magus."

"Hire an assassin," she suggested shortly. "Knives or poisons are wondrous tools of vengeance." *As well I know.* She turned back to her work, and felt, rather than heard, one of them step forward. Heard Ehsan's warning grunt, and lifted her head, watching as the stout one sagged back to where he'd just been standing a moment before. "Was there something more?" she asked, her tone sharp.

"Our associate has . . . protections," the slender one said carefully. "Magical ones. An assassin armed with only a blade or poison will not be successful. Hence our desire to find . . . magical means."

Now, she was more interested. "Does your associate employ food-tasters?"

"Spirits guard his food, yes. And not only does he have

human guards," the slender one's eyes flicked towards Ehsan, "but there are rumors of magical ones, as well." He shrugged. "A trinket, however? A gift of a ring, perhaps, sent to him, which, when he puts it on, turns him to stone? That would be most fitting. A statue of himself."

She snorted under her veil. "Such objects exist, yes, but they were made when Babylon was young." *When we of the Magi had gods to call on for their power.* "I could make one that would cause the blood to congeal in your . . . associate's . . . veins. But I do not think that you could match the price I would charge to create such an object," she murmured, enjoying herself now.

"We are prepared to offer a full talent of silver," the fat one suggested. *He doesn't bargain often. Ah, well, I already knew he wasn't a merchant.*

"I do not trade in gold or silver," Damkina said, smiling behind her veil as she saw their looks of consternation. "I trade in knowledge. Information and secrets. Influence, too. As you are but humble merchants, you have nothing that interests me. Good day."

Ehsan started to push them out of her study, but the fat one blurted, "And if we were to say that we weren't merchants?"

"Then I would say that was the first truth you've spoken since entering my house. Go back to whatever temple you come from, priests," Damkina turned back to her work, her tone supremely bored now — carefully so. "I am not in the business of murdering high priests so that their acolytes may move up the temple hierarchy."

"It's not for a temple elder — " the slender one blurted, and then the fat one seized him by the arm and hustled him out, whispering in Egyptian as they left.

Ehsan gestured at Damkina, and she pursed her lips

behind her veil. "Have one of our men follow them," she told her bodyguard. "They seem inept, but even the foolish occasionally blunder into success." *I do wonder who they want dead so very badly.*

That night, she spent long hours at the Library, only to be alerted by her spirits that something was deeply wrong. When she and Ehsan hurried back, they found the bodies of her servants on the floor, bodies twisted and distorted in death. Huge welts had appeared on their hands and feet, and their faces were locked in rictus grins. Shaken, Damkina lifted her skirts and hastened deeper into the house.

Her study, warded as it was, had been forced open. And as such, the slender half of the pair that had visited her that afternoon lay dead across its threshold, a smell of cooked flesh permeating the air. Beyond, all of her scrolls lay in a wild, tangled mess on the floor, having clearly been rooted through. "Is anything missing?" Damkina asked her spirits, urgently. And then she spotted the open chest, and dug through its contents, her mouth drying with fear.

One cuneiform tablet was, indeed, missing. Along with the more modern partial translation on the scroll she'd tucked beside it. *Damnation.* "We'll need to alert the local guards that someone broke into my home and stole items of value," Damkina told Ehsan. Not that he could reply, beyond repeated gestures that asked why she was so distressed. She swallowed. "And if our foolish priest survives summoning the creature whose Name he stole? We will very shortly know who his target is. And may have to intervene." She hissed between her teeth. "They had enough power to kill all my servants," she told Ehsan, her voice empty as she thought it through. "They weren't just looking for an easy way to reach their target. They wanted a way that reeked of Magi involvement. And not their own."

Alexandria had had a fire brigade for decades, and that fire brigade doubled as a sort of night's watch. Damkina had heard that the last Imperator, Caesar, had been so inspired by the system, that he'd set up a similar one in Rome, and given the Egyptian brigade a Roman name, even here in this ancient city: the *Vigiles*. But many people also called them the *gardia*. They were highly effective at putting out fires. Occasionally helpful in finding lost property. And mostly incompetent to deal with sudden, violent death, unless they happened to have witnessed it as it was occurring.

Those tasked with putting down sedition and riots and dealing with violent crime were the more militarily-organized Urban Cohorts. Who again, were more apt to meet violence with violence, than to investigate its causes. Still, they arrived. Stared wide-eyed at the disfigured bodies of her servants, and the *cooked* intruder. Wrote down her story, frowning intently in the way of men who did not often set pen to papyrus. And then left, taking the bodies with them.

Only then did Damkina sit down at a table, put her face in her hands, and weep, shaking with both anger and grief at once. And she felt Ehsan's large hand on her shoulder. Offering her what little silent comfort he could.

Finally, she looked up at him. "For so much effort, it must be a very important death that they wish," she said, testing the idea out loud.

Her guard nodded, and picked up a wax tablet and a stylus. And picked out, in the modified cuneiform currently in use in Chaldea, *The Imperator of Rome came to Alexandria today.*

She exhaled. "Well, there could hardly be a more important death." Damkina assessed the situation as coldly as she could. "I doubt our priest can read ancient Sumerian. Otherwise, he'd have picked the more deadly, more insidious tablet just below the one he did choose. But the one he took was bad enough, in its way." She rubbed at her eyes briefly. "If that Name is invoked, the very first thing that anyone will do, is come looking for a Magus. I have three choices. Run. Tonight. Get as far from Egypt as we can on the fastest ship available. But that leaves my mission here uncompleted, and I have waited thirteen years for this." Her hands clenched into fists, and Ehsan, across the table, only nodded. "Second, continue as if nothing happened, and pray to all the dead gods that having reported the attack on my servants and the theft is enough to ward off the fury of a Roman emperor."

Ehsan snorted. She pulled back her veil, at ease with him as with no one else in the world. "I didn't say it was a *good* choice." Damkina sighed. "The last option is to find the leader of the Emperor's guards and tell him exactly what was taken, and request that you and I be put someplace where I can be of use, if the Name is invoked."

The gargling sound of a tongueless man attempting to laugh was harsh and horrifying. Ehsan never allowed himself the luxury in public. But Damkina was so used to the sound, she didn't even flinch. She watched his hands sketch out a message on the wax tablet, and sighed. "Yes. I wouldn't believe us, either. But half of the last seven Parthian rulers of Persia have owed their thrones to Roman intervention. Our dear Parthian overlords would, if we fled to Chaldea, simply hand us over at Rome's request, regardless of our innocence, in the name of maintaining good ties. Not that we can go to Chaldea."

You can, he wrote.

"But you can't. Returning home isn't an option for you. They'd all know who you were. And what you were supposed to become." She sighed. "So this is the only option I can think of that doesn't involve half the Empire chasing us down, or both of us being tortured to death, old friend."

He scratched at the tablet again, and Damkina read the words there, and simply nodded.

At least here, death would eventually end our suffering.

Standing at the Palace gates near sundown was something of an exercise in futility, at first. Finally, a guard emerged to tell them to leave, and Damkina drew herself up to her full height—all five feet of it. And announced, "I am a member of the Chaldean Magi. I have information regarding a potential threat to your Imperator's life. I would like to speak to someone in charge."

They didn't believe her at first. She had to bid half her attendant spirits to materialize before the first guard hastened off to find his superior. Then his superior's superior. And on down the line, until, near midnight, she and Ehsan found themselves in a room of the palace clearly usually apportioned for storage. Shelves of oil and the musty smell of grain in sacks. A prized feline prowling among those sacks, looking for mice.

Finally, two men entered—one clearly Roman and much older, his curling hair nearly iron-gray, though his sardonic eyes were clear and sharp. The other didn't appear Roman at all. Oh, Romans could have blond hair as this one did, but he was at least Ehsan's height, and his face lacked the prominent aquiline nose of a Roman. "You claim to be a member of the Chaldean Magi, and you believe there's an imminent threat to our Emperor?" the older man said, raising his eyebrows. "I'd have thought you'd cheer on any assassination attempts."

"When Rome convulses in civil war," Damkina said sharply, "our current Parthian overlords will immediately take arms and hasten to the borders to see what they can carve away. They demand magic of the Magi—but we have yet to give them what they most desire. The Immortals." She snorted. "They aren't kings. They're a drop of oil in a hot pan, there, and then gone again. The Seleucids were kings—though nothing is left of their lineage but the daughters that the Parthians married at sword-point. But your Emperor is descended from a man who called our Seleucids brothers, once." She shrugged.

The younger man smiled grimly. "Perhaps our Emperor should send his brother to Persia, then, and give you a new king."

She shrugged again. "We had hundreds of years of prosperity under the Hellenistic kings. I don't know how another one could do worse than our current masters." Damkina sighed. "But that is neither here nor there. Two men came to my house today to try to buy magic from me, to assassinate someone they called a former business associate. They weren't merchants, however. Their hands were soft, and ink-stained . . . ." She led them through the whole story. And she thought she saw recognition in their eyes at her description of the stout priest.

"What was this spell that they stole?" the younger man asked.

Damkina closed her eyes. "It's not a spell. It's a Name that can be used to summon one of the children of the old gods." She exhaled. "Most of the gods of Sumer and Babylon are dead. Tiamat, the primordial dragon, had many children, however. And one of her sons was chiefly summoned for protection." She opened her eyes once more. "He has not been summoned in centuries. We of the Magi have been careful not to use the ancient Names. For fear that doing so will draw the godslayers down upon us once more."

The older man made a flipping gesture with one hand. "The godslayers are a myth."

"You say that because you still have many gods,

Roman," Damkina told him bluntly. "Young, powerful gods. We have one left to us. And he is old and weary, our Marduk. All the rest are just whispers on the wind."

"Is there anything we can do, if this protection-demon happens to come here?"

Damkina grimaced. "I could try to banish him."

Both men laughed. "Oh no," the older man told her. "Let you invoke power, perform rituals, right here? Without being able to tell precisely what you're doing? Nice try. You will be locked away, gagged and bound, until we can investigate your story more thoroughly."

Of course, she thought tiredly. *Roman rationalism.* "In which case, I will tell you that weapons were said to bounce from the creature's hide. The ancients carried swords of bronze or copper, which did not so much as scratch him. Your iron *may* work. But we have better." She looked at Ehsan. "Give them your dagger, old friend."

With manifest reluctance, Ehsan slowly drew his dagger, and handed it over. "Silver-inlaid," Damkina said, her voice distant. "It's usually effective on spirits, disrupting the bodies that they form. I cannot guarantee that this will work, however." She struggled to remember the rest of the cuneiform tablet, and shook her head. "The lower half of his body is that of a bull. The upper half, that of a man. He sometimes carries a spear, or a sword." She offered her wrists now. "Tie your ropes tightly, Romans," Damkina murmured ironically. "You wouldn't want the real threat running around loose, now would you?"

She saw their frowns. Expected their fists to descend towards her face in punishing arcs. But that didn't happen. They did, however, chain both her and Ehsan. Locked them in the storage room together—though there was, at least, the courtesy of a pot to piss in. And she could hear guards outside, talking to each other in Latin.

Exhausted, Damkina found a relatively clean patch of floor, and sank down next to Ehsan. Put her head on her friend's shoulder, and tried to find sleep. *At least they didn't gag you*, she thought. *Of course, for you, there's no need.*

Februarius 12, 20 AC

Cleopatra had sent messages ahead to tell the palace staff to be ready for a royal investiture, and had also sent invitations to every dignitary in Alexandria — indeed, in all of Egypt. They hadn't been able to set an exact date, due to the exigencies of sea travel and the possibility of rough weather, but they had all known that once they landed, the investiture ceremony — and the attendant additional marriage ceremony . . . their fourth in three years. . . would have to be conducted quickly. Largely because if they waited too long, they would run into the Roman celebration of Parentalia, which took up nine days of Februarius. Since this was a solemn time of the year, spent honoring dead ancestors, marriages and many other public ceremonies were strictly forbidden, Eurydice and Caesarion had opted for setting the investiture for the day before Parentalia would begin — Februarius twelfth.

Eurydice was aware that they had a Magi and her attendant being held in what Malleolus had termed 'protective custody,' somewhere in the palace. She thought speaking with the Chaldean woman would be fascinating, and that she might be able to learn a great deal from a Magi . . . but considering the fact that the entire ostensible "plot" that the woman had brought to the attention of the Praetorians could just be an excuse to get close enough to Caesarion or Eurydice to try to assassinate them? Eurydice wasn't allowed anywhere near the prisoners.

Her time remained well-occupied, however. She spent a substantial portion of each day arguing with her mother, who had clear ideas on how a queen of Egypt ought to appear and behave. Even going out into the city and its outskirts to learn about her new people occasioned disputes. Cleopatra felt that the only proper mode of transportation within the city was a throne-like litter, encrusted with gold-leaf. It had a back, and thus, Eurydice could sit upright in it, but was long enough for her legs to be supported, as if in a bed, and had upright posts and a canopy to keep the sun off her head . . . and curtains, if she didn't feel like seeing, or being seen. The contraption required six men to lift, due to its weight.

Eurydice, on the other hand, had always been subject to nausea in swaying litters, even in Rome. Added to that, she now had a tendency towards nausea at odd points in the day. Never in the morning. But sometimes, she couldn't even make it through dinner without having to excuse herself hastily to throw up in another room. She didn't see a need to add any more reasons to lose her dignity, or what little food she could keep down at the moment. And the ornate carving, gold-leaf, and general ostentation of the apparatus appalled her. For obvious reasons, riding on horseback was not an option at the moment. So she and Caesarion went about by chariot instead. It required a good deal more standing, since the chariot had no seats, but for so long as he was here, he could stand behind her, arms wrapped around her as he controlled the reins.

For better or worse, the chariot was almost as gaudy as the litter, being just as gold-encrusted. But at least in it, she didn't feel like a particularly venerated religious object when passing people in the streets. And while people turned to stare at the chariot, as such things were relatively rare in Alexandria's crowded streets, especially ones surrounded by

Roman guards, few people seemed to feel compelled to kneel at the sight. Though they did make way, as foot-traffic always did for a horse.

No signs, at least for now, that the attack mentioned by the Magus was imminent, though Eurydice had been disquieted by the physical description of a scribe or priest that had sounded so similar to Tahut-Nefer. Prefect Gallus remained entrenched at Thebes, sending several missives by courier indicating that he didn't feel able to leave the situation to his tribunes. Caesarion, his face dark, had already stated that as soon as the investiture was complete, they were marching south along the Nile to deal with whatever was going on down there.

And so, on a bright *dies Lunae*, hundreds of dignitaries arrived at the massive temple of Isis on Pharos Island, under the shadow of the Great Lighthouse. Parthian and Nubian ambassadors. Egyptian nobles and priests from Upper Egypt—though no mage-priests of Thoth had applied to be guests at the ceremony. Hellene nobles, both from Alexandria and from Hellas itself. Roman patricians and wealthy plebeians who made their home in this bustling city. Judeans with heavy beards and expressions of distaste for the temple surroundings. Carthaginians in their white robes and colorful caps, too. All taking their seats on small wooden stools on either side of an open space left as an aisle in the huge central area of the great temple.

Praetorians had been posted at every door, and twenty of them stood on either side of the audience area in a perfect line, their backs to the bulky pillars that supported the temple's heavy stone roof. Braziers flanked either side of the white marble altar, burning sweet incense, sending smoke swirling up before a twenty-foot-tall statue of Isis crafted of ivory and gold, in Hellene style. The goddess had been depicted seated on a throne, holding the infant Horus in her lap, suckling her young son, while her wings reached out from low on her back to encircle both of them—wings that shone with color, the feathers picked out in lapis, carnelian, topaz, malachite, amethyst, onyx, and white agate. Dozens of other statues, all of black basalt, and in a more traditional Egyptian style, had been built into the walls of the temple, and braziers glowed in front of each of them, the flickering light revealing the hieroglyphs and other writings incised and painted on the temple walls and the massive pillars, too.

Eurydice found the temple extraordinarily impressive, but very dim. Lacking in natural light, she felt as if she were entering some cavern or mine deep under a mountain as she walked into the huge chamber, feeling the cool air on skin she didn't normally expose in public. High, thin lyre music and the rattle of a sistrum began as she entered, letting her time her steps to a ritual pace. But keeping her shoulders back and head up was one of the hardest things she'd ever had to do as she stepped slowly towards the altar where Caesarion and Cleopatra, already in position, waited for her. Antony stood near Cleopatra, but with unusual deference for a Roman man, back by several steps, with his hands folded behind him. His eyes weren't on her, or her mother, however. They scanned the temple, constantly evaluating the crowd, the Praetorians, everything.

It didn't particularly help that her mother wore a similar *kalasiris* to Eurydice's own, only hers was completely covered in gold embroidery, in contrast to the stark simplicity of Eurydice's own. Her ample bosom, like Eurydice's, was completely exposed, other than what concealment a large necklace offered. Cleopatra's wig was encrusted in gold, but Eurydice had put her foot down on one thing, and one thing only today: she refused to wear a wig. Her natural hair was long, and she'd let it down for the ceremony, like a Roman bride on her wedding night, and that would simply have to do.

It didn't help that she knew for a fact that both Antony and Caesarion had threatened any man who smiled, leered, or even changed expression at seeing her or Cleopatra dressed so, with immediate expulsion from the Praetorians. She didn't even want to *think* about what barracks jokes would be swapped, out of hearing of their commanders, about how every man of them had seen the tits of both the former and current Empress of Rome.

Courage, she told herself, keeping her eyes locked on Caesarion, whose expression was so grim at the moment, he might have been mistaken for a statue, himself. He wore the white *shendyt* kilt and sandals, along with a solid gold necklace in the form of a Horus hawk, its wings reaching up to his shoulders, and the body covering his sternum, the cost of which would probably have covered the construction of a vast villa on the island of Capri. On his head, he wore the red and white crown of Upper and Lower Egypt. Given the *hate* with which he'd eyed it this morning, she admired him for not showing it in his expression now.

Reaching the altar, Eurydice numbly turned to face Caesarion, while her mother, as queen and priestess of Isis, faced the assembled crowd. The murmuring stilled as Cleopatra, in regal tones, announced, "Today, I am no more queen in Egypt. Today, I give way to my daughter, Eurydice Julia. Descendent of Ptolemy and of the line of kings going back to Ramses and Khufu."

That last, Eurydice knew, was a polite fiction. Dozens of Egyptian dynasties had ruled these lands, some wresting it from each other in open combat, with no lineal claims at all. "My beloved son Ptolemy has been my co-ruler for many years. Now, his sister-wife takes her rightful place at his side to rule this great land. The divine union of Isis and Osiris continues in them, as it has for centuries without count."

As she spoke, Eurydice and Caesarion joined hands, facing one another at arm's length, and Cleopatra continued in solemn tones, "I give the blessing of Isis to you today, my children, though it has ever been with you."

Caesarion pulled her to him, for a public, decorous kiss, which still held all the sweetness Eurydice craved. And when their lips parted, Cleopatra lifted a heavy golden diadem from the altar, passing it to Caesarion. Not the crown of Upper and Lower Egypt, which only the ruling pharaoh could wear, but the crown of a queen. A golden hawk with jeweled eyes and feathers formed a sort of cap, its head dipping low over her forehead, its body cupping her scalp, and its wings flaring out around her face, covering her ears.

Eurydice knelt. And as Caesarion placed this heavy diadem on her head, she felt her lips quiver. It felt like a chain. A trap. "Courage," Caesarion whispered in her ear, bending low enough to do so. "Courage, my queen, my empress, my love." And then he lifted her back to her feet, keeping their hands clasped tightly as Cleopatra finished her oration.

"And I say to all assembled here, that if any have doubts as to the joy of the gods in their union, that your doubts should wither now. For the gods *have* blessed them, and the line of the Ptolemies and the Julii will continue, for my daughter carries her brother-husband's heir." Clear, flat defiance in Cleopatra's voice, and Eurydice's eyes flicked towards her mother. *Oh, gods, how did she* know*? I didn't tell her* – she glanced rapidly at Caesarion, whose face remained impassive, but whose eyes suddenly held rage. *And he didn't either. Oh, gods, Mother, why did you have to announce it!*

The Egyptians in the temple surged to their feet, giving

voice to startled, ululating cheers of unabashed approval. The various Hellenes applauded with a certain restraint. The Romans and Judeans all muttered among themselves with expressions of horrified revulsion—which all gave way to a shocked moment of silence as something in the periphery of Eurydice's vision shifted.

She looked away from Caesarion in time to see the statue of Isis turn its head away from baby Horus, and look down at them. The ivory flesh rippled and groaned, and whatever internal scaffolding held it together shrieked under the strain as one of the statue's hands moved away from supporting Horus to reach out in benediction. And as Eurydice's knees hit the floor in awe, she heard a whisper in her mind: *You have done well, my children. Little hawk, you have so often wondered why I do not speak to you . . . and yet I do. I do not reveal myself often in words, the realm of the rational. I give you dreams, the irrational. Images with which to grapple, mysteries to unfold and interpret for yourself. I give you an idea of what the future may hold, but for me, it is an uncertain business, not the iron-clad fate of Apollo of Delphi. I see myself growing hard and cold in this world, and yet, for the moment, in the two of you, I see hope . . . .*

The goddess' voice faded from Eurydice's mind. And swimming in exaltation, she hardly even registered the sound of the great wooden doors at the far end of the temple being flung open with a resounding crash. The sunlight streaming into the cave-like dimness. But the first screams cut through her awareness, and her head snapped around at the same time Caesarion's did, and she saw a huge figure looming in the doorway, shadowed against the brilliant light outside.

At least twice as tall as a man, its shadow stretched like an inky finger into the audience. Curving, forward-swept horns, like those of a bull, protruded from either side of a humanoid head; and whatever it was, it wore antique-looking armor, verdigris bronze in color, with square plates welded together across its chest, but which left its massive arms bare. Below the chestplate, a kilt of some sort of brown wool, concealing the creature's loins . . . but the legs under that kilt weren't human, but rather those of a bull, down to the heavy hooves. The hooked sword in its hand was a similar verdigris green, and, in proportion to the creature's height, looked no larger than a *gladius* in its massive paw . . . until Eurydice realized that the sword was almost as long as the Praetorians beside the door were tall.

The Praetorians flanking the door, seeing a threat, reacted on instinct and training, lifting both their spears and their shields. One of them immediately paid the price, as the creature, not bothering to lift its heavy sword, reached out with its free hand, seized the *scutum* by the edge, lifted the man by his shield, and threw him, all in one smooth motion. Flung him twenty feet forward, right into the crowd of dignitaries, landing on two wealthy Hellenes.

That was when the screaming started, and people began to run. Eurydice lost track of what was going on, unable to see through all the flailing limbs, but she *thought* that the Praetorian to the left of the door closed on the creature. Rapid stabs with the *pilum*, from behind the shield, just as every legionnaire was taught. But the creature whirled, the green sword rose—and then, behind all the fleeing, screaming, stampeding people, she could see a spray of dark liquid rising up in an arc to stain the temple's walls.

Then nothing but confusion. The Praetorians lining the hall racing forward to form a double wall of bodies between the creature and those they'd sworn to protect, fighting their way through the crowd of dignitaries to do it. Lurio racing from his own pillar to Eurydice's left, throwing himself in between her and the creature, his sword out and shield up. Malleolus racing in from the right, to do the same for Caesarion, but no sword in his hand. Instead, a small, curving dagger was his only weapon. Tiberius and Antyllus, bodily carrying Selene forward out of the crowd to the altar, Antony stepping forward to shield Cleopatra. Caesarion's face turning into the hard, cold mask of combat. "Give me a sword, Mal! Lurio, get Eurydice out of here—"

"I can help—" she shouted over the screams and cries of the crowd, all panicking. All streaming towards the two doors at the rear of the temple, guarded by Praetorians, or the two doors at the sides, all of which just led into other rooms of the temple. Storage chambers, meditation rooms, scriptoriums, which might eventually lead out, but through a maze of other rooms. The only real exit was the one which the creature blocked. Eurydice called the fire of the braziers to her hands, feeling an odd sort of chill as she did so. And, over the heads of the Praetorians forming their shield wall, bracing for the creature's advance, she flung the flame directly at the bull-like demon.

This simple attack, bolstered by her own inner flame, had served her well through two years in Hispania. She'd swathed men in flame from head to toe before. Shuddered at their screams, and prayed for them to die quickly. Mercifully. She expected nothing else from the bull-creature, reverse minotaur that it was.

She heard a roar that shook the ground. But when the flames dissipated, the creature stood, shaking sparks from its long hair, beard, and horns. Completely unscathed. "Oh, *shit*," Eurydice whispered, the barracks word falling unbidden from her lips. Felt Lurio grab her by the shoulders as Caesarion once more shouted for the man to *get her out of here*. Her sandals skidded over the floor as Lurio pushed her right for one of the rear doors of the sanctum. Fleeting glimpse of Antony picking Cleopatra up bodily over his shoulder. Antyllus hurrying Selene in the same direction. Tiberius drawing his sword and, lacking a shield, turning to face the threat. Malleolus letting Caesarion take the *gladius* from his side.

Saw the creature lower its head, as if preparing to charge, like a bull. Pause. And then it *did* race forward, with all the speed of inevitability. Heard one centurion bellow, "Get those fucking *pila* forward, lads! Hold! *Hold*, gods damn you!"

Feel of the creature's hooves on the stone floor, reverberating up through her body like an iron gong. The scream, horribly cut off, as the first man hit by the impact of that huge body was crushed, but the man behind him somehow managed to keep his feet. The incongruous *twang* as a *pilum*, bent under impact, snapped.

And then tumbling through the door, still staring back, desperate to help, but for once in her life, at a loss for how to *do* so. Selene, shoved through after her by Antyllus, who snapped at the Praetorian holding the door, "Go with her! Keep her safe!" before drawing his own sword and turning to run back towards the altar. Antony dropping her mother at the door and shoving her through, with no deference or respect for her royal person at all. "Get your ass back to the palace," Antony snarled. "Get as many guards on the doors as you can, and prepare a ship. With luck, that thing can't *swim*."

And then, he, too, turned back to the fight, drawing his own sword. That he was fifty-nine this year seemed not to make a jot of difference to him as he hastened forward to join the rest of the men. And of all of them, only Caesarion wasn't wearing armor.

Eurydice tried to strain past Lurio's barring arm. Tried

to shout out the door, "Caesarion! Aquilus!" as her mind raced, trying to find options. *Fire didn't work. Fire always works. I don't see more than a scratch on it so far — maybe stone . . . no, if I bring one of the pillars down — even if I could move them, huge things that they are — I'd just bring the roof down on all these people —*

"*Domina, go!*" Lurio finally shouted at her, and, tears streaking down her face, Eurydice let him shove her forward, deeper into the temple. Allowed herself to flee, with one final image burning in her mind — Caesarion, wearing nothing but a kilt, having stripped off his jewelry and crown, and holding a borrowed sword in his hand, forming a last line of defense behind the Praetorians, who had moved to surround and engulf the creature.

Caesarion, mind now eased by knowing that his pregnant wife was being escorted out of danger's way — hopefully — hefted Mal's *gladius*, feeling the weight of the tempered iron. Malleolus flanked his right; Tiberius, his left, both men in full formal armor, though Tiberius lacked a shield. Aware of his Imperator's nearly naked state, Malleolus offered his own *scutum*, but Caesarion shook his head tightly, feeling, more than seeing as Antyllus and Antony run back to form the end of their line. A handful of remaining dignitaries ran out of the way, and then he finally had a clear line of sight to where the bull-creature rampaged in the center of a knot of Praetorians, in the midst of a sea of fallen chairs. Caesarion sucked air around his teeth, fury building in him steadily.

The Praetorians, thanks to their training, had pressed in so closely, shields first, that the bull-creature couldn't get a solid swing in with his oversized sword. But as they jabbed with their *pila* or *gladii*, the creature inevitably lashed out with a kick or a punch, creating space, if only for an instant. And then raised its sword into that gap to swing. "Make a hole!" Caesarion roared over the cries of fear and grunts of effort, the dull thud of metal on hide-wrapped wood. "If he wants me, he can come *get* me!"

"*Dominus!*" Malleolus hissed.

But the Praetorians, hearing that note of command, parted ranks, as ordered. And presented with a straight line of attack, right at Caesarion. . . the creature strode forward, faster than its lumbering gait would suggest that it could move—and then hesitated. Swung its head back and forth, as if looking for its target.

And then raced for the door through which Eurydice, Selene, and Cleopatra had just exited, scattering still more bystanders out of its path, and trampling one Carthaginian completely under its hooves. The man screamed on the ground, a liquid, gurgling sound, as all his ribs were crushed. Antony managed to thrust with a sword as the creature bowled him over, scoring a hit on its shoulder, leaving a thin line of red to join dozens of other nicks and scratches that were the only wounds that the swords and spears of the Pratorians had left. *I'm not the target,* Caesarion realized with a sudden chill. *Eurydice is. She and our child.*

With that surge of cold fear, and without further conscious thought, Caesarion raced after the creature, feeling Tiberius and Malleolus move with him. Mal's sword became an extension of his arm, and Caesarion jabbed, hard, right for the creature's armpit, where a great vein ran, on humans, anyway. The iron sword, held in his god-born hand, didn't bounce. Skin separated, and the blade tasted flesh.

The bull-creature slid to a halt and spun back to face him, its sword coming in a mighty arc that Caesarion ducked just in time, and Malleolus threw himself out of the way of.

Tiberius, shorter to begin with, and the most skilled man with a sword that Caesarion had seen, other than himself, lunged in, aiming not for the armored chest, but for the exposed and hairy knees. "Iron isn't working," Tiberius snarled.

Malleolus managed to roll back to his feet, now behind and beside the minotaur-like creature, and jabbed with his odd, curving dagger—which bit deeply into the creature's arm. "Silver works!" the prefect shouted, his blue eyes glittering in the low light.

"Great, let me throw my coin purse at it!" Antony snapped, pulling himself up off the floor.

"The braziers are silver!" Antyllus shouted, already moving towards the now-dead firebowls beside the altar.

"Go grab one and beat this piece of shit over the head with it!" Tiberius called back, throwing himself out of the way as the creature directed an absent kick at him, bringing its arm around for another backhanded slash at Caesarion.

This time, Caesarion didn't duck. He moved *in*, dropping his own sword to seize his opponent's arm, twice the length of his own, and tried to stop the blow entirely. He could feel the weight of the creature, at least as massive as a horse, and growled, pitting every ounce of his own god-born strength against its weight and power. And he *held* it, locking its elbow in place with one hand. Feeling his feet skid back over the slick stone of the floor, meeting its enraged golden stare with his own. "Hurry up!" Caesarion snapped, feeling his Praetorians swarm now, moving up around him to once more engulf the creature. "Can't . . . hold it . . . for long. . . ."

And then his sliding feet picked up speed, and he found himself shoved out into the open. Both of his hands were tied up, keeping that blade from being used; the creature's other arm was trapped behind its sword arm, off-line from any attacks. But it still had hooves, and one of those huge legs came forward now in a kick that threw Caesarion into the air. Made him sail over the heads of the fleeing bystandards. Then hit the stone floor, his head cracking into the stone. Dim awareness of still sliding, impelled by momentum, several more feet. And then he could see one of the massive pillars looming above and behind him. Impact.

And then, for a moment, blackness.

———————

The brazier was only twenty-five feet away, but looked as distant as Crete as Antyllus ran towards it. Grabbed it by the legs, feeling *heat* still in the bowl from the fires that Eurydice had snuffed moments before. He swung around, seeing his father back on his feet, Tiberius trying to keep the damned creature's attention, Malleolus and the rest of the Praetorians trying to swarm it, and Caesarion—across the room. Unconscious on the floor. *Gods. We have no chance at all if he's out of the fight. Wasn't expecting to die today.*

And with that blank, numb thought, Antyllus charged back into the fight, coming at the creature on its right, and swung the still-smoking brazier at it, aiming for its head at the length of his own arms. The brazier hit—hard enough that he saw the softened silver deform. Two of the legs came off in his hands with the impact, leaving him holding two jagged pieces of silver, one in each hand, while the bowl itself now had formed to the demon's head, like some sort of demented cap.

The creature roared in pain and spun towards Antyllus, ignoring the pinpricks of Malleolus' dagger at its back. Ripped the brazier away from its face with its free hand, and swung that enormous sword at Antony's son. Antyllus threw himself back out of range, feeling the wind of the blade's passage, and shouted, "Tiberius! Catch!" before throwing one of the brazier legs to the younger man, who was already moving in beside the creature.

Tiberius caught the improvised weapon in his left hand, sheathed his sword, switched it to his right, and proceeded to stab at the beast. Always aiming for the armpit if it raised its arm to swing the sword, or ducking down low to jab at its legs, or shifting to cut the angle, and aim for the groin. Vicious, fast stabs, but while the silver clearly *hurt* the creature, there simply wasn't enough of a cutting surface to the broken legs. A sharp elbow from the creature caught Tiberius, sending him tumbling, but Antyllus saw him roll right back up again. Felt his father moving in beside him, trying to help him defend himself.

And then the beast was on him, still clearly furious about the brazier strike to its face. The great sword swung back, and Antyllus once again backed up out of range—and found the damned altar right behind his knees. Caught unaware of his surroundings, Antyllus slipped, falling back over the altar—which, ironically, *saved* him, as the great blade swung in. He felt it catch his chain mail, worn for the ceremony today as part of the honor guard. Felt it slide right through the metal. No pain at first as he tumbled backwards, head hitting the stone, wrenching his neck, and then slamming down with all his weight on his spine, before rolling to a halt against the statue of Isis. Dazed and bloodied, he groped for the silver brazier leg, dimly knowing it was stupid and futile. And watched the creature loom over the altar, bringing its blade back—

Tiberius swore, grabbing a shield from the ground where a fallen Praetorian had dropped it, and ran forward, the silver leg still in his other hand. And managed, somehow, to leap atop the altar, the iron nails of his boots sliding on the slick marble surface. *Shitty footing. Sorry, Isis. Don't smite me for profaning it.* He ducked down behind the shield, taking the hit meant for Antyllus—and promptly slid right off the altar, propelled backwards, and nearly fell onto Antyllus himself. Only by pure luck did he land, shield still up, and one foot braced on either side of the older man. Nothing in him at this moment besides the gray haze of combat. The tight bond of brotherhood that linked him to every other man who wore the same armor, and the need to defeat this enemy—or at least, to buy them all enough time for Caesarion to recover.

"Get up!" Tiberius rapped out, and his shield shook with another hit. He couldn't feel his left arm anymore, and suspected that the bones there had just been broken by the force of the impact. "On your fucking feet, Antyllus!"

On their left, Antony darted in, surprisingly fast for a man his age. Jabbing with his iron sword and dancing back. Trying to buy them time. "Get up!" he roared at his son, and Antyllus responded, managing to slide back and away from Tiberius. Rolled to his feet, and wobbled there, blood creeping down his legs from a wound higher on his body.

"Too bad we don't have rope," Antyllus said, his tone dazed. "We could trip the damned thing—"

"Would take a ship's anchor chain. Come on, stay with me. Circle," Tiberius said tightly, pressing to their left. Watching Antony cede the space to them, and circle to his left, too. While Malleolus once more raced in from behind, stabbing again and again.

This time, the Praetorian wasn't as lucky. The creature, enraged by the bites of this particularly persistent gnat, swung all the way to its right, and, not bothering with the blade of its sword, slammed the pommel of the huge blade into Malleolus' chest, sending the man flying into the crowd of his sworn brothers, knocking several other Praetorians over and back. *Come on, Caesarion,* Tiberius thought, not having the breath to say anything out loud. *We can't hold out much longer here.*

Over his head, though he didn't realize it consciously, the eyes of the statue of Isis had begun to glow, bathing everything around him in a soft luminescence that he put down to the heightened awareness he always experienced in battle.

And that was the moment Caesarion hit the creature from behind at a full charge, driving his sword deep into the back of its right knee.

Tiberius couldn't even see him behind the creature's broad body. His first indication was the creature's flinch, followed by a snapping sound as metal splintered. Then it sagged forward, trying to hold itself upright with only one functioning leg, and Caesarion kicked its other leg out from under it. The beast toppled to its knees, and Tiberius and Antyllus both lunged in at the same time. Both their initial strikes barely scored the creature's face—but the second time, Antyllus managed to drive his brazier leg into the join between neck and throat, and Tiberius felt a shock of triumph as his slid into one of the creature's wide, golden eyes. It screamed in agony, thrashing like a wild thing.

Their moment of triumph was short-lived, as once again, its sword lashed out, this time from a lower angle, and they once more scrambled backwards, slipping on the slick floor. Then sliding backwards like crabs, on their hands and feet, trying to stay out of range, even as the beast tried to regain its feet.

———

Caesarion hadn't had a coherent thought since regaining consciousness. He only knew that this creature threatened his wife, and everyone around him. Therefore, it needed to die. Still dazed, he watched as the creature tried once more to regain its footing. Stepped in. Caught its huge arm at wrist and just above the elbow, before it could move its sword into position for any further attacks. Swung the arm back and down in a calculated arc. And brought his knee up into that braced joint.

Without the strength of Mars in him, it wouldn't have worked. But he *felt* the elbow shatter. Heard the creature, already bleeding from terrible wounds, scream once more. But Caesarion was already moving forward, stripping the green-tinged sword from the creature's limp hand. Too large and unwieldy for a mortal man's hands, it must have weighed over fifty pounds, and once in motion, couldn't be stopped.

Two steps. A pivot. And Caesarion brought the blade around in an arc that made the air hum as he removed the creature's head from its shoulders.

As he watched the head topple away, he saw a look of *peace* cross its features, and stood, befuddled, as Malleolus staggered forward. The Praetorian was battered, sufficiently dazed that he stabbed the slumping, dead body repeatedly, before his fellows caught his arms to make him stop.

And then the great body simply faded away into nothingness. Leaving behind only its sword, still in Caesarion's hands. Breathing hard, he swung around. Checked on the condition of his friends — Malleolus, bruised and battered. Tiberius' arm shield arm hung limp at his side now. Antyllus, bleeding as his father, Antony, helped him remove his armor to inspect the wound. Antony himself, untouched. *He has the gods' own luck,* Caesarion thought, and glanced up, seeing the eyes of Isis continuing to glow. *Or perhaps we all did, this time.* "How many . . . how many did we lose?" he panted, looking around.

"I make it four Praetorians and four dignitaries," Antony said, his tones sharp and precise as he mopped blood away from Antyllus' chest. "Quite a few more wounded, however. And gods only know how many of the guests trampled each other."

Tiberius raised a hand. "*Dominus*, I hate to say this, but there could be other attacks. If I were the one who set this up, I'd have had fallbacks in place—"

Caesarion's mind went blank once more, and he headed straight for the door through which he'd last seen Eurydice—and Antony started calling out orders behind him, rapidly. "Some of you stay here, look after the civilians," he rapped out. "Get *medici* in here—some of these priests must be good for something. The rest of you, form up and follow. You're soldiers of Rome, not a band of deflowered vestals. Get those shields up and *move*."

Vaguely aware that *someone* was at least thinking, and grateful for it, Caesarion ignored the pain of his own head, spine, and ribs as he jogged through the temple, still holding a five-foot sword in one hand. Finding cowering dignitaries and priests in every nook and cranny, until he and his men burst from the temple's rear exit, out into the bright light and sea breezes, and found Eurydice, Cleopatra, Selene, and their escort boarding a barge that would have taken them back across to the palace.

Caesarion never remembered taking the steps that brought him to Eurydice. He was only vaguely aware that she'd somehow flown to him, and landed against his aching ribs with a thud that would have been more objectionable if it had been anyone else. And then, shaking a little, he just held onto her while Selene yelped at the sight of all the blood on Antyllus, and immediately ripped the hem of her gown to make bandages for him and the other men, and Cleopatra went to Antony, murmuring one soft word: "Indestructible."

In a small warehouse in the main city of Alexandria, Tahut-Nefer and several other priests shook inside their binding circle. One man had collapsed entirely, and didn't seem to be breathing. The other six were bathed in sweat, holding their heads as grinding pain surged through them. "What happened?" one of them asked feebly.

"We lost it," Tahut-Nefer snapped. "The beast has been killed, banished, or bound." He picked up the cuneiform tablet, with its impenetrable scribblings, and the parchment scroll that contained a transcription of the demon's name: *Kusarikku*, spirit of protection, and child of Tiamat.

It had taken all seven of them to bind the damnable creature and force it to their will. It hadn't been summoned to this world in over a thousand years, and had been bewildered by their assertions that this city was really the Uruk that it remembered. And that a foreign king and queen were here to assert dominance over the land, and that it should kill them. First the queen, if possible. Then the king. It had refused outright at first, stating, *Queens do not bear arms. It is dishonorable to attack them.*

But they'd borne down on it with their combined wills. Bound it with their own blood, and refused to give to it of their own life-energy. And sent it forth to do their bidding, their reluctant — and very powerful — slave. They hadn't dared get close enough to watch the attack themselves. Which would have been gratifying, but far too dangerous. Anyone could have wandered by them, tucked in some alcove of the Temple of Isis, and seen their ritual circle. Better by far, and safer, to use this warehouse near the water.

"If it's bound by our enemies, it could be compelled to

speak," one of his fellow priests said, thoughtfully, looking down at the dead man in their ritual circle.

"Leave him," Tahut-Nefer said, struck by the words. "We must make haste back to Thebes to consider our next effort. If the demon was in any way successful, we will hear of it shortly."

They cleaned the lamb's blood off the floor. Found their donkeys at the stable where they'd been left. And tried to get out of town—only to find that the Sixteenth Legion had been mobilized, and was working with the Urban Cohorts to block the streets, preventing people from leaving the city. Ships were being stopped in the port for the same reason. "What's happened?" Tahut asked a legionnaire as the man and several of his fellows dragged a wagon across a busy street, barricading it.

"There was an attempt on the lives of the Emperor and Empress," the legionnaire replied shortly. "They wish to see the perpetrators caught."

Tahut raised his hands in feigned shock. "Were either of them injured?" he asked, eyes wide.

"Not a scratch," the legionnaire answered. "Good thing, too. The Empress is with child."

Seething, the priests tried to find another way out of town, before the entire city was blocked off. And Tahut wondered angrily, how it was *possible* that their mission had missed its mark so completely. A mission that not even the high priest of Thoth had known about. One intended to rid them of these arrogant Romans, who, in spite of their power, were not gods. Not *pharaohs*. Who had no respect for the ancient traditions of Egypt.

And once they were gone, replace them with their younger, more malleable siblings. Selene would make a tolerable queen, until young Gaius, taken from Cleopatra, could be raised by priests and nobles who understood tradition. And then, when he was thirteen or so, and Selene was twenty-five, they could be married, be worshipped as living gods, and could continue the line of the Ptolemies. As the gods clearly intended.

Of course, to effect any of these changes, they needed Caesarion, Eurydice, and preferably Alexander and Cleopatra herself, all to die. *How could we have failed, with such a powerful spirit? Perhaps we should have gone with one of the filth spirits, instead. Infected them all with diseases that no medicine can cure. But once those diseases start, it's hard to control them. We could lose the entirety of the lineage. Though . . .* Tahut-Nefer teetered on the brink of an idea so vast, he almost couldn't conceive of it. *Dynasties have fallen before. And the gods have favored new pharaonic houses in the past. But . . . only with their direct blessing.*

He considered that carefully. *Though when Horemheb the general took power after the time of the Accursed Ones, he was followed first by Ramses, and then, at last, by Seti. Whose rule the gods blessed, as they did not bless the short reigns of Ramses or Horemheb.* He contemplated that for a moment. *Perhaps the gods would bestow their power on . . . worthy replacements. Some noble, not even of the line of Ptolemy.* The grandness of it captured his imagination as he rode on his donkey's stolid back. *What a wonder it would be, to excise all that is Hellene and foul from our lands. To send Rome back to its stinking flocks. And all by simply eliminating their rulers.*

It did not occur to him that Rome's strength didn't rest entirely in one family, but in many. And that the very heart of the original Republic's military and social doctrine was that when one man fell, another man would step forward and take his place. His mind was entirely too full of dazzling images of the Hellene temples and buildings around him being torn to the ground, replaced by proper Egyptian ones. The tomb of

Alexander torn down as well, and his body thrown into the sea from which he and his men had come. Pharaohs who were *truly* living gods once more, not the abased descendants of some Hellene horseman.

It passed the time, while they tried to find a road out of the city that had not yet been blocked by Roman troops in Roman armor carrying Roman swords, in the service of a Roman emperor who simply didn't have the courtesy to *die*.

Chapter VII: Truths

The door of the storeroom slammed open, and Damkina jerked awake at its echoes, pulling her head away from Ehsan's shoulder. They'd been held here for days now, and provided enough food and water to keep life in their bodies—though she was guarded while she ate, and her gag re-applied before the guards stepped back out into the hall outside. She couldn't blame them for their caution, but it *was* infuriating, especially since she'd come to them in the best faith she could offer.

A week without bathing had left her miserably aware of her own smell, and her scalp itched, but her attendant spirits assured her constantly that this wasn't the result of fleas, thankfully. Ehsan wasn't in any better condition, but he helped her to stand, her back on fire from having slept sitting up against the wall for so long.

This time, however, when the two men she was accustomed to seeing entered, the younger of the two, the blond man, was bruised and battered. His gleaming Roman armor held scuff marks and traces of dried blood. The older man, with his sardonic dark eyes, appeared unscathed, but impatient. "Come along," he told them, beckoning. "The Imperator wants to see you."

There's been an attack, she thought tiredly, and shuffled behind them as bidden, watching as a dozen other soldiers folded in around them, alertness in their eyes and stances.

Buzz of activity all through the palace, like a hive that had been hit with a stick, as servants and soldiers hastened this way and that. She and Ehsan were escorted into an anteroom, and the younger man removed her gag, though afterwards, he drew his sword and stood behind her, its point resting just between her shoulder blades. "I don't suppose there's a chance that I could get a drink of water?" Damkina croaked, her voice harsh in her dry throat.

To her surprise, the older man filled a cup and brought it to her. She took it in her chained hands, deeply bruised by the constant weight of the iron shackles, and slipped it under her veil to sip it gratefully, before giving the cup to Ehsan. The men around her blinked at this courtesy to someone whom they probably assumed was a slave, but permitted the gesture.

And that was when the others entered, and Damkina's eyebrows rose. The soldiers wore armor, but the pair who entered wore less martial gear. The man wore only a long blue tunic and boots, and had dark hair, gold-tinged skin, and shockingly red eyes, all to go with a grim expression. A huge, hooked sword of verdigris green copper hung over his shoulder, suspended by a hastily-fashioned sling. A young woman walked at his side, in the typical flowing garments of a Roman woman, and her eyes were as golden as those of a lioness.

They've been marked out by the gods or spirits, Damkina thought. She tilted her head to the side, and one of her spirits let her borrow its vision for a moment. She sucked in her breath in awe. The man *seethed* with power, glowing a brilliant crimson in a spirit's vision. And the woman did, too, but there were ripples and distortions over her frame that took Damkina a moment to interpret. Her core glow, a brilliant golden flame, was overshadowed by an aura of red that moved when she did, but didn't entirely overlap her frame. And at her heart, a pinprick of white light that was not of her, but part of her.

Damkina folded her hands together before her heart, bowing over them with the profound respect every Magi showed to those who had equivalent power.

"Imperator Ptolemy Julius Caesarion Philopator Philomator Aquilus," the older man said, a string of names that meant absolutely nothing to Damkina, "and his wife and sister, Eurydice Julia Accipitra. This is our captive Magus, who's given her name as Damkina Banit."

"She could have had co-conspirators," the younger man behind her said. "But on the whole, since she told us that silver might work . . . and it *did*. . . I'm not inclined to believe that."

"The attack was a little too vigorous, and came too close to succeeding, for this to have been an effort to gain our trust, and bring her into our counsels," the older man added, nodding.

Then there was an attack. And they survived it. Praise the dead gods. The Council won't send assassins after me for having caused the death of an Emperor, destabilizing the whole region. Or send me any letters of congratulation, either, for that matter. Damkina sagged in relief for a moment.

The Imperator nodded, staring at her and Ehsan. Anger burned in his eyes, though his face never shifted expression. "The creature that attacked us," he said abruptly. "Twice the height of a man. Legs of a bull, and the horns of one. What was it?"

She exhaled, eyeing the sword he carried. "I hesitate to speak its Name," she said carefully. "To Name something *can* summon it."

"I took its head off with its own sword," the Imperator said coldly, jerking a thumb back over his shoulder at the huge blade. Beside her, Ehsan stiffened, making a noise that she knew was made of pure incredulity. "Then the body vanished, leaving only its sword behind. Unless it can stick its head back on, it's not coming back."

Damkina grimaced, impressed in spite of herself. "Very

well. Generally, when a human has managed to fell the mortal vessel of a spirit, it results in the temporary banishment of that spirit—often for a hundred years, though not always. It depends greatly on the power of the spirit. If they can walk between the worlds at will, or if they need to be summoned. But with its own weapon? In the hands of one such as yourself?" She shook her head. "It may well be truly dead, and that would be a tragedy."

"A tragedy?" the older man rapped out, his expression hardening. Damkina felt the sword dig into her shoulders more pointedly.

"Yes," she said calmly. "Kusarikku, to give him his proper name, is . . . was . . . a protective spirit. The son of the goddess Tiamat. I'd hoped to be able to bargain with him—carefully—for his services in the future. He was summoned in the days of Uruk-that-was to protect children and households." She met each set of eyes solidly. "He was never one for wanton destruction or attack."

"Then explain why he killed four of my men, several foreign dignitaries, and, when given a choice between attacking me, and pursing my wife, started to follow her?" The man's voice held ice.

Oh, by the dead gods. "I cannot say for certain," Damkina replied carefully, "but spirits can be *compelled*, by those with enough will. Or, in some cases, by several people, working to overcome their will in tandem." She swallowed, her throat again dry, this time with fear at the murder currently lurking in those red eyes. "If I may ask . . . did he take any other opportunities to pursue her, past the first?"

Frowns around the room, and then the Imperator shook his head. "We had him ringed. He fought us because we gave him no other choice—"

"Ah," the older man interposed, grimacing. "*Dominus,*

after you were rendered unconscious, the creature really didn't have anyone else who was terribly hurting it. My son and Tiberius hit it with the silver brazier legs, and Malleolus here had that silver dagger that the Magus gave him. But those were . . . flea bites. It could have just walked through the Praetorians around it. It didn't." The man turned and looked at Damkina. "Why not?"

She shrugged slightly. "He is a protector. Was," she corrected herself. "Also, at the moment, the Empress is . . . confusing to a spirit's eyes." Damkina raised her eyebrows. "My own spirits showed me how they perceive both the Imperator and his wife when they entered this room. My guess is, not only would Kusarikku be reluctant to attack a pregnant woman, but he had difficulty perceiving her as his target—"

She hadn't expected how strong the reactions around her would be. Exclamations. The golden-eyed woman moved slightly closer to her husband. The sword at Damkina's back dug in deeply enough that she could feel a trickle of blood run down her spine now. "How precisely do you know of my wife's pregnancy?" the emperor asked through his teeth.

Damkina exhaled. "I said that my spirits shared their perceptions with me," she replied patiently. "At the moment, there is her inner core, her own life-essence. The child's essence overlaps with hers. And of course, there is, ah, *your* life-essence present within her as well," she added delicately, hoping that she wouldn't lose her own tongue for these words.

"My—?" The red eyes blinked, and she could see he'd been thrown off his stride for a moment.

"Through sexual relations," she specified, as delicately as she could. "Malefic spirits, ones that hunt humans at the request of this summoner or that, often have difficulty perceiving pregnant women, because while they might be given a piece of hair or a drop of blood to identify their target's life-essence, when so many overlap, the target becomes warped. Almost invisible. This is one of the reasons why female summoners are often more powerful than male ones. Or at least, safer." She shrugged.

"Must make whores damned near undetectable," the older man opined.

Damkina looked straight at him. "Yes," she said, not lowering her eyes. "That is entirely correct. It is also the core of how many female Magi render themselves undetectable to spirit tracking, and the basis of much of the old sexual magic practiced by the priestess of Ishtar. Before, of course, Ishtar was killed, along with most of our gods." She raised her bound hands uncomfortably, but no one took the hint to loosen her chains.

"So Tahut-Nefer—and I think it's clear that it was him, and not some other priest, because any other priest would have specified me as the first target," the emperor said now, clearly thinking out loud, "—targeted Eurydice, but the creature was either confused by the pregnancy. . . or fought the mission it had been given, because it . . . ."

"It conflicted with his basic nature," Damkina supplied after a moment's pause. "He was, as I said, a protector. Not a killer."

The sword at her back eased, and she took her first full breath in several minutes. The golden-eyed woman lifted her head, her expression suddenly furious. "I should have killed him in Rome," she said, speaking for the first time. Her voice was as chill as her husband's had been.

"He hadn't done anything worth killing him for at the time," the emperor told his wife grimly. "That has changed, however."

"I will do it myself," she added now, her eyes narrowing. "No icicles here in the desert. I'll end him in *flame.*"

Damkina's eyes widened. And, very carefully, she raised one finger. "Ah, my lady? I do beg your pardon, but if you are all not entirely aware of the effect of pregnancy on a spirit's sight, is it at all possible that you do not know about the effects of magic use during pregnancy?"

Every head in the room snapped towards her. And the young empress asked, "What effects?"

Damkina swallowed. "You tap into your own life-energy to *start* every spell, do you not? And the more powerful the spell, the more it drains you, correct? And if you've ever attempted a very great working—one that encompassed a space larger than this room, for example—you would be aware of tiredness. Overextend your will, and you might sleep for a day, or bleed from the nose." She paused, watching as the woman nodded, recognition in her face. "If there is another life in your body, and you overextend your own will, where do you suppose you might take the energy from? Or, failing that, if you weaken yourself, where do you suppose your body will turn to restore the energy lost?"

The young woman's mouth fell open, but no sound emerged. Blank terror in her eyes for a moment, and her husband took one of her hands in his. Tightly, Damkina noticed. "The few female Magi that exist," Damkina added, mildly, "have all learned to store some of our vital will in crystals or other objects. So that we may draw on *those* to empower our spells. If there is need. This also permits our spells to be stored in objects and devices." She sighed inwardly. "So few people in the world have truly *studied* magic. Most are content to call it the will of the gods, and leave it at that."

The young empress' eyes lit up suddenly, and she whispered rapidly to her husband, who shook his head. Emphatically and repeatedly. More whispering, and then, abruptly, he stated, his voice tight, "We've had agents making inquiries about you for the last week. No one in Alexandria has ever seen you socialize with other Chaldean or Parthian residents." A pause, and then a sharp demand, "What are you doing here, Magus? What's your purpose?"

She blinked, taken off-guard. And then looked at Ehsan, whose expression was blank, but whose eyes held grim fear. "I came to Alexandria three years ago to find the men who did this to me when I was a child," Damkina said, pulling her veil away from her face with her bound hands. She knew what it looked like, but could see the shock in their eyes as they saw her disfigured face fully for the first time. The livid color of the scars had faded over the past thirteen years. But the scars themselves never would, long slashes extending from just under her cheekbones to the corners of her mouth.

"My father was not a Magus," she continued tightly. "He was, however, Chaldean nobility. And he took my younger brother and me to Judea once, on a mission to promote understanding and peaceful relations. Some of our fellow travelers did not get that message. They attacked us and our guards. Murdered my father and brother. And would have done the same to me, save that they had another purpose for me first. At the time, I had no spells. They'd thought they'd cut my face, rape me, and leave me the sole survivor, as a message not to bring *spies* into their territory." She looked away. "When the fourth one was raping me, I set him on fire while he was still in me. And managed to run away while his companions were trying to beat out the flames. The three who remained—two Romans and a Judean—I've sought over the years. My spirits have managed to track them this far, but the trail's gone cold." Her voice had long since gone empty, and remained so as she added, "And when I find them, I intend to kill them. Roman citizens or no."

There was a pause, and the man behind her commented, tightly, "The rape of a virgin is punishable by death in Rome, *domina*."

"Magus," she corrected automatically. "A lovely thing Roman law must be. I'm sure it keeps you all warm at night."

"Is that your only purpose here?" the emperor asked, his face expressionless.

"I pass along information I receive to the Council of Magi. Mostly so that they do not interfere with me, or demand that I return home. Ehsan would make the latter very difficult, in any event." She gestured towards her guard, who grunted in what passed for agreement.

"A spy, then." The older man sounded disgusted.

She shrugged. "At present, the only loyalties I have are to the Magi, to what remains of my family, and to my friends." A nod to Ehsan, once more. "I pass along rumors and gossip, and the Council leaves me alone." *And I compromise people, if I can, but that's towards my own ends, not necessarily the Council's.*

Another whispered conference, and then the young empress asked, quickly, "You said that your . . . friend . . . would make it difficult to return home. Why is that?"

Damkina looked at Ehsan, who returned her a brooding stare that said, more plainly than words, *You shouldn't have said anything about me at all. Let me stay invisible, damn it all.*

She sighed. And, committed now to telling as much truth as would keep them both alive, Damkina replied, very slowly, "I mentioned to this one last week," she pointed at the older man, "that the Magi have not turned over the Immortals to our *beloved* Parthian overlords." She swallowed.

The room went silent. "He doesn't look like an Immortal," the older man said, very quietly.

"No," Damkina returned, tightly. "The process for making a man into an Immortal has changed over the centuries. In the time of Darius, a spirit was planted in a living man's body, and he was left . . . intact. Wholly himself. A *reward* to young, promising noblemen for loyalty and service and fealty." She exhaled. "In later days, the kings of Persia began to suspect that some of their companions were less loyal to them, than to . . . Persia as a whole. Or to other nobles. Troublesome issues of free will and trust. So they began to alter the . . . chosen ones."

She licked her dry lips, grateful that her veil once more concealed her face. "None of the Magi were supposed to be making new Immortals," she added now, sharply. "It's been forbidden by the Council, until the kings of Parthia either stabilize, or are overthrown." She looked at Ehsan, misery uncoiling inside her. "A rogue among us decided that the Parthian kings *needed* the Immortals to cement their grip on power. Found in Ehsan one of the best swords of the region. And invited him and several others to his estate, where he drugged them and . . . removed the things that kings usually find detract from loyalty. Tongues that wag. The seat of desire. And then put a spirit in him. But this Magus fumbled the Name, you see," she added, shaking her head. "So instead of a spirit well-accustomed to taking over a human, body and soul, he planted a smaller, weaker spirit in Ehsan's form. He had enough will to fight it. To retain his identity. And, as far as he's ever been able to explain it to me, he broke free and killed the Magus who'd done this to him. Killed half a dozen servants and guards. Then fled, bleeding. And found my uncle's estate, where the servants in turn found him, starving. Trying to eat raw eggs, because nothing else could he manage with a stump for a tongue."

Ehsan looked away, his face rigid with humiliation relived. Damkina sighed, and looked back at the Romans. "If I take him back to Chaldea, there is no one there who won't know what he is. An Immortal, in every way *but* the mindless submission to the will of the king of kings. Someday, I don't doubt that they'll find a way to ensure it," she added, darkly. "But I won't turn him over to be the slave of a Parthian. To have a different spirit forced into his body, and his own mind erased. I *won't*." She looked away. "If you feel a need to dismiss us from your lands for having brought word of this plot to your attention, and because you dare not risk the presence of a Magus in one of your cities. . . " tears prickled at her eyes, which she did her best to hold back, thinking, *Even speaking these truths out loud abases us. I've humiliated Ehsan, humiliated myself, and for what?* ". . . it will be somewhat difficult to find some part of the world not occupied by either Rome or Persia." *Where would we even go? India? They have libraries and magic, yes, but how will I ever find my vengeance, exiled* <u>*there?*</u>

More urgent whispers from the empress to her husband, and reluctance clear in his face, he finally nodded. And ordered their guards, "Let them clean themselves, and give them more comfortable accommodations. My beloved has a few other questions she'd like to ask you, Magus. If you're inclined to answer them once you've had a hot meal and a change of clothing."

The sword withdrew from her back, and she could hear it being sheathed now, an almost-noiseless rustle as the blade slid into its leather scabbard. Her wrists and Ehsan's, both being unshackled. And then, to her utter surprise, the guard who'd stood behind her offered Ehsan the curving silver dagger that she'd told her guard to give him. "Thank you," the soldier said, his voice gruff. "Needed to be about two feet longer if I wanted to do any real harm to that thing, but at least I kept it occupied. Somewhat." He rubbed at his bruised face in explanation, then turned slightly towards Damkina. "If you'll come with me, *Magus,*" stress on her title, "we can see about those rooms. And a bath, and hot food."

Wide-eyed, Damkina nodded, and followed, gesturing for Ehsan to follow.

In another room of the sprawling palace complex, a smell of medicinal herbs and a hint of incense filled the air, as the royal physicians, long denied a change to practice their art on anyone but the courtiers and servants, eagerly offered their services to the wounded Praetorians and the rest of Caesarion's entourage. Their faces fell, however, at being told by Antony, sharply, that they could *assist* the *medici* of the Praetorians, but that the legions cared for their own. And then the new Roman governor of Egypt left, letting the various physicians get on with the business at hand.

Antyllus and Tiberius had biers next to each other. The physicians gave each of them a foul-tasting draught, which made Antyllus even more light-headed and giddy than he already felt. "Should he have that, given that he hit his head?" Tiberius asked. Antyllus heard him as if from underwater, and stared at him for a moment, wondering why it looked as if the younger man's body kept distorting and twisting until he blinked. And then looked solid again, for at least another two heartbeats, before collapsing in on itself again.

"It's a small dose, *dominus,*" the *medicus* in charge told Tiberius. "Enough to keep him from squirming when we put the stitches in."

They set to work, washing the wound in Antyllus' chest with vinegar, which burned like fire, but . . . distantly. He felt as if he were observing the pain, rather than experiencing it, and looked over with mild interest, hearing Tiberius grunt in discomfort as a *medicus* and an Egyptian physician moved the broken bones in his arm around, trying to get them to line up properly before applying the boards of a splint and wrapping it with cloth. "Better run," Antyllus said, his head still spinning. "They might not stop wrapping, and turn you into something fit for a sarcophagus."

That got him dirty looks from every physician present, but he also received a rare half-smile from Tiberius—before another grimace twisted the younger man's face as he struggled not to cry out as broken bones sawed at tender internal flesh. "I owe you," Antyllus told Tiberius, watching as a physician near him threaded an iron needle that had just been held in the heart of a lamp's flame to purify it. "You saved my life."

Sweat trickled down Tiberius' face as the physicians now gently settled his splinted arm into a sling. "You're the one who put weapons in our hands that actually made a difference," Tiberius reminded him. "And you stood side-by-side with me and your father. So I think it's fair to say you'd have done the same for me, if I'd been the one smart enough to grab the brazier, and get pushed back over the altar for my pains." He swung his feet off the bier, and offered Antyllus his good hand for a wrist-clasp. "Don't squirm when they put in the stitches. You'll heal crooked."

Antyllus chuckled, ignoring the increasingly distant pain in his chest. "A jest from Tiberius. The world may end now." But he accepted the wrist-clasp, and then closed his eyes, bracing himself for the tender ministrations of the *medicus'* skilled hands. Clamped his hands on the edges of the bier, and swore under his breath at the first few stitches. After that, the pain dulled into something that resembled familiarity, or at least monotony.

And that was where Selene found him, as she scurried into the warm dimness of the physicians' quarters, having been directed there by a passing servant. She didn't see Tiberius leaving by a different door, but rather, focused on the various men lying groaning on their biers. Most of them had broken bones from having been thrown across the temple, or having had their fellows fall on them with great force. But Antyllus was in the process of being stitched up, and the physicians wouldn't let her near at first, even when she told them, quietly, "But I've read about the process many times — oh!" That last, as she got a look past one of their shoulders at how much blood seemed to be involved. "Oh, Juno and Venus. Is it *that* bad?"

Her world spun for a moment, but one of the physicians, this one an Egyptian, took pity on her and took her aside. "It's actually relatively superficial, my lady," he told her with gentle deference, his shaved head gleaming in the lamplight. "The blade, however sharp it was, and how powerfully it was swung, to cut through an iron breastplate, didn't damage any bones. Just skin and muscle. We're stitching it up, and he'll need to rest until it heals."

Selene blinked, still seeing the red every time she closed her eyes. "He's an archer," she told the physician quietly. "Will it affect his ability to hold his bow?"

A shrug. "Perhaps at first, but most ability and strength can be regained with patience and time. Of course, rumor has it that your brother holds the power to heal in his hands."

"I'll ask him," Selene said immediately. For once, the fear of her terrifying eldest brother was subsumed by a greater fear: an Antyllus unable to go about the world, smiling and doing precisely what he chose, was unthinkable to her. "The tribune is a friend of his, I mean," she added rapidly. "I'm sure he'd heal Antyllus anyway—"

"Is that the voice of a lark that I hear?" Antyllus asked, his voice muzzy, and, after some wrapping of bandages around his ribs, the *medici* propped him up, sitting and permitted Selene to come closer. And her reward was a sleepy smile as he reached out and caught her fingers in his. "It *is* a lark, come to perch on my hand. What a wonder." He closed his eyes for a moment. "Did you come to sing for me?"

One of the Roman physicians leaned over and spoke to her quietly, "He took a hit to the head, too, *domina*. We heard Lord Tiberius ask him why he'd suggested using a rope on the creature a few minutes ago, and Lord Antonius said he didn't remember making the remark. It's best, if someone's taken a head wound, even if it's not bleeding on the outside, that they don't sleep immediately. Try to keep him awake, if you would."

And then the physicians all decamped, swarming to other beds, filled with other groaning men. Selene awkwardly sat on the edge of Antyllus' bed, wondering briefly where Tiberius *was*, if he'd just been here to ask that question. But then her whole world narrowed in focus to the warm hand holding hers, and the urgent need to keep Antyllus awake. So she shook his hand a little, offering, a little catch in her voice, "I didn't bring my *kithara* here. And . . . even if I had . . . I'd, well . . . need both hands to play it."

Antyllus managed to open his eyes, fighting the call of whatever medicines the physicians had given him. "A good thing you didn't bring it, then, for I refuse to give up my prize, now that I've taken it." He lifted her hand a little, pretending to wave it like a banner.

And, as always in his presence, Selene felt her lips quirk up at the corners. "How can you jest at a time like this?" she asked him, warmth welling up in her chest. "You're *hurt*."

His eyes started to drift closed again. "What are my other options?" Antyllus asked sleepily. "I get to lie on my back and hold a pretty girl's hand. Should I weep?" And then he tugged gently at her hand, pulling her closer on the bier, so that her hip landed against his thigh, and he opened his eyes again, looking more alert. "There are four good men lying dead in another room. I'm alive. And the worst I can complain about is that I haven't inherited my father's talent for ducking." A wicked light filled his eyes for a moment. "If you're not here to sing, lark," he added, very softly, "there's another purpose to which those lovely lips could be put."

Selene felt her face turn hot. "You really *did* hit your head," she told him, trying to pull her hand away. But he sat up further, with a grunt of effort, and caught her face with his other hand, catching her open lips with his own. And for several moments, Selene completely forgot that there were other people in the room. Wounded men and physicians, all quite busy about their work or in worlds of their own pain.

When he lifted his lips again, Selene felt as dizzy as if *she* were the one drugged. She touched his face lightly, and watched his expression lighten as she did. "If you want more of that," he teased very quietly, "you'll just have to marry me. No more free samples, *domina*."

And in that split-second, feeling the danger of mortality acutely, she knew that she loved his warmth and light heart, though a voice at the back of her head whispered another name still. And Selene swallowed, and told Antyllus, "So perhaps you should go ahead and marry me, then."

He blinked. "They've drugged me very well, little lark. I'm definitely beginning to hallucinate. I thought you just accepted my on-going and very earnest proposal of marriage."

Selene flushed again at the teasing words. ". . . yes. Yes." She paused, eyeing his still-dazed expression. "I said *yes.*"

He nodded soberly, his mind clearly not working with its accustomed speed. "Well, then. Isn't that a thing . . . you really mean it?"

"How many times do I have to say yes?" Selene asked, embarrassed.

"I don't know. How many times have I asked you?" Antyllus let his head fall back on the pillow, but a wide smile crossed his features, lighting up his dark eyes. "Let's say at least as many."

"You're *horrible.*" Selene writhed a little inwardly, but relaxed as he pulled her hand towards him, and kissed the back of it lightly.

"Best you get used to that now," he told her peaceably. "That way, you can't lay accusations before the Senate in years to come, for grounds of divorce on account of my having misrepresented myself as other than horrible to young women." His eyes closed.

"Don't go to sleep!" Selene said anxiously, her hand tightening on his.

"You're actually worried about a scratch like this, and a bit of a bump on the head?" he asked, chuckling a little. "I'll be up and around and being horrible to you at every opportunity by morning. I give you my oath. On the Styx, if you like."

So immersed was she in all this, that it wasn't until she left the infirmary to go find Caesarion, to beg him to heal Antyllus' 'scratch,' as he persisted in calling the ten-inch gash over his sternum, that reality struck her. And dazed, she stood in a corridor for a long moment. She'd given her word to marry him. And the delight she felt at that realization was suddenly tempered by another realization: *Tiberius gave up his betrothal to Vipsania to come here and court me. Alexander and he have broken off . . . everything . . . for this very reason. And I've loved . . . or thought I loved . . . Tiberius, for years. And even told him so.* She swallowed, putting one hand on the wall of the corridor, just under a brilliantly-colored fresco depicting some important acceptance of tribute by one of her ancestors, from some occupied country or another. *The only reason he did any of that, past the initial offer, was because of my words.* Her throat ached for a moment, and she wondered if she was about to hurt Tiberius.

And standing in that corridor, Selene rationalized it all. *He told me himself that if I chose Antyllus, he'd attend the wedding and wish me well. He said he holds me in affection. But that just means he sees me as a sister, surely. Someone who . . . needs to be taken care of. For Alexander's sake. Maybe . . . maybe he won't forgive me. For not acknowledging what he's given up. But he'd . . . he'd have given it all up anyway, wouldn't he? If he really wanted to marry Vipsania in four or five years, nothing would have stopped him. And if he really wanted to marry me . . . wouldn't he have kissed me by now? Shown some more overt sign? And in the end, I shouldn't choose to marry someone, because I think I might owe them that. I . . . should marry Antyllus. Who's said he could grow fond of me. And this is surely love that I feel for him.*

She stared ahead, down the hall, her eyes burning. *Antyllus was the one who took me to the door, to safety.* Though, in scrupulous honesty, she knew they'd *both* caught her arms and dragged her from her chair, when her legs had been locked in terror. *Tiberius turned back. He chose to fight. Antyllus chose to get me to safety. There can be only one decision. And I've made it.*

"It's the right decision," Selene said out loud, looking

up at the ceiling. "Mother Venus, I know it's the *right* decision. Isn't it? And it's made, and it's done." She covered her mouth with her fingers, swallowing. *I just don't know how I can look Tiberius in the eye and tell him that I chose someone else.*

Tiberius had been halfway to the room he'd been allocated by the palace staff, when, muzzy-headed from his own draught of poppy-blood, he remembered that he'd left his damned sword and kit behind in the infirmary. *Some soldier you are,* he chided himself. *Someone takes your armor off you, and you forget it? Bad form.* He turned and headed back, forgetting in the blissful, pain-stealing fog, that he'd been told that servants would bring his gear for him. He had, after all, only one hand to carry it with at the moment.

On reaching the infirmary door, he'd opened it, and through a sea of bustling healers standing over biers of wounded men, he saw Antyllus pull Selene into him for a deep kiss. Saw, as in the moonlit atrium a month before, her lack of rejection of this very forward overture. She could have pulled away. Her face could have gone cold. Instead, she wore a kind of dazed smile.

And in that moment, all the protective haze of the poppy-blood seemed to burn away. Tiberius turned and left, closing the door softly behind him. Returned to his room, where, yes, the servants had already brought his kit. And quietly, methodically, began packing it away, one-handed, into the chest in which it had traveled with him from Rome. Shaving kit, strigil, the writing kit his brother Drusus had given him years ago. *My entire life can be summed up in one bag or one box. Nevermind the palatial residences of most patricians. My villa in Rome is empty.* Inconsequential thoughts, to keep himself from dwelling on anything else.

A light tap at the door, which opened before Tiberius could even say, *enter*. He glanced up, saw that it was Caesarion, and stood immediately to attention, as if they were in a *castra*, not in a palace. A blank stare from the emperor, encompassing the fact that Tiberius was in the middle of packing, and then a cleared throat. "Brought you something," Caesarion said, holding up a battered silver brazier leg. It was clearly the one Tiberius had used, since it was still stained by the creature's odd, blue blood, covering the entire jagged tip, where he'd shoved it into its eye. "It's not really the *spoila opima*, but it's a suitable sort of trophy of a very fine moment."

The *spoila opima* were considered the preeminent trophies of war. They were the arms and armor of an enemy king or general, taken by a Roman general after defeating the enemy in single combat. No one had taken the *spoila opima* since the Punic Wars, two hundred years ago. And the last person to have taken them was Marcus Claudius Marcellus, one of Tiberius' own distant ancestors.

"Thank you," Tiberius said, accepting the brazier leg, feeling acid burn at the back of his throat. He had no idea how he'd ever look at the damned thing, given that he and Antyllus had fought side-by-side, with the same weapons, just hours before. He tossed it, without much care, into the chest with the rest of his belongings.

Caesarion's face creased into a frown. "Tiberius, why in Dis' name are you *packing*?" He looked around. "And why aren't you having one of the servants help you with that? You've got two broken bones in your arm, for the gods' sakes."

"I don't like letting servants or slaves touch my belongings," Tiberius replied evenly. *Or me.* "Once, long ago, I'd been writing a list of reasons that my mother should let Drusus and me go live with our cousins among the Claudii. I left it on my desk. One of the better-educated slaves took it to Octavian. The next time I saw that piece of parchment, it was in his hands, and he read to me from my list of well-reasoned arguments as he had that same slave beat me." He cast about for what was left to pack, and realized he hadn't put any clothes in the trunk yet. His tunics were in another chest across the room, which he opened one-handed, braced the lid with his right shoulder, and dug for his clothing with his right hand, before bringing an arm-load back across the room to dump loosely into the sea-chest.

A silent blink as Caesarion absorbed that, and then, mildly, carefully, "Yes, but why are you packing now?"

Tiberius straightened. "*Dominus*, when you re-open the harbor, I'd like permission to be on the first ship back to Rome. Britannia and the Tenth await." And before Caesarion could ask the inevitable follow-up question, Tiberius added, his voice colorless, "I happened back into the infirmary in time to see Antyllus pressing his attentions on your sister again. She didn't seem to be objecting, so I rather think her mind is made up. No sense in me staying around. I'll just make the situation uncomfortable." *Well, I'll be uncomfortable. Antyllus definitely appeared quite comfortable where he was.* Tiberius rigorously repressed that line of thought as unworthy, and kept his face blank.

Caesarion put a hand on top of a table, his frown becoming more of a scowl. "Pressing his attentions?"

"Kissing, sir," Tiberius specified clearly. "It's happened before, and I didn't mention it at the time because she didn't slap him." He turned back to the chest, and once more braced it open, one-handed. Finished emptying it out this time, and transferred the contents. *Armor, done, clothing, done, hygiene materials, done, writing kit, done, oils and brushes for armor and sword, done. Maps of Gaul and what we know of Britannia, done.*

I'm done here.

Caesarion's face eased. "Well, kissing's fine, though the *in public* part is unacceptable. I expected a certain amount of that from both of you —" he paused, looking at Tiberius. "You *haven't* kissed her?"

Coldness spread through Tiberius' chest. "No, sir. She's your sister, and Alexander's, and I wanted to treat her with all the *respect* that she's due. The respect it seemed she hadn't been accorded by your mother, or by many others." *That, and it never seemed like a kiss would be welcomed. Always looking away. Always embarrassed.*

He finished latching the chest, and looked around for the piece of rope which had secured it on its way up from the ship. "To be honest," Tiberius said, feeling chill pervade him, down to his bones, "it was a foregone conclusion before we even came here. No one in their right mind chooses winter over summer, or night over day." Not finding the rope, he turned back to Caesarion, feeling somehow clean and very empty. The way he sometimes felt after a bad fever, when he'd vomited and evacuated and sweated out every fluid from his body, and was left shaking and light-headed in its wake. "I should never have come here," Tiberius added with a shrug. *But I wanted her to make that clear choice, for herself. She has.*

Caesarion's heavy brows contracted again. "Tiberius, if you *hadn't* been here, there's a good chance that Antyllus would be dead right now," he said sharply. "You saved his damned life. Antony was the closest to his son when Antyllus went down. Antony's no slouch with a sword, but he's *fifty-nine.* I'd be looking at two dead men now, one of them my mother's husband." He gestured at the trunk, where the silver brazier leg had just been stowed. "I gave you that to remind anyone who sees it, that you're a damned hero. Including you."

"I did my duty, sir," Tiberius said, hearing the words as if from a very great distance. *Please don't say anything else, Caesarion. Nothing that will make me hate myself any more than I already do.* "Any one of the Praetorians around us could have picked up that piece of silver and done exactly the same thing. It takes no great courage to get in the way."

Caesarion looked deeply upset about something, though Tiberius couldn't have said why. "Tiberius, I'm going to ask Malleolus to stay on extra years. As an *evocatus*." *Evocati* were the chosen men of the legions. They'd served their full terms of service, and had been asked, at the request of a legate or consul, to stay on. They were revered, as such. "I want him to stay here in Egypt and keep Eurydice and the child safe—"

"Congratulations, sir," Tiberius murmured, as this was the first he'd heard of Eurydice's pregnant state.

"Stow it. I wasn't finished talking." Caesarion didn't take offense at the interruption, but his brows remained furrowed. "You've been with the Tenth since I transferred you to them in Hispania. I was *hoping* you'd come into the Guard. Eventually even become their prefect. You're the best with a sword that I've ever seen."

Tiberius waited a moment to be sure that Caesarion had finished this time. "My brother will be better than I am, when he's had more experience. He's faster on his feet." He looked straight ahead, not focusing on anything. "While I thank you for the courtesy, *dominus*, the requirement is currently ten years' service before becoming a Praetorian. Please do not waive that for my sake. I would prefer to do my duty." His eyes flicked towards Caesarion. "Do I have your leave to leave for Britannia when the harbor re-opens?"

"And if I said I need you here, to help deal with the mess Cornelius Gallus has made in Thebes?" Caesarion asked heavily.

"I would do as my emperor commands." Empty words. Hollow soul.

"For the sake of the people and the Senate of fucking Rome?" Caesarion rapped out.

"Yes, sir."

There was a long pause. "You may leave for Britannia once I re-open the harbor. Quintus Cicero has command of the Tenth at the moment. Cicero Minor has the Seventh. I have all the Ciceros I need up there. Apparently, I need a Claudius there, too." Caesarion held out his hand, offering a wrist-clasp, as between equals. "Tiberius, for the record, I think she made the wrong decision."

"Right or wrong, it's hers." Tiberius accepted the wrist-clasp. "I'd like to move my belongings to the barracks, sir—"

"You're *my guest*," Caesarion refused, and this time, his tone sounded like iron. "You are my guest, Eurydice's guest, and you will not leave us until the harbor opens."

Tiberius straightened back to attention. "Yes, *dominus*."

And he stayed that way, even when Caesarion reached out, put a hand on his injured arm, and healed the broken bones. A quiet word of thanks, and still, he stood straight, until the door closed behind Caesarion. Then, with nothing left to do with which to occupy his empty time until whenever the harbor opened, Tiberius dug in his chest. Pulled out his writing kit and the maps of Britannia. And sat at the room's low, Egyptian-style table, to plot out how, if *he* were a Briton, he'd go about attacking Gaul and re-taking it.

There was nothing else really left for him, after all. The potential tie with Selene, gone before he'd even realized that it existed. The tie to Alexander, severed, out of honor, because pursuing Selene while remaining connected to Alexander would have been wrong. The tie to his mother, severed, both for Selene's sake, and for his own, because he couldn't bear to hear Livia spew poison any longer. The tie of friendship to Antyllus strained to the breaking point, because the other had capitalized on Selene's feelings for an injured man hours after Tiberius had saved his life. The only things left to Tiberius were his love of his brother, Drusus, his loyalty to Caesarion, and his personal sense of honor.

The plain fact is, I didn't deserve her to begin with. I don't deserve happiness. I don't deserve anything, really. I'm as empty as my villa. The gods did make me for war, and not for love. I said it a month ago in Rome. And now I have the proof of it. The gods made me this way for a reason. I hear them. I obey them. And I accept their judgment.

Caesarion took reports from the urban cohorts and from the men of Eurydice's Sixteenth, who'd fanned out into the city, looking for anything and anyone out of place.

They'd found a body in a warehouse of a middle-aged man, run to fat around the waist, with the hands of a scribe or a priest—soft, uncalloused, and with ink under the nails—but not a mark on him to suggest foul play. The owner of the warehouse swore that it had been rented a month ago by that same man, who'd claimed to have a large shipment of spices and other goods coming in by ship from Syria, but no trade goods were in the empty warehouse.

Alongside the man's body, they found the body of a sacrificed lamb, drained of all blood, but there was little blood on the floor, which had recently been mopped and swept. The warehouse owner informed them that the man's name had been given as Taf-Nekht, but that meant little. No one by that name appeared in any of the official registers of Alexandria, and the warehouse owner, having received his rental payment in advance, hadn't bothered to stop by and inspect his property since.

"Dead end," Caesarion remarked, looking at Malleolus in the room his mother had told him was the palace library. Cavernous and dim, its long, thin, rectangular windows admitted little light, and the whole place smelled oddly from the hundreds of papyrus scrolls in racks along the walls. *Eurydice will make changes here. Roman pillows and a Roman bed, for one, I'm sure.* They'd both been equally disconcerted by the jade headrests, as well as the inclined surface of the royal bed. *And she'll want a lighter, brighter place to do her reading. For however long she's confined here. For her safety.*

The word burned in his mind like a curse, and Caesarion gave it voice here in private, with vehemence. "Mal, I was supposed to leave Eurydice here because Rome wouldn't be *safe* for her if she became pregnant. That, and the damned pact between the Egyptian gods and their mortal rulers." He leaned back in his chair, gesturing in disgust at the palace around them. "How in the gods' names do I keep her alive, if the safest place for her turns out to have enemies at every turn?"

Malleolus shook his head, standing in front of the low table that served Caesarion as a desk, for the moment. "You've asked me to stay on past my term of service, *dominus*. But you want me, the prefect of the Praetorians, to stay here in Egypt with your wife, rather than with you, and the bulk of the Praetorians—"

Caesarion leaned forward, his voice strained as he replied, "Your job is protecting my life, yes? She and the child *are* my life, and the future of the Roman people."

"Yes, sir." Malleolus held up his hands. "If I might continue?"

Caesarion's eyes narrowed, and he leaned back again. "Speak your mind, Mal. I've never asked you to do otherwise."

The prefect nodded. "That being said, sir, I'm not sure *how* I can keep them safe. The merely human threats, yes, I can handle. But at least twice in the past three years, the threat to her has been supernatural. The god-born woman in Hispania, that Aucissa." His jaw clenched for a moment. "And of course, the beast in the temple." He regarded Caesarion somberly. "We need people who can counter those kinds of threats."

Caesarion grimaced. "I am open to suggestions."

"The Roman-born mages that your wife has been training might have impeccable loyalties, but they're too green." Malleolus exhaled. "*Dominus*, I would like to expand our net for recruiting these kinds of . . . specialists. Quietly. *Very* quietly. Hellenes, to start with. Egyptians with no history of involvement in the business down in Thebes, and who have Roman associates with known loyalties, who will vouch for them. Carthaginians and Lydians—"

"You want to trust my wife's life to *Carthaginians?*" Caesarion's voice cracked.

"Whom we'll observe over the span of years to ascertain their loyalty before putting them on any sort of protective detail," Malleolus said, grim-faced. "It will be slow, but I can't see a way around it. In a few decades, maybe even Gauls." The half-Gallic man met Caesarion's eyes. "It doesn't help us in the short-term, but in the long run, it would be a way for people who have been marginalized by their own people to attain Roman citizenship. Which has been, I know, your wife's goal, as well as to build a cadre of sorcerers with similar power to her own."

Caesarion flicked his hands. "Yes, but what do we do as a short-term solution? I don't have decades, or years." *And I can't leave till I know she's safe.*

Malleolus braced himself. "I hate this suggestion," he

noted. "It has a number of risks and uncertainties about it, which I think I can mitigate. But I'd like to put Magus Banit and her bodyguard temporarily on our payroll. She can cast spells, while for the moment, your wife can't—though we have only the Magus' *word* that magic during pregnancy is a bad idea." That last, with dour suspicion.

"You want to put an admitted *spy* on our payroll," Caesarion said, slowly, and he rubbed at his eyes.

"We'll always know where the spy is," Malleolus returned with a note of grim humor in his voice. "If she's in the *domina's* presence, there will always be at least four Praetorians around, as well. Watching the watcher, as it were." His blue eyes were cold. "I can't match supernatural threats. The Magus can. Call her a civilian specialist. She can advise on ways to keep spirits out of the palace and everything else. She just won't be permitted to be alone with your wife, at any time."

Caesarion nodded, a certain relief stealing through him. "Truthfully, Eurydice asked me if the woman could be kept on hand," he admitted. "She wants to learn about the Magi approach to magic. If the Magus is overseen . . . my objections can rest." He eyed Malleolus. "I doubt coin alone will convince the Magus to assist us, after the welcome we gave her."

"No. But if she was telling the truth about the attack on her several years ago, she'll be very interested in Praetorian resources in terms of tracking the men down. I can reach out to your brother, and his *frumentarii*. Have clerks go through records that aren't open to the public. Things of that nature. She may be willing to play along."

Caesarion nodded. "All right. Give it a try. And once you've secured her assent, we'll take the Sixteenth south to Thebes. I think that it's fairly evident that whoever controlled the demon that attacked us was fairly likely Tahut-Nefer, along with other conspirators. All current unrest is centered around Thebes, anyway. Settling the issue in Thebes may result in our finding our attackers." He grimaced. There were too many suppositions, but he had to do *something*. "Dismissed, Mal. And thank you."

As the prefect opened the door of the library, Caesarion could see Selene waiting outside with Antyllus, a shy smile on her face that dimmed when she made eye-contact with him. *I have no patience for her today*, he thought grimly. "Tell my sister and her suitor that they may enter," Caesarion called after Malleolus, who stepped out of the young couple's way, and, with a quick nod, left the room, closing the door behind him.

"*Dominus*," Antyllus began, still clearly muzzy-headed from the blow to his head and whatever medication that the physicians had given him. "If we could have a moment—"

"Sit down before you fall down, Antyllus," Caesarion said, looking at the reports on his table, his own head throbbing from its recent impact on the floor and subsequent impact on a pillar. And as Antyllus gratefully took a chair, Caesarion added tiredly, "I'm fully aware of why you're here."

Silence as the two of them looked at each other, wide-eyed. Caesarion knew that his tone lacked in family feeling, or even basic friendliness at the moment. He lifted his head, set his stylus aside, and went on now, tightly, "You're here to inform me, Antyllus, that Selene has finally made her choice," *After a gods-be-damned month of dragging it out*, he thought, *forcing two men to halt the course of their lives for her convenience*, "and has accepted your offer of marriage. Is this correct?"

Selene's shy smile and quiet glow of joy died. Caesarion would have felt bad about that, but his entire body ached from the thrashing he'd taken from the bull-spirit, and he'd seen the emptiness in Tiberius' eyes not an hour ago. He'd have been happy for his sister, if not for that.

Antyllus, who'd taken a chair at his command, now sat upright, as if stuck with a pin. Uncertainty in his voice now as he replied, "It is. I'd have thought you'd be happier about having the matter resolved, Caesarion." No title for the moment; they *were* step-brothers, after all, and Antyllus was reaching out, on those grounds.

And Caesarion accepted that, for the moment. He leaned back in his chair, regarding both of them steadily. "Does the fact that the two of you are here together mean that Selene has already spoken with Tiberius?" *If so, I can't imagine that you'd both still look quite so happy.*

An awkward glance between the two of them. "Ah, no," Antyllus replied, his back still straight. "I considered it more proper to come to you first, since you're her guardian."

"So Selene couldn't have gone and spoken with him while you were attending to the errand of speaking to me?"

Before either of them could reply, another knock at the door, and at Caesarion's brusque, "Enter!" a centurion of the Sixteenth came in, another scroll in his hand. Approached Caesarion's desk, and murmured, quietly, "We've managed to seal all the major roads that lead away from the city, *dominus,* but we need to push a secondary perimeter out to contain anyone leaving through the fields—"

"Do it. You don't need my permission for that. That's common sense."

The centurion saluted and exited, and Caesarion turned his attention back to the happy couple. "So," he said to Selene directly now, irritation in his voice. "You haven't done the right thing and spoken to Tiberius, whom I last saw in his quarters, packing all of his belongings and asking that he be permitted to bunk with the Sixteenth?"

Selene's face drained of color. "He . . . knows?" she said, her voice barely above a whisper.

Caesarion wanted nothing more than to shake his sister at the moment. *She has to pick today, of all days. While I'm dealing with an assassination attempt on my wife.* "Yes," he told her flatly. "The two of you might want to consider in the future, that kissing in public tends to be noticed, and that the infirmary, surrounded by physicians and wounded men, is not the place to court and woo." He picked up his stylus. "Tiberius returned to pick up his gear, and got to watch the whole show. Not to mention any of the soldiers who happened to be there."

The flush of shame that filled Selene's face, on any other day, would have made Caesarion regret his tone, but today, he rather thought it was her due. *The universe doesn't come to a halt for you, just because you're in love,* he thought grimly. *Gods know, it's never slowed its pace for me or Eurydice.* "You will note that in public, Eurydice and I have, at most, held hands, or she has taken my arm. In public, we have kissed exactly twice, both times to affirm our marriage. Public decorum is important, perhaps more so for us, since we know that most Romans are disgusted by the suggestion that our marriage is more than symbolic." He tapped his stylus against his desk. "That being said, Selene, a little public decorum on your part would be appreciated until such time as you and Antyllus are married, and you're no longer my responsibility, but his, and that of Antony, his father."

He gave her a direct stare now, or tried. As usual, she'd focused her eyes on the floor. *For the past four years — no, five — you have cringed away from me. Hidden. Looked at the floor every time I've addressed you. I've given you time and space, so that you could grasp the fact that I'm not an ogre. I've never reprimanded you for anything until today, but let Eurydice handle your education and corrections of your poor attitude towards her. Apparently, I should have been more of an ogre before now, so that you'd understand the difference between a reprimand for poor behavior, and cruelty. But what's done is done.*

She went from red to chalk-white at his assessment of her behavior. "Yes, Caesarion."

Antyllus' face had gone rigid. "My lord," he said, his voice tight. "I'd like to point out, with due respect, that I was on poppy-blood at the time, and that our feelings were running high."

"Ah, you were drugged. What an excellent time to make life-altering decisions," Caesarion returned shortly, as another tap came at his door, and yet another centurion entered, this time barely waiting for his acknowledgement. He turned his head to listen to the quick report, and his eyebrows rose. "Six men on donkeys managed to cross the fields before the perimeter could be closed? Did you give chase?"

"We sent a patrol of *equites* after them, but they haven't returned yet—"

"Inform me when you've caught them."

The centurion glanced back over his shoulder at Antyllus and Selene, then at Caesarion, inquiringly. "No, I don't mind being interrupted," Caesarion told the man, interpreting the look. "Trying to capture the men who unleashed a demon in Alexandria, attempted to kill my wife, and *did* kill at least eight men, takes priority over everything else."

A quick salute, and the centurion stepped back out of the room.

Clearly smarting from that last remark, Antyllus still waited until the door closed behind the centurion to lean forward and ask, with grim formality at first, "May I ask why, sir, why, when you have previously expressed approbation for my suit," and from formal to familial and wry, in an instant, "you are being a royal *ass* about it at the moment?"

Caesarion stared at him, ignoring his sister completely for the moment. Then picked up from his desk the *second* brazier leg, and tossed it to Antyllus, who caught it deftly, a look of confusion spreading across his face. "Because," Caesarion said evenly, "as I said previously, when I went to go give Tiberius *his* memento of the battle in which he struck a blow to that demon that would have felled any lesser creature—a battle in which he saved your life, and a battle in which you two fought side-by-side, like brothers . . . I found him packing his gear, and requesting that I let him go stay in the barracks of the Sixteenth until he can make his way to Britannia. Because he, who lived in my house for three years, thought it would be less awkward for everyone to absent himself from my house now," Caesarion ground on without mercy. "Because a little damned *discretion* on your part, poppy-blood or no, would have avoided the awkwardness altogether, and you could have told him about the decision like a man. And then it would have been settled with a wrist-clasp and maybe a drink shared between friends."

Or my sister could have shown discretion, and then a little _courage_, *by telling him, herself.* Caesarion stared at Antyllus now. "I need the two of you able to work with each other. Able to save each others' asses, as you've always done. And *you have jeopardized that,* because you couldn't show a little self-control and maybe escort your would-be betrothed to another room for ten damned minutes." He grimaced. "Not for the first time, either, since he'd previously witnessed you kissing in a semi-public place." He turned away towards his parchments, staring at words that had stopped making sense an hour ago. "Make it right, Antyllus."

Antyllus' face had drained of color. "Yes, my lord." No

affect. No *praenomen*.

More kindly now, Caesarion added, not looking up from his reports, "I'll see to your wound tomorrow, old friend. No sense in you wearing stitches for your wedding, but I've already used my healing today on Tiberius." Now he flicked a glance at Selene, who remained chalk-white and very still. "I suggest that the two of you get married here in Egypt, and as quickly as possible. The temple of Isis will be closed for about a week, thanks to the disaster there today, but there are any number of other temples available. Picking an Egyptian temple would get you around the Parentalia restrictions as well.. You could even have the ceremony performed here in the palace, if you wish. I'm sure that Mother and Antony will be overjoyed to witness it." That last, with a shrug.

Antyllus closed his eyes for a moment. "Are you sufficiently angry with me, Caesarion, that you won't attend the ceremony, yourself?"

"Please don't be angry," Selene begged, her voice scarcely above a whisper.

"I'm not angry," Caesarion told them, his voice empty. "I'm *tired* of the matter. Tired of the time taken over the issue. And irritated with you, Selene. You've kept two good men hanging for over a month, and then you make a choice today, while both of them are injured and drugged to the gills on poppy-blood. It's a poor way to make a decision, but at least you finally made one. Gods be praised." *You could have chosen Tiberius, the man who saved Antyllus' life. The man who helped get you to safety, and who helped hold off the monster while Antyllus finished getting you out the door. But you chose Antyllus' charming smile over Tiberius' darker moods. They're both good men. Both loyal, trustworthy, and kind. Gods grant you peace with your choice.*

As Selene flushed once again, another tap at the door, which Caesarion wearily acknowledged. And at this report, he brought his fist down on the desk, making everything on it jump. "How could a patrol of *equites* have *lost sight* of a group of men on donkeys? Go to Eurydice and see if she's feeling up to sending out a hawk or two to try to track them down." Caesarion scowled at the centurion, who kept his wince from showing anywhere but in his eyes. "In between recovering from the attack and throwing up all over the place, she *might* be able to do what *twenty men on horseback* couldn't manage!" Caesarion rose to his feet, not giving the centurion parade-ground volume, but making his displeasure clear.

"Yes, *dominus*," the centurion said hastily, and withdrew as rapidly as he could.

Caesarion, still standing, fixed the happy couple with his stare. "As I was saying," he went on tightly, and with considerably less volume, "I'm not angry with you, Antyllus. On any other day, and if I'd found out any other way, I'd have been delighted." He continued to direct his gaze towards Antyllus. "Fix the issue with Tiberius, and my objections disappear. Eurydice and I will attend your ceremony, assuming you conduct it before we ride south to deal with the revolt at Thebes. After that, I'm bound for Britannia within the damned month." A shrug. "So make haste, if you want both of us to be available." He paused. "When the harbor opens, you have my permission to depart for Syria to fetch your bows and bowyers, Antyllus. I encourage you to take your new wife with you."

Antyllus wet his lips, clearly unsure of how to take that set of statements. "You don't want me to go south with you to assist?"

Caesarion looked at the ceiling. "And take you away from your new wife's arms?"

"I'll do my duty. I always do—" Antyllus' voice was tight.

"It's not necessary." Caesarion picked up a scroll and squinted at the words there. "One man with a bow won't make much of a difference."

"With respect, I feel that I need to prove myself —"

Caesarion looked up from the scroll with as much patience as he could muster. "You've proven yourself every day since I've met you. You don't need to prove anything further to me."

Antyllus hesitated, his easy smiles nowhere in evidence. "Afterwards . . . am I to remain in Syria, *dominus*? Or to go to Britannia with you, once I'm done in Syria?"

Caesarion sighed, setting the scroll back down. "Do you even need to ask? How many times do I have to stress the importance of you being able to work with Tiberius? You're slated to leave your Cretan auxiliaries and take over as legate of a full legion inside the year. Gods help me, you might even wind up as Tiberius' commanding officer. I *need* you and your Cretans in Britannia. With your damned Scythian bows. Your men are waiting around without a leader in Gaul, so finish up your business in Syria quickly." He shrugged. "Whether your wife accompanies you on the campaign in Britannia, will, of course, be between the two of you."

And if the gods are kind, you'll have the sense to leave her in Rome. Where she can't make matters any worse than she already has. Caesarion exhaled, and tried to remember that his sister was fifteen. *Gods __damn__ it, Eurydice was fourteen when she took over running the house, meeting with ambassadors, assisting with reconnaissance, learning magic, reading dispatches from Egypt, and assisting with policy decisions. Then again, my beloved is an exception. Selene is . . . not.*

Antyllus exhaled, looking deeply relieved. "Thank you, Caesarion."

"Don't thank me. Make it right. You may go now."

Caesarion paused. "Selene, congratulations on your impending marriage. I recommend that you inform Eurydice next, so that you will have someone to stand with you when you tell our mother that you're acceding to her will in this matter. Mother's delight can be a hard thing to bear."

He seethed with things he wanted to say to his sister. Things he didn't dare give voice, because he didn't want her second-guessing her decision and dragging the two men through another round of vacillation. It wouldn't be fair to any of them. But what he wanted to say was simple. *You made a snap decision today, on the basis of a wound and a kiss. I hope it's a good one, sister. Because you're going to have to live with it.*

———————

Eurydice heard the tap at her door, but was busy throwing up into a basin. Nesa answered it, and Selene rushed through, in tears, babbling a tumble of other uncharacteristic words, which fell into abrupt silence as Selene surely realized that Eurydice wasn't particularly in a listening place. The older sister's shoulders heaved, and, after a few more struggles, she finally managed to convince her stomach that there was nothing left to bring up besides bile. Nesa handed her a damp cloth with which to clean her mouth, making clucking noises of sympathy, and took the basin away to empty and clean it. "Selene," Eurydice said, with a wan smile. "You looked wrung out after the attack. Are you feeling better?"

Selene stumbled over her own words in her haste, the story tumbling out in bits and pieces. Eurydice finally managed to put together that Antyllus, while in the infirmary, had kissed her, and renewed his suit, and that Selene had accepted, but that Tiberius had somehow seen, and that Caesarion was angry.

Eurydice found a chair. Poured herself a cup of tepid water from a pitcher to wash the taste from her mouth. And let Nesa, on returning with a clean basin, place a damp rag on her forehead, all while listening to this uncharacteristic effusion of words from Selene. Finally, Eurydice said, simply, "Congratulations. I'm sure you'll be very happy." And after a pause without a reply from Selene, she added, "So, Caesarion suggested that I go with you to see Mother? Give me a moment to finish drinking my water, and I'll do so." *My head's still splitting from trying to control the hawks while not throwing up, but that's another story.* She snorted under her breath. "Be warned. If you thought she was difficult when you didn't agree with her, she's almost worse when you go along with her will."

Selene stared at her, her mouth dropping open. "That's . . . that's all you have to say?" Her usually timorous sister looked almost angry. "Eurydice! Caesarion shouted at Antyllus for my telling him *yes*. That's *not right*—"

"No," Eurydice said patiently. "If I understood you correctly, he yelled at Antyllus for jeopardizing his working relationship with Tiberius, when Caesarion needs *both* of his finest young commanders in the field, and able to operate together without friction." She regarded Selene, whose mouth fell open. Not without sympathy, Eurydice added, "Caesarion loves you, Selene. But in that moment, he probably didn't give a damn about your feelings, because while you're important to him, the military needs superseded the personal ones." She paused. "Also, you've made it damned hard for him to talk to you. You never look at him, and give him every indication that you find him an object of mortal terror."

Selene curled in on herself. And in a very small voice, she said, "I thought you'd take my side. You married Caesarion for love. In the face of every convention. When it could have brought Rome to another civil war."

Eurydice's heart ached for Selene, but another wave of nausea also gripped her. *What do I say?* "I don't have a side," Eurydice finally said. "I don't even think there *are* sides in this. We'll all be happy so long as you're happy. But Antyllus should have waited until you were in private to renew his addresses, and that's really that. So long as he makes it right with Tiberius, it'll become a non-issue—oh, *gods.*" She lurched upright, and Nesa immediately brought her the basin again. After several wretched heaves, Eurydice asked her old nursemaid, wearily, "How long does this part usually last?"

"My first child, the one I nursed at the same time as Alexander, my lady? Only the first three months. My second, the one I nursed with you? I never had a day's sickness at all. It will pass, my lady." Nesa patted her hair gently.

"So, another month. Maybe more. Maybe less." Eurydice groaned under her breath. "How can the child *grow* if I can't keep any food down with which to feed it in my belly?"

"I don't know, but they do," Nesa told her cheerfully, and changed out the damp cloth for a fresher, cooler one. "You'll soon know all about this, too, my lady," she added, turning towards Selene, who flushed and then went pale.

Eurydice heaved herself upright. "Come along," she told Selene tiredly. "I have just enough time to go with you to see Mother before Malleolus said he should have come to terms with Magus Banit, and might be able to bring her to me." She didn't want Selene to feel marginalized, but there were more important things afoot than her sister's marriage plans. "Caesarion agreed to let Magus Banit stay here at least long enough to teach me about her magic—and, possibly, join my bodyguards here, at least for a time. Which will be a help. Come along, Selene," she repeated, standing at the door of the huge royal bedchamber now, trying not to look at its wide expanses or the ancient frescoes on the walls, which made her feel like an intruder on her own family's history. "Let's go find Mother and get this over with."

Selene walked beside Eurydice, deeply dispirited. In the first delicious moments of accepting Antyllus' proposal at last, she'd been dizzy with happiness. Now, everyone seemed intent on stealing her joy. Caesarion was angry. Eurydice didn't even seem to *care*. Though a little voice at the back of her mind whispered, *Someone did just try to kill her. While she's pregnant. And she has to take over the rulership of the Empire's second-most important region inside this month. Maybe I'm being selfish. I . . . I am.*

Chagrinned, Selene retreated into silence as Eurydice and she made their way through the royal quarters, finding the rooms Cleopatra now shared with Antony. And on finding themselves admitted, Eurydice said wearily, "Mother, Selene has some news for you," and just looked at her. Waiting for her to speak.

Selene's stomach clenched as she looked at her mother. And suddenly, she didn't even want to share her happiness. Her mother would just spoil it, anyway. But the die was cast, and she had no choice but to speak now, otherwise she'd just be wasting Eurydice's time. "I've accepted Antyllus' proposal," Selene mumbled.

"Ah, excellent," Cleopatra said, smiling. "I knew you'd see reason eventually. He has too much of his father's charm not to succeed with any woman with whom he's determined to court." A brisk nod. "So, we'll set the wedding for a month from now—"

"Caesarion said to make it quick," Selene said, looking at the floor. "Else he and Eurydice would not be able to attend, given the need to travel south to Thebes."

Cleopatra turned towards Eurydice, frowning. "This is as royal a wedding as your own, not that your ceremony in Rome at the Temple of Isis had much grandeur to it," she told her older daughter crisply.

"I rather thought that the one we did for ourselves, in the gladiatorial arena, covered everything that was needed," Eurydice returned mildly.

Cleopatra waved that away. "Selene is entitled to all the majesty due to a princess of Egypt. Barges on the Nile. A week of festivities for the commoners—and that sort of thing is just as important here, as providing bread and games in Rome. You and Caesarion will surely be back from Thebes by the time everything can be made ready—"

"Perhaps," Eurydice said, her tone brittle, "we might ask Selene what *she* wants." She looked over at her sister now, and Selene raised her eyes from the floor, swallowing.

Cleopatra sighed, folding her hands in front of her. "Selene," she said, her tone not unkind, "has gone out of her way to turn herself into a mouse. But she is a princess of Egypt, as well as the daughter of the Emperor of Rome, and it is time that she takes up her public role, and that she stops *hiding*."

"No," Selene said, her voice shaking, and she raised her head to look her mother in the eyes.

"No?" Cleopatra repeated, clearly finding the word unfamiliar.

"No," Selene repeated herself, feeling her knees weaken. "I don't want all that fuss. I'm sure Antyllus would find it just as repugnant as I do—"

"Oh really?" Cleopatra asked, sharply. "Have you asked him? Have you asked the young man who wants a public career, particularly a career that involves reaching out to Rome's provinces, and any manner of foreigners, if he's unwilling to make use of his wife's political and familial connections to add luster to his own name? Have you asked your betrothed if he's willing to give up the shine that a public marriage to royalty will give him?"

Selene swallowed, her tongue feeling thick in her mouth. *No,* she thought, dimly. *He kissed me. He said his heart would be mine, if I wanted it. It's not just about politics.* But the sinking feeling she always had, when subjected to her mother's political mind, returned, and the last vestiges of happiness tore away from her. "Caesarion said to marry quickly, and for us to go to Syria as soon as the harbor opens," Selene whispered. "I don't think he wants us to stay here and . . . and prolong this." *As he made it clear I've already dragged it out past all reason,* she added, silently, feeling coldness steal through her. *I don't think at this point he even cares which of them I marry, so long as I do so.*

Cleopatra sighed. "Caesarion is a fine fighter and a wonderful general, but he has the political acumen of a bedbug sometimes," she replied uncharitably. "This is a marriage that firmly allies the Julii and Antonii families—much more so than mine, since you're a daughter of Caesar. Of *course* a fuss must be made. I don't think Antony would tolerate anything *but* a fuss."

"Have you asked him that?" Eurydice suddenly interposed, a dry, direct thrust that stole their mother's previous words to Selene and threw them in Cleopatra's face. "Don't answer," Eurydice added, raising a hand as Cleopatra's brows lowered into a frown. "For the moment, I'm done with this conversation. Selene, with me, please. I have a Magus with whom to discuss magic, and I will address *everyone's* concerns when I've had time to think about the social, political, and personal needs of everyone concerned."

"Daughter, I have not finished talking to you—"

Cleopatra began.

Eurydice's eyebrows rose. And Selene had never loved or admired her sister more than when Eurydice said, calmly and evenly, "But I have finished speaking with you on this topic, Mother. You are, as always, my cherished advisor, as is your husband, the governor of Egypt. But for the moment, I do not wish to hear more of your counsel. Selene, accompany me. Now."

And Eurydice *swept* out of the room, dragging Selene in her wake. Small ships might have been pulled along with her, so thoroughly did she sweep. Though, two passages down, Eurydice muttered under her breath, "I enjoyed that too much. She's going to make me *pay* for it."

"Thank you," Selene whispered.

"Don't thank me," Eurydice replied, unknowingly echoing Caesarion. "Just talk to Antyllus and figure out what you both want, and I'll try to arrange it so you get it." She made a shooing gesture. "Go."

And on entering her apartments, Eurydice found four Praetorians, including Malleolus, standing around Damkina Banit. No weapons drawn, but the Magus appeared highly conscious of their presence, eying them all sidelong. "Thank you for agreeing to at least speak to me," Eurydice told the woman, smiling. "I've been doing my best to scrape up information on magic, so that I can learn, and those of our people who have similar gifts, can learn to use them. But it's been slow going. The Hellene tradition of magic is wrapped up with Hecate, and most of her priests live as quietly and out of sight as they can. The rest are the mage-philosophers of Crete—"

"They had a stronger tradition of magic, once," Damkina murmured. "When the godslayers walked the earth."

Eurydice gestured at a chair, inviting the other woman to sit. "I've been struggling," she admitted candidly, "with both the traditional spells locked in the Book of Thoth, which seem terribly limited to me, and with the traditional philosophical notions first put forward by Aristotle, of four major elements, and a fifth one, divine and pure. Why *is* air so damnably heavy to move, for example? It's weightless!" Eurydice sliced her hand through the air in demonstration.

Damkina's brow creased over her veil. "Because there's so much *of* it," she answered, her tone confused. "Air is still something that is present; it's still a thing. We've conducted experiments in which we've managed to remove all air from a glass vessel, using magic. Every time we've done so, the vessel collapses in on itself. Why?"

Eurydice's mind raced. "The *weight* of the air around the now-empty vessel . . . crushed it?" she offered. *Air can crush. So can water — look at how strong waves are, as they beat on a ship or a quay.*

"That was the supposition put forward by Nebo Bel-Zikri, the Magus who first made the attempt," Damkina replied, her eyes alert. "You have an apt mind, my lady."

Eurydice smiled and asked, "So talk to me about earth, Damkina. I've seen how water and air can behave the same way, pushing at whatever it touches, impelled by . . . force. Wind propelling water. Water propelled by . . . the tide, I suppose. I've seen water, in frozen form, ice, come down a mountainside in the form of a wave, too. If water in both solid and liquid form can behave like a wave, can earth behave like either of these things?"

Damkina's eyes lit up behind her veil. "Yes," she replied, with enthusiasm. "Both when rendered liquid by heat, as by a volcano, or when the pieces of earth are very small, like grains of sand slipping down the side of a dune — "

Eurydice lifted her head and gave Malleolus a beatific smile. Which garnered no response from the Praetorian at all; his attention remained locked on the Magus, almost entirely.

That didn't deter the two women from talking, non-stop, for the next hour. Eurydice removed scrolls from out of the chests she'd brought to Alexandria. And Damkina asked if *her* scrolls and cuneiform tablets might be retrieved from her house and brought to the palace.

With a sigh, Antyllus tapped on the door of Tiberius' room. He had a bottle of wine and two cups with him. *This is not at all how I thought the day of my betrothal would go,* he thought, wincing. He'd informed his father next, and received Antony's blessing, in between his father shouting at the various members of the urban cohorts to *deal* with the merchants who were objecting to having their wagonloads of fish go bad in the sun, unable to leave the city for the fish processing centers on the outskirts of town.

When Antony's attention had returned to Antyllus, he'd smiled briefly and told him, "Good show. Brought the unicorn in from the hunt at last. Now get the marriage sealed, and her with child as quickly as you can." A quick nod, and Antony directed his attention towards a centurion, being at least as busy as Caesarion at the moment. "In the meantime, if you're feeling up to walking around, why not put on some armor and help with the search for the attackers?"

His father's famously blunt manner did sometimes grate. "Ah, thank you," Antyllus muttered. *How nice to know that all the work I've put into making her smile simply boils down to 'Good job. Now get her pregnant before you get killed or she regains her sanity and divorces you.'* "Caesarion asked me to go patch things up with Tiberius before anything else—"

Antony's head lifted with a frown, which turned into a grimace. "Most of the time, I'd say 'too bad for him, you got in first,'" he told his son with brutal frankness. "However, I'll admit that it makes it easier to work with men when their eyes don't say 'fuck you,' while their mouths say 'yes, sir.'" He shrugged. "Once you get things 'patched up,' drag him out of whatever hole he's hiding in," Antony added. "A broken arm shouldn't have him prostrated on his bed, and I need commanders out in the street, helping to coordinate this mess." A gesture of impatience at the scrolls heaped on his own desk, and the string of couriers scuttling in with information every few minutes.

Now, Antyllus stood in front of Tiberius' door, holding two cups and a clay bottle of wine, chafing a little at reality. He'd always somehow imagined that having his proposal accepted would mean a quiet half hour or so in an antechamber of the girl's house, not out of earshot, but definitely unseen by her parents, to be spent in blissful contemplation of the kinds of silent conversations two pairs of lips could hold.

And received no answer at his tap. *Perhaps he already left to go join the search? Caesarion did heal his arm, and my father doesn't have eyes everywhere.* Antyllus tried the door's latch gently, and found it swinging open under his fingers.

And to his surprise, Tiberius *was* inside, but didn't even look up from his desk as he continued to work at whatever he was writing. "I said go away. I don't need any—" the younger man snapped, and, looking up, cut his words off short. Set his stylus down on his desk, and stood behind his desk.

That was when the awkwardness of the moment set in. *Caesarion was right. I* do *need this addressed before we're in the field. Damn it.* Antyllus stepped inside, closing the door behind him, and approached, trying to find some portion of the desk that wasn't covered in parchment. Finally finding a thin strip near the edge, he set the cups down on it, commenting, "These don't look like maps of Alexandria."

"Britannia. Gaul." No inflection in Tiberius' voice.

Antyllus poured the wine into both cups, adding, "My father's asked us both to join the effort to find the attackers—"

"I'll go directly." Tiberius moved out from around his desk, heading straight for the door.

Antyllus caught his arm, and felt every muscle in the younger man's body stiffen at the contact, and for a moment, he thought Tiberius might spin and punch him. But all the younger man did was rock to a halt, looking at the door, a muscle working in his jaw until Antyllus let his hand fall. "You really don't like being touched, do you?" Antyllus asked, mildly.

He'd been at the baths last year with Tiberius, Alexander, Caesarion, and a handful of other young nobles, and Tiberius had declined, repeatedly, the suggestion that they all leave the waters for the *tepidarium*, where they could all get massages. Only when Alexander had told him that the services were already paid for, and to continue to decline would be unsociable, had Tiberius reluctantly left the pool. And he'd scowled the entire time the slave had been working on his back and legs, in spite of the bath attendant's quiet, plaintive requests that the young lord please relax now.

"It depends on the person." Tiberius remained precisely where he was. "Your father's waiting for us. Let's go."

Antyllus sighed. "I thought we might share a drink together first."

"We're about to go on duty."

"Fuck duty for a moment, Tiberius. My father's out of line even asking us to volunteer. We were excused duty today after being wounded, for the gods' sakes." Antyllus took a deep breath. "Just . . . sit and have a drink with me, all right?" He'd rarely found anyone he couldn't charm or talk around to his point of view, given time. *Other than Octavia. Nothing worked on that woman. Not smiles, not reason, not humor. Nothing.*

Tiberius turned. Picked up one cup, and said, clearly and distinctly, "To your impending wedding." He snapped his head back to drink the whole thing in one go.

Antyllus reached out to stop him, unsure of how to do that without *touching* him, and finally grabbed his friend's wrist, anyway. "That wasn't—damn it all!" Antyllus swore under his breath. "I didn't come here to make you drink to my *wedding.*" Incredulity filled his voice. "Dis, do you think I'm *that* devoid of understanding?"

His friend didn't answer. Antyllus gestured at one of the room's chairs, and repeated, "Please sit down."

Tiberius obeyed. Drank when Antyllus filled his cup again. "Caesarion threw one of the legs of that brazier at my head," Antyllus offered, after a moment. "That's going to be a conversation-starter in my tent next time I'm in a *castra.*"

Tiberius heard the words, but couldn't come up with anything to say in reply. So he nodded. That was, more or less, what trophies were for. For helping to remember what you'd done. Or reminding other people of who and what you were.

Antyllus drank from his own cup now, looking uncomfortable. "Caesarion said he'd given you the other one."

Tiberius nodded once more. Again, there didn't really seem to be much he could say that would add to this one-sided conversation. So he emptied his cup and put it aside.

"You plan to hang yours up in your tent?" Antyllus felt lost. He had no idea what to do or to say to get Tiberius to *talk.* React. Anything, really. If Tiberius had gotten raging drunk and *punched* him, Antyllus would have understood it better. They could have had a nice, cleansing fight, and gotten whatever jealousy or rage was in Tiberius out of his system, and while the expensive furniture of the palace might have taken a beating, and some teeth might have been loosened, it would have been done.

But all Tiberius did was shake his head in reply. "Why not?" Antyllus said, more sharply now. "I'll put mine up. We fought together. We *won* together." He cast about for words. *And both of us having one is important. It shows that we're brothers, in a way.*

"No point," Tiberius replied shrugging, and the words hit Antyllus somewhere in the pit of the stomach, as if Tiberius had just denied that bond of brotherhood. *Because I . . . betrayed a brother today? Did I? By pursuing my own interests?* Antyllus wavered. And then decided, *I could have put it off by a day, but Father's always told me, when Fortuna arrives, grab her by the forelock. I'm not sure Tiberius would have done any differently.*

And then a little cold stole through him, and Antyllus wondered, fleetingly, if *Tiberius* had been the one wounded badly enough to stay in the infirmary a little longer, if Selene would have chosen him, then, instead. *Does it all boil down to which of us she felt sorrier for?*

But Tiberius, oblivious to Antyllus' sudden inner qualms, had found a store of words somewhere. "Caesarion won that battle. He's got the demon's own sword to prove it. We didn't do anything but distract it till he got up off the ground." Another shrug. "Doesn't seem worth bragging about." He quickly put his hand over the top of his cup as Antyllus once more went to refill it. "No, thank you." *I wouldn't be drinking with you if you hadn't demanded it.* Still, there was nothing for it but to endure until Antyllus gave up on whatever his goal here was. Sooner or later, he would.

"Caesarion healed you?" Tentative words now, and again, Tiberius nodded. "You'll be going with him south to Thebes, then?" Antyllus added.

"He didn't ask." Tiberius cast around for something that would satisfy the older man and end this discussion. "I requested assignment to Britannia. My brother is there. As soon as the harbor opens, I'm gone." *Seventy days' travel at this time of year. Maybe I'll be able to make the trip faster alone, without keeping to a legion's marching pace. Though it might be more dangerous to be a lone traveler.*

Silence, and Antyllus, staring into his wine cup, made one last sally. "Tiberius, just hours ago, we clasped wrists as friends." He looked at the younger man. "You don't give friendship easily or often. I'd like to keep yours."

Tiberius snorted, a sound that scraped the back of his throat. "Cicero says that the first law of friendship is that we demand of friends only what is right. And that we do for the sake of friends only what is right." He paused and added, his tone formal, "He also says that friendship is only possible between two people of virtue, who have no conflicting interests, such as the pursuit of a wife."

Antyllus half-laughed. "While I hope I'm counted as a person of virtue in that statement, it's best not to quote Cicero the Elder around my family." A quick, wry smile. "When my father was out of favor with Caesar, Cicero once got on the floor of the Senate and libelously accused him of playing the woman to Gaius Scribonius Curio—down to wearing a bridal stola for him." He snorted himself, now. "Cicero's name and writings weren't allowed in our house for years." *Of course, the odd thing is, Cicero actually was great friends with Curio and Curio's father. And Curio's wife, Fulvia? Divorced him, married my father . . . and became my <u>mother</u>.* Roman politics was a tiny, crowded stage on which all the great families played out their dramas.

Tiberius stared at him, taking the point behind Antyllus' words. Pithy quotations weren't needed in this conversation. *How much virtue did it take to leap for the opportunity to secure her regard? But . . . her feelings for me were a child's fantasy. Let it all blow into dust. Because that's all it ever was. The things I gave up? Probably didn't matter, anyway.* "I told you in Rome that it didn't matter which of us married her, so long as she was happy and had a home. That remains true." He stood and moved away, towards the door of the room. "Alexander asked me to court his sister. As a friend, I did so." Perfect, polite formality now, nothing more. "He thought it was the right thing to do. Plainly, he was wrong." He swallowed. "I remained your friend even while there was competition between us. I remain your friend now." Tiberius paused to allow Antyllus to consider that. "You seized the opportunity to secure her regard when you saw it. You truly deserve her." He nodded, adding, his tone blank, "Gods grant you both much joy."

"So . . . you and I will be able to work together in the future?" Antyllus asked, standing up from his chair, starting to feel the first trickles of relief.

Tiberius remained by the door, looking at nothing in particular. "I don't see why not," he replied, shrugging. *What in Dis' name do you want me to say? That I'm going to help sacrifice doves at your wedding?* "When I next see you, in six months, or a year, or whenever you report to the campaign in Britannia, everything should have blown over. Consider the time and my absence the best wedding gift I can give you." *Assuming I'm alive in a year. The Britons are fierce fighters, and they have their druids solidly involved now. And even so, by then, she'll likely be pregnant, and setting up dinners in Rome. Or, if you're daft enough to bring her to Britannia, she'll be so occupied* *being an officer's wife in a <u>castra</u>, and getting ready to have the child, or nursing it, or changing it, or whatever else, that she won't even have time to play her music, let alone remember childish fantasies.* He added tonelessly, "You needn't worry about jealousy on my part. Once a woman is married, assuming she's not being shoved down the stairs or some such by her loving husband, she ceases to exist for me in that way."

"That's . . . fair," Antyllus said, setting his cup aside, and crossing the room to offer Tiberius his hand, his expression oddly uncertain. Antyllus *never* looked uncertain. Always appeared ebullient and in total control of his surroundings.

Tiberius looked at the offered hand for a moment. Then accepted the wrist-clasp. "Please inform your father that I will assist him with the efforts to find the attackers shortly."

And he was as good as his word, joining a group of *equites* sent out to follow the trail of the six donkeys that Eurydice's hawks had just found. However, even Tiberius was surprised at what they actually found.

Chapter VIII: Shifting Winds

<u>Februarius 2, 20 AC</u>

Back in Rome, Jocasta sat in a back room of Agrippa's princely villa, shivering a little as her sister worked diligently, sewing a new dress for Livia. "You're quite certain you like it here?" Jocasta asked Viola for the third or fourth time. Her sister had been paralyzed since she was ten

"Oh, *yes*, sister! No more drunk hands rattling the latch while you're out, and having to have Ianos here pick up a piece of firewood to stand guard, just in case someone kicks the door in and comes through, thinking it's their home. Or in search of, well, you." Viola looked downcast over that piece of truth, and threaded her needle again. "It's clean here, and Lady Livia is ever so kind. Her physicians couldn't help me, but the food is so much better than we could ever afford, and Ianos isn't the only one who has to, well, help me clean myself and use the lavatory." She flushed again. Two years younger than Jocasta, she'd turned fifteen this year, and had been paralyzed below the waist since she was ten. Having lost their parents to the same fever that had taken Viola's legs, Jocasta had become a whore that same year to ensure her sister's and her own survival.

Jocasta had seen a lot in the past five years. Enough to make her doubt that any fancy Roman noblewoman would do so much out of the simple kindness of her heart. She swiveled in her seat to regard Ianos, the eunuch she'd scraped together enough coin to purchase three years ago. A year her senior, he still shrank in on himself whenever anyone looked at him directly; he'd been a *puer* to some Roman patrician who liked his boys *young*. Castrated at the age of ten, he had the high, pure voice of a woman, no facial hair, and a generally softer appearance than a man should. But apparently, he'd still grown too tall and developed too much musculature for the taste of his lord, and had been thus, sold at the age of fifteen to a whore a year his junior, for a less than princely sum. She'd kept his hair cut short since then, instead of making him keep the long, flowing locks his old master had favored. Had given him male clothing, too. "Ianos," Jocasta asked, "is the rest of the household treating you well?"

He shrugged. "As well as can be expected, mistress," Ianos told her softly. He rarely said two words when one would do; she'd heard other slaves in the street mock his high-pitched voice more than once. She'd picked up cobblestones and thrown them at the taunters, as she would have at any other mangy curs. "I stay with Mistress Viola and take care of her needs, as always. They all know what I am, of course." He looked away.

"What you are, is a very good person," Jocasta told him, with feeling. She occasionally debated the notion of taking Ianos to her bed and showing him that regardless of what had been cut away, he could still be as much or as little of a man as he wished. But such fancies usually passed after her second or third customer of the night, with the exhaustion and ennui of having to deal with so many others' desires. And in the gray light of dawn, when she usually staggered home, a bottle in hand to let her sleep through until at least noon, and Ianos met her at the door and politely tucked her into bed, it never seemed entirely fair to turn him back into what he'd once been. Or what she was now, herself.

The door opened behind her, and to her consternation, the lady of the house stood there, her blond hair so pale it was nearly white. *Probably is white, under some dye,* an uncharitable part of Jocasta's mind whispered as she rose to make a low bow before Livia Drusilla. "My lady," Jocasta murmured.

"Ah, there you are. I've always *just* missed you when you've made your visits to your sister. Come along, Jocasta. You and I have much to discuss."

Jocasta looked over her shoulder, seeing nothing but peace in Viola's face. But Ianos' eyes looked worried as she found her shoulder gripped by fingers that felt like claws, drawn into another of the small, cold rooms occupied mainly by the serving staff of the great villa. "Let me see you, child," Livia said, smiling. "Why, you're quite charming. You could do better for yourself than employment as a common whore, you know." Livia brushed off one of the stools in this room, looking at it with distaste before taking a seat there. "Do sit down, dear. Let's talk about your future."

My future? Good gods, let's hope she doesn't want a female lover. I've been paid to do that before, but it's so boring that it's difficult to pretend to being interested the whole time. Jocasta sank down warily onto her own seat. "My lady," she said uneasily, "I don't have any talents or training, and no man in his right mind would take me for a wife. But at least I've never been a beggar." *Taking bread and wheat at the dole line isn't the same, of course. Everyone does <u>that</u>. And the times I spread my legs for food and not for coin . . . those were business transactions, not begging.* She had her pride, after all.

Livia smiled, a distant, chill expression, which warmed a little, even as Jocasta watched. "Oh, my dear girl, do you really think there's so much difference between the high-born and the low-born in Rome?" The genteel accent and manners never changed, but the warmth in the words increased as Livia added, gently, "Why, at least the low-born girl gets a price for what's between her legs. We high-born? Our fathers have to buy us husbands, you know. That's what the dowry's for. To tempt them to take us, and to pay for the costs of the household, at least initially. And to make sure the man feels the sting of it when he divorces us, because then, he has to give the money back!" A little laugh, covered by the patrician woman's hand. Jocasta laughed uneasily, knowing that it was best to go along with the high-born when they smiled.

Livia continued to smile, and then said, confidingly, "Honestly, I once brought another girl who shared your, ah, profession into this house. A *hetaira* of Athens, actually, so very, hmm. High-brow."

Not a trull like me, one step above walking the streets, Jocasta interpreted, but invited confidences with her eyes and smile. "Why would you do that, *domina*?"

"Because when my last child was born, the physicians butchered me," Livia replied, with charming frankness and startling intimacy. "The poor thing was stuck inside me. They had to cut it up to get it out and save my life. And they cut me too. Infection. Nothing healed *quite* right. You know how it is." She reached out and put a hand, lightly, on Jocasta's shoulder.

Jocasta cringed. She'd watched the same damned botched operation a year ago, conducted on another whore in the house where she worked. And had even more diligently painted herself inside with white lead, and rinsed herself with vinegar after every customer, and be *damned* to the burning sensation of the acid in her most tender places. "Oh, my *lady*," Jocasta said, with sudden, deep compassion. "I am so *sorry*."

"So was I, my dear, so was I. But we were discussing you, and your future, and the last young woman of your, ah, profession, whom I had brought here." Livia smiled. "I brought her to me so that she could . . . teach me. I wanted to hold onto my Octavian's love, you understand, but I couldn't *bear* his touch. Not there. I couldn't bear his body inside of mine, and the thought of going through all of that again? If it had almost killed me the last time? Never again. But she was *quite* skilled, and told me of all *manner* of things I'd never even considered before."

Jocasta laughed, this time freely. "Oh, there are things that I'm sure fine ladies aren't much taught," she acknowledged cheerfully, and missed the glitter in Livia's eyes completely. "But what has this to do with me, my lady?"

"Why, I'm quite fond of Viola, and I know it distresses her that you've been forced into your, ah, line of work, simply to support her. And I know that you're suspicious of my motives, dear." Livia patted her shoulder as Jocasta looked up with a start. "And you're *wise* to be, for everyone in Rome wants something. Nothing for nothing, as the saying goes." She smiled again. "That's why, even with your sister's needs entirely attended to, and with her making enough money as one of my servants to support *you* for once, you haven't quit a job that you must hate. Because you're uncertain of what will happen if you become dependent on me."

Jocasta licked lips that suddenly felt dry. "I mean no disrespect, *domina*—"

"Of course you don't." Nothing but affability in Livia's tone now. "But if I can't convince you to leave your deplorable employment, because you're afraid of what might happen, and because you wish to remain in control of your own life—a distinction which so few Roman women possess—then the least I can do is give you the means with which you might *improve* your conditions. And pass on a few of the *hetaira's* lessons to me, which, I must confess, my Octavian dearly loved." A very becoming flush stained the older woman's cheeks. "Things that perhaps, might not be commonly available in your particular, ah, establishment."

Jocasta's eyes widened. Of all the places this conversation could have gone, this was the *last* she'd have ever considered. "My lady?" she asked, trying not to laugh. "Surely, I think I've had it shoved all the places it *can* be shoved, if you'll pardon the crudity."

The warmth faded for an instant, and then returned as Livia smiled once again. "Oh, *no*, my dear. I'm sure your expertise far surpasses mine in that area." She went to the door and summoned a servant, murmuring quietly for a moment or two, and then came back with a bottle. "This, for example, my dear, is a delicious concoction—olive oil and warming herbs, mixed with wolf's blood. Not to be eaten or drunk, mind you, for it can make someone very sick. But rubbed into the skin, it soothes. Tingles. Makes *everything* feel that much better, you understand." Livia's little, secretive smirk make Jocasta perk up her ears in more interest. "And if you give a man just enough, why, he thinks that he can fly. He sees the gods. Murmurs his deepest thoughts, gets out all the hates and vileness. Never remembers a word of what he spoke when he dreamed, and when he wakes up, refreshed, why, he feels sated as if he's had you all night, and all you might have had to do was rub it out of him once or twice while he dreamed." Livia shrugged.

Jocasta's spine snapped straight. "All of that, from a few herbs?" she asked, incredulous. "Why doesn't everyone do this?"

"Because most men don't *want* to bare their souls," Livia murmured. "No matter how much good it will do them, no matter how good it will feel to fly with the gods. They want to think that they're in control, all the time. Hold it all in their cramped, little hearts. But so long as they don't *know* that they lost control, and all they know is that they feel the best they've ever felt? My goodness, girl. You could name your price."

Jocasta stared at the bottle consideringly. And then

looked at Livia and asked, "And what would be *your* price for giving me this potion, my lady?"

Livia set the bottle in her hand. "The first? Free. See if I'm wrong about its effects. And mind that a strong, healthy, young man may need quite a bit more to unlock his mind and heart." A sly smile. "After that? You can bring me their secrets for more of the potion. But no telling any of them about it. We wouldn't want word to get around, and for customers to avoid you, for fear of what they might say or do when they're flying with the gods, and not firmly in control of themselves."

Jocasta considered that. *It's no different than what I already do for Lord Alexander,* she thought pragmatically. *And involves much less risk of pregnancy and disease, and the ache between my legs and in my stomach might abate a bit, if I have a few nights off a week. I can still give Lord Alexander his information when he comes around — maybe all the same information that I give Lady Livia. And all this, and Viola keeps living here, in this wonderful house. Clean and well-fed, useful and safe.* The more she thought about it, the better it sounded. "How do I rub it in?" she asked, dubiously. "Won't it have the same effect on me?"

"Oh, no, no," Livia murmured. "It only affects men. Another reason they've tried to keep wolf's blood out of women's hands for centuries."

If Jocasta had been literate at all, or had had a country girl's education in basic herbalism, she might have recognized the term *wolf's blood* as another name for *aconite.* But she wasn't and she didn't. And, profoundly grateful to Livia, she accepted the bottle, made her bow, and left to start her night's work.

Februarius 13, 20 AC

Alexander awoke in the villa of the Julii at dawn, and reached for the amulet of Sekhmet around his neck. It felt cold to the touch—like ice, really—and he frowned over it, puzzled. *It's never done that before.* A little tingling warmth now and again, let him know that it was more than an inert lump of metal. Which also provided a polite warning not to go any further into the bedchamber with this person or that. Not that in the past six weeks, he'd really felt the need for extravagances in that regard.

He'd been *busy*, reading all the reports that usually crossed Caesarion's desk, as well as those that usually crossed his own. Maintaining his network of contacts. Establishing new ones, when he found himself invited to Sulpicia's theater, and whisked to the *skene,* or scene-house, where the actors changed between acts, put on their masks, and, apparently, got *roaring* drunk after each performance. Sulpicia herself had never been inside the scene-house, and the persnickety Hellene slave who'd been purchased to be her manager for both the theater and the vineyard was *scandalized* that his mistress wished to go and *meet* her actors—on the arm of a noble of the Julii family or no.

Alexander had done his best not to laugh in the man's bearded face, and had continued to insist that he would provide all the protection the patrician woman would require from the *infames.* And as such, they'd gotten a hard, clear look at an entirely different world than the one they both usually occupied. Some of the actors had running sores around their mouths, concealed by the wooden masks they usually wore. Some of the men were incredibly effeminate, so much so that they got on Alexander's nerves with their breathy diction and swaying walks. He might have enjoyed every minute he spent wrapped in Tiberius' arms, rocking together, the play of muscle against muscle, but he'd never considered himself a *woman* because of it, and what he chose to do in bed, and who he chose to do it with, had nothing to do with *who he was.*

On the outside, he smiled. Complimented people on their performances. Listened, discarding the least intelligent of the crowd rapidly. Scanned the remainder for faces with whom he might be able to work. Not the ones who got drunk immediately. Easily compromised, they could be bought by anyone for the price of a bottle. Not the ones who immediately dragged a lover off to another room — be that lover man, woman, or boy. Again, their weaknesses were evident, and easily played.

No, Alexander wanted the ones who were *still acting.* Even off-stage. The ones who didn't have evident weaknesses or vices, who could put on the façade of normal social behavior, or take it off, at a whim. Not the ones who reveled in standing outside of society's dictates. Those, he recruited gently. Pulled over to the side of the *skene* with himself and Sulpicia, the poetess on his arm, and remarked, lightly, "You should write these good men something that they can get their teeth into, love. All we have these days is Plautus, Plautus, and yet more plodding Plautus. I'm tired of twins switched at birth and girls dressed as boys dressed as girls. And Plautus died almost two hundred years ago."

"Well, there *is* Quintus Novius," Sulpicia demurred, and the various actors made scoffing sounds and rude noises. "No, no, the one he wrote about the Hellene *hetaira* wasn't bad! I laughed at it, anyway."

"Yes, *domina,* but he's written *three* about the cloth-fuller, the cloth-fuller's wife, and the cloth-fullers who went on holiday," came a quick, wickedly dry response. "I think either he's in debt to his tailor, or he's plowing the cloth-fuller's daughter."

Sulpicia laughed out loud, her eyes sparkling. "How

about *Hercules the Money-Collector?*" she offered, recovering. "Surely that one wasn't all bad."

"*Domina*, if we run that one again, he'll throw us a script about *Hercules the Tender of Infants*," came the reply, and Alexander laughed himself now, getting a feel for these people. "If you write something for us, lady, make it better than *that*, and we'll bless you for it."

"Just for the gods' sakes, don't write it under your own name," came an addendum from the back of the crowd. "No one will take it seriously if they know a woman wrote it."

Sulpicia's lips curled down at the corners. Just a hint, but Alexander knew that mobile face well enough by now to read every nuance of it. "I'll keep that in mind, particularly if I feel myself take a tragic turn," she assured the actors, however.

And Alexander drew the conversation gently on. Talked with them about politics. Noted which of them turned to walk away when he drew the subject there, and which showed real contempt for the Octavianites. Noted which of *those* mentioned having been solicited for sex by members of that faction. Tucked that information away at the back of his head, and murmured that it was a pity that so much of the finest acting in the city seemed to go on in daily life, and in noble houses, rather than on the stage. Not full-on recruitment, not at first. Just finding those with sympathies and talents he could . . . encourage.

And then he'd whisked Sulpicia away. It had been the only time they'd gone somewhere together publically, since he was, after all, a betrothed man, and because it wouldn't do to have people linking their names. It would damage her ability to hear all the things that he couldn't hear from inside the Julii villa, after all.

But in private, he met her at least once a week. Not on

the same days, or at the same hours. But often at *Merges*, where he had his private room converted into a study for her, where she could retreat to whenever she liked. To her marked surprise, he read every scrap of her poetry that she brought him. And each day, after having exercised and bathed, eaten dinner and finished his dispatches for Caesarion, Alexander found a little peace of mind by sitting down and copying her poetry out for her. He'd trained as a military scribe, where legibility of orders and dispatches were of the utmost importance; therefore, his lettering was open, wide, smooth, and evenly-spaced. Her handwriting was crabbed, ran uphill across a page, and she had a tendency to jam all of her ideas into corners, as if her 'twiddles,' as she called her poems, weren't of great importance.

He copied them all out, neat and clean and clear. Even the ones that were about her erstwhile lover. Three copies in all, just to start with. One for his own pleasure. One to send to the Library of Alexandria, with Caesarion's seal on the letter stating that a record of this famous Roman poetess should be kept, and a space allotted for her future works. And one, which he handed to her on the evening of the thirteenth, neatly rolled, before they were to eat dinner together in the private room at *Merges*. Sulpicia unrolled the scroll, and flushed a little with pleasure at the sight. "Oh, it all looks so . . . official this way," she told him as he slipped onto the eating couch behind her. "All of them together, not tossed in with Tibullus' works." A note of wonder in her voice. "My twiddles. Why, they look somehow more real this way."

"Stop calling them twiddles," Alexander advised in her ear. "Another copy of that codex went to the Library of Alexandria by boat this morning. Nothing can be more official than that. Your poems will be housed in a niche somewhat to the west of the shelves on Homer and his commentators."

She looked back over her shoulder at him, her eyes wide, and then turned, kissing him fervently. Alexander had no objections to this, though when her lips broke free, he did murmur, "Dinner will get cold."

"Would you rather have a hot dinner or a warm sheath?" she whispered against his ear, and Alexander had her on her back in an instant, gently pushing the scroll out of their way, lest it be crumpled.

He found it very difficult to be careful with her. To let himself glide back and forth between her thighs, as he'd always done with Tiberius, just tantalized him with how close her warm and welcoming depths really were. And she always offered herself so sweetly, and while she made ardent sounds of enjoyment for lips and fingers and tongue, it was when he was hilt-deep in her and giving her everything he had that her sounds turned feral, and tonight was no exception. Finally, bodies cooling, Sulpicia picked a piece of now-cold quail from off the platter in front of the couch, and offered it to him with her fingers. He accepted it, and asked, stretching, "Have you picked a name yet, Via?"

He liked calling her Via, from *Servia*. By itself, the word could mean *through* or *by means of*, though she'd given him a look the first time he'd used it, and told him that she wasn't a *street*, thank you. "But if you ever write a philosophical tract of poetry, you could call it the *Via Servia*," he'd told her, teasing, and there the matter had ended.

She rolled to her side, smiling, and told him, "Aurea, I think."

"Golden. Like dawn's golden fingers. I like it."

"And if you really want me to write a play or two, it could be made to Aureus without much trouble. Except that sounds like the playwright's made of money." She rolled her eyes expressively. "Gods forbid a woman write a silly play—"

"What, and associate yourself with all those *infames*?" Alexander made a rude noise, sitting up on the couch. "I really think you should. You could make fun of all the hypocrites in society today."

"And, after offending a consul with my sharp tongue, get myself exiled to Carthage, like Gnaeus Naevius, and have to open my veins after composing my own epitaph?" Her eyebrows lifted, and Alexander leaned down to kiss her hungrily again.

"Never happen," he told her when he paused for breath. "Just disguise it a bit. Set the action in Hellas, give them all Hellenic names."

"And make the hero a brave and dashing former Roman legionnaire?" A twinkle in her eyes as he kissed her again.

"Just . . . so long . . . as it's not a *miles gloriousus*. I *hate* the braggart ex-soldier type. In his fifties, and the victor of a thousand battles he never actually took part in." Alexander sighed as a tap came at their door. "I haven't eaten, and I need to get on with my rounds, darling. *Aurea*." That, just to practice saying the new name.

"You know, now that I hear you say it, I'm not sure I like it." She tapped a finger against her teeth consideringly.

"You like Via better?"

"I'm definitely more *used* to it." She made a face at him.

Alexander chuckled. "Why don't you stay here, and write? I'll be back before morning, and then we can say a proper good-bye for once."

She just smiled, and he pulled on his clothes, and left. Once more wondering why the amulet of Sekhmet seemed so damned *cold* around his neck. He had to tuck it between his tunic and his toga to shield it from his skin, in fact.

Alexander made his rounds of his informants, a

frumentarii and former Praetorian shadowing his steps, as usual. Ducked into his last stop, the brothel where Jocasta worked, made what sounded like idle chit-chat with the rest of the staff, and, once Jocasta presumably finished with her current customer, was ushered to the back, where his *frumentarii* protector took up a post down the hall, as discreetly as possible.

Jocasta had found over the past two weeks that Livia's magic potion did indeed enhance the experience for most of her customers. Some of the older men in particular commented that after a good massage from her, their aches and pains had diminished, and they felt younger than they had in *years*, more able to move their hips, knees, and shoulders. But sadly, as far as she was concerned, this led to an increase in their libidos, rather than the more magical sleep that Livia had suggested might happen. Still, the tips added up, even though she'd been careful to give the *special* treatment to only a few customers. A few *had* been drowsy and comfortable enough afterwards that they'd talked far more than usual. And Jocasta, with her terrible handwriting, had made two sets of notes. One for Lord Alexander, and one for Lady Livia. *A year like this, and I can quit,* she decided. *Steal off to the countryside and buy a little farm somewhere. Bring my sister and Ianos with me.*

Of course, she knew that that would require some doing. Livia might not *let* her take her sister. Or let her quit, a thought that gave her qualms of foreboding. But that was a problem for another day.

She'd been doing well enough that been able to take a night or two off from what Livia referred to as her deplorable employment. She'd spent those nights over in the servant quarters of Livia's great house, watching her sister smile, and without the need for a bottle to put herself to sleep. And after one too many snickers from Livia's servants in the direction of Ianos, Jocasta had simply tucked herself in bed beside her slave just last night. Had felt his tears against her neck in the early hours of the morning, and had turned over to wipe them away, gently, whispering, "What's wrong?"

"Nothing." That, muffled.

"Well, there must be *something*."

"It feels good to hold someone. To be . . . worth something."

She'd kissed him then. Let her hands explore whatever he was willing to let her touch. There were differing levels of castration, she knew. Some poor men—such as the *gallii*, the devotees of Cybele who eventually dressed like women, assuming they *survived* their self-mutilation—had had the whole thing cut away, and the surgeons had to put a reed in while they healed, so that they'd eventually be able to urinate. Just a mass of ugly scar tissue left behind.

More practical, but still brutal, was the removal of just the scrotum; that prevented erections, and left the voice as high as a woman's, but with more power. Some singers had that done to them as children, but if they were Roman-born, castration was forbidden. Thus, some singers wore instead a ring around the base of the penis, called a fibula, which was meant to prevent bloodflow from reaching the member, and thus prevent them from achieving erections that might make their voices suffer in purity. She wasn't sure how one affected the other, but that was the common belief, anyway.

And then there was the third, most surgical and precise method of castration, reserved for *prized* slaves. Just the removal of the testicles, leaving the rest intact. Eunuchs of that sort could actually achieve erection if they were vigorously stimulated, and even achieve release.

She'd never asked Ianos which procedure had been conducted on him. To her surprise, he'd proven to be of the third type, as she discovered as she stroked him lightly through his tunic. And in the very dim moonlight filtering in the windows of the servants' quarters, she'd watched his head fall back and his mouth open, slack. Another tear streaked down his face, and she'd stopped, only to have him catch her hand. Kiss it. And then they had, tentatively, fumblingly, as if neither of them had ever done this before, joined their bodies.

It hadn't made time stop in its tracks, but it had been sweet and tender, and all the things that Jocasta hadn't realized were missing from her life. He'd *thanked* her, softly, and in their whispered confidences, told her that he'd been taken as a *puer* by his master for the first time at no more than eight years of age. They traded stories; she confessed that she *hated* servicing other women, so that her patrons could watch, and he noted that his master's wife had taught him to perform those same services for her, just after he'd been castrated.

Two lifetimes of degradation. And somehow, for a moment or two, she'd felt *clean*.

This morning, however, Lady Livia had caught her before she could slip away. "Ah, there you are, my dear. How's my potion been working for you?"

"My lady, I left a list of all the information I've heard so far on your desk—"

"Yes, yes. But I can't help but notice that a few names are missing. I know, for example, that Alexander Julius is one of your regular clients. Why haven't you provided anything on him?" The blue eyes were penetrating.

Jocasta had taken refuge in the truth. "Actually, my lady, he's not been to see me in several weeks." She blinked, and then added, tentatively, "I think that the potion might be a little weak, my lady. Many of the men report feeling quite relaxed, and very healthy, but they don't seem to sleep."

"Use more of it." Livia handed her another bottle, her eyes gleaming. "I'm particularly interested in what young lord Alexander might have to say under its effects. If and when he comes to see you? Use at least half this bottle on him, dear. That should have the desired results."

Half? Jocasta thought, swallowing. *But Livia does seem to know her business. I owe Alexander a good deal . . . but he hasn't given my sister a new home. Hasn't given me a way out of my* deplorable employment. *Well, not that Livia had, to be honest. If he tells me anything, I'll make sure that Livia only hears the things that I want her to hear. Nothing that would hurt him. But it would be interesting to know what goes on behind those dark eyes of his. And in the end, while I told Alexander that if anyone* threatened *my sister . . . Livia hasn't threatened her. She just* has *her. Well-kept. Comfortable. Useful.*

So this evening, as Alexander entered and took a seat in her room, Jocasta dithered a little. "My lord," she murmured, smiling genuinely, for she liked both Alexander and Tiberius. Alexander for giving her a way to stick it to her noble clients, and being a very considerate lover. Tiberius, for being an incredible lover, and for always treating her, out of bed, as if she were fully clothed even if she was naked. It had started off as somewhat annoying, and had become a challenge to see if she could get him to react . . . till she'd become accustomed to it. She cherished the way he always bowed over her hand, as if she were a lady. "You haven't been here in six weeks. I'd thought you'd forgotten me." She lay on the bed, spreading her legs invitingly, while Alexander took the chair across the room.

"Forget you? Never. You're one of my best agents!" A quick smile. "I've simply been run off my feet. I wasn't expecting how much administrative nonsense my brother has had to deal with, every single day," Alexander told her, exhaling as he leaned back in the chair. "I'm here to collect your reports. At double your usual rate, to apologize for my long absence."

Jocasta laughed, and dug the scroll out from where she'd hidden it, teasingly holding it just out of his reach—even after he'd put the small bag of coins on the table, where she could get to it. Alexander, however, reached in and deftly snagged the scroll, reading through her results from the past weeks. "Interesting," he murmured, his eyes scanning over the words. "Thank you, my dear. I'd best be getting on, however. You're my last stop for the evening."

Jocasta blinked and sat up on her bed. "You haven't been here more than ten minutes!" she said indignantly. "You're going to destroy my reputation!"

"Sorry," Alexander told her, a twinkle in his eyes. "I have an appointment to keep."

"You said I was your last stop."

"On the tour that duty impels me to make, yes."

"You don't want to fuck me?" Jocasta wasn't sure if she should be outraged or not. *Did I age in the past month? Am I some old and stringy harridan all of a sudden?*

The twinkle in his eyes became more pronounced, but his lips barely curved. "I'm feeling remarkably sated at the moment. But if it will do your *reputation* harm for me to leave so soon, I can stay here and we can talk. How's your sister doing?"

Jocasta gave him a narrow-eyed glance, wondering if he was making fun of her. "If you won't take your one solid fuck a day, as any *medicus* would prescribe," she told him, rolling to her feet, "at least let me give you a massage."

He frowned. "No more than twenty minutes," he told

her, taking off his toga and tunic, revealing the cleanly-muscled torso underneath—and the vicious scar right over his heart. The amulet of Sekhmet, she'd seen many times before, but it almost seemed to be glowing tonight.

"You really are concerned about this appointment," she murmured as he lay on the bed, face-down.

"You have no idea," he replied, and then she felt his muscles go limp as she began to work the wolf's blood oil into his back. Shoulders. She straddled his narrow hips, feeling the oil tingle in her palms, as it always did, and along her thighs now, too, as she poured more on his skin. *Half a bottle, Livia said. This is going to get my bed even messier than it usually is.* Down to the buttocks now, though he'd not taken off his *subligaria,* for some reason. Sliding back, and then down the backs of the hard thighs, too, thumbs working in circles. Hearing soft groans of pure pleasure and relaxation as she did. "So what's her name?" Jocasta asked, feeling a prickle along her tongue. "I'm sure your *appointment* has one."

"She told me she wants to be called Aurea." Alexander's voice was slurred, and very close to sleep.

Jocasta moved up again, straddling his hips once more, though now they were slick from the oil. Felt a bit more of a sting than she expected in her own most tender places, but ignored it; it had never really been an issue before with the wolf's blood. "Aurea? That's not a name, that's just the word for a coin I'll never see," she laughed, draping herself along his back, rubbing her breasts enticingly against his shoulder blades. "Why do you want to meet with her, anyway?"

"Because I'm in love with her," Alexander replied sleepily. "Didn't even know there was a difference between loving someone, and being *in* love with them. I hope Tiberius likes her. I . . . hope she likes Tiberius."

Jocasta suddenly felt deeply sleepy, herself. Prickling

warmth radiating up from all along his body, like a toasty fire. "Why . . . would that matter?" she asked, her tongue thick in her mouth. *Something isn't right,* her mind nagged at her. *Why am I . . . so sleepy? He said . . . no more . . . than twenty minutes . . . ?*

"Might not matter at all. But I'd like them to."
She never heard the answer.

Alexander snapped awake, feeling the amulet against his chest burn with cold. Heaviness over his back, not a crushing weight, but definitely about a hundred pounds more than he'd like. His entire back felt as if it were on fire, his heart stuttered in his chest, and raw nausea filled him, making him spew uncontrollably into the pillow just in front of him. He could smell his own bile as it tried to fill his nostrils, and he recoiled, very distantly grateful that he hadn't eaten much dinner at all. Whatever was on his back slipped free limply, rolling away from him with a thump, and he threw up again, his vision skewing.

He tried to get to his feet, failed, and fell out of the bed. Crawled to the door. Managed to remember, after several moments, how to work the latch. Got the door open, and called in a low voice down the hall, "Help. I . . . need help. . . ."

Minucius Spurius, the *frumentarii* agent who'd been accompanying Alexander on his rounds, hastened down the brothel's hallway, aware of various other doors cracking open along his path. He scowled in the direction of both whores and customers, and the doors shut once more. He found his young employer sitting half-naked against the plaster wall, barely able to hold his head up, a strange, medicinal smell around him. *Poison*, was the first thought that crossed Spurius' mind, and he got his hands under the younger man's arms, feeling oil on the skin, making it slick and harder to move Alexander. He kicked the door open, and half-carried him back into the room—and saw the limp body of the young whore Alexander was here to visit, sprawled across the bed. In here, the medicinal smell was much stronger, and he could feel a faint tingling in his hands now, himself. *I fucking hate poisons and poisoners*, he thought grimly. He'd seen far too much of this kind of shit in the east.

Spurius let Alexander fall into a chair. Checked the girl's pulse in her wrist, and could barely feel the flutter of a heartbeat there. Wiped his hands free of the oil on a piece of cloth, and got Alexander's tunic over his head. Wrapped the white folds of the toga around the girl's body, already pragmatically trying to determine his best course of action. *Throw her over my shoulder. Get the young lord on his feet, his arm over my other shoulder, walk him out of here. Get him on his horse, belly-down . . . looks bad, but can say he's had too much to drink. Get him to the villa of the Julii, and drop this harlot in the Tiber . . . no. Too public.*

Alexander's eyes fluttered open. "Spurius," he said, his breathing labored now.

"Yes, *dominus*. Trying to work out how to get you to the villa—"

"No! Too . . . many . . . eyes." Alexander struggled upright. "*Merges*. And . . . call for Ianthe. At the winter camp . . . of the Sixteenth."

Spurius felt a chill go through him. He knew of the priestess of Hecate. He'd managed to avoid being on Alexander's detail any of the days on which the young lord had visited the Empress' private *school*. "You're sure?"

"Knows . . . her poisons. Knows . . . antidotes."

Spurius swallowed. "Yes, my lord. Can you walk?"

"With help." Sweat trickled down Alexander's face, and his head swung almost blindly towards the bed. "Jocasta?"

Who? Oh. The whore. Spurius frowned. "Not quite dead yet. Probably best to get rid of the evidence—"

"I didn't kill her!" That was a stark whisper.

"No, my lord, it's fairly evident she tried to kill *you*, but no one outside this room will believe *that*."

"Bring her. With us. To *Merges*." Each cluster of words punctuated by a gasp for breath, Alexander managed to get himself upright, and then his knees buckled, and Spurius had to catch him. "And the bottle of oil. Had to come. From somewhere."

Spurius groaned under his breath. The young lord needed to lose some of his sentimentality. It was baggage that only weighed him down. But an order was an order. He got Alexander leaning against a wall. Stoppered the bottle and tucked it in a fold of his own toga, praying to all the gods of the underworld that none of the shit in it would bleed through onto his own skin. Tossed the girl's limp body over his shoulder, wondering if she were even breathing still, and then put Alexander's left arm over his shoulder. And somehow got them all out the door.

Aware of the doors cracking open behind him, Spurius got Alexander onto one horse, where the young lord listed, but managed to sit more or less upright. Put the girl in front of his own saddle, and held her up, while paying the servants who'd been holding the horses. And then added, tersely, "There's an *assarius* in it for you, lad, if you run to Flavius the fishmonger on the docks, and tell him Spurius needs fresh eels sent to *Merges*."

"Fresh eels?" the boy said, staring at the reeling Alexander and the unconscious girl.

"Yes," Spurius said, deadpan. "Good eating for when you've had as much to drink as these two have."

And then he kicked his horse and led Alexander's back to the *taverna* near the theater. Hoping that Flavius, damn his hide, would remember the code, and would bring several slippery *frumentari* agents with him, and not a basket of eels fresh-caught from the Tiber this morning.

Servia Sulpicia had spent the evening since dinner happily occupied at the desk in what she was slowly coming to consider a home away from home. She'd decided that her cast of characters wouldn't be the commoners usually found in comedy, no matter *what* Aristotle had to say about that. *Nobles are for tragedy and commoners are for comedy, my ass,* she'd decided. *If Alexander wants to see a play about high-class hypocrisy, how can I possibly show that with a flock of Hellene shepherds?*

Her mind had drifted, and she'd decided on the title, first and foremost: *Masters and Servants. There. Something for everyone. I can have the low-brow clowns that everyone turns out to see, and the high-born people that Alexander wants to mock. We need young lovers, since this is a comedy. Forcibly separated by their families. Should I bring in Marcellus, scurrying off to marry a woman he hadn't seen since he was three years old, because his family demands it? No, too easy to recognize, unless I disguise it – ahh, our young hero, just back from the wars, is in love with one of the family slaves, an Egyptian girl, and wants to free and marry her. Except his family has betrothed him elsewhere, and his beloved slave also has another possible lover – the butler. His father is . . . like Rullus, I think. All stern lectures on how even if the girl was free, she couldn't make more Roman babies . . . whoops, no. This has to be set in Hellas. Or does it, really? Do I really need that much distance? At any rate, he's all stern lectures in public, but behind everyone's back, he's sneaking out at night to visit his favorite male prostitute, like in Aristophanes''* The Frogs. *Oh, this has potential. What's the mother like? Why, she's sleeping with the same butler who has designs on our maiden fair!* Sulpicia's stylus cut into the wax, and she chuckled to herself, already imagining bawdy, farcical scenes that she'd couch in the best poetry she could manage. *And our hero's bride-to-be?* Sulpicia tapped the stylus against her teeth, and then laughed under her breath. *Why, none other than Octavia Thurina. Suitably disguised and exaggerated. Do I dare have her ask our hero if he'd please bring a cyclops home from Etna, the next time he visits Sicily?*

She snickered under her breath and launched into the prologue, light banter between two slaves in verse, to set the scene. Then heard a thud beside the door. Turned with a smile, expecting nothing more than Alexander coming through the door to greet her with a kiss.

And then her smile vanished as a strange man helped Alexander through the door. Her lover's face was nearly gray, and his toga was missing, his tunic stained across the shoulders with some sort of fluid. He staggered to the bed and dropped there, convulsing briefly as he tried to retch, but brought nothing up but a thin trickle of bile on the floor. "Darling," Sulpicia said, dropping to her knees and stroking his face. "You didn't eat dinner—it *can't* be that! What *happened?*"

"Poison," Alexander managed to whisper, and then another thud from the doorway got her attention.

The man once more appeared, this time carrying a slim form wrapped in a white toga. He dropped this person unceremoniously on the floor, and regarded Sulpicia herself now, warily. "Careful, *domina*," the man told her forthrightly. "Think the poison went in through his skin, so mind where you touch the young lord, right?" He took a bottle from inside his own toga's folds carefully now, with two fingers, and set it more cautiously on Sulpicia's desk.

"Ianthe," Alexander said, raising his head, making eye-contact with the man.

"Already sent a man for the priestess of Hecate. She'll be here inside twenty minutes, if I know Flavius."

Priestess of Hecate? Sulpicia blinked.

Alexander heaved himself upright, and Sulpicia looked from him to the bundle on the floor. Saw long, dark hair streaming out of the folds of the toga. Her eyebrows rose, and she gave Alexander a less friendly look. "Who is she?" Sulpicia asked, her heart twinging suddenly.

"Jocasta. Informant." Alexander's shaking hands found the bottom of his tunic, and he pulled it up and over his head. The thick wool had been a very good thing; it had concealed that his amulet now glowed almost blindingly with magic. And that his back and shoulders were almost scarlet, as if with sunburn . "She's . . . a whore. But . . . I didn't . . . didn't sleep with her." He caught her hand now, pressing her fingers tightly with his own, and she could feel the tremors wracking him as he slowly listed back down onto their sleeping couch, face-first. "Haven't . . . with anyone else. Not since you." He turned his head to the side, trying to meet her eyes, and Sulpicia leaned in closer, so she could make out words among his mumbling. "Love my family. Love Ti's spirit. Love your mind, Via. Love you."

He closed his eyes, and Sulpicia, her mind whirling, rose. Unable to make sense of half of what she'd just heard, she seized her *stola* from the bed — she'd never bothered putting it back over her tunic — and a pitcher of wine. *Water won't do it. Water doesn't clean oil worth a damn.* Poured the wine into the soft wool, and started scrubbing at his back, as carefully as she could, trying to avoid touching his skin, or any of the folds of the cloth. *If it came in through the skin, through the oil that's making his skin shine, and has left him as red as if stained with beet-juice, then . . . I need to get it off of him. Before any more of it goes through into his body.*

Within twenty minutes, more people entered the room. More of the strange, cold-eyed men. All older, usually with scars that spoke of old military service. And a woman in a *peplos,* in spite of the Februarius chill. Dark-haired and dark-eyed, she entered the room, looking at first timid . . . and then straightening her back and lifting her chin as if she were a queen. Picked up the bottle when it was pointed out to her, and sniffed it, once. "Aconite," she muttered. "Wolfsbane. Someone knew their art fairly well." She knelt and checked the unconscious woman on the floor, her face a mask of concentration. "This is the poisoner? Strange that she'd be affected by her own brew."

"It's possible that she didn't know what she was using," one of the men replied curtly. "Is she alive?"

"Barely. Get me a brazier with coals. I need to brew antidotes. In the meantime, elevate her feet with some cushions and get her a blanket." Firm, authoritative tone, and then the woman moved over to examine Alexander. Her eyebrows rose. "Very good thinking," she complimented Sulpicia calmly. "You've taken most of the poison off his skin. Are your hands tingling?"

"A little," Sulpicia admitted.

"Wash your hands in wine, then in vinegar, then in water, and then throw all of the fluids straight into the lavatory. No sense you getting ill, as well." She checked Alexander's pulse with impersonal fingers, and peeled back one of his eyelids—at which point he awoke, groaning a bit. "You're in better shape than you have any right to be, considering the strength of the dose in that bottle—ah." As he sat up, the amulet against his chest once more appeared, its glow diminished, but still present. "Sekhmet appears to have protected you. You should give her thanks for your life."

"It's been cold all day," Alexander muttered shakily. "Since dawn."

"Didn't Lord Tiberius have a matching one, my lord?" Two men entered the room, carrying a brazier with coals, setting it down nearby, and the woman turned away to root through the bag she'd carried into the room, coming up with a strange, bifurcated root, which she quickly peeled and chopped, muttering under her breath as she did.

"He does," Alexander confirmed, wrapping his fingers around the amulet. "You think . . . something could have . . . happened to him, too?" He looked dazed. "Coordinated attack?"

"Doubtful," one of the cold-eyed men replied. "If something happened to him, it's coincidence, my lord. You have any orders for us?"

Sulpicia helped Alexander sit up as the woman in the peplos brewed something *foul*-smelling from the root in the pot. He leaned against her unashamed, and managed to raise his head again. "Get someone to Jocasta's house. Check to see . . . if her sister's still there. Or if anyone else is watching the place. Doubt . . . doubt she'd do this on her own. Or even . . . or even knowingly."

One of the men saluted and left immediately, his boots thudding on the stairs. Another man prompted, "And the brothel, *dominus*? Quite a few people saw you leave. Quite a bit worse for wear."

"So long as I'm out in public tomorrow . . . will just . . .

add to my reputation. . . as a reprobate. . . . but have to make sure. . . Jocasta lives." Alexander doubled over again, retching, but as much as he heaved, nothing came up. Sulpicia could feel every spasm wrack him with all the strength in his body. Finally, weakly, he added, "Don't . . . need a reputation . . . as a killer of women . . . dose her first, Ianthe."

"You took more of the poison than she did," Ianthe replied tersely.

"And Sekhmet's . . . little gift . . . is doing more . . . than I ever thought it would. Help *her*. I need to know . . . who's behind this."

Sulpicia stroked his sweat-soaked hair. Gave him water to drink, which he almost immediately brought back up. Rubbed his back, a piece of cloth over her hand, trying to help him breathe. And watched as Ianthe, clearly the priestess of Hecate, took a carefully-measured dose of the brew she'd concocted. Let it cool a little, and then ordered two of the men in the room with them, "I need a reed about nine inches long, and a funnel. Get them from the man downstairs who runs the bar. When he comes back with it, you will need to hold her sitting up. Use the sheath of your knife to prop her jaws open. And I'll need more light."

"What are you going to do?" Sulpicia asked, fascinated.

"If I pour this brew into her mouth, chances are, most of it will wind up pouring down her breasts, which does us no good at all. It needs to get into her belly, and without going into her lungs and drowning her." Terse, cold, professional tone. "I'll put the reed down her throat, aim for the gullet, and pour it in. Unconscious, she shouldn't have a gag reflex."

"She's a whore," one of the two men left in the room pointed out darkly. "If she's apt to gag, I doubt she makes much coin."

Sulpicia glared at him, feeling oddly protective of the

limp, mostly naked girl — an odd reaction, she realized, when just a few minutes ago, she'd thought Alexander had fucked the girl just hours after giving her bliss. "I don't think the comments are necessary," she informed the man crisply.

"Might not be necessary, *domina*, but doesn't make them less true." That, from the other man, with a roll of his eyes.

"Peace, Spurius," Alexander said wearily, as one of the others entered the room once more, reed and funnel in hand. And Sulpicia winced, watching the woman's body quiver, even unconsciously, as the warm tisane was poured down her throat. "Keep her up!" Ianthe said sharply. "She *must* keep it down, or else I'll just be guessing at how much has stayed in her body. And what I'm giving her is just as surely deadly if it's not kept in strict balance with what she's already had."

The woman's body convulsed, and her eyes opened. Rolled. She retched, and some of the fluids came out her nose, at which point Ianthe had the men roll her to her side, so she wouldn't inhale bile and the tisane and everything else. Another convulsion, and Sulpicia felt Alexander tense. "Is she — ?"

"Breathing," Ianthe said after a moment. "It's in the gods' hands now. Perhaps they'll show her a little mercy tonight." She put a blanket over the girl once more, and measured out another draught, this one larger, handing it to Alexander. "Drink it *all*," she told him, evenly.

"What is it?" Sulpicia asked warily.

"Mandrake root," the priestess of Hecate replied calmly, and Alexander almost dropped the cup.

"Mandrake? That's poison — " one of the men objected.

"As I said, it's almost as powerful as the toxin already moving through them, but it counters the aconite. *Drink*, if you would like your heart and your bowels to function again as they should."

Alexander exhaled, and then drank the whole cup in one go, turning his head to spit at the flavor when done. "Via," he said, slipping back down onto the bed.

"I'm here." Sulpicia kept her fingers locked in his.

"You said . . . Rullus and Livia. . . were the ones saying. . . what a pity it would be. . . if I died?"

"They did say that," she replied, stroking his hair again. "But there's no proof right now that either of them were behind this."

"If they were, I will see them *dead*." No inflection in his voice.

"You can't execute a sitting consul. They're immune from prosecution, among other things." She stroked his back, this time letting the cloth fall away. No additional tingling in her fingers. *I must have gotten most of the poison off of him.* "Rullus is quite safe for the rest of his term."

"Then I'll have his fucking *reputation*. I'll have you . . . write epigrams . . . about his preference . . . for being shit on . . . by pretty girls. And who says . . . anything about . . . *prosecution*, anyway?"

The words weren't as labored, but he did sound deeply sleepy now. Sulpicia gave Ianthe a concerned look. "Should we let him sleep?"

"Keep him awake. Talk to him. The longer we can keep him alert, the better I'll feel," the priestess admitted, from where she was looking after Jocasta on the floor.

So through the night, Sulpicia kept Alexander awake. Forced his mind to stay active. Watched as his men helped him to the lavatory, so he could evacuate his bowels—several times. By dawn, he was weak as a day-old kitten, but *alive*, and Ianthe declared that he might sleep now.

Sulpicia leaned down and kissed him. "I have to go,"

she whispered. "I should have been back at my father's house hours ago—"

"Stay." His hand wouldn't unlock from hers.

"He doesn't know all the things I've been doing for you and my uncle—"

"Spurius, go to the house of Corvinus and tell him to make excuses for his niece to her father. She fell ill last night at his house, and will be home when she's feeling up to it. Or some such." Alexander looked up at Sulpicia. "Stay. Please."

She lay down beside him, ignoring the various men in the room. And stayed.

Two hours later, Alexander's eyes snapped open as one of his men tapped on the door. "My lord? We found someone at the house rented by Jocasta, and brought him here."

Alexander managed to heave himself upright in bed, feeling weak and light-headed. . . and not at all hungry yet. Ianthe had dozed off by the hearth, Jocasta in a sort of makeshift bed of blankets and pillows at the priestess' feet, on the floor. He could feel a warm arm slide off his chest, and looked down, realizing, *She stayed. Sulpicia stayed.* "Is whoever it is, safe?"

"Don't think he's much of a threat, *dominus*." Dry tone, that. "Brought you some clean clothes, before we bring him up."

Alexander looked at his soiled tunic on the floor and shuddered. *I couldn't possibly look commanding in something stained with oil and vomit.* Thanking the gods for Spurius, Flavius, and the *taverna* owner, Titius, Alexander managed to find his feet as the door clicked open. Put one hand on the wall, and accepted the fresh tunic and toga, as well as assistance putting them on. By this point, Sulpicia and Ianthe had both awakened, and Alexander nodded at Jocasta on the floor. "Any change?"

"Still breathing," Ianthe reported. "A smaller dose than you took. But she has a much smaller frame. And the gods weren't looking out for her."

"Not so," Alexander said tightly. "Any of the rest of her customers would have left her there to die, I'm sure." Feeling at least ninety percent more human for being clothed, he found a stool to sit down on and caught Sulpicia's hand. "I don't suppose you found clothing for my lady, too, Spurius?" Her dark blue inner tunic only came to her knee. Made of thin silk, it would have been damnably distracting under any other circumstances. A *stola* over it made the whole thing perfectly innocuous, of course.

A sour look from the *frumentarius*. "I'll put it on my list of things to do, *dominus*," the older man growled. "But first, the fish we caught?"

Alexander nodded, and then wished he hadn't, as pain radiated through his head even as his agents propelled a young . . . man? . . . into the room.

No older than Alexander, he had the look of Cupid himself, for all that he wore the undyed, sleeveless tunic of a slave. A hint of gold to his skin, but with curling blond hair, clipped rigorously short in an attempt to make him look more masculine. Honey-amber eyes, long lashes, and an incongruously soft face—no whiskers at all. Little muscle to his long limbs, though he was above average height for a Roman man. And when he saw Jocasta on the floor, the young man immediately dropped to his knees, anguish plain in his face as he shook her shoulder gently. "Mistress! Mistress Jocasta!" An odd, flute-like voice completed the entire package, and Alexander blinked in surprise. *He's been castrated. Early in life, though he hasn't developed breasts yet. Poor lad, he might yet.* The boy looked up, staring at everyone in the room. "What—what have you done to her?"

"Watch your tongue, slave, or I'll have it out of you," Spurius snapped.

Alexander raised a hand, noting distantly how it still trembled. "Peace, Spurius. The young man is right to be concerned for his mistress." He sighed, trying to lean forward. "What's your name?"

"Ianos, my lord." The slave stayed on his knees, but picked Jocasta up. Gathered her to him as if she were a precious, fragile thing.

And Alexander blinked. *It's . . . strange. We think we know people. But they pass through a door, and become someone else, out of our sight.* "Ianos," Alexander said, nodding. "Jocasta was poisoned by the same thing I was. An oil she rubbed on my back, that nearly killed her. And me."

A flutter of expressions, all minute, and ending in a blank wall that shuttered even the young man's eyes. *He's been trained not to show his feelings. Heavily trained.* But Alexander took a stab at understanding, anyway, having read dislike in the first expression. "I was there for information," he said mildly. "I'd already told her I wouldn't be requiring any other services of her, but she informed me that her *reputation* would be damaged if I walked out after only ten minutes of conversation. She was insistent on the massage. I asked her how her sister was . . . and honestly, that's almost all I remember, before crawling to the door to call for help."

The slave's eyes rose tentatively, only by degrees, but still stayed somewhere south of Alexander's chin. "Can you help us understand what might have happened?" Alexander asked, as gently as he could.

"The girl's sister wasn't at their apartment," Spurius put in.

Alexander looked at Ianos now. "Well, where is she? I can't imagine she went far, with both of her legs paralyzed." He caught the inhalation of shock from Sulpicia beside him.

Ianos swallowed. And then the words came out in a tumble. "The lady came six weeks ago, with her guards. Made me carry Mistress Viola to the lady's house. Set her up as a seamstress for her, in her household. Made me stay there, too, until Mistress Jocasta came looking for her sister. The lady kept taking Mistress Jocasta aside for long conversations. Mistress Jocasta wasn't stupid," he added, cradling her to him still. "She kept asking if Mistress Viola really was comfortable. Really felt safe. But with her sister getting three meals a day, and me getting two, I think she felt she *had* to do whatever the lady asked." He swallowed.

"And the lady's name?" Alexander asked, quietly.

"Livia Drusilla," Ianos muttered, looking at the ground. "Mistress Jocasta told me that she'd given her some sort of magic potion to make men very relaxed. So relaxed that maybe she wouldn't have to let them fuck her so much." His soft face tightened a little. "Relaxed enough that they'd tell her things that they wouldn't normally say. She said she'd give everything they said under the potion to you, as well as to Lady Livia. Because she owed you. But . . . Lady Livia has her sister." He glanced up. Made fleeting eye contact with Alexander, and then looked down again.

"It won't hold up in court," Spurius muttered. "Not unless we torture him." And as he spoke, Ianos looked terrified, and clutched Jocasta to him all the more closely.

It was a quirk of Roman law, that testimony from a slave was only admissible if the slave had made the admission under torture. The law was a holdover from an earlier time, in which many slaves were the sons and daughters of the men of the household, fathered on their female slaves. As such, these slaves were assumed to have almost the same filial loyalty as the trueborn children of the house. Alexander snorted, feeling another spasm of pain sear through his head. "Who says that this will go to court, Spurius? I can't make a case against Livia for attempting to murder me. She'll make it all sound like she was just doing *charitable work* among the downtrodden, and that Jocasta misunderstood how much of the potion to give her customers."

"If she told the girl to put the oil on your skin and rub it in by hand," Ianthe said suddenly, "she undoubtedly intended the girl to die as well. That bottle was *very* potent. How much worse for the Julii, if Lord Alexander was found not just dead, but dead, with a dead prostitute beside him? And if he happened somehow to survive, for him to have to deal with the repercussions of the dead girl, too?"

Alexander's eyes fell on the bottle on the table, beside Sulpicia's writing kit. "I'd like to pour Livia's wolfsbane oil right down her throat," he said. Clear, cold words. Not a snarl, not a growl. "I'd like her to taste it all, right before it takes her to meet Pluto and Proserpina."

Ianos looked down at Jocasta's slack face. "Please . . . will Mistress Jocasta be all right?"

Ianthe stood from where she'd been sitting against the wall, and moved forward, putting a hand on his shoulder with surprising gentleness. "Her heart beats. She breathes. She may just need time for her body to recover. How were you able to leave Lady Livia's house today, slave that you are?"

"I'm slave to Mistress Viola and Mistress Jocasta, and Mistress Viola asked me to check on her sister. That was enough for the other servants to let me leave," he mumbled, and then looked up at Alexander, a flicker of profound hate suddenly passing through his eyes before he remembered to focus his gaze below Alexander's chin. "Lady Livia did this to her."

Alexander nodded, slowly. "Yes."

"Mistress Jocasta's the only person who's ever treated me like a human being," Ianos said, his soft voice becoming surprisingly cold now. "If you want Lady Livia dead, I can do it. I can put a knife in her heart. And I wouldn't even care if her guards cut me down afterwards."

"But I think Jocasta would," Sulpicia said suddenly, with so much compassion and insight, that Alexander turned and looked at his lady, startled. "Wait until your mistress wakes up, Ianos. You can stay with her and tend her until she . . . either wakes, or passes. And that will give Lord Alexander time to decide what to do about Lady Livia."

What to do, indeed, Alexander thought, his head still burning, making it difficult to think. *Having the slave do it would be fitting, but . . . what a possible waste if the guards kill him. He couldn't be traced back to me, but. . . he can pass for either male or female. He's used to controlling his face. A little training, and he might be a better resource than any of Sulpicia's actors. But if he does it, then Jocasta's sister is still in that house, and could be killed. Though that might just be . . . unfortunate collateral damage.*

And against his heart, the amulet of Sekhmet winked out, and warmed to the same temperature as his skin, at last.

Chapter IX: Breath of the Desert

It had been late in the afternoon when the *equites* had left Alexandria, following a trail that would have gone cold, but for Eurydice's hawks in the air. They knew that their quarry had yet to leave the Nile's lush delta area, but had made good time, for all that the six men were ambling along on donkeys, and staying at the periphery of the green, farmed area. The *equites* had a local guide with them, in case they needed to talk to locals, who might not speak Latin; their guide called over to Tiberius, "They are being very cautious for the moment. Close to the river, more people will see them. And with the sun so close to setting, many animals in the river become more active, too."

"What kind of animals?" Tiberius called back.

"Crocodiles, snakes, and hippopotami," the man called back, a wide smile flashing across his olive-toned face. "At least, crossing through the farms at the very edge of the desert, all they need to worry about are lions and jackals. And snakes, too."

"Crocodiles and hippopotami are worse than lions?" Tiberius asked, not entirely interested at the moment.

"Much worse," their guide affirmed, laughing. "You Romans say, as brave as a lion. *We* say, as brave as a hippopotamus. At least a lion will only attack for good reason—you've startled it, you're interfering with its hunt, you've come too close to its cubs. A hippo? Sometimes attacks a boat four times its length, for no other reason than that it's in the water." A grimace. "And wins." The guide paused. "They'll probably make for a river landing at some point, and try to take a barge further south. It's faster by far."

No more words for a while. Just watching the fields

pass by to their left, and the desert pass by to the right. The fields were bare at the moment, though their canals still held a little water and mosquitoes buzzed constantly around them. Date palms clustered here and there, both near the farmers' huts, to provide shade and food, and also here, at the far edges of the fields, where the canals ran along the edge. A thin and rustling wall to break the desert winds.

That rustle was the only sound for the moment, besides the jingle of harnesses and armor. Tiberius' horse, shield, and the light spear the cavalry favored were all borrowed from another *equite* attached to Eurydice's Sixteenth, but his sword, *pugio*, and armor were his own. Sweating a little under the last rays of the sun, but then night's chill, spreading across the desert with startling suddenness. "We need to make up time on them," the lead *equite* called. "There's a clear enough road, and enough moonlight. We can press on."

"We also don't want to overshoot their campsite in the dark," Tiberius muttered under his breath. They'd lost the support of Eurydice's hawk with sunset. If she'd managed to find a friendly owl, the bird had yet to land on anyone's shoulder to let them know of its presence.

Night sounds joined the jingle of harness. Strange, hooting laughter from the darkness set them all on edge, but their guide identified it tersely, "Hyenas. Small ones. Peasants eat them — if they can catch the cowardly things."

"I heard that if you get ahold of a male hyena," a voice from Tiberius' left, "and kill it, you can take the anus, and bind it into an amulet. Wear it on your upper arm, and you'll be irresistible to women."

"Manius, women already know you're an asshole," someone else called back. "That's your whole *problem*. You don't need to add to it."

Rough guffaws of laughter. Tiberius wished he could

join in, but even the heat in his body from exertion, the feeling of being part of something larger than himself, that he always got from working with other legionnaires, had failed to warm him for once.

Finally, they made camp for a few hours, mostly to let the horses rest. Caught what sleep they could, themselves. And before dawn, were back in the saddle, following the faint tracks in the hard-beaten road that they'd been tracing out for hours now. Stopping to talk to farmers hauling plows out into the fields to break up winter's sleeping soil along the way — wary, suspicious eyes, regarding their Roman armor and faces. "Still ahead of us, but not by much," the patrol's leader, a man with the odd cognomen of Libo, announced after one such conversation. "Let's pick up the pace."

And thus, with the first rays of the sun's light peeking over the horizon, they finally set eyes on their quarry. Six men on donkeys, hastily trying to cut through a farmer's field now, heading off the road towards the Nile. "Look, they're heading for behind that farmer's hut, to hide and let us pass them by!" the *equite* who'd spoken so knowledgeably about the properties of hyena rectums called.

"Form up," Libo shouted back. "One of them, at least, is a mage-priest. We all know what that means. Get in close as fast as you can, and they can't concentrate for shit to use their magic. So in we go, lads — at the gallop. Watch for holes in this field, though. No one needs to break a horse's leg today."

Two hundred *pesi* away, they spread out into a rough wedge shape, using the leader as the point of the simple triangular shape. Twenty men, four rows, more or less, with Tiberius just behind the leader, in the second row. They kicked their horses, and their legs, conditioned and strengthened by just this exercise, clamped to the horses' sides. That hold and their innate sense of balance were all that would keep them atop the beasts, even at the full charge. Still, it took raw nerve for infantry to hold in the face of a cavalry charge. Horses outweighed humans, usually by about eight hundred pounds. And a trained war-horse didn't flinch from trampling right over soft human flesh with their bare hooves. Were trained to bite and kick as well. Infantry only stood a chance when they had long spears, and were several rows deep—and preferably, had some sort of barrier in front of them. Spears. Ditches. *Tribuli*, or caltrops. These priests on their donkeys couldn't have had time to set up such defenses, and were, in fact, still in motion. Trying to crowd behind that farmer's hut in the distance.

One hundred *pesi*. Libo shouted to the fleeing priests, "Stand down! Dismount! Hands where we can see them!"

In response, the last of the donkeys crowded behind the hut. Tiberius could just see the door of the hut opening. The surprised look on the farmer's face was lost to the distance and the gray light of dawn, but the rough door slammed right back shut again.

Sixty *pesi*. "Watch for spells! We're almost in their range now! Watch for fire, and stay spread out!"

One man beside Tiberius shouted in fear and reined in, his hands flying to his face and eyes in consternation, even as the other riders thundered past him. "I can't see!" he bawled over the noise of hooves. "I can't fucking *see*!"

Another man screamed, and Tiberius caught a brief glimpse of something horrific—scarab beetles and scorpions, somehow clinging to the horse's sides, swarming up the beast's legs and scrambling up onto the rider. The horse reared, panicking, throwing the man, and then he was on the ground, covered in the creatures—if they were real. Tearing at his own flesh, howling with pain at the stings and the bites—

No time to wonder. Just enough to grit his teeth, pray

to any gods that were listening for protection, and continue in. "Right flank, west! Left flank, east. Move around the house and pin them from both sides!"

Fifty *pesi*. Tiberius could *just* see the priests leaning around the western edge of the house. Could see their mouths moving.

And then the winds rose, slamming in from the west, carrying sand with them like a wave from the sea. Scraping over armor and skin. It wasn't enough to stop the momentum of the horses, but then there was so much brown dirt in the air, it looked as if they were riding into the heart of a wildfire. They couldn't see more than five feet ahead of them, and, unconsciously, every rider leaned back, and the horses responded, easing their pace as they all tried to ensure that they wouldn't run into anything. "Steady!" Libo shouted, his voice almost lost in the wind. "Keep going! It can't reach far!"

But somehow, the winds seemed to blanket the entire area. Whipping in a furious circle, the sandstorm intensified. Tore at their flesh. Tiberius couldn't keep his eyes open, and his horse spooked under him, trying to bolt. He clutched the reins, sawing at the creature's mouth, and clamped his legs tightly, trying to keep the beast under control, when *another* burst of wind came in, buffeting him from behind, making him reel. The *sound* of it was like nothing he'd ever heard before—not the shattering clap of thunder, but a steady, continuous deafening roar.

Their charge faltered. Turned into a nightmarish crawl as this horse or that spooked, throwing its rider, and galloped off, away from the freakish wind. Blind, they could only move forward. Deafened, they couldn't coordinate. Tiberius' horse finally bucked one time too many, and he flew off, hitting the ground in an agony of abraded, tortured flesh. Only where his metal armor stood between him and the wind, was there any relief from the pain—his legs, arms, and parts of his face felt as if they were weeping blood. On the ground, the dirt came up to cover him, relentlessly, and the wind shrieked and pummeled him every time he tried to rise.

He got his shield up over his head and *crawled,* his spear still in his right hand. Blind. *I'm a worm in the earth,* he thought, half-delirious, as the sand piled atop him. *On my belly. Buried alive.* The sand grew heavier atop him, but the shield provided a pocket of air, and at least the heavy sand gave some relief from the stinging, cruel wind. *Keep going. Keep going. If you stop moving, you're dead. Or you died already, and just don't know any better.* He'd have laughed, if he had any breath. *Can't see. Can't hear. No idea if you're going forward or up or down. Just a worm in the earth. They died and buried you, and the worms came to eat you, and now you're one of the worms. Crawl on, Tiberius, son of Nero. Crawl on, like a worm. Like a ghost. You're your own mane . . . .*

Not enough air left. Every movement took more and more effort, and his head ached fiercely. *See? Dead. Dead and buried. Just didn't have the sense to stop moving.* Tiberius managed to open his eyes in the darkness under the ground, and whispered, with what felt like his last breath, "Pluto. Proserpina. I give myself to you, to curse these fucking priests. I spit at them, and all enemies of Rome. May my death be their scourge."

The curse of a dying man was held to have great power. And *devotio,* the rite in which the general of a Roman army promised his life to Pluto in return for victory, hadn't actually been practiced since the Punic wars. But as his ears rang with the lack of air, Tiberius suddenly felt . . . comforted. Felt as if he had a legion of brothers all around him. And somehow found the strength to lift himself up, through the two feet of heavy sand over his head, and found that the wind had died. Nothing but sweet, blissful air.

He gasped for a lungful. Blinked rapidly, tears pouring through his reddened, painful eyes, clearing the dust, so he could see that he'd somehow wound up near the edge of the farmer's hut — which had been in the middle of an arable field, with a plow set at the edge of one of the canals, waiting for the farmer to begin his day's labor. Now, the walls of the hut were pitted and scored. Sand had piled up around it, halfway up the door, and the shuttered windows were silted in. Behind him, Tiberius realized distantly, five or so of the *equites* were struggling up from the sand, just as he had — some up to forty *pesi* away. He, on the other hand, was close enough to hear voices from the other side of the building. Voices speaking in Egyptian. Harried. Hurried.

And then one of them laughed.

Tiberius found his feet. Set them atop the shifting, uncertain drifts of sand. And came around the corner of the building, spear in hand and shield up, feeling nothing but empty coldness all the way through him. Caught a glimpse of wide, shocked brown eyes and a mouth rounded in horror, and jabbed, hard, catching the first priest in the throat. The priest clutched at the wound as Tiberius yanked the spear back, and blood poured through the man's fingers as he choked. Gasped. Fell to the ground, trying to hold his life in. *Try all you like. You're already dead.*

Two steps, over the body of the dying man as he writhed. Five more priests, backing up, eyes wide in surprise. But they weren't afraid. Not yet. One of them gabbled in his own language, twisting his fingers in the air, and *something* came up from under the sands. Agitated by the sudden storm, and drawn by the mage-priest's command, a cobra rose up, flaring its hood, and struck, sinking its fangs into Tiberius' left knee, coated as it was by an armor of his own blood and the sand that had entombed him.

He barely felt the bite. Didn't feel the burn. *Did* feel the amulet hanging at his heart turn suddenly cold, but it didn't matter. The only thing that mattered was killing these enemies. Now. Before they could do any more harm. *My life for this, Pluto. My life for their deaths.*

His first stab with the spear missed; on the second attempt, one of the priests shouted something, and the wooden shaft splintered in his hand. The fourth man shrieked the words of another incantation, and fire roared towards Tiberius. He ducked behind his leather-covered wooden shield with its metal rivets. The shield burst into flame; his legs, covered by that armor of blood and sand, felt the heat, but didn't blister.

And treating his fiery shield as just another weapon, Tiberius slammed it into the face of the closest priest and bore down on the man. Hit him in the face with it, hard, and then held the shield right to the man's reeling body. Heard the screams of pain and panic as the man's wig and clothing caught on fire. Smelled burning skin and flesh as the priest staggered back. Saw the pattern of blisters left by the hot rivets, embossed into the man's face and body as he rolled back and forth on the sand, trying to put the flames out. *Too bad you filled in the canals with your sandstorm,* Tiberius thought distantly, drawing his sword now, and stabbing down. Killing the wounded man mid-roll.

Footsteps behind him, as some of his fellow *equites* finally made it around the corner. The stoutest of the priests, who looked vaguely familiar to Tiberius' dazed eyes, lifted a hand, and both *equites* locked in place. Shook. One of them took a step back, and then the iron conditioning of the legion kicked in. *No retreat. We never retreat. We only go forward.* Fighting some unseen compulsion, both *equites* continued forward, trembling in what looked like mortal terror. But forward they came. Inexorably.

The cobra struck one of them, coiled and ready—he shouted in pain, and staggered, trying to move in. The other man attacked one of the priests, and somehow, shaken by the magic used against him, missed. Giving another priest time to incant, and suddenly, the weapons held by all three of them turned red-hot to the touch.

Tiberius shouted in agony, the leather wrapping around the hilt of his gladius going up in flames in his hand, but held onto it anyway. *It doesn't matter. None of it matters. I'm already dead. They buried me in the ground, and my breathing this air is just an illusion. An anomaly. An extra chance granted by Pluto to exercise my own curse on them.* Two decisive thrusts at the torso of the closest priest, and the red-hot blade sank into vitals both times, once again with the smell of burning flesh, and the rending howls of a dying man.

Neither of the other *equites* managed to hold onto the forge-hot blades, but even the man bitten by the cobra stepped forward now. Shields became weapons, hitting the faces of two of the remaining priests. And that freed Tiberius to chase after the last man, the stout one, who'd turned to flee now, heading for the line of date palms that marked the edge of the next field over.

Tiberius was limping on the bitten leg, the only reason he didn't catch the man immediately. The priest swung around, and Tiberius finally recognized him through the haze of pain and battle-fury over his eyes. *That's Tahut-Nefer. I saw him at the Julii villa often enough.* "Surrender," Tiberius rasped, still holding his *gladius* in a hand that seemed to be made of equal parts pain and numbness. "You've got nowhere to run, priest."

Tahut spun, but kept backing away. "Surrender? So

you can crucify me in the name of Rome? I think not!"

He took another step back, and Tiberius followed him. Eyed the priest's path. Noted how Tahut was backing right for the farmer's wooden plow, which protruded up through the sand now, anchored in place by the weight of it. The curving wood that normally comprised the handles and the actual blade—bronze-tipped, pointed up into the air like a single sharp tooth.

And then Tahut's hands lifted, and two fist-sized balls of fire formed in the air in front of him. Tiberius got the smoking remnants of his shield up in time, but they burned through the scorched wood, searing his arm behind it. And then he limped closer, inexorably. "I'm already dead," he told Tahut. Saw how the words jarred the man, and added, quietly, "You can't kill what's dead."

And then he was on Tahut, jabbing with the sword that seemed an extension of his arm, and the pain and misery of his burned right hand seemed to transmit right through to the blade's tip. Caught the priest in one thick shoulder, but that was hardly a killing blow. *Many gladiators keep a few extra pounds of fat on their frames. So it's that much harder to find their gullets with a sword's point.* Blank, absent thoughts, and Tiberius took another step in. Slammed his shield's rim into Tahut's teeth, making the priest take another step back, spitting blood.

And then, as the blood hit the ground, the priest said a *Name*, which rang out through the air. "Kebechet!" Tahut snarled. "My blood for you! Kill this man!"

Something rippled through the air in front of him, a feminine figure that seemed transparent as water. Cold, clammy, wet fingers gripped his throat, and a second hand covered his nose and mouth, and water poured down his throat, and for a terrible instant, Tiberius thought he was about to drown on dry land. It *burned*, forcing its way into his lungs, and his mind screamed for an instant in mortal fear.

And then the terrible, stubborn part of him that Octavian had hated so much rose up, and Tiberius jammed his iron sword through the sleek, watery form of whatever spirit this was. And when his hand, bleeding freely from where it had been burned, rammed through the spirit's body in the wake of the iron blade, it recoiled. Pulled away with a hiss, and he was able to strike it again and again with the blade, until it fled, turning into a white vapor and undulating away through the air.

Gasping and choking for air, Tiberius set off after the fleeing priest once more. Chest burning, leg on fire now, he managed one final sprint. And, mid-stride, kicked with his good leg, hitting the priest in the lower back, sending him tumbling face-first . . . right atop the upturned plow's bronze-plated blade.

There was a meaty sort of sound as the blade ripped through the priest's body, but it was low, through the intestines and out through the man's back. Far too low to kill him cleanly. Tiberius stood there for a moment, coughing up pink-tinged water from his lungs, watching the priest squirm and writhe, trying to lift himself off the two feet of the curving blade that protruded from the sand. Listened to Tahut begging various spirits to help him — each *Name* rippled through the air, but nothing answered. Frantic invocations of the Name of Thoth, each one weaker than the last. Tiberius couldn't understand a word of it, and yet, he understood the meaning all too well. *Mercy, my lord. Mercy and life, please, mercy, I beg of you.*

Watching this man beg for life, while Tiberius had consigned his own to the underworld to stop him, somehow grated. But there wasn't any conscious thought at all as

Tiberius brought the point of his *gladius* down, jamming it through where the bald scalp showed the hollow where skull met spinal column. Felt it crunch through the bone, and into the softer material of the brain. Felt the whole body spasm, once.

And then went limp.

Tiberius dropped to kneel, exhausted, beside the dead man's body. Realized that his right hand was so badly burned, he couldn't unflex it from around his sword. Tried to pull the blade free of the skull, and realized that it was stuck fast, for the moment. *Bad form, that. My old trainers would have a fit.* Mechanical, useless thoughts.

He groped at his belt, left-handed, for his *pugio*, and tried to pry his fingers apart, only to give up as pain lanced up from the damaged tendons and screaming nerves. And then he just leaned there, feeling a lighter wind now against his abraded cheeks. And waited for Pluto and Proserpina to take their due. *I'm ready. A bargain is a bargain. My life is yours.*

Except, for whatever unaccountable reason, he kept on existing. Eyeblink after eyeblink, he remained conscious. No darkness. No Styx. No Charon. Just the pitiless light of dawn streaming over the Nile in the distance, and the hooting of strange birds in the palms above. *What, don't you want your sacrifice? Take me.*

And then the other equites were on him, panting and in pain, just as he was. "He's dead," they told him, misinterpreting the *pugio* in his hand. "He's already dead. Come here, let's have a look at you—"

"Manius took a bite to the leg from a cobra—we've got him lying down, a belt around his knee, trying to keep the poison from swelling—"

"Anyone see Libo?"

"I think he bought it—"

"Hey, the sand over here is moving—might have a survivor! Help me dig, gods damn it!"

Tiberius let the others pull him away from the body. Let one of them take a look at his knee, where the cobra venom mysteriously didn't seem to be spreading. Let them uncurl his hand from his *gladius,* clenching his teeth against the pain. Let them wrap the wound, for what good it would do, and generally provide the half-tender, half-joking concern that legionnaires showed each other, when no one else was around to see how much they cared. "Hope you don't masturbate right-handed, lad. Otherwise, that's strictly a non-issue for a while."

"Hey! Did you see that last priest? Did you *see* what our lad did to him?"

"Yes! Our Tiberius *plowed* him! Fucked him right up!"

"You need a cognomen, you know. Fancy *Agricola*?"

The word for farmer rang through the air, and Tiberius raised his head slowly. Stared at the man speaking. "Exanimis," he said, his voice a dull croak. *Without life.* "Funestus." *Defiled by death.* "Damnatus." *Damned.*

"Ah, shush. No one wants to hear ill-omened shit like that. Mark my words. Tiberius Claudius Nero Agricola it will be." The speaker, a man in his late twenties, helped the younger tribune to his feet.

No. It'll be Tiberius Claudius Nero Damnatus. What <u>else</u> do you call a man who died, was buried, and whom not even the gods want when he freely offers his life?

Wandering thoughts, however, had to be set aside, as he was now the ranking officer. On his feet now, it fell to him to deal with the frightened farmer and his family. To ask them for water to soothe parched throats. And then he sent someone off to try to collect the terrified horses. Sent another off as a courier, ahead of everyone else. Put the two remaining more-or-less able-bodied men to the task of helping the severely injured man whom they'd dug up from under the sand, and finding the bodies of the dead, while allowing the other man who'd been bitten by the cobra to rest in the shade. Nothing more they could do for him, or so it seemed. Tiberius moved to his side, offering him the amulet of Sekhmet that still burned cold around his neck, but the other man refused. "No. The snake took me second. Shouldn't have had as much venom left after the first bite." Still, his face dripped with sweat, where they'd lain him down with his feet propped up. "Just get me moving, trib. I need a *medicus* to look at this. Frown. And pour some damned tea down my throat and mutter prayers in the general direction of Asclepius."

Of a patrol of twenty, fourteen men had died. The man who'd been blinded had perished in the sandstorm. One man, when dug up, had hundreds of swollen bites and stings over his body, and Tiberius shuddered at the recollection of the beetles and scorpions. *That could have as easily been me. Or any of the rest of us.*

They built sledges for the bodies of the fallen, and a separate, smaller sledge for their injured comrades. Hitched them, roughly, to the recovered horses. And then, very slowly, they rode back north, towards Alexandria.

Tiberius wondered, as he rode, the reins in his left hand, and still looking like a creature made of the earth itself, if he'd ever know peace or respite again. *Agricola. Damnatus.* The two words spun in his head in tandem, like the beat of a drum.

In Alexandria the night before, Eurydice had been watching through the eyes of her hawks, while still conversing with Damkina Banit, their new Magus acquaintance, with Caesarion, Malleolus, Antyllus, Selene, and Antony in the room. Plenty of people to keep an eye on the Magus for her, while her own were otherwise occupied. She'd frowned after a moment or two, and then held a hand up apologetically to check Damkina's words as she turned towards her husband. "Caesarion?" she said, blind to the room around her, but knowing that he was nearby, at the sand table with Antony and Antyllus, looking over a model of Thebes. "Why is Tiberius with this band of *equites* riding out of the city? He was wounded three hours ago. Shouldn't he be resting?"

She'd been able to hear the frown in Caesarion's voice. "I healed the bones in his arm, but I considered him stood down for the day, yes. He did us good service, holding that demon at bay. And you say he's riding out in search of that group that slipped the perimeter? The one we think might be the priests we're looking for?"

"A hawk's eyes do not lie," Eurydice replied crisply. "He's distinctive, armor or no, and I took a low pass in front of the column of horsemen. It's him."

"Who the fuck put him up to this?" Caesarion said, the barracks oath slipping out unchecked.

"I did," Antony returned evenly, and Eurydice wished she could release the hawk to look around her, without having to grope for the mind again. But at such a distance, her grip on the bird's mind was tenuous enough without adding to the difficulty. "I thought keeping him occupied would be the best thing for him, honestly. Work's a damned fine tonic. Would have done me better, years ago, than all the wine I wound up drinking instead."

Uncomfortable shifting of feet, scraping against the smooth tiles of the floor. "Besides," Antony went on, his shrug practically audible in his voice, "he's helping to chase down a clout of priests. Our empress already met Tahut and outstripped him in power inside of a year. If twenty men can't handle that, they don't deserve to be called legionnaires."

Damkina cleared her throat during Antony's oration, and then chuckled uneasily. "Ah. You haven't often fought the mage-priests of Thebes, then."

Eurydice's head turned towards Damkina, and she frowned. "What do you mean? I honestly didn't find much noteworthy about Tahut-Nefer. Even the spells in his Book of Thoth seemed . . . rudimentary. Things learned by rote."

Damkina sighed. "Yes. They do tend towards a very . . . basic understanding of the world around us. One locked in the past. Fortunately for those of us who serve the Magi, anyway. Individually, a mage-priest *isn't* much of a foe. However, they're incredibly dangerous when found in larger numbers. Even I would hesitate to fight a group of them without other Magi for assistance."

Antyllus, his voice moving closer as he spoke, said sharply, "What do you mean? What makes groups of them so dangerous?"

"Because they have a gift that we Magi do not," Damkina replied simply. "Those very simple spells, the ones that aren't very effective when cast by a single person? Become extraordinarily dangerous when cast by a large group of mage-priests. They don't just add to one another's power. It . . . concatenates. For example, if one mage-priest can usually cast a spell that throws a rock ten feet, he and a friend working together don't just double it. It's not two rocks, thrown ten feet. It's two rocks thrown *twenty*, with twice the force. Four mage-priests? That's four rocks, all thrown forty feet, with four times the force."

Eurydice bolted to her feet, suddenly shaking and sick to her stomach. A vision of her own firefan spell, learned from

Tahut-Nefer's Book of Thoth, flared across her vision. *A fan of flame, ten to fifteen feet long. What would it look like with six men all casting it at once?* "But Tahut said that they couldn't cast outside forty *pesi* with any accuracy—"

"How much accuracy," Damkina asked softly, "do you need when you start a whirlwind, centered forty feet from you, and then a friend joins in, and then another, and then another? The winds will spread their effect on their own. Shear into each other. Churn the area around them—"

"That's how they did it!" Caesarion said, his voice tight. "That's how they took out Prefect Gallus' century, the one he sent to Thebes to investigate the missing tax collectors. *That's* why there are reports from the survivors of men being buried alive." He moved across the room, sound of rapid steps on the floor, and he caught Eurydice's arm in his hand. "Can you tell them to stop?"

Sick at heart, Eurydice shook her head. "No," she whispered. "I'm looping the hawk back and forth in front of them, but they just keep following the trail. Gods, for a way to *talk* to them at a distance—"

"You don't have spirits tied to any of them, whose Names you know?" Damkina asked, sounding surprised.

"Most Romans don't have more than house-spirits," Caesarion told her curtly.

"And none of mine know the smell of your men's blood," Damkina returned, her voice regretful. "I can't help you in this."

"Gods *damn* it," Antyllus swore, pacing back and forth, his feet rasping on the tile. "I should *be* there with them—"

"What, and get yourself killed, too?" Antony snapped at his son. "Think! What's one more man going to do in this situation?"

"Shoot the fucking priests in the *eye* from farther away

than they can cast any spells," Antyllus returned, just as sharply, and Eurydice heard Selene inhale in shock at her betrothed's choice of words. *Yes, sister, there's more to him than the kind and gentle man who courted you. He's just as much a legionnaire as all the rest.*

"Send a century after them," Caesarion ordered Antony. "Even if all they do is arrive in time to pick up the pieces and bandage the survivors, it's the least we can do."

"I volunteer—" Antyllus began.

"No," Caesarion said curtly. "You, too, have done enough. You're *still* wounded, since I can't heal more than one person a day. And you just became betrothed a few hours ago. You can sit still for a day or two. And that *is* an order, since apparently I need to make these things *explicitly clear*."

With sunset, the *equites* rode on. Out of Eurydice's range. She'd thought that she'd have trouble sleeping, but instead, her body betrayed her, and she fell asleep almost as soon as they left the range of her eyes, awakening near dawn, groggy and only partially refreshed. As soon as she stirred, Caesarion rolled over in the bed next to her, and pulled her close. "The child makes you sleepy," he muttered against her hair.

"Sleepy and sick," she mumbled. "Though Nesa tells me the first months are the worst. The next three months, she informs me, are quite enjoyable."

"Mmm." Caesarion apparently woke up a little further then. "What's that?"

"She says I can expect to feel considerable ardor," Eurydice informed him, rubbing his forearm, snugged tight to her ribs at the moment. "Of course, with you in Britannia, *that* will be a complete waste."

Caesarion groaned and kissed the side of her neck. "Wonderful. I would take you with me, love, but . . . if you can't use your magic, then you're a great potential prize for the enemy."

"I've been thinking about that—"

"Of course you have." Caesarion sat up and squinted at their windows, which overlooked the port below. Cool sea breezes wafted in through these openings, left unshuttered against the night air. Even at this hour, lights were moving across the blackened waters of the pre-dawn sea. "I thought I ordered the harbor closed."

"Local fishermen, as the people of the city need to keep eating. Mother requested an exemption, so long as they stay within sight of the Lighthouse. Any of them try to slip away, and there's a quinquereme ready to take off after them and sink them. No quarter given. Signals are all set up." Eurydice sat up with him now. "About what I was thinking—"

Caesarion lay back among their sheets. "I take back everything I said about the boredom of our trip here. I suddenly long for the chance to sleep in and not think about any of this." He rubbed her arm. "Go ahead. I'm listening."

Eurydice swallowed. "Remember outside the baths a few years ago, when I touched your mind for the first time?"

He went still. "Gods, yes."

"I remember wondering what we could do if we joined our powers." She slipped down and pillowed her head on his chest. "If the problem is draining too much power from the mother's body, and *that's* what puts the child at risk, what happens if I take the power from you, instead?"

His fingers found the base of her neck, and stroked against her scalp for a moment or two as he thought about it. "I don't know," Caesarion told her at last. "I don't think I want to experiment with it at the moment. It seems risky, and we do have other options."

She nodded against him. "Just something to consider.

Mother does keep mentioning the royal magics. Which we need to do at Thebes anyway. I expect it might have something to do with, well, exactly this."

"You touch my mind every time we join our bodies. I can *feel* the power coursing between us." Caesarion's voice had become almost inaudible. "I'm fairly sure that we're doing what we need to be doing, every time we do *that*." He rolled to his side, dumping her gently on her back. "Speaking of which? Would you like to ensure the fertility of the land and the fecundity of the Nile some more?"

She laughed, but a little guiltily. "I'm a little worried about that patrol," Eurydice admitted.

"So am I. But we can't do much for them from here. The century we sent after them will either arrive in time. Or it won't." He kissed her, gently, and then more ruthlessly as they both woke up more thoroughly.

But before they'd even finished, there came a tap at the door, as servants tried to wake them to start their day. "Not yet!" Caesarion snapped.

"My lord, my lady, you have meetings scheduled over breakfast—"

"Five damned minutes, and if you open that door, you'll be dismissed!" Caesarion put his forehead against Eurydice's shoulder, as she couldn't help but chuckle under her breath, and then got back to what they'd been doing. It was better to laugh, than to weep, as she'd been doing too often lately. Because every embrace felt like a long, silent farewell at the moment.

Then, yes, breakfast. Meetings with the commander of the Sixteenth, Balbus, about the lockdown of the city. Meetings with at least three irate merchant princes, whose cargos were starting to rot in their ships. "Once we determine that all the perpetrators have been caught, then yes, I will open the harbor," Caesarion said sharply, and Eurydice touched his elbow lightly with her fingers. He glanced back at her, caught her silent message, and went on more temperately, "This is a security decision for the protection of my wife, but it remains a short-term one."

"I expect that normal trade will resume within a day," Eurydice put in calmly. "Two, at most, though that could change."

And when the merchants left, Caesarion caught her hand lightly. "I need to let you do more of the talking, don't I, if they're to see you as queen in your own right, and not just an adjunct to me."

Eurydice smiled faintly. "The pharaoh rules. The queen rules through him, unless she's a pharaoh in her own right. I don't really plan to wear a false beard in public, so I think we're fine."

More meetings. More reports. Agitated ambassadors who couldn't receive messages from their countries. "And, as official spies, can't send reports to their countries, either," Caesarion muttered under his breath.

Finally, around noon, Selene slipped in to remind them, quietly, that lunch was ready, and that the cooks were likely about to waste food by cooking another version of the same meal, to be able to present it at optimum freshness. Eurydice and Caesarion joined their sister for the meal—which was presented in Hellene, style, reclining, in the formal dining area. Duck braised with figs and coriander, fresh pomegranates, and unleavened bread. Caesarion insisted on eating first, though Eurydice reminded him that her spirits would likely recognize most poisons. *Except perhaps random herbs like catmint and silphium, which threaten the baby, and not me,* she thought grimly, and then concentrated simply on keeping her food down where it belonged. While the duck smelled amazing, she kept to bread and fruit for the moment.

And noticing how downcast Selene seemed, for a newly-betrothed woman, Eurydice attributed it to Antyllus' absence from the meal, and addressed their sister bracingly, "You know, Selene, you're quite fortunate. Whenever you return to Rome with Antyllus, why, even if he decides not to move out of the Antonii villa, you'll largely be the woman of the house! Mother will be staying here indefinitely . . . though Antony told me two days ago, with what I considered surprising tact and thoughtfulness from him, that he planned to build his own house here in Alexandria. A true governor's residence, separate from the military enclave where Prefect Gallus has been living." She nodded. "You won't be under Mother's thumb, regardless of where you and Antyllus wind up living." With no response from Selene but a nod, Eurydice continued on, forthrightly, "And while I wouldn't trade in Caesarion for any man in the world, I envy you one thing, Selene—the freedom you and Antyllus will have to travel. Why, coming here, Caesarion and I had to call up most of a flotilla. To see the Alps last year? Half a legion went with us. You and Antyllus just need a light guard, and off you go to Antioch or Palmyra or wherever you choose."

"You won't even have a Praetorian escort anymore," Caesarion said, picking up on the cues. "I'm sure that will make you happy."

Selene nodded at the appropriate junctures, until Eurydice sighed internally and gave up.

Selene looked up from the lists and lists of things her mother's servants had sent her, regarding her wedding. She'd shuddered over half of them. *No, I will not wear a bridal kalasiris, with my breasts exposed. Eurydice had to, to make the*

Egyptians happy. I don't have to make anyone happy. Except Antyllus. It was a novel thought. *And I'm fairly sure he just wants a normal Roman ceremony, or as normal as we can get here, given that I can't carry a torch from my family's hearth all the way to his. I'm quite sure it would burn out before we got across the ocean.*

But at the moment, two hours postmeridian, there was a commotion at the palace gates, and any distraction from the conundrum of how to tell her mother *no*, without needing Eurydice to do it for her, was welcome. Selene let the papyrus scrolls fall from her hands and slipped out of her room to see what was going on.

Foot soldiers filed through one of the gates into the palace complex, ahead of four men on horseback, all of them unrecognizable. The *equites'* armor appeared pitted and scored, nearly matte from the damage they'd taken. Any inlay or decoration each of them had previously had, had been utterly destroyed by wind and sand. Their brave red cloaks were tattered, and had turned a faded brown in color, saturated by dust. Any crests their helmets had once had, were no more; torn away at some point in the past day. Their arms, legs, and faces were swathed in blood-dotted bandages. And wherever they weren't bandaged, sand appeared to be embedded in their skin, so thick was the dirt on them. They all slumped in their saddles, virtually indistinguishable from one another.

Behind them, escorted by the infantry, came a cart with six bodies on it, barely covered by a tarp. Flies buzzed over them, and hands and feet stuck out here and there, bouncing limply as the wheels of the cart found the pavement of the courtyard less than even.

Selene's hand rose to cover her mouth in horror, even as Caesarion, Eurydice, Cleopatra, Antony, and Antyllus hurried out of other buildings in the complex, coming to meet the survivors of the *equite* patrol. *I can't tell which of them is Tiberius,* Selene thought, going cold. *Did he . . . did he die?*

A warm hand landed on her shoulder as Antyllus found her, and the lead rider slid off his horse. Advanced, limping heavily, through the massed ranks of the infantry. And brought his hand to his chest to salute Caesarion and Eurydice. "Your assailants did not make it far from Alexandria, *dominae,*" he said, his voice so rusty, that it took Selene a long moment to recognize Tiberius' tones. And as she did, relief rushed through her. "Report six priests of Thoth dead, including Tahut-Nefer, slain by my own hand." Empty voice, empty words. No affect at all. He jerked a thumb back, as the infantry started unloading the dead bodies so that they could be seen and identified. "Report loss of fifteen men. One casualty died on the way here. Last sustained a cobra bite, as I did myself. He might lose his leg without your assistance, *dominus.*"

Stunned silence in the courtyard. "You were bitten, but you're on your feet," Caesarion said, his voice distant.

"Amulet that Alexander insisted that I buy a few years ago appears to have more potency than either of us thought, *dominus.*" No inflections.

"Fifteen men," Antony said, striding forward. "You lost *seventy-five percent* of the patrol taking down six men? How the *fuck* did that happen?"

"Buried us alive under three feet of sand," Tiberius returned colorlessly. "Blinded one man before that. Another was swarmed by about fifty scorpions and other creatures. Fire. Heating our weapons in our hands to red-hot." He held up his right hand in explanation, pulling back the bandage on it, and Selene choked, seeing blackened skin there.

Caesarion and Eurydice had stepped apart to look at

the bodies, and Antyllus joined them now, leaving Selene by herself. She couldn't bear to follow him over to survey the corpses. She knew that in war, men died, but she'd never been even this close to such . . . messily dead bodies before. And knowing that Tiberius had personally slain half of them made her stomach turn queasily. The completely empty look in his eyes didn't help matters.

Now Caesarion called over, "Yes, that's Tahut-Nefer. Hard to recognize him without the expression of disapproving sanctimony, but that's him. The wound in his belly is too big for a *gladius*, though."

"What in Dis' name did you hit him with, Ti?" Antyllus asked, spreading his hands. "A scythe? Half a ship's mast?"

"A plow, *dominus*," one of the other *equites* put in, when Tiberius seemed disinclined to reply. "He killed two of the other priests single-handed, chased the fat one down, fought off some sort of water-spirit, and then kicked the fat fuck straight onto an overturned farmer's plow. Was glorious, sir. Only caught the show from a distance, since I was still dealing with the two remaining priests, and the man with me had lost the use of his damned leg, thanks to the cobra bite." Chuckling among the men now. "Keep telling him he needs the cognomen of *Agricola*."

Selene's other hand crept up to cover the first now. "Permission to clean up, *dominus?*" Tiberius asked now blankly. "And then board the first ship heading north?"

"Clean up, yes, ship, no. I'll heal the man with the cobra bite as soon as I can get to the barracks, since your bite doesn't seem to be spreading. But you need to wait till tomorrow for your own healing." Caesarion crossed to put a hand on Tiberius' shoulder. "You'd be welcome to come with us to Thebes. It's time we put an end to all this nonsense. And having Tahut's head, and these others' atop spears when we go there, will make that easier. Thank you."

"With respect, *dominus*, Britannia is where I would prefer to go."

"A good sea voyage with nothing to do but heal would probably be best for you right now, yes," Caesarion agreed, his voice light, but his brows furrowed. "Go get cleaned up, all of you. Have the palace physicians look over your wounds. And you're all staying here till I know you're properly healed. Understood?"

"Yes, my lord," Tiberius answered, along with the other men Turned away as smartly as he could, and his knee gave out—at which point, Antyllus leaped forward to help steady him, while Caesarion kept a tight grip on his shoulder, too.

"I've got him," Antyllus told Caesarion. "Come on, Tiberius. You've won enough *gloria* for any two men for now." He helped the younger man across the courtyard, passing by Selene. The gray eyes glanced in her direction momentarily.

And looked through her, as if she were as invisible as she'd always thought she was. As if she didn't even exist. Selene recoiled, at least as much from the emptiness in those eyes, as from the blood and the dirt and everything else.

Februarius 15, 20 AC

A legion's marching pace remained four miles an hour—five, if the men were instructed to hustle, but that wore on them, in the long run. And with over five hundred miles between Alexandria and Thebes, the math was remorseless—sixteen days, minimum, to reach Upper Egypt with all their forces. Or less than a week, if they all somehow crowded onto enough river craft—the river craft that Prefect Gallus had commandeered to send his *own* men south.

Chafing visibly at the delays, Caesarion had directed the Sixteenth to move out at dawn. As good as his word, he'd healed Tiberius, and given the young man leave to board a ship in the re-opened harbor. The early healing helped; infection had already set in all over Tiberius' body, everywhere that the sand and dust had cut into his skin. As such, if Caesarion hadn't stepped in, Tiberius would have been left with layers of pitted scars everywhere, but only a few had wound up being deep enough to leave visible marks on his face, arms, and legs.

Antyllus had made a point of clasping wrists with Tiberius before letting him walk up the quay for the ship. It faintly disturbed him that Tiberius didn't look up at the great Lighthouse with awe. Didn't turn his head to study the sprawling harbor and its forest of ship masts. Just looked straight ahead, towards the horizon, almost at all times. "It wasn't your fault the men with you died," Antyllus felt compelled to remind him as Tiberius started up the ramp of the ship that would take him to Ostia, and from there, he'd arrange transportation to northern Gaul.

"I know," Tiberius said over his shoulder.

"It's on the mage-priests, not on you. Don't let my father's words bother you."

"They don't." A pause, and Tiberius, now on the deck of the ship, called back down, "Good hunting in Thebes." And then vanished below deck.

Antyllus sighed and left, feeling ill-at-ease, somehow. He headed back to the palace, climbed the long stairs up to the headland, and a servant caught him and redirected him to Eurydice's study, where it sounded like an argument was taking place behind the closed door. A tap, an "Enter!" from Caesarion, and Antyllus walked in, raising his eyebrows at finding Selene, her siblings, and Cleopatra already inside. Selene looked flushed and near tears, which didn't bode well. "What's the problem?" Antyllus asked warily, moving to take her hands in his.

"There you are," Caesarion said in a tone of quiet relief. "I've been putting together Selene's dowry for you. Father had the coin set aside for both her and Eurydice years ago." A quirk of his lips as he added, "It was rather pleasant not to have to pay Eurydice's. It might have bankrupted our war effort a few years ago. We'd still have fighting in Illyria, I'm sure, if I had."

"Caesarion!" Eurydice gave her husband a look.

"It's true," he told her mildly. "I can give you the whole amount now, Antyllus, but if you'd rather not carry that much coin, I can give you half now, and a letter for you to carry to Rome, where Alexander will disburse the other half later."

Antyllus moved over to the desk, drawing Selene with him. "There's no rush. I know you're good for it, and it's quite common for the dowry to be paid out over three years anyway." He shrugged. "How much coin are we talking, anyway?"

Dowries ranged from a token amount, sometimes paid by someone other than the family—in which case, they were expected to be repaid if the girl died—to quite large amounts, intended to allow for the maintenance of a wealthy household. A single skilled laborer made a denarius a day. As such, Caesarion shrugged as well. "Father set aside about twenty thousand denarii for her. Enough to cover household expenses for the first three years of marriage, assuming you have a relatively small staff. I can give that to you in solidi, but that's still a lot of coin to carry."

Antyllus grimaced. "I wasn't planning on bringing a pack mule with me wherever I go just to carry her dowry. Just give me a letter for the full amount, and I'll settle up with you or Alexander whenever we get home to Rome. It's not as if I don't have money of my own." He glanced at Selene. "If you want to buy slaves or servants to help around the *castra* when we're on campaign, I'll make sure you have enough coin to do that, all right?"

Her eyes had gone wide, and she nodded now, silently. He had the distinct impression she'd never thought about these sorts of realities before. *She's so damned young in so many ways. Ah, well. We all grow up.* Antyllus accepted a wrist-clasp from Caesarion on the matter, and watched out of the corner of his eye as the Imperator carefully began writing a letter in his own handwriting, to be marked with his personal seal, regarding the matter. "Was there anything else here that needed my attention?" Antyllus asked.

Selene nodded fervently, and then said, quickly, in a tumble of words, "Do you want a big Egyptian ceremony, with hundreds of people from Alexandria here, and a priestess of Isis, or do you want a quiet ceremony here in the palace, with a priestess of Juno, and just our family?"

"Selene!" Cleopatra remonstrated sharply. "If you're going to ask the question, ask it honestly. Does he want a ceremony that will assist him in his later political career, especially if he *does* wish to be some sort of diplomat, a public face for Rome to foreign countries? Or does he want the marriage of a private citizen, one uninvolved in the public life of Rome?"

Eurydice delicately rubbed at her eyes, but didn't intervene.

Antyllus frowned. Looked over at Caesarion, and asked, mildly, "Can I recuse myself from answering that one for about a year?"

Caesarion didn't look up from the letter he was

drafting. "It's your problem, Antyllus. Happily, it's not mine."

Antyllus wanted to make a rude noise in the general direction of his friend, but their respective social ranks, and the presence of Cleopatra and Selene, if not Eurydice, precluded that. Instead, he looked down at Selene, and told her, gently and apologetically, "If it were just about me, as a private citizen, yes, I'd prefer to get married tomorrow. No fuss at all, and then you'd just join me as I head south to Thebes with your brother and sister. Or leave Alexandria for Syria and points beyond."

"I did say you were free to go to Antioch in Syria, and from there north to Scythia, if you can't find bows there," Caesarion noted, still not looking up. "You need them. Go get them. I won't be able to heal your chest till tomorrow, but that's only applicable if you come with us. If you come with us, you won't have time to go *get* the weapons you want. Not in time to join us right at the outset of the campaign season. Seven days by sea to Antioch from here. Forty to fifty days to get from Antioch to our camps in northern Gaul. And that's not counting any travel northwest into Scythia, which could take up to a month, if not more, depending on how the tribes move around up there. That puts you in Gaul somewhere around Maius at best. I'm looking at two weeks down to Thebes, two weeks back, and then thirty-six days or so of *hard* travel with the Sixth, once I get them back from Gallus, up to northern Gaul. I'll beat you by a month, unless Fortuna favors you, and you find hundreds of Scythian bows sitting in a market stall in Antioch."

Antyllus frowned. "Every man needs an interesting scar or two," he told Caesarion, turning his grimace into a smile. "This can be mine. You're right. If my eyes are on arming my Cretans better, then I can't afford to come with you to Thebes. That would add a month to starting off for

Antioch. I'd reach Britannia by *Iunius*, at that point. Much as I'd like to go with you to Thebes to ensure that Tiberius doesn't get all the glory." The flippant words concealed real concern. *I want to go with you. Gods only know what waits at Thebes, and the world is a better place with you and Eurydice in it. But . . . we have to keep our eyes on the target. And at the moment, the _real_ target is chastising Britannia and their druids, firmly, for their meddling in Hispania.*

Antyllus turned back toward Selene and Cleopatra. With his eyes on the mark on the horizon, it was easy to deal with both of them, really. "Selene, while your mother is substantially correct about my future career, what we really need at the moment is speed." *Which Caesarion understood, bless him. He gave me a way out.* "We can set up a grand celebration when we get back to Rome. But if the intention is for us to get married before I leave for Syria . . . let's find a priestess of Juno and be done with this."

Cleopatra threw up her hands in exasperation. "Very well. But if you let your lives be dictated by the exigencies of a military campaign, if you don't give your wife all the honor she's due now, or take advantage of the political connections you can make with a large state wedding here, you'll only have yourselves to blame when you look back and wonder what else you should have done."

"Mother," Eurydice said quietly.

"I'm done. I'll fetch you a priestess of Juno, and they can be off on the evening tide. I'll have the servants pack their belongings." Cleopatra glided out of the room, a frown stark on her features.

"It's all right," Eurydice told Selene. "I'm honestly not sure if there's *anything* you can do to please her at the moment, beyond giving in completely. And even that doesn't please her, because then, you'd just be spineless."

"I'm aware," Selene said, her voice tight.

Antyllus shrugged and put a hand lightly on her shoulder. "By this time tomorrow? She won't be your problem anymore, except when children are born. And since she'll be living here in Egypt for however long my father's here as governor, and my youngest sister will come here to live as well, until she's old enough to marry Tiberius' brother, Drusus? You won't, very likely, see her again for years." *If ever,* the back of his mind told him sharply. *I should say good-bye to my father with some care. Even if I weren't going off to war, he's getting older, and he won't be in Rome often after this. This could be the last time I see him. "Indestructible" or no, age always wins the battle, in the end.* "You might want to say your farewells to her with that in mind," was all he said out loud, however.

And thus, the Sixteenth Legion waited an hour or so longer to depart for Thebes, as Caesarion and Eurydice witnessed the wedding of Selene and Antyllus. Eurydice kissed her sister good-bye and wished her a safe journey to Antioch, and Caesarion gave Antyllus a quick, firm wrist-clasp. And then they rode off, Eurydice ahead of Caesarion on his horse for as much safety and speed as they could arrange. In the distance, even from the palace, Antyllus could see the legions marching out of town, along the roads they'd blockaded until today. His throat tightened a bit. *I wish I were going with them. But . . . eyes on the mark. We'll get where we're going. Just by another path.*

And he looked down at Selene, now his wife. Saw the look of shocked apprehension in her eyes as she started to realize exactly how much her life had changed inside of three days. Gave her hand a quick squeeze as they ate one last meal with his father and her mother. Bade them farewell—and Antyllus saw the moisture in Cleopatra's eyes as she said goodbye to her youngest child by Caesar. And then they boarded a ship for Antioch, just in time to catch the evening tide.

The ship wasn't a military vessel, so it had passenger cabins. Dark wood, with a smell of the pitch that sealed the boards of the ship, and old cookery. Selene had only one personal servant, Ranno, the older woman who'd been her wet-nurse — but as Egyptian nobility, Ranno, like Nesa and Salatis, had asked permission to remain in Egypt and live with their families for the first time in years. "We'll pick up a new servant or two for you in Antioch," Antyllus promised lightly. "We'll need to hire guides and guards anyway, as we'll need to skirt Parthian territory to reach the Scythians and Sarmatians. Until then, I think I can help you fasten this and unfasten that. Though, fair warning. I haven't a clue what to do with hair." A very sober nod to go with that assertion, though his eyes twinkled. "Other than the taking down bit. That, I can manage."

They had guards in the cabin beside theirs; long-term servants of Antony's family who'd also helped carry their bags of clothing and chests of gear aboard. Selene sank down onto the edge of the bed, and acknowledged, deep in her heart, that she was terrified. She was leaving her entire family behind, venturing to an unknown city, followed, probably, by a completely foreign land filled with barbarians, with not one person around her that she could say that she really knew. She'd married this man hours ago, placing her hand in his before a priestess of Juno, and suddenly, he looked like a complete stranger. And neither Eurydice nor Caesarion had said one word, beyond congratulations, quick talk of the dowry, and wishes for a safe journey.

Selene closed her eyes, swallowing as she felt the rocking of the boat around her, and listened vaguely to the sound of Antyllus' voice, talking with the guards outside their door. *Oh, gods. This was a very bad idea. This was the worst idea in the history of bad ideas. He thinks that life is an adventure, something out of Homer. He wants to see the world. And taking a trip from the villa to the baths has been, to date, the most I could really manage without fear.*

And added to all that, I'm quite sure he's going to want to . . . do all the things Mother told us men like to do. Here, on this boat, with probably his men listening from outside the door, or the next cabin over. What had sounded vaguely interesting a few years ago, and had provoked delightful, vague fantasies about kissing for years, now seemed both quite imminent, and all too real. *Eurydice did pull me aside to tell me that the first time wasn't nearly as bad as Mother made it out to be, but oh, gods, why did I agree to any of this?* Her breathing sped up. Her heart pounded. And she yipped as Antyllus' hand fell on her shoulder.

Antyllus chuckled a little at the reaction initially, but when he saw genuine fear in her eyes, he stifled his laughter and sat down on the bed beside her. Saw the way she leaned away subtly, and sighed under his breath. "Lots of changes, very quickly," he acknowledged, as gently as he could, doing his best to master a trickle of impatience that muttered, *Am I back to being a monster in your eyes again? Just hours after taking my hand before the priestess?* "You know, I don't think you've played your *kithara* once since coming to Egypt. Why don't you dig it out and play something?" He reluctantly took his hand away from her shoulder, and stood to look out their tiny window at the great city as their ship began to slip away from the quay. Listened to the sounds of her hesitantly fishing through their bags and chests, finally finding her *kithara* "We didn't have a chance to see much of Alexandria at all." An unintentional note of longing filled his voice. "We'll have to come back. So long as your sister's here, or my father, we should have a warm welcome. And next time, we can see the tomb of Alexander the Great, and everything else we missed this time."

Her fingers touched the strings, and he glanced back over his shoulder at his new bride. "Would you like that, love?"

She gave him a look of confusion, and shrugged. "I doubt we'll have as many attacks next time," he pointed out, sitting back down on the bed, and closing his eyes, composing himself to listen. To not move a muscle, until he was sure she'd relaxed.

It took several songs before he didn't hear missed notes, and she shifted between Hellene modes to some Egyptian air or another. "When did you hear that one?" he asked, trying not to break the spell.

"At dinner a week ago," she replied quietly. "One of the entertainers played it."

"And you can play it from memory after only one hearing?"

"Oh, I don't remember it perfectly. The main melody, yes, but I'm sort of . . . making up all the rest as I go." Her voice sounded easier now, and he exhaled in relief. Edged closer, cautiously, not disturbing her playing, and thought again of his joking words to his father, about trying to hunt a unicorn. *Maybe I should have just settled for a deer,* he thought, finally managing to stretch out fully on the bed beside her, and kicked his boots off at the foot. His sudden movements made her fingers catch the strings awry, a harsh dissonance, and Antyllus lay back. Put his right forearm over his eyes, and said, simply, "Go on playing. You're enjoying yourself, and gods know, between your mother and everything else, you haven't done much of that since leaving Rome." *Cleopatra's not a monster. She genuinely wants what's best for her children. But she can't let go of the reins for even an instant.*

As the notes spilled out again, Antyllus shifted his left arm, and rubbed the small of her back gently, feeling smooth skin through the layers of stola and tunic. *Slowly,* he told himself grimly. *A unicorn startles worse than any deer. But if I move slowly enough, and carefully enough, I might be able to slip the halter up and over her head before she knows what I've done.*

Not looking at her directly, all he had to go on were the subtle cues of muscle tension in her back, and the stutters and stops of her fingers on the strings. Finally, he eased to his side, feeling the stitches in his chest pull a little, and put his own hand on the kithara. It had grown darker since he'd covered his eyes, as the sun had now set, and only a faint, gray light came in now through the tiny window. She'd been playing by touch for quite some time, it seemed.

He eased the instrument from her suddenly limp hands, and set it down in its case on the floor. "I think it's my turn to play," he told her quietly. "I'm not a musician, but there's one instrument I play, and I'm told I do it fairly well." Antyllus tried to keep his smile audible in his voice, but felt her muscles tighten again as he brought his right hand up to cup her face. "It's just me," he reminded her, trying once more to leash his impatience. "You've liked kissing quite well before. Remember? And we're in private, and we're married, and it's right." A little light teasing, and then he leaned in to taste her lips again. Eased her back against the bed, trying not to rush, but he hadn't had a woman under him in some time, and it was glorious, knowing that she was his, and he was hers, and he didn't have to go hunting for this anymore. "Here," he said after several fervent moments. "Let me light one of the lamps. I want to see you."

"Aren't . . . aren't we supposed to . . . in the dark?" Her

voice was a squeak.

"That might be what's deemed proper by old dead men like Cato the Elder, but he threw a man out of the Senate for kissing his own wife in public, for the gods' sakes. I'm not going to base my life around what people like him think." He fumbled for a sparkstriker. Stood, and lit one of the tiny lamps hanging from a hook on the wall, where it couldn't fall and set the ship on fire. Then turned back towards her, pleased by what the golden lamplight did to her face, casting her eyes into shadows and mystery. And got back to what he'd been doing.

He eventually got her clothing off. Felt her shiver in the cool air coming in the open window, and moved to cover her with his own body. And in desperate need of a distraction, so that he wouldn't do what he ached to do, which was to slide into her, hilt-deep, all at once, he whispered against her ear, "You do know what comes next, yes?"

"Mother explained it when I was ten." Her voice was small. "And the love-spell, too, of course. Not that it works."

He pulled back, raising his eyebrows, hoping she could see his expression in the dim light. "I don't know. Have you ever worked the spell on me?" Antyllus asked.

She shook her head, rapidly. "It . . . didn't seem fair," Selene admitted. "I . . . wanted you to like me for me. Again, not that it works."

"I do like you. What's involved in the spell?" he asked, grateful for the distraction. And then looked down, surprised, as she shifted her legs further apart. And sucked in a breath as he saw where her hand slid next. Fingers moving, dancing. "Oh, gods," he murmured reverently. "Now that's a pretty sight. Show me how to play you, Selene. There you go." A quick, wicked grin. "You definitely want me to get the fingering right, don't you?"'

A squeak of embarrassed laughter, and then he replaced her fingers with his own. Saw the look of startled, dazed pleasure that told him more clearly than words that she'd never gotten quite this far before on his own. A wave of lazy triumph, and then he pulled off his own clothes, and joined their bodies at last. Soothed her through the yelp of pain—"only the first time, I swear, Selene,"—and generally tried to do more good than harm as he finished.

"There," he told her as he held her in the golden light of the lamp afterwards. "See? Not so bad, was it?"

She shook her head against his chest, and he asked, teasingly, "Actually, since I have a certain amount of evidence that you did enjoy yourself. . . I don't suppose you might be ready for a second song?"

"I'm . . . very sore," Selene whispered, and Antyllus kissed her hair.

"I know. At least we don't have anyone outside the door, counting how many times I take you tonight. There are houses where I've seen that done at weddings. And the guests were all drunk, and cheering the groom on." Antyllus felt her stiffen against him in mild horror at the thought, and laughed. "The last one I went to like that, they stopped counting at nine. Fortunately for the woman, it was her second marriage."

"Oh my dear gods." Selene's voice was tight.

He kissed her again, and told her lightly, "I'll wait till tomorrow night for that."

"Oh, gods."

"Oh, very well, the night after that." He got up and blew out the lamp, coming back to bed and gathering her up in his arms again. "Are you at least happy you married me?" *Say yes.*

"I think so," Selene whispered softly. "But I think I'm going to disappoint you. I'm . . . not very adventurous."

His chest ached. "I don't think you know what you are. It's not as if you've ever had occasion to find out. Why not try an adventure or two with me, before you decide if you like them or not?" Antyllus paused, and then added, trying to keep the resignation out of his voice, "And if you really don't like adventure, well. I can leave you at home in Rome. The way many men do." *I want a wife like my own mother. Minus the shouting that could be heard across the castra. She went everywhere with my father. Camp after camp, province after province. I don't want a wife like Octavia. Sitting like a toad in Rome, never budging from her rock.* "But at least try it first?" he coaxed. "You never know. You might like it at least as much as you liked what we just did, right?"

A tiny, muffled laugh, and he had to be content with that for the moment. And closed his eyes, thinking, *It's far easier to make my Scythian maiden smile, than to make this one do so. To make my wife smile. I never thought that would be a goal of mine. Nor that it would be so much work to attain.*

Chapter X: Thebes of a Hundred Gates

Februarius 15-Martius 1, 20 AC

The long march from Lower Egypt to Upper would have been enervating, had it not been for the earliness of the season. Even so, the men sweated under their armor, and were left with no other recourse but drinking directly from the Nile, and some of the legionnaires who bathed in the river complained of stomach discomfort later, even urinating blood. The *medici* had their hands full, and consulted with the local physicians, to no avail; red urine was considered almost normal in some villages along the Nile, and no one knew the cause. Caesarion did his best, but he could only cure one person a day, and he generally preferred to hold back on the blessings of Isis until after they'd made camp, in case there were actual wounds over the course of the march.

Eurydice found the stares of the locals as the legion passed to be almost as depressing as the looks in the eyes of the natives of Hispania, three years ago. Women and children fled into their tiny houses. The menfolk retreated as far as their doorsteps, watching warily. Might go so far as to offer water, and smiled with relief when the legion's quartermasters asked to *buy* food, rather than simply taking it from them. "Gaius Cornelius Gallus hasn't made a good name for Rome here," she told Caesarion on the fourth afternoon.

"No. He really hasn't. But that's partially my fault. I've been concentrating on other provinces." He sighed, and they rode on.

At their mother's recommendation, Eurydice had opted

to wear a modified *kalasiris* dresses every day of the march south. She couldn't *fathom* cutting her hair as short as a man's, and wearing a wig over it, but she did wear a diadem, even on horseback, perched just ahead of Caesarion. He, naturally, wore armor. *Try to look as if at least one of you embraces your heritage,* Cleopatra had advised, her lips curling down.

Eurydice knew that none of her mother's ancestors had even spoken Egyptian; Cleopatra was the first of the Ptolemaic line in hundreds of years of rule to reach out to her subjects, and adopt some of their culture. *And she — and they — are afraid she'll be the last. I'm trying, Mother. I'm really trying.*

Several days into the journey, they passed close enough to the Giza Plateau that they could see the pyramids from the banks of the Nile. Eurydice gaped at them, her eyes wide. Each of their sides were sheathed in white limestone, and the largest had a cap of pure gold at the top. At this distance, she couldn't make out the details of the temples that crouched at their feet, but the pyramids themselves were among the most impressive things she'd ever seen. The largest was easily the same height as the staggering Lighthouse of Alexandria, but spread out from its peak like a mountain, reflecting the blazing light of the Egyptian sun searingly off its gold-capped peak — it looked as if the sun itself had found a new place to rise. "Men made those," she said, stunned. "How on *earth* did they manage it?"

"With quite a bit of manpower, and some good engineering," Caesarion said against her ear, but he sounded as awed as she did. "We'll take a closer look on our way back. When we're not so pressed for time."

Seeing the pyramids, sleek and perfect, and utterly alien to the smooth pillars and arches she was accustomed to seeing in Rome, gave Eurydice really her first inkling of how *different* the Egyptian mind-set really was. Oh, she'd grown up reading demotic texts—Egyptian by way of Hellene writing—and had had hieratic pounded into her head over the past few years. She knew many of the legends, but again, understood them from a Hellene perspective.

A Hellene looked at Thoth and saw *Hermes*, with an oddly-shaped head. *Your god and our god both handle knowledge and magic, and ours is a trickster, and yours is solemn, but really, they're the same, aren't they?* And the Egyptians, as a people conquered from time to time by the Nubians, the Kush, the Assyrians, the Persians, and most recently the Hellenes under Alexander the Great, tended to reply, *If that's how you choose to understand our god, we have no real objection.*

But, as she and Alexander and Caesarion had been discussing of the problems with Hispania and Gaul, where the locals were angrily refusing to worship in temples built by Roman hands, that were for Jupiter and Taranis alike, they *weren't* the same. Jupiter might throw thunderbolts, and so might Taranis, but they weren't the same gods. And while polytheists like themselves might willingly nod to whichever god currently seemed to be helpful, there were too many differences to say *Thoth is Hermes and Hermes is, well, whatever the Goths or the Gauls call their gods of knowledge.*

Traveling south, the Nile unwinding for what felt like the better part of forever as they kept to the pace of the Sixteenth, she began to understand, dimly, how *old* this place was. Rome accounted itself great, because the city had been built, supposedly, seven hundred years ago. The city they were journeying towards, Thebes? Had been populated for over *three thousand*. That was a number that inspired awe, and not a little humility. And yet, as they continued along the Nile, she felt as if they were traveling not just in space, but in time. For the farmers here wore the same clothing that she'd seen on the ancient walls of temples in Alexandria. Used the same types of tools and plows. Went to worship in the same temples that their great-great-great-great grandparents had used — or at least, it seemed that way. Their guides and scribes were quick to point out which temples were 'new,' or at least, *only* five hundred years old or so. "That one is new," they told Eurydice. "Put up by the Persians when Cambyces came here five hundred years ago, before he was deposed by the Magus Gaumata, who posed as his younger brother successfully for seven months, ruling the whole of Persia, before being deposed by Darius."

And then Alexander conquered Persia, and my family came into power, Eurydice thought numbly. *And they consider this to be* new. *No wonder they have a hard time accepting Roman customs and laws and beliefs. We're even newer than the Hellenes. And here they are, farming the same land that their grandparents farmed, as far back as the dawn of time. Because what else are you going to do, if you were born on that farm?*

She swallowed. Changeless, because in spite of the *waves* of conquest that had hit this kingdom, time after time, there was no real *need* to change. The Nile provided its abundance, for so long as the pharaohs, no matter their original extraction, comported themselves by the pact made by the ancients with the gods of Egypt. *And over time, each set of conquerors either retreated, or came to an accommodation with those gods. Which is . . . precisely what we're doing. But Egypt needs to change. At least a little. If we're to change a little to accommodate them.*

She did ask Damkina, quietly, if Gaumata had been a real person, and if he'd really successfully impersonated Persian royalty, and killed a Persian king. "Oh yes," the Magus replied simply. "He's a hero among the Magi. We have a secret history of his life, which we've kept away from the eyes of our various Persian, Seleucid, and now Parthian masters. He was a master of illusion and disguise. And only one of the wives of the real younger brother saw through the deception. Or at least, only one of them *cared*, which says something about the man whom Gaumata impersonated, Bardiya." The magus snorted behind her veil—garnet-colored silk today—as they sat in the command tent, waiting for the sun to go down. "The world would be a very different place if Gaumata had maintained control of the Empire," Damkina added, flatly. "Darius and his son Xerxes would never have headed west into Hellene lands. The Hellenes would never have mustered the interest in heading east, and Alexander would have had no purpose in conquering in our direction. Gaumata was Median; he was committed to *knowledge* and the Magi. Persia would have been more insular, but more peaceful. But he made mistakes, and Darius was able to wrest control from his hands. More's the pity."

It was a very different view of history than the one presented in Herodotus and the other classical Hellene and Roman authors that Eurydice had read. Her head spun, trying to imagine a world in which Thermopylae had never happened. In which Macedonia had remained a pastoral backwater. *Would Rome as I know it even exist, if this Median man had successfully held the Persian empire?* Eurydice wondered. *Would we have our grand, pillared temples in the Hellene style? Or would we just be . . . Etruscans?*

Dizzying thoughts, ones she couldn't maintain for long, not without feeling somehow small, dwarfed by the whole of history.

And then, finally, after sixteen grueling days, they reached Thebes. Sacked during the turbulent reigns of Ptolemy Lathyros and Ptolemy Alexander, the two brothers who were, well, both her great-grandfathers. They'd quarreled viciously, stolen the throne from each other two or three times, each bedded the same sister (Cleopatra Selene) with her bearing them each offspring, but it was Ptolemy Lathyros' son by *another* sister that had married Ptolemy Alexander's daughter by another woman, and thus had carried on the line. Eventually. Eurydice was *fairly* sure that was how her mother had explained it to her a few days before her own marriage to Caesarion.

Thebes had been reconstructed in part since then, mostly with the sanction of Cleopatra herself. The city, and indeed, most of Upper Egypt, had been rebellious all through the rule of the Ptolemies; culturally, the region had closer ties to Nubia than to Hellas, and it showed. The people working the farms along the Nile had skins that weren't tawny, as those closer to the coast, but the same rich brown as the fertile soil of the river's banks, for example. But everyone in Egypt with the means to do so, eventually traveled to Thebes. To pray in the great temples of Karnak and Luxor. To trade in its marketplace for gold, ivory, ebony, and incense, imported from deeper in Africa, or from across the Red Sea. And once again, Eurydice's mouth hung slightly agape at the sphinx statues that lined the sun-beaten roads, each one far larger than a man. The images of long-dead kings that stared blankly back from the fronts of temples. *How can I possibly rule this land, or even claim to?* she thought, desperately. *I can't even begin to grasp it.*

For better or worse, however, there were plenty of things to distract her from her awe. As they drew closer to the huge temples, which loomed in the distance, they could also see the neat, orderly, utterly familiar lines of a *castra*, drawn up with Roman military precision. The headquarters *here*, the barracks for the *equites* and their horses *there*; the mess over there, the latrines over there, all surrounded by a palisade and entrenchments. It would have looked exactly the same in

Hispania or Gaul or Syria. And here it stood, facing some of the most ancient buildings and monuments in the world, and the legionnaires in their red cloaks went about their business inside those walls, as if the staring eyes of ancient kings didn't exist. *I need to absorb a little of that,* Eurydice thought as they rode towards the gates, the men of the Sixteenth streaming behind them, and the standard-bearer of her Hawks keeping pace beside them. *Not unconcern, no. Not superiority to, either. But I need to be aware of all that history . . . without drowning in it. Somehow.*

At the wall of the camp, the guards took one look at the red eyes and grim expression on the face of the Imperator of Rome, the full legion of fresh troops behind him, swallowed, and opened the gates. "Where is Prefect Gallus?" Caesarion demanded, letting Eurydice down before dismounting, himself. She'd seen and heard him angry before, but rarely so much so. The rage seemed leashed at the moment, but given a target at the moment? She knew he'd tear strips out of that person's hide.

"In the command tent, *dominus*—"

That was directed at Caesarion's back as he strode on, Eurydice on his arm, and the members of their honor guard surrounding them. Mostly Praetorians, including Malleolus, with Damkina and her own guard, Ehsan, trailing behind. Legionnaires scrambled to attention as they passed, and Eurydice got good looks at men who were as sand-scoured as Tiberius and the other equites had been. Men with bandaged legs and feet, too swollen to slip into their boots, trying to stand outside their tents. The storied Sixth Legion—the *Ferrata*, or "Iron-clad"—wasn't beaten. But it was hurting, to be sure.

Near the command tent, Prefect Gallus emerged hastily, looking mildly frantic, but quickly smoothing his expression as he advanced. He was a tall, gaunt man in his late forties, with white at his temples, but otherwise black hair, combed back from a receding hairline, and a hawk-like Roman nose. Eurydice rapidly ran through her mind what they knew of him. *Supported our father. Long-term, scandalous love-affair with Cytheris, a freedwoman who'd been Mark Antony's lover, briefly, about fifteen years ago, and had borne him one of his many bastards. She was one of Rome's few female actresses—a* mima, *who couldn't act in classical tragedy or comedy, but could sing, dance, and recite commonplace verse. Things not written by dead Hellenes or that referred to the gods, anyway, but Gallus brought her with him into Egypt on being appointed prefect. He's written four books of poetry, all dedicated to her. Great friend of Virgil, but Sulpicia turns up her nose at his verse. And most recently, has been corresponding heavily with Agrippa, Rullus, and other members of the Octavianite faction.*

"Imperator!" Gallus exclaimed now, saluting. "You arrived more quickly than we expected—we haven't had the chance to expand the *castra*, set up a second command tent—"

Caesarion stared at him, his expression tight. "I sent riders ahead of us, prefect. They should have arrived a week ago."

"Ah, yes, they did, it's just that, what with everything, we've simply been too busy—" The various tribunes exiting the command tent behind their prefect had gone blank-faced. Their eyes found a horizon and locked on it. Eurydice winced internally, knowing what was coming now. *Gallus is making excuses in front of his men, instead of inviting us inside. Caesarion wouldn't usually dress someone down in front of his own men, but—*

"And yet, no guard sent to meet us, aside from a few sentries on patrol that we happened to encounter when coming from the north. Not your second-in-command, or even a damned tribune at the gate to greet us, and now you're keeping us out in the sun with excuses?" Caesarion's voice never rose. He didn't shout. But every word had the weight of lead behind it as he addressed a man over twice his age. "I believe that my pregnant wife would much appreciate a chance to sit in the shade. Once you've seen to her comfort, Prefect, you may continue to tender your excuses."

Gallus' mouth snapped shut. His face went rigid. And then he bowed very slightly, extending a hand to the command tent, and Caesarion stepped forward, past him, once again drawing Eurydice with him. Just past the flap, Caesarion murmured, "Do you wish to handle him, beloved?"

"You're taking him and the *Ferrata* out of Egypt?"

"They've stirred up enough unrest with the locals that fresh faces might be in order, yes. Your Sixteenth has to start all over again with preconceptions about Egypt, but . . ." Caesarion shrugged.

"You handle him," Eurydice murmured in reply. "I'll handle the priests. I already have a notion of how to go about it, and I need to live with them." She'd been thinking about the problem for four weeks now, and the perfect stick had arrived in her thoughts just last night. *Now I need some form of honey to go with it, and they should fall in line. It's a pretty big stick, however. It might not need much honey.*

He found her a comfortable enough camp stool, just as the others came in behind them. Gallus clearly wanted to put a better foot forward now, and gabbled an apology, commenting, "Ah, I will pray to Juno for the safe delivery of a healthy child—" the quick flicker over his expression said more clearly than words what he thought the chances of *that* were, before he straightened his features again, "—we had no idea at all that the Empress was with child—"

"We hadn't planned to make a public announcement

until she was further along," Caesarion said brusquely, moving to the map table as people continued to file inside. Eurydice felt Malleolus take position directly behind her, shielding her back with his body, standing between her and the tent flap. "Now. Explain to me the current situation here. Have you recovered the tax-collectors? Have you put down this very important rebellion that you mobilized an entire legion to deal with two months ago?"

Gallus threw his hands up. "*Dominus!* The entire population of Thebes — a not inconsequential forty thousand people! — are in a state of unrest! We arrived here six weeks ago, and sent emissaries to each temple complex as well as to the *nomarch* — the, ah, governor of the region. The *nome*, as they call it here — "

"*Sepat*," Caesarion corrected, putting his hands on the map table. "*Nome* is the Hellene term for the regional prefactures. *Sepat* is the Egyptian one. At any rate, you spoke with the *nomarch*. That would be Sebichos, if I remember my briefings correctly." He raised his eyebrows. "And?"

Gallus appeared nettled. "He promised that he would send his agents among the people and recover our men, *dominus*. After three days, I felt a show of force was in order, to communicate that we weren't merely here to pick flowers. I sent out four cohorts — " *Just under two thousand men, one third of his legion,* Eurydice translated, "to enter Thebes proper, and gave them orders to search every shop, every home, every stable, until some trace of our agents was found." Gallus grimaced. "Some of the residents resisted opening their doors, and threw stones at my men. The men retaliated as they've been trained to do at any attack."

Caesarion exhaled. "I assume this turned into a bloody riot?" At Gallus' tight nod, Caesarion asked, grimly, "How many civilians and how many legionnaires dead?"

"Fifteen hundred civilians, and forty legionnaires" Gallus replied, very quietly. "Someone started a fire, in and around the riot. That caused the bulk of the deaths, that we know of. My men could only account for seventy, all told, when they counted off how many they'd each slain, on reporting back to camp."

Caesarion's fists clenched. "And since then?" he asked through his teeth. "Have you made any attempts to help drag the debris from the fire away? Reached out to the *nomarch* and offered to help with rebuilding efforts?"

Gallus' brow creased. Eurydice knew that he had a reputation as a thoughtful man, and certainly, when in Rome, he and Virgil usually spent time drinking together, and commenting on each others' verse. But he seemed to be a step behind Caesarion at the moment. "*Dominus*, they're in a state of rebellion. You don't help rebels; you chastise them."

Caesarion glared at him. "Someone started that fire, you said. If that someone was one of my own legionnaires, even by accident, then you and your men have killed hundreds of people who might not have been rebellious at all, and have certainly solidified the ill opinion of most of the locals against you. And if that fire was set by some of the rebels, and you again didn't reach out to offer the assistance of Rome *to one of its provinces*, you missed an opportunity to win the hearts of the people here." He drummed his fingers on the table now. "What since then?"

Gallus' lips compressed together until they nearly looked white. "Every time I send men out on patrol, they're hit, sir. Hit and run attacks by archers, trying to draw them into the desert. If they give chase . . . magic. There's no other explanation for it, much as I hate to use the word. Sandstorms *don't* blow up that fast, hit only my men, and then vanish, once they've bloodied and buried the lot. Scorpions don't naturally *swarm*. We've been hit here in the *castra*, too. A mist rises at night, every night. And in the wake of that strange, unnatural fog. . . I have dead and injured men. The *medici* have never seen this many snakebites—even with the soldiers shaking their bed-rolls every night, I have over ninety men in the infirmary, with gangrenous, poisoned bites that may require amputation. I have another thirty who didn't survive the bites." Gallus looked away, swallowing. "I've had guards on the wall fail to report in, and when the watch commander investigates the sound of screams in the mist, the men are where they were supposed to be . . . but they're smoking piles of ash, grease, and burned bone, with the remnants of their armor slowly cooling." He swallowed. "I've served for decades. I've never seen anything like it. And there's nothing *natural* that can explain that, my lord." He shook his head. "I've sent out patrol after patrol, trying to find the attackers, but they get lost in the fog, and are set on with fire and blades in the darkness. They've gotten lucky a few times, and have returned with the bodies of their assailants. All young men. Soft hands. Soft bodies." He grimaced with contempt. "Priests or scribes, or some such."

Caesarion looked across the tent at Eurydice and Damkina. "All magical effects we've seen. They're using the fog they raise to get close enough to pick off men on the walls, yes?"

Eurydice nodded. "I'd recommend setting up a line of caltrops, hidden under the sand, forty *pesi* from the perimeter," she suggested. "Also, saturate the sand, hmm, ten feet in front of the walls with pitch, and when you hear the first screams, light it. The mages have to get close enough to be able to see their targets, and thick fog should blind them just as much as it does our men. A sudden pool of fire around their feet should make it very difficult for them to concentrate." She smiled without humor, keeping her back very straight as she sat on the camp stool.

"Blind, perhaps, yes. Unless they have spirits to help them aim," Damkina put in, her tone neutral from behind her veil. "However, they are not alone in that regard. If you wish, it would be my pleasure to remonstrate with them this evening."

"Gallus, start setting up those precautions," Caesarion ordered. "Also, get archers on the walls. It might seem like a waste of ammunition, but when the fog rolls in tonight, I want the men to start firing volleys out, at random intervals, anywhere that there's a man on watch. You can recover the arrows in the morning." He glanced around. "In the meantime? I want a message sent to the *nomarch* of Thebes and to the high priest of Thoth. Their *pharaoh* and his queen are here. And requires their presence in his tent *immediately*."

Gallus gaped at him. "You . . . don't mean to go to them—?"

"A pharaoh doesn't dance attendance on lesser men," Caesarion said, his voice icy now. "Neither does the *imperator* of Rome, but a pharaoh is precisely what they need to see if I am to undo the damage you have done here, Gallus." He swung towards Malleolus and his own tribunes. "Get our men working on setting up our own *castra*. I'll meet with the *nomarch* and the high priest of Thoth in my own tent. And ensure that the, ah, marks of our *equites'* good service are in full view at the gate. I want those heads clearly visible as our guests enter my camp."

"Heads?" Gallus asked blankly.

Caesarion gave him a dark look. "Yes. The heads of seven priests of Thoth who made their way out of this rebellious area, which you have under such good control, prefect. Seven priests who made an attempt on my life, the life of my wife, and the life of the unborn heir of the Julii that she carries under her heart." Eurydice knew that Caesarion was taking out some of his bad temper on Gallus; the man probably didn't *entirely* deserve the tongue-lashing. That being said, he'd responded heavy-handedly to what seemed like deliberate provocation, giving the residents of Thebes an excuse to rebel . . . and giving the mage-priests, whether universally or independently of each other, the opportunity to strike. "You will forgive me, prefect, if I am not particularly in a good temper. This month, I meant to settle my wife in the *safety* of Alexandria, and perhaps take an enjoyable tour of our mother's ancestral homeland." That, without so much as a blink, threw their marriage and mingled ancestry right in the Roman prefect's face. "Instead, I'm forced to deal with assassination attempts, quell uprisings, and generally clean up a mess that shouldn't have been allowed to happen in the first place. I am not pleased, prefect."

Gallus swallowed, hard, his face devoid of color. "Does Rome require my life in reparation?" he asked, tonelessly.

"I see no compelling reason for you to open your veins," Caesarion informed him tautly. "You were already slated for replacement by a full governor. Whether the Senate chooses to offer you any further positions will be up to them." *Your career isn't necessarily over, and I'm not sending you into exile in shame, so there's no need to commit suicide to efface the dishonor. But your political allies in Rome may find your actions here embarrassing, especially if I succeed where you failed, so keep your knife handy.* Eurydice didn't smile over her mental translation. The stakes in politics at this level were very high, indeed.

Caesarion extended his arm to Eurydice, who accepted it and stood. And then they walked out together, heading for the men of the Sixteenth outside this *castra*. Caesarion stopped at the infirmary of the Sixth along the way, where a terrible smell of suppurating flesh emanated from the men inside, and asked for the man who was the worst off. And healed him, immediately. Eurydice, beside him, wished profoundly that she shared his gift for healing, and simply pressed as many hands as she could, whispering prayers as she did. *But while Caesarion's gifts from the gods are in perfect balance, harm and healing in the same hands, the gods didn't grant me the same gifts. Or if they have, they have yet to reveal them to me.* At the back of her head, a nagging concern now, for the infant inside of her. *The spark of power to heal must come from within, too . . . .*

And then they headed into their own camp, through the bustle of men rapidly working to set everything up. Inside their own command tent, Eurydice asked Caesarion, with a certain dry irony in her voice, "If you wish our *nomarch* and the high priest to see a pharaoh and his queen, does this mean you're going to break out the regalia?"

Caesarion grimaced at her. "Yes. Probably. Any man who laughs, I will personally punch."

Damkina, who'd lurked at the entrance of the tent, asked now, her voice interested and concerned, "Will you require me for this meeting, my lord, my lady? You will, I expect, have to demonstrate power to the mage-priests. And in your current condition—"

Eurydice raised a hand, cutting the woman off. "I've learned a little in the past three years," she said quietly. "There's power, and then there's *power.* I made the mistake once, of showing Tahut-Nefer how much magical power I have, when all I really needed to do was order him to leave, and have a few guards throw him out of the villa. Concentrated to a point? You don't need a lot of power to have the effect you want." She felt her own lips thin. "And in this particular case, information is power." She looked up, met

Damkina's eyes, over the woman's veil, and made herself smile. "Stay outside the tent, if you would. Let them see you. I'm quite sure they'll know what you are, at a glance."

"I should certainly hope so, my lady," Damkina replied, gesturing at her clothing. "I do not dress this way to blend in. I wear the garb of Chaldea to proclaim as loudly as I can, who and what I am." Her strange, green-bronze eyes were hooded as she added, "It saves much time and effort, in the end."

Caesarion gave her a look as the others cleared out of the tent for the moment. "Do I want to know what you have in mind?" he asked.

She considered it carefully. "I'm going to do my best to frighten the high priest of Thoth and all his adherents into complete obedience," Eurydice told her husband. "And this is how."

When she finished her explanation, Caesarion had to sit down for a moment or two to digest it. Shook his head. And then told her, "Yes. That might just do it." His crimson eyes held concern, however. "You're going to have to act as if you're completely in control, beloved."

"I know." She nodded. "Act as if you're in charge, and half the time, people will believe it. And at the moment, we *need* them to believe it. More than they believe anything else."

Padubast, the High Priest of Thoth, had just passed his sixty-fifth birthday. He thought it possible that he might see his sixty-sixth, but that really was in the hands of the gods. He could feel death inside of him, reaching its cold fingers from his heart to every extremity. Clenching its fist around his heart and lungs, making it difficult to breathe, and forcing him to bring up blood when he coughed, now and again. Thus, he was carried to the camp of the Roman Emperor—the *pharaoh*—on a bier, by six of his attendants, while three other, lesser priests of the temple, rode small donkeys behind his litter. Another attendant walked alongside his litter, handing the high priest fresh cloths into which he could spit when he had need, or clusters of aniseed on which to chew, to make his breath a little sweeter.

Twenty feet ahead of him, entering the hastily-erected gate of the camp already, he could see the *nomarch* of Thebes on his own litter. Nomarch Sebichos was a tall, thin man by Egyptian standards; his position was hereditary, and his ancestors had intermarried frequently with Nubian and Kushite royalty to strengthen bonds with the kingdoms to the south of Egypt. Hence, his skin was darker than Padubast's own, contrasting with the pure white of his *shendyt* kilt and the crisp white linen that covered his head and neck at the moment. As regional royalty, Sebichos was entitled to, and wore, a leopard skin cape over his shoulders, in addition to heavy gold jewelry. Politically astute, Sebichos was certain to blow whichever way the wind was strongest—and Padubast could see him suddenly lurch upright on his bier, staring at something just past the gate. *Unusual. I suppose I'll see whatever it is, in a moment.*

And as his own bier moved through the gate now, Padubast sat up himself, anger and sorrow coursing through him in equal measures. For just past the gate, on seven spears driven butt-first into the ground, were seven heads, severed at the neck. They'd been crudely preserved, probably in salt. And Padubast recognized all seven faces, battered though the visages were, with their mouths hanging agape and their eyes missing, pecked out by the crows and other birds that still hovered nearby, looking for a quick meal.

His stomach churned, and he sat back in his litter,

coughing once more into a fresh piece of linen. *What do I tell my pharaoh? That we met in the last part of the dying year, and my brethren voted <u>against</u> rebellion, seven to four. And the four who voted for rebellion vanished, along with three lesser priests, a week later — after the tax-collectors went missing. That I suspected their involvement in the whole sorry mess, but could do nothing more than support my people against the heavy hands of armed troops, who started a massacre in the city streets?*

The tent at the center of the camp hardly looked grand enough to be the pavilion of a pharaoh. It should have occupied most of an acre, and have been constructed of light, translucent linen to admit the breeze. There should have been slaves on hand to wash the feet of the guests, offer them wine and honeyed dates, and stir the otherwise unmoving air with palm fronds. Instead, this tent seemed to be made of heavy wool, like the tents of the desert nomads. A few servants were on hand to open the flap for them, and Padubast shakily took one of his attendant's arms, grateful for the support as he made his way into the depths of the structure.

Inside, there were servants, yes, pouring wine and water into cups around a table. At the head of that table, an eagle, a living one, trod back and forth over a tall wooden perch. Not chained there, nor caged, it seemed restless and huge. All of the guests eyed the predator warily, and most elected to sit well away from a creature that could, on a whim, attack and destroy their eyes and faces.

Padubast, for his part, took a seat gratefully, as did his lower-ranked priests, but he waved the cup away. *"I have not managed to live so long by drinking water,"* he wheezed in Hellene, which he spoke fluently.

"I've given orders for all my men to boil their water before drinking it, and then to pass it through a Hippocrates' sleeve to remove any further impurities. That should take care of whatever in the Nile is causing so many of them to piss blood," a deep voice said from behind him in Latin, and Padubast turned, his eyes widening. And then tried to rise so that he could kneel respectfully, but again, he required aid.

The pharaoh—for surely, this young man was he!—was as tall as any Nubian Padubast had ever met, at least seven large spans in height, but lacked the whipcord frames of those who dwelled in the southern regions. Instead, he was broad across neck, chest, and shoulders, with his arms in proportion, all of which were bare at the moment, for he'd chosen to wear a *shendyt* as if born to it, instead of a Roman tunic and toga. His hair was dark and slightly curly, though very short, and utterly exposed, for he'd eschewed crown and head-covering entirely. No jewelry, beyond a heavy gold ring on one finger. And not sandals, but Roman boots, shod with iron nails. And while his eyes lacked any kohl, they were red. The same red as drying blood. And they carried with them a world of authority, and a certain icy irritation, too. *This is not a good man to annoy*, Padubast thought tiredly. *The last several generations of Ptolemies were fat and quarrelsome, but fearful to behold when enraged. Plump and stupid, they still razed Thebes almost to the ground. What will this one do?* "My lord," Padubast wheezed in Egyptian, slowly lowering himself to the ground, even as those around him did.

The young man held out his hand, and a woman emerged from the depths of the tent, with its thick smell of wet animal. And she, too, somehow outshone her surroundings. Their faces held the unmistakable signs of the same heredity. Roman noses, high Etruscan cheekbones, and the same determined jaw, more prominent on him than on her. Her skin had seen less of the sun, being paler, and her eyes were the same gold as the eagle on its perch. While she wore no wig, she did wear the golden crown of a queen, with the hawk of Horus spreading its wings alongside her ears, and a necklace of a dozen huge amethysts, each carved with the image of a different god, wrapped around her throat, above a pure white *kalasiris*. Deceptive in its simplicity, the dress skimmed her curves. A *kalasiris* was tight for a reason—it showed all of a woman's fecundity. And in this case, it quietly flared over a waist slightly thicker than it might have been. Stating, subtly, but unmistakably, that the queen was with child. With all the *power* that a pregnant woman had, of potential, mystery, and connection to realms inaccessible to men.

Never changing expression from the regal calm and distance with which she had entered, the queen took her husband-brother's hand, and allowed him to escort her to the head of the table, where a servant placed a basket of raw flesh. And now, seeming not to care that the flesh would dirty her fingers with blood, she began to offer gobbets of it to the eagle, which hopped down from its perch to land on her shoulder. Accepting the morsels from her delicate, bare fingers as gently as a child.

Padubast swallowed, but the *nomarch* of Thebes fortunately took the lead in conversation, immediately and obsequiously stating, "My pharaoh, my agents have been unable to find the missing Roman tax-collectors. But they have been much delayed in their search by the events that have transpired since they began looking—"

"We are aware of what's happened since the men went missing," the pharaoh said sternly. "Full-scale riots, resulting in the deaths of hundreds of people. Followed by attacks on this *castra* and patrols sent out from it. This ends today, gentlemen."

The *nomarch* spread his hands placatingly. "My lord, many times in ages past, this province or that has shown signs of unrest. Your ancestors often chose to forgive, and thus ensured that trade from the south and east would not be interrupted. I hope that you will embrace this wise policy."

The young pharaoh looked at his queen. And she was the one who responded now, calmly. Distantly, "My beloved husband and I are united in our desire for the prosperity of Egypt, *nomarch*, because the prosperity of one province contributes to the prosperity of the entire empire. But there is one thing that must be had in an empire of this size—an empire that covers over six times as much land as Egypt does, alone." She fed another gobbet to the eagle, and went on, after a pause, "There must be *order*, Lord Sebichos. There must be the rule of law. Taxes must be paid—and we understand that the grain harvest was poor this year. And since the tax is a *percentage* of each farmer and land-owner's yields, this means that the tax burden on each individual was less this year, than in years past. Perhaps this was not communicated properly to the peasantry. We will rely on you to make this clear to them, and to your fellow nobles as well." Unspoken in that calm-voiced statement was an underlying threat: *We suspect that you deliberately did not communicate this to people in this region, so as to stir up unrest and anti-Roman sentiment.*

The pharaoh added now, his voice cold, "And we will send scribes and other officials from Alexandria to finish the tax collection, and examine the records kept by you, and all other nobles of this region. It would be distressing, if there were discrepancies between the amount reported collected by the peasantry, and the amount turned in to the coffers of the state."

Padubast translated, *You may have an underlying reason not to have found the tax-collectors rapidly, <u>Nomarch</u>. You might have been collecting the same amount as last year's taxes from your direct subjects, and passing along only the amount demanded this* *year. Lining your coffers with the difference, while claiming to the populace that it was all the fault of greedy Rome.*

Sebichos lifted his chin. "Your inspectors will find that my records are in order."

"We certainly hope that this is the case. Because if any noble's records are found to have serious discrepancies, we will give them to your own peasants, and allow them to look for their missing coin and grain inside the coffer of the noble's own flesh," the young queen said, tilting her head to the side, just as the eagle did the same thing. An avian, alien look. Not interested on a human level but . . . calculating. Assessing. "In the meantime, we will render assistance to the citizens of Thebes, and the engineers of the two legions encamped here will begin removing rubble and marking the ground for the building of new homes and shops. This will be a glorious chance to *improve* Thebes by straightening what looks to have been a maze of crooked streets. Perhaps even a chance to build, if not sewers, then at least lavatory pits. Better, I think, than simply letting all the filth wash into the Nile."

The *nomarch* choked. "Where is the coin for these improvements to come from, my lady?" he asked.

"I can't help but notice that the cost of grain has gone up staggeringly," she returned, her expression still remote. "The largest land-owners in Egypt have become even wealthier in the past year, while paying that reduced tax rate. I was rather hoping that, being civic-minded men, well aware of the needs of society, that some of you might be prevailed upon to donate some of the funds. I will, personally, donate half a talent of silver to help the reconstruction effort along." Her expression shifted, minutely. "After which, my lord Sebichos, there will be no more unrest in Thebes."

It wasn't a question. It was a direct order. The *nomarch* threw up his hands in exasperation. "I do not control the hearts and minds of the entire populace!" He looked at Padubast in frustration. "The priests will need to speak out, if you wish the current situation to . . . abate."

"I have spoken," Padubast wheezed. "On several occasions."

The queen placed one red-daubed finger to her lips, and then asked a question that froze Padubast's already slow-moving blood in his veins. "Tell me, respected high priest of Thoth, how many of your brethren here today have been initiated into the mystery of the Seven Gods?"

Padubast went rigid. Then coughed into a square of linen to give himself time to think, as two of his three underpriests murmured to each other in bafflement, and Sebichos turned to look at him in puzzlement. "My lady," Padubast said, at length, "I take it from your words, that *you* have been."

A very slight inclination of her head. The high priest sighed. "Leave us," he ordered the two most junior priests, but gesturing for Riei, the second-most senior priest in his order, to remain. "I would take it . . . as a courtesy . . . if Lord Sebichos were to leave us, as well."

"Go," the pharaoh ordered the *nomarch*, and Sebichos left, turning to peer behind himself with evident curiosity. Every servant left now, as well, dismissed with quick, sharp words in Latin.

And when they were all safely out of earshot, the young queen offered her eagle another piece of meat from the bowl, and said, softly, "Ah. So the two of you know the great secret."

Padubast did his best to sit upright without coughing. "I'm surprised that you do, my lady." He paused. *Of course, she could just know the* words*, but not the meaning behind them. I'll give her no confirmation.* "What is the reason for your inquiry?"

he asked, feeling another wheeze coming on. "How does this relate to the question of . . . tempering the rebellion? I *have* spoken against it. Repeatedly."

"And yet, as you saw on your way into our camp, seven priests came to Alexandria and attempted to kill my wife," the pharaoh said evenly. "They stole the grimoire of a Magus—the one you surely saw outside our tent—and summoned a demon whose Name hasn't been spoken in over two thousand years in an effort to murder her, me, and as much of the line of Ptolemy as they could."

Padubast closed his eyes, wanting to rail at the stupidity of Tahut-Nefer and the rest of his associates. "We did not know where they had gone," he managed after a moment. "Tahut and three others of my higher-ranking priests spoke against you in conclave a few months ago, but the rest of our brethren denounced them." *Denounced* was a strong word. *Voted against and then politely ignored* was probably more accurate, but he needed to convince this pair not to execute him and the rest of his priesthood. "Then they vanished, along with several younger priests. Three of whom adorned your spears, yes." He swallowed.

"You must exert more control over your brotherhood," the queen said quietly. "And this is why. If you do not bring them in line, and if the rest of the temples of the Seven Gods—Aten, Amun-Ra, Isis, Thoth, Sekhmet, Horus, and Set—do not back our rule, to the hilt? Then my brother-husband has given me leave to dissolve all of the temples of the *dead* gods. There are literally thousands of temples that would be affected, from those of Anouke to those of Tawaret. I will evict every one of these false priests from their temples. Confiscate all treasures belonging to them, and all their lands. Put their coin in the coffers of the state, put their artifacts into the collections of the pharaoh."

Padubast stopped breathing. "You can't *do* that, my lady," he protested. "The economic disruption alone would take hundreds of years to abate." He gasped for breath, foreseeing consequences that he doubted the young woman before him could envision. "The temples, even of the dead gods . . . do much good. Almost . . . all artistry . . . sponsored by them. All . . . dance and music . . . taught by priestesses of Bastet . . . ." He wheezed. "Almost all physicians . . . train in the temples of Ptah. Thousands of scribes, all employed by temples. Thousands of craftsmen . . . employed to keep up the temples. Provide food. Whole economy . . . hinges on them."

Beside him, Riei shook his head. "And concentrating so much power into the seven priesthoods—no pharaoh has ever done that. It would be your undoing, and it wouldn't serve any ends—"

She smiled, and Padubast quailed inwardly at the expression, so cold and confident. "Oh, undeniably, it would give great power to the priests of the seven living gods, yes. But there's a reason you yourselves have never announced the *truth* to the people of Egypt. After all, what happens if you do? I'm sure that most of the priests of Bastet and Ptah and the rest don't know that their prayers are directed at dead, deaf ears. They might be rightly irritated at having lived a lie. They might decide to take that anger out on, say, the priests of gods that still exist. The ones who've lied to them, and had real power all along." She leaned her head against her knuckles now, propping her elbow on the arm of her chair. "And the commoners! If someone were to tell them that they've been *lied* to for over a thousand years, they might rise up and kill all the priests who've been doing the lying. Both the ones who've been representing the dead gods, and the living ones. And goodness only knows what they'll do then. Why, they might decide that if gods can die, they might not need gods at all."

Padubast's mouth had gone completely dry. "You . . . you are god-born of Isis," he managed, swallowing. "Do you say these things . . . is this her will?"

"She speaks to me in dreams and in portents, and expects me to derive my own interpretations and make my own decisions. She does not lead me by the hand, or drive me along like a brainless sheep towards a stream." The queen's eyes were hooded now. "I look at Egypt, my lord priests, and I see a land that has achieved greatness, but has stagnated, too. It's locked in a dream of its own magnificence, little realizing that the world has begun to pass it by. To my way of thinking? Gradually eliminating the cults of the dead gods, over the course of centuries, would be greatly in the interest of the seven living gods. And their temples." She stared at the two men, unblinking. "But to do that, rather than simply making the announcement and letting the common people rip you apart with their hands and teeth, and then marching in the legions to impose order once every priest in Egypt is dead?" She paused, and then gave them a sweet, empty smile. "That is a policy decision I will find it easier to make, knowing that I, my brother-husband, and Rome, have your unconditional support."

Put that way, there wasn't much Padubast could say in the way of protest. He lowered his head in deep homage, and rasped, "I will reach out to my brethren at the temples of Karnak and Luxor. You will have their full-throated support, my lady. My lord."

The queen flicked two fingers at the tent flap, and, dismissed, Padubast and Riei stumbled out. "They wouldn't," Riei whispered furiously as Padubast settled himself in his litter once more. "They *can't*."

"In less than a year, I think, you will be on your own to make that determination," Padubast told him, coughing into yet another linen square. "I will be in the afterlife, beyond the reach of peasants and pharaohs alike. Though I'd prefer not to have my mummy dug up and burned by an angry mob." He closed his eyes as the bearers lifted him up. "You may take your chances then, Riei, my old friend. For now? I believe them. I believe that they will do what they say. I even believe *her*, when she says that change may be . . . what is best . . . for our people. And it may even be the will of our gods. Thoth doesn't speak to me often. But I noticed no flickering of the lamps in their tent. No . . . sudden storms have appeared. No packs of lions have emerged to roar at the walls of the camp." He sighed.

In the command tent, Eurydice allowed her expression to relax. Inhaled and exhaled deeply, then yelped a little as Caesarion leaned over, lifted her bodily from her chair, and pulled her into his lap, startling the eagle into flapping wildly back to its perch. "What are you *doing* – " She blinked rapidly as he stood, propping her backside on the table in front of them, and kissed her. Fervently.

"Accipitra," he murmured against her lips. "You played the role perfectly. You showed them the beak and the talons. And I *love* it when you do that." He laughed, a rare sound indeed from Caesarion, and rested his forehead against hers. "The threat *is* the bribe. The bribe is the threat. Either way, you promised them that the truth's coming out . . . and the only thing they get to choose is whether it comes out fast and bloody, or slow and controlled. Beautiful, my beloved. Simply beautiful."

She swallowed, letting the fear she'd felt recede. "I thought for a few minutes there that I'd have to *do* it the bloody way. I might still have to. I've never tried so hard to imitate Mother before in my life—"

"*Don't* spoil it," Caesarion told her, and pushed her back onto the table, gently pressing his weight along her body.

A tiny, muffled laugh in reaction, and then a light tease as she ran her nails along one of his shoulders. "You know, I was looking forward to just after the investiture ceremony. You in this same kilt, me in that *ridiculous* dress—"

He bit her gently under her ear, cutting off her words as she gasped. "*Want me to speak Egyptian while I take you?*"

"*Gods, yes, but not in here, the servants are going to walk in at any moment*—" Her voice was dazed suddenly.

"*The bed's not that far away.*" He picked her up, whirled her around in a quick, exultant circle, and carried her the fifteen feet or so to the private area of the tent. "*You proved that you can rule them,*" Caesarion told her, settling her down on the bed. "*Never forget that.*"

Martius 24, 20 AC

They spent the better part of a week in Thebes, making sure that the various priests took Eurydice very seriously indeed, and then instructed the priests of the sprawling Egyptian pantheon to send delegates north to Alexandria, with lists of the names of major spirits who'd escaped the purges of a thousand years ago . . . and lists of major temples that were dedicated to dead gods, which could be easily merged with the worship of existing living ones. "Nothing that Egypt hasn't really done before," Eurydice pointed out in private. "How often have gods like Amun and Re seemed to be combined, anyway? And in fifty or a hundred years, the names of the dead ones can be gently eased out of living memory." She shrugged. "The most conservative elements of society will protest, of course. But they won't be much interested in truth. Just in maintaining their own power."

"Just keep your Praetorians around you at all times. And work with Damkina on protections." Caesarion had told her, his fingers tightening on her hand. "I won't be here to, ah, provide you with masking from spirits. And once the child's born. . . ."

"Once the child's born, I should be able to go back to protecting myself, at least in part," Eurydice reminded him. "I do feel annoyingly like a glass goblet, packed in straw and cotton, lest I fall and break myself."

On the journey back, they did take the opportunity to explore the pyramids on the Giza Plateau. Eurydice was faintly surprised, and a little dismayed, to discover how small the passageways inside the great structures were. She had to drop to a crouch, and Caesarion needed to fold to his knees. And the spaces inside? One was a tomb, certainly, but many of the rest were simply engineering necessities. Open places to relieve the weight of the structure, lest it fall in on itself.

The keepers of the regional temples seemed happy to tell them that the Sphinx itself had been lost to the sands at least once before, and had been dug up at the command of Thutmose IV. That the statue had to be repainted once every five years, to keep its colors bright. "All this effort," Eurydice murmured to Caesarion, looking up at the greatest of the pyramids, "all the preservation required to keep the limestone and gold shining, in spite of the sand tearing at it, year after year, century after century. And it's all just for one man's tomb. It's not even a building, really. It can never be used for anything, other than to be a . . . symbol."

"You have to admit, they're damned impressive symbols," Caesarion commented, staring at the face of the Sphinx, with its noble nose and impassive eyes. "I wonder what a Roman version of a pyramid would look like."

She chuckled, subtly elbowing him as they turned away. "It would be functional," Eurydice informed him loftily. "And there would be arches and pillars and statuary."

"So, basically, square levels, stepped, with rooms inside?"

"And stairs that people can actually walk up and down. And it wouldn't just be one man's grave. Romans wouldn't stand for that." She looked up at him, smiling. "Maybe a tomb on the very top floor. With a good view of the sky."

"And below that?" he asked, chuckling.

"Temples. Libraries. Places of learning. If you're going to devote that much space to something, let it be for something that matters."

The words sank into the back of his mind, and lingered there. *It would be a good thing, to build a kind of symbol of unity in Rome. Not quite Egyptian, not quite Roman. But the engineering needed for it would be quite difficult. And costly. Will have to wait to see if those gold mines in Hispania pan out. Building us a new villa on the scale we really need to entertain diplomats and governors and everyone else is going to be expensive enough – and that's with Alexander insisting that the Senate pay for half.*

A slew of letters awaited them in Alexandria. A half-dozen from Alexander alone, including one in the hieratic code that only he and Eurydice used. Eurydice translated it, and gave it to Caesarion. Caesarion dictated a reply, grim-faced. Giving their brother permission for what he needed to do. But neither of them felt good about the decision. Nor did they feel clean.

Neither of them slept the night before he left. Caesarion spent a good portion of the evening wondering what it would be like just to . . . stay here. Somehow. *But in the end, I sent men to Britannia. The war season began two weeks ago, and the salii leaped and danced in Rome, and I wasn't there to watch. It's time I lead my men, damn it.* "Write to me," Eurydice told him quietly, just before dawn, as he started dressing to leave for the ship.

"I will. Every day." He gave her a faint smile. "Did you know that Father wrote several books of poetry?"

"Mother's mentioned it. I've never had the courage to read any of it."

"He was just as good at it as he was at oratory and history. I don't think I inherited any of those skills. But I'll send you maudlin poems in my letters, how's that?"

As he expected, she burst out laughing at the mere thought, and he came over to the bed. Leaned down and kissed her as she laughed. And, as she stilled, he spread a hand across her belly, wondering if he'd feel anything there. He didn't, of course; it was too early in the pregnancy. "I keep telling myself that thousands of legionnaires miss their wives every year," Caesarion told Eurydice quietly. "Thousands of men don't get to hold their children just after they're born. There's . . . nothing special about us, in that respect." He sighed, and gave her one last, tight embrace.

"Stay alive, and be victorious," Eurydice whispered, her voice tight.

"I'll try to do both those things. And the instant I get the men into winter camp, I will cross that narrow bit of sea and take a horse relay from Gaul to Rome. My backside won't love me, but I'll be here before the year ends, if Fortuna smiles." He kissed her hand, and picked up the bag that held his armor and weapons; he wouldn't suffer anyone else to carry it for him. "Goodbye, Accipitra. I love you."

"I love you, too, Aquilus." Her eyes were suspiciously bright, but he knew she was holding back the tears as best she could, not wanting to weep before him.

Nothing more than that. He left quietly, and looked

back once he'd reached the docks below. Caught sight of a single figure in white up on the headland, looking down at the ships below. . . and a particularly persistent gull landed on the ship's deck beside him. Caesarion chuckled under his breath, though his heart wasn't really in it. "You'll see me off, then. As far as you can reach."

Chapter XI: Blood

Februarius 15-20, 20 AC

Octavia Thurina wandered the grounds of the Julii villa, bored and discontent. She'd long since found herself drifting out of her friendship with Selene Julia, though they lived in the same house, and Eurydice Julia was powerful and frightening—and usually incredibly *busy*. The Empress of Rome had delegated household oversight to Selene quite willingly over the past three years, but between constantly meeting with ambassadors, studying magic, conversing with priestesses of Venus for whatever reason, and periodically riding off on campaign with Caesarion, she never seemed to have time to sit down and *talk*. There were always injunctions for Octavia to concentrate more on her studies, to improve her mind, to read more. But never a moment to chit-chat about the latest fashions—for all that Eurydice seemed to be *setting* the style among younger Roman women, with her tendency to wear Egyptian bracelets and Roman *stolae*, and whatever else. And certainly never a chance to talk about what they'd seen at the last games, or who'd been betrothed of late, and everything else.

If Octavia had been a little more aware and intelligent, she could have parleyed gossip into a more political awareness—who was betrothed to whom was one of the most important weathervanes for shifting politics among wealthy plebeians and patricians in Rome. But she wasn't, and she didn't particularly feel the lack. Being relatively inclined towards kind-heartedness, her gossip never tended towards the malicious. But she was *starved* for conversation at this point. Since the rest of the household had left, Alexander, her betrothed, occasionally ate dinner at the house with her. Politely nodded through her conversational sallies, but had an air of preoccupation through every meal, as if he were reading as they ate — even if there wasn't a single scroll in front of him at all!

Midway through Februarius, he'd come down with some fever or another, that had resulted in him being pale and ill for several days — though he'd insisted on going out and about throughout the illness as if nothing at all was wrong. "Just ate something that didn't agree with me," he'd assured her blithely at the door, and had mounted up to leave. "Much to do."

"I'd really like to speak with you about our wedding!" Octavia had called after him, and, as the servants closed the door between them, had stomped her foot on the tile floor of the lobby, hurting her heel in her vexation.

Stalking through the villa in her agitation, she'd blundered along through the chilly *peristylium* garden, where she'd not ventured since winter began. And had noticed, to her surprise, that on the upper story, where there were a half-dozen usually unused rooms, there were *guards* on duty along the balcony. In curiosity, she'd gone upstairs to find out what was going on, to be firmly rebuffed by men twice her age, but surely with half her social standing. "I *live* here," she told them, folding her arms across her chest. "I'm Lord Alexander's betrothed, and in the absence of the Empress and Selene Julia, I am the lady of this house."

It . . . wasn't strictly true. No one had handed her the keys, to her chagrin. She remained precisely what she'd been before the general exodus of the Julii; an honored house-guest.

And these men, with their unshaven faces and hard eyes, seemed to know it, too. They exchanged glances, shrugged at one another, and simply wouldn't let her *pass*. In exasperation, Octavia stood on her tiptoes, trying to look over their shoulders, and caught sight of a male slave she didn't recognize—relatively tall, with short, curly, golden hair—assisting a woman out the door of one of these upstairs bedrooms. Octavia couldn't see her face, only the red-gold hair, and the fact that she wore only a thin tunic, exposing most of her legs. Octavia's eyes widened; the slave assisting the woman caught sight of her, and he immediately hustled the woman back into her room, closing the door behind them.

"It might be for the best if you were to go now, *domina*," one of the men said pointedly.

Bristling with indignation, Octavia did precisely that. At a loss for anything else she could do, she waited until Alexander came home, and tried to brace him on the subject at dinner. "Why are there guards around one of the bedrooms? Who is our guest, Alexander? I have a right to know who's . . . who's living under this roof." She tried to put firmness in her voice, but Alexander, who was sharing the same eating couch with her, but hardly doing justice to the meal before them, looked as if she'd jerked him back from a thousand miles away.

"I'm sorry, what did you say?"

"Who is staying in the guarded room?" Octavia's mind teemed with sudden suspicions. She'd *seen* how he looked at that horrible Sulpicia months ago. Her with her *obviously* dyed red-gold hair. *While mine is dyed, it's at least blond to start with,* she fumed to herself now. *Mine's tasteful. Hers is not.* And then the suspicion, already forming, fermented completely: "It's Servia Sulpicia, isn't it?" Octavia accused, watching Alexander's eyes widen slightly. "You're having an affair with her, right under the same roof where I live. Well, I won't *have* it!" She sat up, bristling now. "You may make every excuse there is to put off our wedding, but I won't have you keeping a mistress in the same house as me!"

Alexander stared at her for a long moment, and then laughed. Uproariously. Octavia felt herself dwindling under that laughter, like a pig's bladder, inflated with air, and then popped with a pin. "No," he said, picking up a knife and peeling an apple with it. "My guest is not Sulpicia. You'll note that she hasn't been to dinner here more than twice in the past several months?" He cut off a slice of apple and put it in his mouth with every evidence of enjoyment, but didn't offer her any. "As for the rest? This isn't your house." His eyes shuttered. Went blank and cold, and she realized numbly that she'd never seen this side of him before. Ever. "It is my brother's, and for the moment, I speak for him. Who the guests of the Julii are, are none of your affair. You will not attempt to enter those rooms or speak with their inhabitants again, Octavia. I say this for your own safety."

Octavia gaped at him. And her mind took a leap, and landed somewhere entirely elsewhere. "Are they *ill?*" she asked, her eyes wide. "Do they have some horrible sickness?"

"As far as you're concerned, they're lepers." His dark eyes glittered in the low light from the oil lamps illuminating the room. "Stay away from them. Forget they exist. And," he cut another slice of apple with the knife, adding with slow, cool purpose, "I'd take it as a courtesy if you never mentioned Servia Sulpicia's name to me again."

A rush of relief passed through her. *He hates her,* Octavia thought with glee. *He despises that old creature with her kohl and her would-be Egyptian jewelry and all her airs and pretensions to poetry,* she thought, consigning a woman of only twenty-one years to the same mental midden to which she'd assign a woman of sixty.

When her step-mother, Livia, summoned her to lunch later that week, Octavia went, relieved to have *someone* to talk to at last, even if it was Livia. Her own mother, Scribonia, from whom Octavian had ensured that she'd be estranged for the first ten years of her life, had died this past year. Octavia had found it almost impossible to mourn the woman. The Julii had permitted her to become acquainted with her mother over the intervening four years, but it had been solely on social occasions. No real *bond* had ever been established. And so, she was left with Livia, Cleopatra, and Eurydice as the closest things to motherly figures in her life. None of whom really fit that description at all.

But in Livia's house, drinking watered wine, Octavia felt, for the first time in her life, as if her step-mother sympathized with her. "Alexander simply won't set a date for the marriage," Octavia complained. "He says he's too busy, what with working with the architects on the plans for the new Julii villa—"

"So that's actually going to happen. They're going to build that monstrosity right on the Palatine." Livia shuddered delicately. "And then the *reigning monarch* of Egypt and his incestuous queen will daily walk the sacred soil of Rome. As no king or queen has been permitted to do in hundreds of years."

Octavia nodded, but she was preoccupied with her own complaints. "And all the other things he has to do," she went on. "He doesn't dine at home more than once a week. I never see him."

"Well, you may expect that to continue as you have allowed it to begin," Livia told her wisely, nodding. "Unless you make your displeasure clear to him."

Octavia shuddered. "Oh, I wouldn't dare. The way he *looked* at me when I asked him about the woman he's keeping in rooms in the villa. I thought at first it was Servia Sulpicia— that obviously *fake* red hair—" she touched her own dyed tresses gently, "but he hates *her*. He made no bones about *that*. But still, he told me not to concern myself with whoever it is. Told me that I should act as if she has some horrible, contagious disease, like leprosy. And yet, whoever it is, is still there!" Octavia threw her hands up. "It's an outrage, isn't it, to be forced to live under the same roof as his mistress? I mean, it's one thing if he's just . . . you know . . . with a slave. That's just physical. He might actually *love* this woman." Face crumbling, she drained her cup, and missed the expression in Livia's eyes as she did. "Livia—step-mother, please. Tell me what I should do."

Livia took her gently into her arms and rocked her, as she'd never done in all the years that Octavia had lived with her and her father, Octavian. "There, there," Livia crooned. "I was against this marriage from the beginning, as you might remember, but my dear Agrippa insisted on some sort of tie to end the strife between your father's supporters and these false Julii. And now Alexander has not only corrupted my poor Tiberius, but dishonored you, too."

Octavia raised her head, confused. "Corrupted Tiberius? I don't understand—"

"Oh, my dear, you didn't know?" Livia said, her face contorting in a perfect mask of anguish and shame. "I'm so sorry—I shouldn't have spoken—"

"Tell me!" Octavia demanded, her stomach twisting.

"Why, it's common knowledge that Alexander's used Tiberius like a woman. They've been at *that* for at least three years. I've tried and tried to separate them, to have my son act like a man again, but to no avail. I'm fairly sure that some of it has gone on under the same roof where you have lived, too— to your further dishonor." Livia sighed heavily, and Octavia sat, rigid, unable to believe what she was hearing.

Finally, nauseous at the incredible insensitivity of the

horrible man to whom she was betrothed, Octavia told Livia, "Please tell your husband Agrippa that I absolutely *cannot* marry Alexander. That I *refuse* to do so. Or to live in the Julii house even one day longer."

"Oh, I will, I will." Livia nodded understandingly. "But I think it might be best if you were to be subtle about this, for a few days. A week at most. I think that you should certainly have your revenge on young Alexander. And whoever his current mistress is—the one he has all tucked away in his brother's house."

"And how am I to do that?" Octavia wailed, covering her face with her hands, trying to hold back the tears. It was all too much. The humiliation was so intense, she didn't know how she was going to live. *I am the laughingstock of Rome. Everyone who's seen me on Alexander's arm for the past four years — everyone who's come to dinner at the Julii house — they've all known. They've all known and laughed.*

Livia smoothed her hair. "It's very simple," she crooned. "Bring the poor, *sick* woman a basket of medicaments and soothing foods. I'll have the cooks here prepare something suitable myself. Get a good look at her face, and see if it's someone you know. And if it's a young woman with a tiny scar, right here," Livia said, drawing a line by the corner of her right eye, "do tell young Jocasta that you're sorry that her sister's health has taken such a turn for the worse."

Octavia blinked. "And *this* will be vengeance?" she said, dubiously.

"There is such a thing, my dear, as killing people with kindness," Livia told her gently. "Why, I imagine that if you say such a kind, good-natured thing after she's eaten from the good things you bring her? She'll be overcome by remorse. Wouldn't you be?"

Octavia thought about that. And, for the first time in ages, feeling as if she had someone's support, she decided that it all made perfect sense. "Of course," she told Livia, managing an uncertain smile. "You're right. You've always been right."

Februarius 21, 20 AC

Alexander spent an intoxicating evening with Sulpicia, listening to her read scenes from the play he'd asked her to write, and laughing uproariously for the better part of two hours. The father figure of the play had a catch-phrase: "For the family is everything!" and he used it at every inappropriate moment possible — when being *mounted* by his male courtesan, for example.

The mother, by the end of the play, on realizing that the patriarch of the house actually preferred to play the woman's part, threw up her hands in exasperation. "Well, why didn't you *say* so years ago?" she exclaimed. "I could have given you that pleasure, without you ever having to leave the house! You've never left the lamps burning while you did your marital duties, so my deepest secret has been, till now, something between me and the gods alone. For they saw fit to give me the parts of both sexes — I am Hermaphroditus, reborn!" she said, lifting up her skirts.

"I have never loved you more!" her husband cried.

"I am undone!" the butler, her erstwhile lover mourned. "No one will ever believe that I didn't know!"

And in the meantime, the noble maiden who'd been betrothed to the son of the house, had been so nervous about her wedding night, and so desirous of ensuring that her betrothed would love her, that she'd gone to the same bawdy house frequented by the father, and had paid for *instruction* in the arts of love. The same concubine who'd mounted the father, now mounted the prospective daughter-in-law, and she enjoyed the act so thoroughly, that she declared she'd never leave the house—she'd become a *hetaira*, shame to her family or not, and pleasure herself and anyone else she chose, for the rest of her days.

So in the end, the son of the house was able to marry his half-Egyptian beloved, and the butler exiled himself to Syria, lest anyone in Athens see his face again. The father and mother, reconciled and newly enamored for . . . very obvious reasons. . . waved from the balcony of their house to the audience, before both disappearing back inside, while the young groom below carried his wife into the house, asking her, somewhat nervously, "Is it all right with you if I leave the lamps on, my love? For while the family is everything, I'd rather not have any surprises."

Alexander curled in on himself and *laughed* until tears ran, unashamed, from his eyes. "Oh my dear gods," he gasped after she'd finished reading. "I don't have enough money to bribe the censors to show that unedited at your theater, love."

"It's set in Athens, not Rome," she said, making a rude noise. "And I don't even have any of the actors wearing enormous fake phalluses, like when they play Aristophanes. All the sex takes place off-stage, too—all I have them do is make noises. Very loud, barnyard noises, I will admit, but noises, nonetheless." They were sitting side by side on the sleeping couch at *Merges*. "You really like it? The verse is very rough so far—"

"Like it? I love it. It's a breath of fresh air. Ends in *gamos*, male-female union, like every other comedy, reaffirms the social order but overturns it completely. Aristophanes has nothing on you." He meant every word, sincerely. "I think you should change the title to *The Family*. And maybe a little more polish on the final lines. But once you're happy with the verse, I will spend every night copying it for you for a month." He kissed her hand. "And now, I need to leave you."

Sulpicia sighed. "Duty calls?"

"It never really stops." Alexander stroked her face. *Octavia is more perceptive than I gave her credit for—or her accusations are proof that even a blind man can throw a dart and hit a target now and again. I've haven't dared have Sulpicia over for dinner, for fear people would be able to read my face, or hers. And what would someone like Livia do with information like that? Target her. Try to kill her, or use her to get to me.* "My goal in the next several years," Alexander told her softly, "is to make myself one of the most hated men in Rome. So that Caesarion doesn't have to. It'll be dangerous for anyone associated with me—"

"I know how to keep secrets," Sulpicia assured him. "Have you decided what to do about Livia yet?"

"I've sent Caesarion a coded letter on the subject, but there's one more person I need to speak to about the matter. Who's also, similarly, too far away to speak with readily."

"Tiberius?" Sulpicia regarded him steadily. "When you were poisoned, you said you loved his spirit. And my mind."

Alexander blinked as he pulled his tunic over his head. "Then the poison loosened my tongue more than it should have." *I've only known I loved this woman for a few months. My emotions could run off with my mind. I can't tell her all my secrets, much as I want to. Not yet. Not until I'm as sure of her, as I've ever been of Tiberius.* He sighed, taking her hand lightly in his as he stood by the bed. Soberly, Alexander said, "I asked my brother, in the same letter about Livia, if he'd object if I broke my betrothal to Octavia. So that I could pursue marriage with you."

He watched her mouth open, soundlessly, and went on,

quietly, "It wouldn't be at first. It's probably better—safer, anyway—if no one knows about us. For the time being. So that you're not a target for poison and knives. But I *do* want to marry you, Via. Aurea. My love, by any name." He closed his eyes. "For the moment, let that be enough. I'll tell you everything you *ought* to know. But some secrets aren't entirely mine to give. Can you respect that?"

Sulpicia sat up, and as his eyes opened, he met her gaze. "Of course I can," she said, simply. "We've only been together for *months*. That's enough to know how I feel about you—now, today." She half-laughed, a rueful snort through her nose. "To know that it's more than I felt about *Cerinthus*, years ago. But I trusted then, and look where it got me." Her lips quirked. "And that was just one woman's heart, not the secrets of the Julii, or the Empire. You *shouldn't* trust me entirely. Not yet. And I won't ask twice about things you're not ready to tell me."

Alexander gripped her hand tightly. "There are dark places in me," he warned. "I've helped torture men for information. I've killed men for treason. And I *sleep well* at night. The only nightmares I suffer are for . . . far different reasons." *Yes, I see myself dying again, only this time, Caesarion doesn't pull me back, and then I'm trapped in the nothingness for all eternity, just on the verge of oblivion. Or I get to watch everyone I care for, murdered. Eurydice poisoned, Tiberius suffocated, Caesarion drowned, Selene garroted. And I'm powerless to help. Or worse, I'm not me, but Octavian. And I arranged it all.*

Sulpicia kissed his hand. "You do what you need to do. Not just because the family is everything, with all the pride of place and name with which so many people say those words," she added, quoting the ironic lines of her own play, "but because you *love* your family, and Rome. And those are no bad things."

Ianos had spent the last week caring for Jocasta as if she were a babe. He was used to having to pick up Viola and carry her to the lavatory — the public ones, for the rooms in which his two mistresses lived, were up several flights of stairs in their tenement, and Viola couldn't quite manage those easily with her withered legs. There were several lavatories in the lavish Julii villa, but Jocasta had been severely weakened by the poisoning, and hadn't been able to walk at all, the first few days. After that, she'd struggled to her feet, but had needed to be held upright while she took one shaky step after another. "Why is Lord Alexander being so generous?" Jocasta had whispered to Ianos, over and over. "He knows I betrayed him!"

"You didn't betray him, mistress," Ianos told her, carefully. He hated the sound of his own voice, but for her, he'd speak more than a handful of words. "You didn't mean to kill him. He'll explain it all for himself, when he's less busy, and when you're well."

"Oh, but I did betray him," Jocasta said, wretchedly. "I was going to listen to his secrets. He has to know that. He knows he can never trust me — at least for so long as Livia has my sister." She closed her eyes. "I should have told him. I should have told him that Livia had Viola, but Viola seemed so . . . peaceful there . . . ."

"It's being taken care of," Ianos assured her. "You just need to be better, first."

He couldn't tell her that *he* was going to be the one taking care of it. That Lord Alexander had promised him, that if he survived his mission, he'd be manumitted. Given the Julii *name*. As a freedman, he'd always be under the supervision of Lord Alexander. Always look to him for employment. But . . .

eunuch or not, former *puer* or not, he could maybe even take care of Jocasta—if she let him. She had her pride, after all. *Which is all people like us have, some days.*

And then, in the late afternoon, while Jocasta dozed, trying to regain her strength, and Ianos struggled through a scroll written in his native Hellene—his previous master had ensured that he could read and write enough to make decent conversation, on those occasions when the mistress of the house wasn't available, and the master wanted someone to share his couch over dinner—there came a great commotion from outside the door. A female voice, rising sharply as the guards prevented her from advancing.

Ianos went to the door and cracked it open, spotting the lady he'd seen before. Younger than Jocasta by a few years, in spite of her heavily-embroidered *stola* and elaborately-coiffed hair—only this time, tears rolled from her eyes as the guards seized a basket from her hands. "I know what she is!" the young woman wailed, as the guards walked her back from the door—gently, but with authority. "I know she's his mistress! He's supposed to be my *betrothed*, and he brings his mistress here! You tell her—you tell her that I brought those medicines in good faith, to . . . to make her well! And you tell her that her sister's very sick now, too! My step-mother Livia said so!"

Ianos stared out the door, hearing Jocasta stir behind him in the bed. "These high-born have complicated lives," he whispered, looking back at her. "He's betrothed to the daughter of that harpy. Gods have mercy."

Jocasta had managed to sit up on her own, her face white. "My sister's sick? I . . . doubt that. That's a threat." Hands shaking, she tried to get out of the bed on her own, and would have fallen, if Ianos hadn't bolted to her side to catch her. "I have to *go*. I have to go to Livia's villa."

"No, mistress," Ianos whispered, crouching beside her.

"If you do that, you'll *die*. You're the only evidence linking her to an attempt on Lord Alexander's life. Right now, she doesn't *know* if you're alive or dead. Her daughter hasn't seen your face, I think." He smoothed her back. "Lord Alexander has promised that I will go to Lady Livia's house at least once more. If Mistress Viola's able . . . I'll bring her home with me. I promise."

Gradually, she let him put her back to bed. Snug the sheets up to her neck. But her hand crept out from under the coverlet, and clutched his until she finally drifted once more to sleep. And then, Ianos dared to kiss her forehead, lightly. *Perhaps, once I'm free . . . she'll let me marry her. She might not. It was only one night. And she probably only did it because she felt sorry for me. Which is a terrible basis for marriage. I can never give her children. Never give her a* family. *The priests will object, since I'm not much of a man. But I can dream of being something more than a* puer.

Alexander arrived home to a tumult. Octavia was screaming and sobbing at some of the *frumentarii* guards from her room, where they'd *locked her in*, to Alexander's consternation. "What's going on?" Alexander demanded of Spurius, one of the men on duty, frowning.

"The young *domina* tried to get past us again," Spurius said, grimacing. "This time, with a basket of sweet cakes and medicines for the *invalid*. When we wouldn't let her past, and took the basket, she lost her head," he went on, shaking his own. "Started shouting past the door that she *knew* what your guest was. And rambled on about the young woman's sister being in poor health. The slave kept his mistress from the door, so her face still hasn't been seen. Shot in the dark, my lord, is my guess. A damned bad one, since we tested the medicines in the basket on some rats in the barn. No survivors." A snort. "*Medici* usually have a better rate of success that that, especially when they start with entirely healthy patients."

Gods damn it, Alexander thought grimly, spinning and heading for Octavia's chambers. *I have at least a week still before Caesarion receives my letter. I can't change time or speed up the passage of a ship over the sea.*

The scene with Octavia was ugly; he'd expected nothing else after what Spurius had said. She sobbed as she spewed Livia's venom, probably almost word-for-word as the older woman had fed it to her, clearly never having given it a moment of analysis before accepting it as the kind of truth that came from the gods' own lips. "You've systematically humiliated me and everyone I call family for years. Tiberius is my *step-brother*, and you've . . . you've . . . turned him into a woman! For years! With me under the same roof! And now low-class harlots, again in the same villa! I told my step-mother that I want my betrothal broken!" Octavia shouted, her face blotchy with tears of humiliation and rage. "She said Agrippa would take care of it directly. And that she'd find someone who'd treat me with *respect*, like Rullus or Gallus or someone like that!"

Alexander's eyebrows rose. And, calmly, almost without affect, he replied, "I'm glad you've decided that we won't suit, Octavia. I'd come to that conclusion years ago, but felt obliged to follow through on the agreement between Agrippa and my brother. I'll ensure that the servants gather all of your belongings immediately, and escort you to Agrippa's villa forthwith. We of the Julii won't even demand compensation from him for the *magnificent* education you were offered under our roof, largely as it's evident that you never once partook of it."

He saw her mouth drop open in outrage, and he went on, still without raising his voice, "For the record, however? Your step-mother is a wondrous inventor of fiction. Neither Tiberius nor I have ever taken it up the ass." The crudity was deliberate, and enough to make her flinch, though he'd not so much as taken a step further into her room, from where he leaned against the doorframe. "Though I'm sure many have joked about the closeness of our friendship. You see, we're both of the opinion that if you're going to fuck someone that way, it's about power. And since he and I are equals, freeborn men of high birth, it would be utterly impossible for either of us to disrespect each other in that way. Which should be evident to anyone with even *half* a brain." *That part? Complete truth. But now for a few more truths to do the service of lies.* "And for all the common Roman jokes about Hellene love? It's the same for them. They even think that for a man to shove his cock into another man's mouth is to dishonor him, if they're of the same social class." *Truth, that. That's reserved for prostitutes and slaves, male and female alike.*

Octavia wilted. 'Then you're saying you've never — ?"

"I'm prepared to swear on the Styx that I've never turned Tiberius into a *woman*." *No, when we've fucked, we've both been men about it. And it was magnificent. Thank you for asking.* Alexander's lips didn't move, however. His face remained as hard as marble as he added, coldly, "I'm sure that whoever you *do* wind up marrying, Octavia, would greatly appreciate it if you subjected your step-mother's tales to a little more analytical thought in the future. Also, as a side-note, Eurydice long ago told me about your kissing games with the maids. You might consider *that*, in and around your personal indignation with me."

Octavia's face went white. "Those . . . those were just games. Practice for kissing a man — "

"Yes, yes," Alexander told her, impatiently. "Notice that none of us has ever confronted you about it, or shamed you for it? However, if you speak one lie more that previously dripped from your step-mother's lips, about me, Tiberius, or the invalid I've been trying to help, I will ensure that everyone in Rome knows about the kissing games, Octavia. And just how far they've gone. Is that clear?" *Also, best of luck to you with Rullus, who likes it when pretty girls shit on him, or Gallus, who's had an actress for a mistress for twenty years, or anyone else that Livia picks for you. But that will hardly be my concern anymore. And once you're out of this house, I may, locked in my study where no one can see, cavort and caper like a Hellene dancer at the thought of freedom.*

Octavia nodded, her expression dazed, as if suddenly understanding how alone she was. Alexander felt an instant of sympathy for her; she wasn't a bad person. Merely a silly and easily-manipulated one. But his sympathy died the moment he remembered that his agents had fed some of the medicines in the basket to some rats in the barn. And had watched the creatures die, one by one. She didn't know. But her ignorance is a liability. "Get your things together," Alexander told her, more kindly. "I'm sure Livia will embrace you when you return to her villa."

He chafed for the next week, unable to move against Livia just yet. He needed confirmation from two sources before he took action: Caesarion, and Tiberius.

On Martius 1, a letter arrived at the villa in the latter half of the afternoon, bearing Tiberius' seal, to his surprise. *Good, this should be news of his betrothal to my sister,* Alexander thought, never doubting that outcome for a moment.

Thus he read the contents with some consternation.

Alexander —

I'm at the _Leaena_ inn, in Ostia, with a day or two of stopover before I can catch a ship heading for Colonia Narbo Martius, on the shores of Gaul. That should get me heading properly to Britannia, at long last. I know you're busy, so don't take horse and come to meet me. The news I have isn't good.

In short? Your sister decided that M. Antonius Antyllus would suit her better than I would. It's for the best. I couldn't offer her more than an empty villa, anyway. He'll take excellent care of her, and I'm certain that your mother will be far more pleased by this union, than by any other.

There was an attack on your sister and brother during the investiture ceremony, undertaken by a priest you might recall. Antyllus and I kept the creature set against your siblings occupied, until the Emperor was able to recover and finish it off. I later had the honor of killing the priest in question myself, with the aid of several other _equites_ from the Sixteenth.

But enough about that. I'm sure you'll get full details from P. Julius Caesarion in his next letter, though last I heard, he was riding south to Thebes to deal with a revolt there. Your brother rarely sits still for long.

Best wishes to you and yours, and may the gods keep you in their hands.

Your friend,

T. Claudius Nero

Postscript: Please do not let any rumors about Egypt get around. I particularly do not wish for the proposed cognomen of "Agricola" to be promulgated publically. The men of the Sixteenth can go hang on that count.

Alexander read the letter, and then immediately called for his horse, knowing that the two and a half hour ride would put him in Ostia, at the door of the *Leaena*, by no later than eight, if he skipped dinner now. And with no one else in the villa to discommode besides the servants, that was an easy decision to make. He couldn't leave a message for Sulpicia at *Merges*, but that was fine; many evenings, their schedules simply didn't coordinate, and that helped keep people from seeing patterns in their visits to the *taverna*.

As he rode, however, he turned the terse, short words of Tiberius' letter around in his mind. The tone had been extremely formal throughout; the only moment of humanity had been the acerbic postscript. Alexander cursed his sister Selene repeatedly and viciously under his breath. *We did everything but stop the course of the moon in the sky to please her, and she decided to vacillate the other direction. After explicitly telling Tiberius that she was in love with him. Gods. The news I have for him is bad enough. I don't need him in a foul mood before asking him what I need to ask him, and yet I have no choice. I can't do what needs to be done behind his back. If hears about it after the fact, he'll spend his whole life trying to find out who did it, and I won't do that dance. Not with him.* A flicker of bleak humor crossed his mind, then. *I'd hoped that when I put the question to him, he'd see it as the best thing for his relationship with his soon-to-be-wife: a life together, without his mother involved in it.*

Just past eight postmeridian, Alexander finally reached the correct inn in Ostia. Tossed the reins and a small coin at one of the loafing servants at the front, and strode in, covered in road dirt. Smelled lamb stew and the sweat of the dozens of men already occupying trestle tables, and called the *taverna's* owner over, asking for Tiberius by name. A quick flash of the Julii signet on his finger got him a startled look and an admission that the man of the Claudii was indeed in a private room upstairs. And off Alexander went, tapping on the correct door.

"I said I didn't want to be bothered," Tiberius' curt voice came from behind the door.

"It's me, Ti. Open up."

After a pause, the door opened, and Alexander met Tiberius' gray stare, noting that his friend had acquired a tan over the course of two sea voyages in the past six weeks. A faint scent of wine on his breath, but not too much; he wasn't drowning his sorrows. "And I told *you* to stay in Rome," Tiberius said quietly. "You're rotten at taking suggestions, you know that?" He stepped out of the way, letting Alexander in.

"After receiving a letter like that? I'd have been on my horse even if I *didn't* need to talk to you about something too urgent and too dangerous to put in a note," Alexander said, stepping through.

Tiberius closed the door behind them, and Alexander put an arm around his shoulders, gently. "I'm sorry. My sister is a complete idiot. I hope for her sake that Antyllus is the only man of the Antonius name who's capable of being faithful—"

"Antony seems singularly faithful to your mother," Tiberius replied, his voice empty and very precise. Like a judge offering a verdict. "The indiscretions with that actress were when his first faithless wife was in the picture. And I can't blame him for anything he did when married to Octavia.

Your sister will be happy with Antyllus, I have no doubt." He pulled away from Alexander's arm, gesturing to one of the two seats in the room, the single chair beside the bed. "Pour you some wine?"

Alexander took the offered chair. Tiberius sometimes said more with gestures than with words, and this was one of those times. "I'll take the wine, but only after I'm done apologizing," he said, simply. "It was my damned fool idea that you marry her. None of the rest would have happened, if I hadn't been greedy. Wanting to keep you in my life as a brother, when I should have known that your friendship, once given, is eternal." *And yet, here I am, about to ask you something else that will jeopardize that friendship.* He swallowed.

"I wanted to punch you about two weeks ago," Tiberius admitted, taking a seat on the bed and looking at the nearby window, its shutters drawn against Ostia's sea breezes. "Then I realized that it's no one's fault. Things happen as the gods will it."

No. It's not the gods' fault. It's my sister's, for being a flighty child. *But if you're choosing to be magnanimous, I can't say more.* Alexander nodded. "We're all right?"

"We're fine."

"And *you're* fine?" Alexander pressed, gently. *The emptiness in his eyes — it's like the self-loathing fits. But . . . different. This isn't the black pit of despair, which I've seen even in the eyes of people like Ianos. This is just . . . nothingness.*

"As I am likely to be." Tiberius poured fresh wine and watered it. "I only have the one cup. We'll have to share it."

"We've done *that* many times."

A silent nod as Tiberius handed the cup to him. And then his friend began to describe the demon attack at the Temple of Isis, and Alexander nearly choked. Followed by the fight against the mage-priests, which had claimed so many lives. "In the end, as I was trying to crawl under three feet of sand, the *weight* of it pressing down, no air left . . . I prayed to Pluto and Proserpina. I offered my life, so that we could destroy these enemies. I don't know why they didn't *take* it," Tiberius said, frowning over the cup as Alexander passed it back. "Perhaps I didn't use the correct prayer. I know that when you offer *devotio*, you're supposed to invoke Quirinus and Jove, too — "

Alexander lunged forward, putting his hand on Tiberius' shoulder, his heart having gone cold inside of him. "Don't! For the gods' sakes, *don't* invoke them now — "

A faint, wintery smile as Tiberius looked at him. "I think the gods know what's their due, old friend. Sooner or later, they'll collect it. When they're ready."

"And maybe you just found the strength to stand up on your own, in a moment of desperation and courage," Alexander shot back angrily. "Perhaps the gods had nothing to do with it at all." And he leaned in, kissing his friend. Hard. Trying to remind him of life, damn it.

Tiberius responded, but slowly. Wrapped one arm around his neck, and finally pulled his lips away, but didn't retreat further. "And what's new with you? Did you finally seek out your poetess?"

Alexander sighed. Put his head on Tiberius' shoulder. "I did."

"Did you find a way to fuck her mind after all?" A hopeful sign; there was a slightly humorous lilt to the question.

"*Gods*, yes," Alexander returned fervently. "I ask her to recite poetry in bed, and when she starts forgetting words, I know I've found the correct path to that beautiful mind of hers."

"You sound smitten." Tiberius kissed his cheek. "It's a

pleasure to hear."

"I am," Alexander admitted. "She's writing a play for me. And I'm going to marry her. Someday." He turned his head to look at Tiberius. "I have to admit, she's the one thing I don't *want* to share with you. I thought about it at first—incessantly. And then I realized that I didn't want to take the chance that she might like it better with you." A flicker of a smile for the insecurity of that admission.

A snort from Tiberius. "Does this mean we're growing up?"

"No. It means I *know* you're the better swordsman. In every way. And I can't take that chance with her." Rueful humor.

Tiberius' lips actually quirked up for that. "You give me too much credit, and yourself not enough." He raised his eyebrows. "So, if you marry her, won't that make for a crowded bedchamber? What with Octavia in there, too?"

Alexander sighed. Pulled back. "That's not going to be an issue," he told Tiberius tiredly. "Octavia ended the betrothal a week ago. On the grounds that your mother had told her that I'd fucked your ass smooth for four years."

Tiberius' head snapped up, a look of rage and offended pride crossing his face. *That's the most human he's looked since I sat down*, Alexander thought, concern vying with the *need* to make Tiberius understand everything. To agree with what needed to be done. "What did you just say?" Tiberius demanded furiously.

"As I live and breathe, your mother told Octavia that I'd made a woman of you. I'd already asked Caesarion if I could be *shed* of this betrothal, so it was a damned relief for me—"

"Why?" Tiberius snapped, lurching to his feet. "Why would my mother dishonor me so? Why would she put those words in the mouth of a chatterbox like Octavia, to be spread all over Rome—"

"I took care of *that*. She says one word, and she'll be known for the *Sapphic* dalliances she's been having with some of our maids. It'll put a stain on her virtue that no amount of coin in her dowry will ever remove." Alexander regarded Tiberius, his throat tight. *And now, we come to the point that might break our friendship in half.* "Ti. Your mother didn't just tell a bunch of half-truths and distortions to Octavia." All the words now in whispers so soft that he almost had to strain to hear himself. "She got ahold of Jocasta's sister. Took her in, made her comfortable, indebted Jocasta in so doing, and then made her listen for information, too. I didn't know about it. And Jocasta surely didn't know what was in the bottle of oil your mother gave her, with explicit directions to pour half of it over my back and rub it in the next time I visited—"

Tiberius' eyes locked on Alexander, and the other man finished now, quietly. Simply, "Wolfsbane. Aconite. Jocasta nearly died—my agents got us both to Ianthe in time. I'm sure that the only reason I survived was the amulet of Sekhmet. I had no idea it would handle poison. Though it started burning with cold at dawn that morning—"

"The thirteenth?" Tiberius said, hoarsely.

"Yes, why?" Alexander asked, frowning.

"I was bitten by the cobra at dawn that day. Couldn't understand why the amulet woke me up near midnight, with it burning cold against my skin." Tiberius took a seat again, one hand over his face as he fought through the emotional responses. Finally, he looked up. "The amulets are linked, then. We'll always know when one of us is in mortal danger, I expect."

"You'll see more of that than I will. Britannia won't exactly be a wedding feast." Alexander said nothing more.

Tiberius worked through things in his own time. At his own pace. Pushing *never* helped.

And Tiberius worked through it. Step by step. "My mother targeted you, through Jocasta. Nearly murdered both of you. She went after you, because . . . you're of the Julii. Because she's ambitious. . . on my behalf, or Drusus'. Because you're in her way." And then, very softly, so that even another person standing in the same room wouldn't have heard it, "And because I love you."

Alexander nodded. Tiberius closed his eyes. "Do you want me to kill her?" he whispered, his voice empty. "She's dishonored me, in word and in deed. I should do it—"

"No! No, Ti, I would never ask you to commit *matricide*." Alexander caught his friend's hand in his.

"Who better than a dead man, to bring another to dissolution?" That wasn't quite a joke.

"Even if Pluto has a marker for your soul—the same as he has for every man born!—that doesn't mean you don't get to live in the meantime," Alexander retorted hotly. "No. It won't be by your hand, Ti. I have it arranged. I just . . . needed you to know."

"Knowledge, in this case, is a heavy burden," Tiberius muttered, his voice taut. "Knowing that my mother is a would-be-murderess. Knowing that she *has* to have tried this sort of thing before, to be so good at it. Knowing that my best friend—my *lo*—"

"Shh," Alexander said, putting his other hand over Tiberius' mouth. "Don't say it."

"Knowing that you're going to have to kill her," Tiberius finished, quietly. "Can we ever look at each other the same way again?"

Alexander's throat hurt. "I had to tell you. Otherwise, you'd have gone digging afterwards. And there was the potential that you'd feel betrayed when you found out."

Tiberius exhaled. Lay back on the bed with a forearm over his eyes. "The only person who's betrayed me," he said quietly, "is Livia Drusilla. She's a murderess. She'll try again and again, if you let her." He uncovered his eyes, regarding Alexander steadily. "Do what you need to do. And don't feel badly about it. She hasn't been my mother in years. You will *always* be my brother. And my friend."

Alexander let out the breath he didn't realize he'd been holding. Slid into the bed beside Tiberius, and just lay there. Not moving. Not touching. Not talking, at least not for a long while. Tiberius finally took his hand, and told him, gently, "You need to sleep, if you're going to ride back to Rome in the morning. Please tell Sulpicia that I very much would like to meet the woman who captured my brother's heart. And that if her play is ever performed in public while I am in Rome, I expect good seats for Drusus and myself."

"You're a good man, Tiberius," Alexander told his friend, with deep conviction. *Better than I am.*

"No. I'm not. But I can pretend, now and again, can't I?"

Aprilis 1, 20 AC

While on one side of the Mediterranean, Caesarion Aquilus took ship for Rome, in Rome itself, Alexander Cerastes took pains to earn his name once more.

"It's time to earn your freedom," Alexander told Ianos quietly. "Victory or death. The same rules as the arena. Except, if you succeed, you'll never hear the roar of the crowd. And if you lose, you'll probably be tortured to death, and I'll disavow all knowledge of your actions."

Ianos nodded. Jocasta was well again—at least as well as could be expected, for someone who'd been so near to death a six weeks or so ago. And to his shy, stunned delight, she'd begun to insist on sharing the big, warm bed in the room she'd been given by Lord Alexander. *You're up all night taking care of me. You need to sleep,* had been the excuse at first. Followed, slowly, as she began to feel better, by little kisses, butterfly light. Stroking. Touching. And, gloriously, sex, too. He was sure he couldn't be particularly good at it. But she made such pretty sounds, that even if she was pretending enjoyment out of habit, he forgave her, because with her, he came as close to feeling like a man as he'd ever been permitted.

Lord Alexander had sworn that no matter what happened, Jocasta would be safe. Whisked away to Capri, perhaps, or Sicily. But *safe.* "I know what to do," Ianos murmured. "I won't let anyone down."

And then he left, a small, wax-sealed box filled with innocuous white powder in a pouch dangling from his belt. He knew better than to open that box for any reason other than seeing Livia Drusilla's face in front of him. In the box was a death so terrible, he wondered why the gods would permit such things to grow in the bark and seeds of such common, inocuous plants with their pretty white flowers.

He went around to the servant's entrance of Lord Agrippa's villa. Was greeted by the staff there with a mix of derision and interest. "You haven't been around in a while, *puer,*" the housekeeper said, her lip curling with scorn. "Forgot all about your poor crippled mistress?"

"Oh no! Not at all! Mistress Jocasta was dreadfully sick these past six weeks. Took every last *denarii* she had for the *medici* to save her life." Meek, sober words, his eyes firmly on the floor. "Even now, they're not sure she'll make it."

"Oh really? What sort of horrible pustules did she have up her cunny, then, anyway?" one of the stable-boys asked, laughing. "Did they explode?"

Ianos kept his eyes on the ground. The master had taught him that early. If he looked up, if he cried out, if he protested—no matter *what* was being done to him—he'd be punished. And the punishment was often even worse than what was being done to him to start with. *When the master sent men to hold me down, and a <u>medicus</u> to cut out my balls, I cried then. I protested. I begged them not to do this to me, after so many other things had been done. And then the men hit me so hard I lost consciousness. And when I woke up, I knew I'd never be a man. I wasn't a woman, either. Just something in between. Forever.*

A little thing like words—even horrible words about Jocasta—couldn't make him react now, beyond the meek-sounding reply of, "Oh, it wasn't that. She ate something with mushrooms in it. The cook must have bought a bad batch at the market. She's lucky to be alive, she is."

"So, what are you here for, then, *puer?*" The housekeeper again, grabbing him by the ear. She had to reach up to do it. Even hunched over as he usually walked, his head down, he was taller than the tiny, wizened old woman with her talon-sharp nails.

"She sent me to ask her sister to come to her. I'll carry Mistress Viola to her. It won't cost anyone a thing." Ianos held his breath, but the servants and slaves all seemed to believe him. And, as expected, they put him in a side room, and called for Lady Livia. *Who of course needs to know where Jocasta is,* he thought, the words burning coldly in his mind. *So that she can finish things off, if there's a need. And who certainly won't let Mistress Viola go. Not while Jocasta still draws breath. And she'll come with two or three men. To put the fear of torture in me. Or to rape me, so that I'll <u>beg</u> to be allowed to tell the truth.*

He pulled the little box from the bag at his waist when he heard steps in the hallway. More than one set of feet, as he'd known there would be. And then Lady Livia entered with two of the other slaves of the house, both male. He could see her smiling out of the corner of his eyes. "Well, now, look who's returned!" Honeyed tones disguising venom. "I'm told your young mistress was very ill?"

"Yes, my lady."

"Something she ate?"

"Yes, my lady." Not a word offered more than was asked.

"And where has she been recovering? I sent men to her home to check on her, when neither you nor she had appeared in some time." A little titter of laughter. "Why, there were those who'd thought you'd had a quarrel, and that you'd dropped her in the Tiber!"

Slow burn of rage inside of him; he tucked it where he always put his anger—deep down in his bowels. Where no one could see it. *No one said that. She's saying it now to test me.* "She told me to take her to Tiber Island, my lady," he said quietly. "To the temple of Asclepius there."

"Those quacks are never cheap." Scornful tone. "How did she pay them?"

"It took all her savings, *domina*. But they gave her a blessing for her sister before she left." That, the only unasked-for piece of information so far. Ianos kept his eyes on the ground, but watched everything out of the periphery of his vision. This, too, was a skill he'd perfected in the master's house. He'd learned that if he could keep enough people around him, it was less likely that the master would start caressing him. Or take him off to the room where pain lived. The result was that Ianos always knew *exactly* where people were around him. How close. How many. He knew that at the moment, there was a group of serving women in the hall outside, carrying loads of laundry downstairs. He could hear them chattering and laughing. *Not yet. Soon. They'll be passing the door any moment now. Has to be when they're past, or the powder could catch them, too.*

"Hah. A blessing. That costs them as much to speak the words as the blessing itself is worth." Livia studied him. He could feel her eyes boring into his skull. "You haven't spent the past weeks with Lord Alexander?"

"My lady?" Carefully blank tone, and he flinched a little as her fingers caught his face. He couldn't help it; he flinched when *anyone* touched him. He'd even flinched at Jocasta's touch once or twice, when she caught him unawares.

"Lord Alexander," Livia repeated, impatiently. "You stayed with him, didn't you, and not at the Temple of Asclepius."

Now came the *real* test. Ianos looked into her eyes. And, as he'd been so carefully trained for years, filled himself with all the things that the master had always wanted to see in him. Weakness. Fragility. Beauty. Innocence. And a broken spirit. Even *thinking* of the master made bile rise up in his throat. Made his hands shake, but that only added to the believability of his illusion. "*Domina*, I don't know a Lord Alexander," Ianos lied, with perfect sincerity in his voice. "I don't know any lords and ladies anymore, excepting yourself."

And as he'd hoped, she was distracted. "And once you did?"

He dropped his eyes. "Yes, my lady."

"I'd be most interested to know which lord kept you, *puer.*"

I bet that you would. He choked the thought down. Put it with the rage and the nausea. Flicked a glance at the two slaves, and listened as the servants passed outside.

Taking the hint, Livia waved her two slaves away. "Go on with you," she told them indifferently. "This one's so well-trained that I'm sure he'll do everything necessary to ensure that our young Jocasta comes home safely to her sister."

The two slaves left, looking dubious. Ianos allowed himself one exhalation of relief. He wouldn't be responsible for more than one death, hopefully. "So," Livia murmured, her smile predatory as they left, closing the door behind them, "what *was* the name of your former master?"

Ianos glanced up timidly. "My lady, I was told never to tell anyone. And I should be bringing Mistress Viola to her sister—"

"You *dare* to presume?" Livia's face contorted for a moment with rage, and she struck him, hard, across the face. "You *dare* to put the requirements of your little harlot before my request for information?"

She was close enough now. The door was closed. Ianos, his face still stinging, flipped open the box in his hand and ducked away, as if to protect himself from more blows . . . and threw the entire contents of the box in Livia's face.

White powder bloomed out, looking nothing so much like talc dust. Ianos leaped back, immediately, getting away from the cloud, trying not to breathe. "Oh, no!" he wailed loudly. "The blessing! The priests gave this blessing for Mistress Viola!"

Coughing and choking on the powder, some of which had gotten into her mouth and nose, Livia furiously beat at the powder that now covered her face, hair, and *stola*. "Imbecile!" she shouted, and the door opened behind her, revealing those same two slaves, looking angry. Ianos backed up another step, truly apprehensive, and found his back against a window that opened into the *peristylium*. And he was on the ground floor, gods be thanked. "I'm so sorry," Ianos cried out, and leaped through the shutters of the window. It didn't matter if they caught him and beat him till his ribs broke. He needed to get away from that cloud of dust.

The slaves *did* catch him. They kicked him and punched him, and Ianos curled into a ball, protecting his head and stomach, grateful for once in his life that when they kicked him in the groin, it was uncomfortable, but not debilitating. Aware that all the servants had turned out to watch, over the rails of balconies. Most of them cheering the two brutes on. *Kill him!* they screamed. *Kill that uppity little* <u>puer</u>*. So pretty, you'd think he was a girl. Thinks he's so much better than us, never had to work a day in his life? Mess his shit up but good!*

He was aware, too, that Viola was one of the people looking down into the garden. Alone, on her crutches. Unable to stop what was happening.

Livia had no further use for him at that point. She had him thrown out of the house, once the slaves had had their fun. Ianos was simply grateful that they'd stopped with a beating, and *hadn't* decided to rape him, or shove a stick up his ass.

Bleeding from the eyes, nose, and mouth, and hunched in on himself like an old, old man, he staggered through the streets of the Palatine, among all the houses of the rich. Until a hand came out from behind a tree and pulled him into cover. He flinched, but he couldn't do anything to prevent the contact. "Dis' teeth and toenails," Spurius muttered, wetting a cloth with water from a flask, and mopping with surprising gentleness at Ianos' face. "You look like someone who got the wrong end of his *contubernium's* fists when the centurion said 'you know, I don't care which of you idiots was responsible, so I'm going to pick one man and the rest of you get to beat him to set an example.'"

"Feels like it, too," Ianos mumbled through his swelling lips.

"Did they get you anyplace important? Besides the pretty face?"

"Couple good kicks in the groin." Ianos shrugged. "I'll survive that."

"You've definitely had worse in that region." Dry humor, but not hurtful.

"It's the fact that I can still . . . feel their feet . . . under my ribs in my back. . . ."

"Fuck. Sounds like kidneys. You'll probably piss blood for a couple of days. Depends on how thorough they were." Spurius gave him another wipe with the cloth. "Let's get you to a *medicus*. Set most of these with stitches, and won't be able to tell you were cut up in a month or so."

"Scars . . . would only . . . improve things for me." Ianos coughed, felt a rib scream to life as he did so, and tried to breathe shallowly. "Wouldn't be . . . so fucking pretty . . . anymore."

"*Dominus* says you stay as pretty as the job lets you. It's all right. Most of us wear our scars on the inside, anyway. Makes it harder for people to identify us." Spurius smirked. "I'm the exception, of course. Did you get the powder in her face?"

"On her. On half of the room. I'm hoping . . . that the fuckers who did this. . . got a couple of good lungfuls." Gone were his earlier compunctions about the collateral damage to the two slaves. Now, Ianos hoped they died just as painfully as their mistress would.

An hour later, Livia sat in her room. She'd called Viola to her, and ordered the girl to brush out her hair, to ensure that all the flour, or whatever it was, was *gone. The last thing I need is anything to make it whiter than it already is,* she thought grimly, watching the young woman, leaning on one crutch, comb out her tangled tresses. The bronze mirror in front of her gave everything a somewhat jaundiced color, but she *knew* that white was creeping into her blond hair.

The little Hellene slave who usually took care of Livia's needs was, unfortunately, unavailable. Agrippa had taken her off with him into his rooms early this morning, and whatever they'd been doing, they hadn't so much as poked a nose out of his chambers during all the contretemps earlier. So Livia made do. She had Viola help her remove her flour-covered *stola*, and had the girl toss it on the bed, for the moment. "Impudent wretch," Livia muttered under her breath. And Viola, not daring to reply, said nothing at all. Just combed the white powder out of Livia's hair, sweeping it off her shoulders with a horsehair brush. Stirring up fresh clouds of the finely-milled stuff.

"It looks a little like face-powder, my lady," Viola ventured. "I wonder why he'd have been carrying that."

"He said it was a blessing from the priests of Asclepius. For you. After your sister spent all her savings, trying to cure herself of food poisoning." Livia snorted. "Fat chance they'd just *give* that away. I'd be willing to bet that it *was* just face-powder. Something to try to buy back your good-will, my dear."

"Yes, *domina.*"

She grimaced as Viola's hands hit a tangle. *Alive she has to stay, until I know for sure where Jocasta is, and have taken care of the problem. I'm quite sure young Ianos will lead me back to her. The men I set to following him, however, lost him somewhere in the Palatine. No matter. He stands out. More, now that he's been beaten. We'll find him again. And with him, her.*

Livia found that she simply couldn't sit *still*. She wanted to be up and moving around, but forced herself to calmness, though her knee bounced up and down—a clear violation of the self-control on which she prided herself. Her neck hurt, too—a pervasive soreness that she simply couldn't get away from. "Be a dear and rub my neck, girl. That's it— not too hard now."

A muscle fluttered by her eyelid, and Livia raised her fingers to press against the tic for a moment. *I've been overdoing it,* she decided. *My body's telling me that I've spent too many late nights trying to hold together this far-flung faction of Octavian's former officers, friends, and social conservatives like the distant relations of Cato the Younger.* "I think I might like to lie down for a bit. Clear my clothing away, girl! Doesn't do to be a slattern, with everything lying around, out of place."

When the first spasm hit, Livia felt her legs and spine contort, as if she were trying to give birth to something that wasn't even *there*. She moaned with the pain of it, and sat up, panting and sweating, as soon as it passed. And with a shock of horror, she recognized all the symptoms. *Strychnine. Oh, dear gods, how did they get it to me? I haven't had anything to eat or drink that I haven't had tasted by three different slaves. How did they—could it have been the powder? Oh, gods.* "Girl!" Livia called imperatively. "Viola! On the shelf here—the ivory and gold casket."

But Viola, shuffling in from another room, had a tic under her eye, and, balancing on only one crutch, couldn't quite reach the costly container. Livia managed to raise herself upright, and then another spasm hit, making her feel as if her jaw were about to rip itself off of her face. "Oh, gods," she whispered as it passed, and heaved herself up. Managed to reach the casket down herself, and, opening it, found the rich, spicy smell of *mithridate* inside—the universal cure, the recipe seized from the defeated Parthian king Mithridates, and carried to Rome by the hand of Pompey the Great himself.

Livia broke off a piece of the crystallized cure. Dropped it in a cup, poured wine over it, her hands shaking so much that she slopped it everywhere. Brought the mixture to her lips. Another spasm hit, even as the precious elixir coursed over her tongue. Found the back of her throat.

But she couldn't *swallow*. Her limbs seized. Her back arched like that of an acrobat, and searing pain flooded through her. "This . . . is . . . his . . . fault," Livia panted. "The snake . . . the snake murdered me. . . ."

With the last glimmers of her consciousness, Livia saw Viola pop a fragment of the universal curative in her own mouth. And took the pitcher of wine, and drank from it directly. Trying to preserve her own life. *It won't work*, Livia thought, the thought dissipating. *It's as much a crock as everything else . . . .*

"Is it done?" Alexander asked Spurius tightly. Jocasta had held Ianos' hand the entire time that Ianthe, the priestess of Hecate, had gone about the business of swabbing the cuts and stitching them up.

"Agrippa's villa looks like a kicked anthill," Spurius returned, glancing through several slips of parchment.

"Anyone shouting *poison* yet?"

Spurius shook his head, his eyes narrow. "No. Too many people in the villa have come down sick, it seems. The girl who helped Livia change and brush her hair is ill, or so our man on the inside says." He frowned over something, then handed Alexander the parchment, going on calmly, "The two slaves who beat our lad here are convulsing. Several others who *weren't* in the room are coming down ill, as well—

not typical for poison, as they're all likely to know. They're closing down the house, saying it could be some sort of disease."

"So less evidence to come back to us," Alexander noted. It had been the most compelling reason to use strychnine in powdered form, in spite of the terrible burden that potential collateral damage put on his conscience. That, and trying to get it into Livia's food or drink would have been next to impossible. Which left somehow getting it into her blood—difficult, without jabbing her with an arrow—or getting her to inhale a substantial amount of the toxin. *Unfortunately, that also means that there will be collateral damage. Ianos was willing to take the risk of becoming a casualty, himself. Brave man. Though he'd quickly tell me he's neither of those things.*

He sat on a bench in the atrium as Ianthe continued to clean Ianos' wounds, and read the scroll that Spurius had handed him. One sentence beat at him. *Viola was the girl pushed into service, helping Livia brush her hair. No one could have known it would happen. It certainly wasn't in the plan. She was weak before this; even a trace of the poison will likely kill her. Jocasta will never forgive me if her sister dies. And I've promised Ianos that she will be taken care of in return for his on-going service. Gods, I don't ask for much, or very often. But if you could arrange to spare this poor girl's life? I'd be grateful.*

"I couldn't get her out, *domina*," Ianos mumbled now thickly, drawing Alexander's attention once more. "Lady Livia wasn't going to let me get near Viola, Jocasta. I'm so sorry."

"You can stop calling me *my lady*," she muttered, looking embarrassed. "You're about to be a freedman."

Ianos nodded, looking pained as he did so. "Yes, my. . . I mean, yes." He paused. "Hopefully, once this all passes, we can get in there, and bring her out."

"Not you, lad," Spurius told him firmly. "You need to disappear from sight for a while. Resurface later with a different name, even if Lord Alexander has your proper one inscribed as a freedman on the rolls of his family. I'll go over myself . . . once the anthill quits boiling." His face and voice revealed nothing.

Alexander stared at the scroll, feeling ill. He'd taken no joy in the planning or the execution. It was murder, but he preferred to think of it as. . . extra-judiciary punishment. Livia had attempted his murder, and Jocasta's. Bringing her to trial wasn't an option. It would expend enormous amounts of political capital, and she would turn the trial into a circus in which she could expound upon her opinions of the Julii for weeks or months at a time. And in the end, they might not get a conviction, since everything hinged on the word of a young foreign whore. No, it had needed to be taken care of. Quickly. Quietly. Decisively. And Caesarion had told him to exercise his best judgment. Which was tacit agreement. Tiberius had given his acquiescence—which made him something of a co-conspirator, from one point of view. Or a fellow judge and juror, from another perspective.

But he'd never intended so *many* other lives to be affected. So he sat, staring at the scroll in his hand. Feeling the warmth of the sun beating down on him. And prayed as he'd rarely done since his own death.

Several days later, they knew more. Something in the order of half of the servants in Agrippa's villa came down with similar, though lesser variants of the same symptoms that had carried off Livia and her two male slaves. Agrippa and Octavia never contracted the 'disease,' and Alexander carefully encouraged gossip from the surviving servants, who'd heard Ianos' wail that she'd broken the blessing of the priests of Asclepius. The superstitious Roman soul caught ahold of this interesting tidbit, and soon, all of Rome was convinced that this was nothing more than divine retribution. A man had brought the blessing of the god of health, and when it had been scorned, disease struck the house.

Alexander cultivated those rumors carefully. Pruned them. Shaped them. Smiled to himself when people began to spread new permutations—that it had been a *god-born* of Asclepius who'd gone to Livia's villa, to heal a crippled girl there. Tall, he'd been, and more beautiful than any mortal. And she'd had him beaten and thrown from the villa. "How does it feel to be a god-born?" Alexander asked Ianos, whose cuts were healing—and who was undergoing knife training from Spurius in the *peristylium* of the Julii villa.

"I'd feel much better if we knew what happened to Viola, *dominus*," Ianos replied, ducking a knife-jab from Spurius.

So would I, Alexander thought.

In the end, Jocasta was called to the villa for the sad duty of tending to her sister. Viola had held on, somehow, through the worst of the symptoms. And when Jocasta returned, white-faced, with red-rimmed eyes, she brought with her a treasure, hidden in a fold of her *stola*.

"*Mithridate*," Jocasta told them, putting the gold and ivory cask on the table in front of Alexander and his various agents. "She told me . . . before she passed . . . that Livia tried to take this before she died, but she couldn't swallow it. And thank the gods for it, because Viola said that the medicine *worked* on her." She stared around them, and then covered her mouth as she laughed a little, half-bitterly, half in wonder. "The poison didn't take her," she told them all, giving Alexander and Ianos each a firm look. "The cure *worked*. It was just. . ." Jocasta sighed. "It was just time. I spent so many years trying to keep her alive. . . ."

Alexander murmured what he hoped were comforting words. Let Ianos take Jocasta off to weep in private. Made arrangements for a better funeral than the pauper's grave Viola might otherwise have had. And, just as quietly, arranged for a nice little house outside of Rome for Ianos and Jocasta. He had *work* for his new agent. And Ianos couldn't work, if he was constantly worried about Jocasta. So, a little house. Some land. Chickens in the dooryard, and a garden he frankly suspected that Jocasta wouldn't know what to do with at first.

And then he quietly and fervently thanked the *gods* that Viola had survived, because he didn't for an instant think that a lump of honey, boiled with sixty or so conflicting and contradictory herbs, some of which were poisons in themselves, had had a damned thing to do with Viola's survival. *A perfectly white bull and a lamb,* he promised Pluto and Proserpina. *Thank you for not offering your hospitality too quickly.*

Chapter XII: The Wider World

Februarius 22-Martius 27, 20 AC

The jolting gait of the donkey on which she perched rattled Selene's teeth with every step the animal took. It was a short-legged creature—so much so, that when she'd balked at learning to ride the little gray thing, Antyllus had laughed, picked her up, settled her on its back, and told her, "Put your feet on the ground."

Selene had done so, sheepishly realizing how much smaller the creature was than even Roman horses. And Roman horses were short, compared to the great beasts that came from Hispania and Scythia—only about twelve hands high, in all. Still, she'd never ridden before, and the donkey had looked like an enormous, self-willed machine of destruction.

It wasn't. After their first short break, after three hours of riding, her donkey led by its reins, attached to Antyllus' saddle, she gave in and named the little creature *Flora*. Not for the female donkey's sweet smell—donkeys didn't smell particularly good, Selene had noticed—but for the beast's persistent habit of eating any flowers it found along the side of the road.

She'd been married just over a week now, and still couldn't quite wrap her head around the concept. They'd landed in Syria after seven days aboard ship, and from there, Antyllus had piled her on Flora's back for the ride east to Antioch. She'd asked about taking a *carruca*, and Antyllus had given her a patient look, and asked her, "Do you suppose they send many of those up into the mountains, my lark? Do you think we can skirt Parthian territory dragging one of those, and get into Sarmatian and Scythian territory quickly? We'll bring pack horses and wagons, since we'll need goods to trade with the nomads, in case they don't want coin. We'll need guards as well, to make sure none of the trade goods get stolen. But while I realize that enclosed carriages are usually considered fitting for a patrician woman's dignity and comfort . . ." his smile turned lopsided, "Eurydice rides a horse. I think you can manage a donkey."

There were, however, *reasons* for the tradition of riding in *carrucae*, Selene learned rapidly. Travel dust and mud splatter from the hooves of the animals caked her *stola* and her sandals. The sun, not precisely hot, for this was still Februarius, still burned her face until she gave up and pulled her *palla* up over her face and shoulders, trying to ward off the rays.

By night, her entire body *ached* from exhaustion, and being as stiff and tired as she was, she found it stupefying that Antyllus had only requested one bedchamber for them at the inns. "Ah . . . isn't something missing?" she asked tactfully, still in her travel-stained clothing. One room for him, one room for their guards. . . .

"No, I think the servants brought up all our belongings," Antyllus replied, already pulling his tunic over his head, the new-healed scar over his chest red and angry in the lamplight. "I told the innkeeper to send up a cask of warm water. That'll take off most of the dirt, and I'll give you a good rub with oil and a scrape with a strigil in a bit. And then you can return the favor before we go to bed. What do you say?" They were traveling light, for the sake of speed; still only two guards, who doubled as servants.

She blinked, looking around in consternation. It had been one thing aboard the ship; cabin space was at a premium, even for wealthy nobles. But now, in a relatively clean,

Hellene-style inn? "I meant, where's *my* room?" Selene finally asked, as a tap at the door announced the arrival of the tub and buckets of warm water from downstairs.

Antyllus didn't answer till the tub had been set up, and the servants had been sent away again. In fact, he didn't answer until he'd helped her take off her clothes, and had gotten her into the tub, where the warm water started doing some good for her aching muscles. "Selene," he finally said, as he rubbed her shoulders gently under the water, his tone a little taken aback, "I'm somewhat under the impression that, ah, your brother and sister share a bedchamber. Don't they?"

"Well, Eurydice does have Mother's old bedchamber, next to Caesarion's, which used to belong to Father," Selene replied sleepily. "I think she mostly uses it as an office."

His fingers tightened on her shoulders. "Then why on earth would you think I'd be any more inclined to antique patrician notions like separate bedchambers than they are?" His tone remained a little odd. "My family's plebeian, love. Through and through. Octavia brought her chilly notions with her, but before she came along, the only time the room beside my father's saw use when my mother was sick, or was nursing Jullus. Not that we spent much time at the villa, back then. It was mostly this *castra* or that. Always in a tent or a command building. Where they stayed together."

She shrank a little in on herself, feeling foolish. "Oh." Selene swallowed. "Then . . . how will I . . . practice music without bothering you?" *Or sew. Or anything, really, that you won't want to be around for?*

"Whenever we get back to Rome, we can worry about it then. But I'd imagine that you could use that room beside mine, the way you say Eurydice uses her room as an office." A shrug in his voice. "Just don't get the idea that you'll be sleeping in there often," he added, his voice droll. "I'm *entirely* too fond of the notion of waking up and finding a wife beside me to give that up easily." He helped her out of the tub at that point, adding, lightly, "You know, sooner or later, I'm going to enjoy hearing you say my name."

"Marcus," she said immediately and politely, wrapping a length of towel around herself to try to catch all the drips.

He made a face. "No. That's my father. Actually, *Antony* is my father, too. Anyone says either name, and I turn around to see where he's standing." He paused, raising his eyebrows, clearly hoping for a laugh from her. "I actually *prefer* my cognomen, strange as it might sound."

The six days after that had set the tone for the entire journey. She hurt every night from head to toe, and felt exhaustion deep into her bones. Yet his energy seemed indefatigable. And she couldn't really fathom how he could still be so interested in marital relations after eight hours a day spent riding. He was very considerate about it, always making sure most of the soreness had been rubbed out of her body first. But also politely and kindly insistent. She decided drowsily one night that this was probably just a result of what he called *being hardened to the saddle*; he just didn't *feel* the tiredness. Also, she decided, there was probably a bit of a novelty aspect. She'd often worn the same new *stola* three days in a row, simply because it *was* new. But when she'd grown a little accustomed to it, then it might lie in a chest for weeks on end, until she remembered that she owned it. *It's probably something like that,* she thought, and let herself go to sleep.

On the twenty-ninth, they reached Antioch, and Selene let her *palla* slide back from her face, staring ahead of her in awe. Hundreds of wagons and horses and thousands of people lined the road leading into the great city, which had its back to the Amanus mountains, which were wild and green with all the rain that winter brought the region.

A huge citadel loomed over the city, up on the slopes of Mt. Silpius, but the city itself sat on the Orontes River, with its baths, circus, and small stadium all clustered on an island formed where the Orontes split briefly, and then rejoined. Golden walls girdled each area of the city, running up and down the rugged hills like water leaping over stones in a brook. And just past the great gates, Selene could see a mix of architectural styles—many buildings with Hellene pillars and porticos, along the neatly intersecting grid of streets that made her think of Alexandria. But in and around these greater buildings, stood smaller, humbler structures, with fewer arches and no pillars at all. Spare and lean, they'd have looked out of place here, if they weren't made of the same golden stone, just as weathered as all the rest.

"Antioch was built by the Seleucids," Antyllus called back to her, looking over his shoulder as he did. "There was a town here, of course, before Alexander the Great passed through. After he died, and his generals carved up his empire, Seleucus Nicator, whom I'm sure got along *beautifully* with your own ancestor, Ptolemy," a laugh in his voice as he added that, "decided that this would be a good place for a city. He built it up into the seat of his power, and from here, he controlled Armenia, Persia, Parthia, Arabia, and Mesopotamia. Basically, everything from here, to the Indus River." He gestured towards the east with a sweeping gesture. "I think he got a better deal than Ptolemy did, don't you? The gold mines of Egypt notwithstanding?"

Selene stared up at the hilly city, which, in spite of its exotic architecture, still spoke to her far more than the alien hieroglyphs and paintings of Alexandria, and nodded, fervently. "It's wonderful," she said, managing to find her tongue, but then they were crowding through the gate as part of a long line of people, and she tried to nudge Flora a little closer to Antyllus' horse. She couldn't remember the last time she'd had so many *people* around her; even at the games, the Praetorians usually managed to keep a little bubble of space around the Julii family. And she certainly hadn't gone to the Lupercalia any of the last three years, in spite of Eurydice's cheerful invitation to come with her. There were so many faces and voices, and all those *hands* reaching out of the crowd.

Flora finally took the hint and ambled a bit closer to Antyllus' horse. Selene breathed a little easier; he wasn't in armor, since that was the function of their guards for the moment, but she felt better for being beside him. Though, clearly, he didn't feel any of her anxiety; he just smiled down at her from the top of his tall horse, and told her cheerfully, "We'll take a few days here. Pick up servants, guards, trade goods, and, most importantly, *guides* for the trip northeast."

By nightfall, they'd found another inn, this one in the teeming Hellene quarter of the city—which had a surprising number if Judean people bustling around. She hadn't seen many Judeans before. The men tended to wear long beards; the women, veils. She couldn't fathom why; in Rome, only the Vestals wore such, usually in saffron yellow. Or perhaps elderly widows. *Then again, maybe it's just to keep the sun off their faces. I can see a need for that.*

Selene found that Antioch didn't even *smell* like Rome. For starters, if it had a sewer system, she had yet to see evidence of it. Since it was a Hellene city in its bones, there were efforts to keep the horse and ox manure from the carts from piling up in the streets; she'd seen men sweeping the mess up and carting it away, at least. But ordure made up a constant undertone to the odor of the city, and she decided she wouldn't enjoy the place much in summer. But there were other aromas, too—cinnamon and coriander and truly exotic notes like *sandalwood*, imported all the way from India.

During their stay, they passed through the crowded marketplace on foot, Selene once more trying to adhere herself to Antyllus' side, which seemed to amuse and please him, and she gaped at the delicately-worked silks there. "I'm starting to understand," Selene said, very quietly, while examining one of the bolts of material, "why Eurydice keeps telling me not to bother with weaving for her. When you can buy silk *this* fine, and just sew it into whatever you want? This is amazing work." *Far better than anything I've ever made.* The individual threads were so fine, she almost couldn't see them, and somehow, a pattern of leaves was *in* the weaving itself; the pearl-like luster of the cloth became matte periodically, outlining the leaves. The whole thing had been dyed a rich, vibrant red, and it needed no embroidery; the skill of the weaving was its own adornment.

"From Persia!" the man running the booth had told her, with a bright smile, clearly smelling a sale. But she'd turned away, leaving the silk behind. *A fine waste of money that would be,* Selene told herself ruefully. *Every night, my stola and undertunics are filthy almost to the waist. I haven't had the heart to wear a different stola in a week, nevermind the smell of sweat, lest I ruin any more of my clothes with travel. And there's only more of this ahead. Because life is such an adventure.* That last thought held a hint of sarcasm to it, which she immediately repented and repressed.

And yet, that night, she found that precise roll of silk, tucked in among their belongings in the room she now shared with Antyllus. "I didn't buy this!" Selene blurted, raising her hands as if she'd found a poisonous asp in the luggage.

"No, I did," Antyllus said, looking up from one of the many lists he'd spent the last several nights drawing up. "You seemed to admire it. And it'll look lovely on you."

"Th-thank you," she mumbled, feeling about two *uncia* tall. And hoped that Antyllus couldn't read minds.

She had no practical advice to give regarding the trip north. Stayed firmly in the rooms in the inn, guarded by one of their men, while Antyllus went out and recruited guides, mercenaries, cart drivers, and such for the journey north. He took her to the slave market to find herself a female servant to replace Ranno, the Egyptian woman who'd been first her nursemaid and then her servant for most of Selene's life. *As if someone like that can be replaced,* Selene thought, wishing Ranno were here. *But that's selfish. She's Egyptian nobility, sent by her family to serve my mother for fifteen years. She deserves to see her home again. But I wonder what she'd think of Antioch. Would she snort and say it didn't have a patch on Alexandria, the way she always sniffed and said that, whenever I had to go through Rome with her?*

"Look through the lists of qualifications," Antyllus said, bringing Selene's attention back to the present, where they sat in a brightly-lit overseer's office, sipping mint tea and reading through records. "This one might do. She's highly recommended. Served for seven years as a pedagogue for a Hellene nobleman's family here in Antioch, and then another five as a lady's maid to the oldest daughter. Thirty years old, no children born to her, impeccable credentials. Speaks . . . gods. More languages than I do. Latin, Hellene, Hebrew, Aramaic, and Persian." Antyllus looked at her, his expression a little anxious. "What do you think?"

Selene blinked. She'd never seen that expression on his face before. *He wants to please me?* "I'm sure she'll do," she replied, hesitantly.

The overseer, a fat local man in his late fifties, immediately smiled and began to talk price, but Antyllus held up a hand. "Could you give us a moment alone?" he asked the overseer, and the man heaved himself to his feet and lurched off to another room. When the door shut behind him, Antyllus frowned a little at Selene. "This is someone that *you* have to feel comfortable with," he told her, gently. "It's your decision, not mine. It's probably best to meet the various candidates first, don't you think?"

Uncertainly, Selene nodded. Antyllus sighed. "I've been trying," he told her softly, taking one of her hands, "to get you to see that you're not a child in your brother and sister's house anymore. You have a say in things—maybe not about the *carruca*, because we really do need to move quickly—" a swift, rueful smile over that "but in matters of the household, especially the servant who'll help you with all your needs? Absolutely."

He always made her warmer inside, just by being there. But in spite of having felt for most of her life as if she were invisible, Selene had never felt more *isolated* than she did here, in Antioch, as far away from her family as if she'd somehow been transported to the moon or one of the other celestial bodies. "I understand," she replied. *He wants me to act like a wife. I'm trying. Gods, please know, I'm trying.*

She found the Hellene slave, Hebe, to be motherly enough, though she still terribly missed Ranno, and knew that her own grip on Egyptian was going to slip without anyone around with whom to speak it. But at least now she had someone who could help her wash her hair with astringent herbs when it itched after a stay in the wrong inn, and who could at least *try* to get road dust out of her clothes. Selene also found herself miserably sick just before they left Antioch, probably due to something she'd eaten. She'd thought for a day that she was never going to be able to leave the lavatory again, and it seemed unfair that Antyllus was completely unaffected by whatever it was. "Legion rations give you a stomach made of iron," he told her as Hebe fixed her a soothing tea. "You'll get used to the road."

It passed, fortunately, after only two days, leaving her able to ride her ambling donkey behind Antyllus as they left the city, with its hum of humanity and its smell of spices, and headed northeast, through the mountains. This time with twenty guards, all hardened Hellene mercenaries, two guides, Lydian boys not much older than Selene herself, and four carts of goods. Selene occasionally envied the carters their seats on the bouncing, jostling wagons. But Hebe, who rode with them, told her loftily that the carters were low men, crudely-spoken and very disrespectful.

Weeks passed in a gray blur for Selene as they crawled through valleys, mounted hills, and followed winding, narrow trails around mountains. Several times, they had to camp close enough to Parthian territory that Antyllus wouldn't allow any campfires at night, and Selene had no idea how she'd be able to sleep, for fear of a Parthian patrol finding them—until, of course, she woke up the next morning. Still wrapped in a haze of fatigue that never seemed to end.

The mountains, she found beautiful; stark and uncompromising. The music of the shepherds who lived among them, played mostly on pipes as they endured the boring task of watching the flocks? A lonely, pervasive sound that followed them down this mountain, and up the next hill, where the last tune dwindled, to be picked up afresh by a new shepherd and a new flock. She tried to pick out the notes on her *kithara* at night once or twice, with fingers made numb by exhaustion, but Antyllus reminded her that they were close to Parthia and that sound carried at night. So she set the *kithara* back in its case.

Finally, one last set of mountains lay behind them. And

ahead of them, a vast and rolling plain. Almost featureless, it seemed to go on forever, a sea of winter-yellow grass just becoming tinged with fresh green, and drab, low bushes. If the mountains had been beautiful, if exhausting to travel through, this was . . . a wasteland. A desert of grass, if not of sand. Impossible to believe that people *lived* here. Why, there were no cities in sight—and even the people of Cappadocia, through which they'd traveled to get here, had villages.

They'd picked up another guide in one of those Cappadocian villages, a man who spoke broken Hellene and, by his own account, some of the various Scythian dialects, and had traded with them and the Sarmatians before. "*Herdsmen,*" he said now, pointing to the horizon. Squinting, Selene *thought* she might see something that might have been smoke.

"I wish I had Eurydice's eyes," she said glumly.

"It would be somewhat helpful. But on the other hand, I'm glad you're along, and not her," Antyllus told her lightly, and turned back to their guide. And switched languages to the perfect, fluent Hellene that always surprised Selene when he spoke it. He had a different accent than she'd ever heard in the language before—a legacy, he'd told her, from commanding Cretan archers for several years now. "*Is it better for us to go to them, or to let them come to us?*"

Their guide chuckled uneasily. "*Depends on how their chieftain feels today, and if their gods are angry or not. Sarmatians worship a fire-god first and foremost of their pantheon, not the goddess of nature that the Scythians revere. But Scythians will take captives in war, and sacrifice them to their war-god, whose name they won't teach to outsiders.*" The bearded man shuddered a little.

"*Are there any signs we can give, to show our intent is peaceful trade?*" Antyllus asked sharply.

"*Set up camp. Don't let the horses eat the grass — give them fodder. The herdsmen get angry if they come to an area where the grass has already been cut down. They have very specific circuits that their clans are allowed to follow, from this camp to that camp, over the course of the seasons. If any clan strays into the territory of another, it can lead to violence.*" The Cappadocian scratched at his hair. "*They'll ride up and probably circle the camp several times with their bows in their hands. Testing your men's mettle and your own. Don't flinch, but also, don't start anything. They respect courage above everything else — that's true of all these tribes. Scythian, Sarmatian, royal Scythian —* "

"*What's the difference?*" Antyllus asked immediately.

"*They don't tell us that. All I know is, the royal Scythians have an extra god, only worshipped by them. They seem to rule over the rest of the Scythians, pretty much from their big city. It's the only one they really have, other than small farming villages that the herders go around. They trade with each other, and everyone's very polite, since they all go around armed at all times — even many of the women. The Royal Scythians dominate the slave-trade. Have the biggest tombs. And gods, never go near their tombs. I've heard rumors that they flay tomb-robbers alive.*"

Selene swallowed, and asked, in her own Egyptian-inflected Hellene, "*Excuse me, but you said that the woman are armed, too? So these are the Amazons?*" She had vague impressions of Pentesilea from the *Iliad* to go on here, and little more.

Their guide laughed. "*If only they were that kind. Depending on the tribe, the women might rule over everyone, yes — or not. But a woman who chooses to become a warrior, it's said, has to kill three men before she can choose to marry and lose her virginity. They're strict about those who take the warrior's path.*"

Antyllus commented in Latin, very dryly, "No easily taking back *that* decision, eh?"

Selene wondered, not for the first time, why on *earth*

Antyllus had brought her here. Between the words of their garrulous guide and the tales she'd heard since the cradle of Amazons, she fully expected hairy people, dressed in skins, with the women bare to the waist to expose one breast—the other cauterized with a hot iron in infancy, to prevent its growth and to allow them to use their bows unimpeded in adulthood.

They didn't have time to set up the tents; instead, the men got the wagons into a sort of triangle, giving themselves both the chance to protect the trade-goods and the draft animals, and potential cover from any incoming arrows. Antyllus moved Selene purposefully into the shelter of one of them, and told her, tersely, "If it comes down to it, get under the cart. We've taken the pack horses off for a reason. Shouldn't be an issue, though. They *do* trade with others." A quick, light smile. "I'll do my best not to antagonize them."

In the distance, Selene could hear the drumming of hundreds of hooves, and could just make out the cloud of dust that foretold the coming of the main herd. She could just make out small, cloth-covered wagons that looked like tents on wheels, moving alongside the herd, and watched, watched, wide-eyed, as the outriders now sped towards the camp.

As their guide had predicted, the scouts rode in dizzying circles around the cluster of wagons, not holding the reins of their horses, for they had their bows in their hands. Bows that looked identical to the one Antyllus had in his own hands at the moment. But while the tribesmen rode with arrows on their strings, Antyllus just stood there, unflinching. Allowing them to take their aim, but simply watching each of them as they passed before him. Selene clutched the wooden side of the cart and wished that she had one tenth of her husband's courage. Or some measure of Eurydice's magic.

Finally, the riders ceased their dizzying maneuvers

around the camp. Slowed the horses to a walk, and the leader advanced. Selene's eyes widened. These people weren't at all as she'd pictured them. For starters, they all wore their hair long, flowing out from under their oddly peaked caps, and were universally either blond or red-haired, with gray or blue eyes. The men did wear beards, close-cropped, for the most part. All of them wore long tunics and pants, but these weren't crude fabrications pieced together from animal skins, but carefully woven wool in bright colors. And they wore gold jewelry—some of it fantastically elaborate—which jingled from their arms and throats as they rode.

And the leader? Was indeed a woman. She wasn't stripped to the waist, and she certainly appeared to be in possession of both breasts. Selene flushed a little, remembering how Antyllus had laughed at that legend, and told her, smiling, *I fail to see how a breast could get in the way of a bowstring.* And the woman, with her flaxen hair and tanned skin, nudged her horse forward with her knees, staring directly and boldly into Antyllus' eyes. Selene's heart twisted a little inside her as she saw Antyllus smile up at her.

A flurry of words in some indecipherable language, which their guide began to render into more-or-less comprehensible Hellene. Antyllus quickly established that they were here to trade. *"I command archers in our lands, far to the west. But I have never seen a better bow than this one, which I found in Illyria. I would place these bows in the hands of my men, who go to fight enemies even further to the west."*

"What lands do these enemies hold? What do they call themselves?" Rapid-fire words.

"They are no allies of yours," Antyllus assured her. *"They are called Gauls. Some of their distant kin pushed as far east as Thrace, hundreds of years ago, and still dwell near there. But these live on an island in an ocean so far from here, that we will take*

nearly two months to cross the lands and rivers to reach them."
Antyllus paused for the translation to catch up. *"They call themselves by many names—Caledoni, Cantiaci, Dobunni."* He gave her an appraising look, clearly admiring the horses, the bows, and the people themselves. *"If they were not so far from your lands, I would ask if any of your young warriors wished to make a name for themselves, fighting them. We of Rome often bring warriors of other people with us on our battles. Many hands are stronger together."*

Selene had never seen Antyllus exercising the famous Antony charm on someone else. His eyes gleamed, but, clearly watching the faces of those around him, he didn't smile as much. Tailored his facial responses to theirs. All the gentleness he normally displayed towards her was in abeyance at the moment; nothing in his face and eyes but a stern soldier admiring the skill of other warriors.

And these Scythians or Sarmatians, or whatever they were, responded to that. Their demeanor lightened. They promptly gave permission for Antyllus' party to put up their tents, and extended the group grazing rights—for a few days, anyway. So that Antyllus could meet with the elders, and speak more seriously of bows, bowyers, and what might be traded for them.

Selene again watched, feeling useless, as their guards set up their tents—and the nomads, who'd driven their horses and cattle into the area around them, set up their own camp around the foreigners. Parked their tent-covered wagons in a series of circles, hemming them in. "Well, they certainly know how to keep an eye on us," Antyllus said lightly, taking Selene by the hand. "Come on. One of the scouts is going to introduce us to their leaders. It'll be helpful for you to be there when I meet their elders. Generally, a man doesn't bring his wife places where he intends to make trouble."

"How can you be so calm?" Selene hissed as he pulled her along in the wake of the same flaxen-haired woman who'd met with them at first, their interpreter following behind them doggedly, through a small city that hadn't been *there* a half hour ago. People were taking items out of their wagons and setting up their homes more comfortably. Curved pieces of wood, stowed in the wagons, were removed, and each family raised these in circles, spreading cloth over them to form odd little huts, with peaked roofs. Wicker hutches with chickens in them, which had been bundled along the sides of the wagons, were settled onto the ground, and the birds released to forage for the time being. Selene almost tripped over one of the chickens, which flapped out of her path, squawking. "How can you joke?"

Antyllus glanced down at her as they walked, and told her, in that same light, almost affable way, "Well, just about four years ago now, I was riding along a mountain path, being shot at now and again. My legate and the rest of the senior tribunes were up with the regular legion, and had just sent me back to chivy the auxiliary cavalry along a little faster—I'm always sent to deal with the auxiliaries. I usually speak their language." He shrugged. "And when I looked up, an avalanche was coming down the mountainside. If I'd been up with the legate and the rest of the regulars, I'd have been killed. Probably wouldn't even have had time to feel the pain—at least, I hope *they* didn't. That avalanche was a force of nature, if one unleashed by men." He patted her hand, where it sat on his arm. "I was never one to get worked up over the small things even before that. Now? If they're not actively pulling out my fingernails, I can work with them."

Selene felt as if all the blood had left her head. She'd never even considered how close Antyllus had been to death in Hispania. She swallowed, and let him pull her into the wagon that they'd been directed to, which smelled oddly like cheese and wool and other things. Nodded politely to the wizened elders inside, who had faces like apples that had been dried in a kiln, their eyes almost invisible among the wrinkles. And the elders opted to put off talking of details, saying that they could only speak of business once they'd extended their hospitality to the foreigners. "Another way of taking our measure," Antyllus assessed. "I'll talk to our guards, and tell them to stay *away* from the local women. Too many chances for misunderstandings here."

So that first night, the nomads, safely arrived at their spring grazing grounds, put on a feast, and the foreigners, including Selene, as the wife of the guest of honor, were required to attend. There was roasted calf—fresh-slaughtered, the pick of the herd. Flat, unleavened bread. And a horrible, thick, sour drink that fizzed slightly as they passed it around in leather drinking skin, and clearly expected everyone to drink communally. Selene managed one mouthful, and felt quite proud of herself for not spewing it onto the ground, in spite of the laughter from the nomads all around her. *"What is that?"* she asked their guide.

"Fermented mare's milk," came the reply in Hellene. *"It's a rare favor to be given it—cow's milk is easier to obtain, and usually subjected to the same process. They say it's safer to drink than water."*

"Fermented?" Antyllus said, smiling, and took the skin from her, drinking from it. He gave the skin an evaluative look, and then took another quick swig before passing it along. Selene had no idea how his expression hadn't changed either time. "Apparently, they want to see who I am when I'm drunk, eh?"

And as the night wore on around the bright bonfire, various of the nomads' women came over and . . . there was no other word for it. They flirted with him. Touched his short-cropped hair and shaved face. And said things that their translator choked on his mare's milk before rendering into Hellene. *"That one says that you should sell your little wife, and let a real woman take you to her bed,"* the Hellene man said, very obviously choosing not to look at Selene. *"She asks what good your wife is, since she carries no weapons, and does no work, not even setting up your tent?"*

The slow burn of humiliation passed through Selene, and no amount of telling herself that she was a daughter of the Julii and a princess of Egypt, and that these barbarians who smelled of horse had probably never heard of either place, did any good. She turned her face away, and stared into the fire. Pretending that none of them were there. Pretending that she wasn't there, herself.

Antyllus shook her arm gently, and, roused, she looked back at him. "I said," he repeated patiently, "I sent Hebe for your *kithara*. Perhaps you could play something for them." His lips quirked at the corners. "There isn't a tribe anywhere that doesn't know music. It's as close to a universal language as there is."

When Hebe returned with the instrument, Selene took in in numb hands. She hadn't been able to play in over a month, but the strings felt like the hand of an old friend, taking her own. She'd never played for so many people before, but put them out of her mind resolutely. If she could just immerse herself in the music, they'd . . . go away. She wouldn't have to watch them touching Antyllus anymore. Or hear what they were saying, translated so carefully.

She struck the strings. Invoked the quiet ripple of a stream over rocks, and then switched modes into a hymn to Poseidon, with the strings wavering and wailing, like the first breath of a gale. Another shift, to a hunting song, usually sung in praise of Artemis, but she didn't feel like celebrating the maiden goddess of the moon right now, so her fingers shifted. Caught the last note and wound into another song—one she'd heard in Egypt, with the elaborate, serpentine progressions favored in that land. Which triggered another association, this time the lonely pipes of the shepherds of Cappadocia.

By the time Selene looked up, her hands ached, for she hadn't played in so long. *I'm surprised I didn't strike more false notes,* she thought, and as the strings stilled, she was startled to realize that the various herders had gone respectfully silent. Unnervingly so. And when the last note no longer shimmered in the ear, they gave voice to ululating cries that she desperately hoped were approval, and slapped their thighs, which certainly seemed to be applause. They were smiling, anyway. And their guide translated one of the elders' comments, *"They ask if you are a poet, as well as a keeper of songs?"*

"Tell them that I have memorized some of the poems of my father's people, and those of my mother, too, for they are the history of two great peoples, but that I am no poet. I have no gift for words." Selene looked away.

A moment, and then the translation came back. *"They say that remembering the deeds of the past is what every singer must do, and that it is good that you remember the great deeds of your ancestors. They respect that, and your gift for song."* The translator's smile showed white through his dark beard. *"They also say you must drink more mare's milk. That you are too small and thin, and will have much difficulty bearing your husband healthy children if you do not make yourself stronger."*

Selene flushed, grateful that the firelight washed away the color. And, when Antyllus, laughing, put the skin of horrible drink back in her hand, she resignedly took another sip. A very small one.

By midnight, Antyllus was slightly tipsy from the fermented mare's milk, and he took her off to their tent, smiling and telling her when they reached its confines, "You did very well tonight. They were testing us. They respect skill, honor, and strength. And these are Sarmatians, if you didn't catch all the conversation while you were playing. They told me all about the Goths that are on their western flank, pushing them east, into the Scythians. They don't share a language with the Goths, but there are . . . similarities. All those female warriors." He picked her up off the ground and twirled her. Selene, her stomach lurching from the mare's milk, roasted veal, and everything else, pushed at his arms and begged him to stop. Which he did with a laugh. "They liked you, my lark. I think that tomorrow, they'll be willing to talk trade."

Selene certainly hoped so. The sooner they did, the sooner they could leave.

Antyllus didn't think of himself as an idiot or blind, and it would have taken being both of those things not to realize that there was something amiss with his pretty bride. For him, marriage hadn't fundamentally altered the nature of his existence; he could still largely go anywhere and do anything he wanted, so long as it wasn't illegal, and didn't interfere with his duty to his family or his duty to Rome. The biggest change had been a welcome one — ready access to a female body, without having to worry about disease, unwanted pregnancies, or the issue of payment. And he did his best — and thought he usually succeeded — in making that a pleasure for her, too.

But still, something remained . . . amiss. He'd pondered once, in Rome, asking Caesarion who'd beaten her, but he knew that no such thing lurked in Selene's past. At first, he'd put it down to a lifetime of being overshadowed by three brilliant, accomplished elder siblings, two of them god-born. More recently, he'd made himself slow down with her, yet again. *She's left home for the first time. I did that at fourteen, myself—a year younger than she is now, surely, but I'd also been in at least five different* castrae *by the time I was ten, all in my father's command tent. I'd already seen more of the world than she has.* He still didn't think that was the whole of it, however. *Also, she's . . . well, she's not* alone. *I'm here, after all. But she doesn't have anyone at all familiar around her. When I joined the legion, I had all the other young nobles around me, fresh tribunes and young* optios, *for the most part. I might not have known them all, but they all were my brothers. Some for better, some for worse. She doesn't have that.*

He reminded himself of those facts night after night. Tried to do little, considerate things for her, making sure that she had a lady's maid with whom she was at least comfortable, to help her with all the female necessities with which he was wholly inexperienced. Gave her small gifts now and again. Not trying to buy her love—he thought he'd made fairly good progress on wooing her in Rome and Alexandria, and love couldn't really be bought—but trying to show her that he cared.

But the longer their journey lasted, the more Selene seemed to shrink in on herself. He'd pull her out of the tent at twilight to show her a magnificent sunset throwing the stark mountains of Cappadocia into inky black cutouts against the horizon, and she'd silently drink it in for a while. And then she'd go back to the tent. There had been areas where he wouldn't let her play her *kithara* or allow a fire to burn, but that had been at the recommendation of the guides, and only a fool hired guides to ignore their advice. So there had definitely been danger along their route . . . but she didn't leave the tent even in safe areas.

He'd tried asking her to sit with him under the stars at night, something he'd loved since he was a boy. But with the wide band of the Milky Way trailing across the sky above them, she'd seemed uneasy and uncomfortable. Antyllus had shaken his head over it all, repeatedly, where she couldn't see him. *I never asked for a grand passion, he thought,* tiredly. *I've spent my entire life watching what passion usually leads to, reflected in my father's life. All that anger at his first, faithless wife. A solid marriage with my mother, till she died. The embarrassing incident with the actress, who, freedwoman or not, still owed her loyalties to her former owner, one of Caesar's political rivals, so Caesar told him to drop her, resulting in one of my <u>many</u> illegitimate half-siblings. All the infidelities with Octavia – not that I can blame him, honestly. Whatever happened with Cleopatra, years ago, and now a stable marriage with her. All of that tumult. I never wanted any of that. Just . . . contentment. Peace. Someone I could love a bit, and someone who might love me a bit, too. I didn't think there'd be this <u>constant</u> effort to get her to smile – and those smiles seem to be dwindling, day by day.*

And I have no idea why.

He'd been delighted by her music for the Sarmatians; she'd played a panoply of different styles, all alien to the herders, invoking a variety of moods, from solemn grandeur to elegiac sorrow. But Antyllus had also noted that none of the songs had exactly sounded cheerful. And again, he couldn't wrap his head around it. *There's fresh air around us, beautiful scenery, new people to meet. No <u>buccinae</u> to wake us up in the morning, and no duty, except to <u>get to Britannia</u> with the weapons I'm here to buy. If it weren't for how withdrawn she's been, I'd have called this the best two months of my adult life so far.*

So, for the next six days, in and around haggling with the locals — who sent outriders to fetch people from the spring camps of neighboring tribes—he tried to draw Selene out of herself. Took her around the camp of the Sarmatians. Pointed out the thick, beautiful, elaborately woven rugs with which they covered their dirt floors. "Looks like a mosaic floor at home, but so much more portable," he pointed out, trying to make her smile. "Quite a few more flowers, too. Think we should bring some back with us?"

Then he found a group of women weaving, and when Selene stopped to watch an activity he'd never put any thought into at all, he paused with her. "What do you think?" he asked her, trying to draw her out.

"I've never seen anything like it," she admitted, staring. All three of the women were working on the same rug, kneeling on the ground. The loom itself was vertical, as most looms in the west were, but it stretched across the ground, rather than being an upright mechanism. As such, the women knelt right on the bottom edge of the carpet as they worked, on hands and knees, rapidly moving threads and combing them down. "My back aches just watching them."

He nudged her gently, and disentangled her hand from his arm. "Why don't you go talk to them?" Antyllus asked. "You know about weaving. I'm sure they'd enjoy talking with you while they work."

Selene's eyes went wide. "I can't speak their language! How can I talk to them without a translator?" she protested, looking around for their guide.

"I think interest speaks a language all its own. Go on. I'll wait over here. I'm sure there's something around for me to look at." *Please work,* he thought, and withdrew. Glanced over now and again, as Selene hovered near the women, finally kneeling down beside them to look more closely at their work, though clearly trying to stay out of their way and their light. Inside of ten minutes of her trying to gesture at them, they'd pulled her down with them, and were showing her how they tied the knots—and then handed her a comb, letting her pack down their work, rather than risk her inexpert hands damaging a pattern that clearly might take a year to finish.

"Was that at least interesting?" he asked a half-hour or so later, and got a quick nod. And, gods be praised, a slight smile.

"It seems almost a sacrilege to offer coin for something that must take so long to make," she told him. "And yet, I suppose they must sell them, because once a family's covered the floor of their own tent, what else is there left to do?"

The answer, however, lay inside each of the tents that they visited. Because the rugs weren't just used on the floors. They hung from poles inside the tents, creating divisions and rooms. Hung beside the actual walls of the tent, too, offering more protection from the winds of the steppe. Entering any tent, however drab it was on the outside, was to experience a cacophony of conflicting colors and patterns, with no uniformity or structure at all, which dazed a Roman mind accustomed to balance, harmony, and simplicity in interior design. "There's your answer," Antyllus told her, chuckling, and took her faint smile as his reward once more.

Everything took time, and Selene tried not to chafe visibly with her desire to leave. Bows like the one Antyllus wanted weren't just lying around; they were made to each warrior's measure, and if a man or woman died, their bows were often buried with them.

Their hosts sent riders to the spring camps of neighboring tribes, who brought back more Sarmatians, and even some Scythians—Selene wasn't really sure how to tell the difference, except that the Scythians seemed to wear more gold clasps and pins and studs on their clothing.

With Hebe to walk beside her, she might have been free to wander around the Sarmatian camp. But she'd shrunk from the idea initially. She didn't speak the language, and the herders and warriors—particularly the female warriors!— frightened her. Their voices were loud, and even the women who carried weapons tended to walk with a certain swaggering confidence, that to her sensibilities, seemed to border on braggadocio. Yet when she ventured that opinion to Antyllus, he chuckled and said, mildly, "You haven't been inside of an enlisted barracks often, then. Because I see plenty of swagger and bluster there, too."

And having ventured that opinion, she found her arm taken, and Antyllus marched her around the camp several times. It felt like punishment at first, but meeting the weavers had alleviated some of that reaction. After that, she did ask Hebe to walk with her back to the weavers several times. And once, managed to get the attention of their Cappadocian guide, and brought him with her, so that she could actually speak to the women. Ask them what they used for dye— common madder for the reds, onion and chamomile for the yellows and browns, acorns for black, as it turned out. Cautiously pulled out her own, very limited sewing kit, and showed them silk thread and linen, which they touched in wonder at its fineness, but told her, through the translator, *"Cloth woven with such thin thread must be quite useless, except perhaps in the warmest days of summer. Wool is better. Wool is warmer. But this is so soft, and it shimmers so."*

Not knowing what else to do, Selene gave them the silk thread. *"Perhaps they can embroider with it,"* she told the translator.

"My lady, I don't know that word in their language,"

he said, looking annoyed with the whole conversation. As if she were wasting his time with all these women's dealings.

Selene nodded, and simply pressed the loop of silk thread into the hand of the nearest woman. *"Tell them that I thank them for letting me watch how they work. Their rugs are beautiful. Each one a labor of love."*

The translator conveyed that, clearly trying not to roll his eyes.

Selene was quite startled the next day, when one of the women appeared at her own tent. And gave her a tiny rug, worked in similar fashion to the huge one that the three had been making all this while. A babble of words in Sarmatian — no translator around to help interpret — and a little bow. And then the woman turned and walked away, leaving Selene to stare after her. *I don't think that this is a fair trade at all. I gave them silk threads. They gave me something beautiful.*

From what little she could see, the nomads had a layered, hierarchical culture, with the warriors on top, priests either co-equal or slightly above the warriors, skilled craftsmen like the goldsmiths and the weavers below that, and slaves below that, with farmers — drawn from the sedentary parts of the population — occupying a nebulous place below the craftsmen. Still, they were generally treated with respect, and the nomads traded with them for vegetables, fruits, and grain.

Women could be priestesses of their various goddesses, as well as warriors or wives or craftsmen. Selene had read her Herodotus on the way here; she'd expected the male priests, called *enarei*, to be somewhat like *galli*. Of course, Herodotus had claimed that the *enarei* were hereditary priests; a full caste all to themselves, they had been granted the gift of prophecy by the Scythian gods, and that male children of this caste underwent certain rituals in adolescence that barred them from becoming warriors, and forever after, wore women's clothing.

Since it would be rather difficult to have a *hereditary* priesthood without *propagating* that lineage, and since Selene couldn't see any distinction between men and women's clothing, since they all wore the ubiquitous trousers, she rather thought that Herodotus might have had some bad information mixed in with the good. With the high status of women, a male-only caste that dressed as women to set themselves apart—when the women could have status as warriors!—made little sense at all. But she couldn't ask such questions; their interpreter was usually busy with Antyllus. And even if their Cappadocian had been at hand, Selene couldn't think of a single way to start that kind of conversation with the people standing around their carts. At least not any that wouldn't cause serious offense.

And then Antyllus told her, behind his hand, that he'd figured out the mystery at the privy trench dug at the side of camp. "There's one of those *enarei* here, a very old one. Woman's breasts and, as I inadvertently found out while pissing, the genitals of both sexes. They're full hermaphrodites," he told her, shaking his head a bit. "Not eunuchs. Either it's the gods' will, to set them apart, but it only seems to occur inside their caste, and only once, maybe twice in a generation. Like red hair, maybe it just runs in some families. I asked. Politely, you may be sure. They're regarded as prodigies, the same way they would be in Rome, and considered to have great magical powers. Though I have *seen* magic, and this elderly *enarei* has yet to do so much as light a lamp with it here in camp." He shrugged. "Their beliefs, not mine. They'd probably find great portent in the birth of a two-headed calf, too."

Antyllus had hoped to be able to purchase bows in the

thousands; he wound up with several hundred, but with something perhaps a little better, in the long-run; two young bowyers from different tribes indicated that, for a price, they'd come with him on his journeys, and equip his troops, assuming he could provide them with materials. Both were young men in their early twenties, without families. They had decent prospects ahead of them, but were hungry for more wealth and renown than were available to them at the moment. And, since the goods they'd brought were worth so much to these nomads—salt, gems, glass, olive oil, and even spices from far-off India—they wound up with several pounds of beautifully worked Scythian gold necklaces, several new, clean rugs, worked in patterns that made Selene sigh in appreciation, and a few Sarmatian slaves in trade as well, though Antyllus muttered that he had no idea what they'd do with them.

All three were female, and Selene had little difficulty interpreting the looks their new bowyers were giving them. "Hebe and I can try to teach them Latin," Selene offered shyly. "They'll find better places in Rome, if you decide to sell them later, if they can at least speak the language. And . . . might not wind up in brothels." She paused. "And I think *that* one was with the weavers when I visited with them. She might be trained to weave their rugs. That wouldn't be . . . that wouldn't be terrible, would it?"

Antyllus shook his head. "I have *my* Scythian maiden," he said, tapping the bow slung over his shoulder. "I've been quite content with her. I didn't need to add any living ones to my household. We can sell the other two on the way home, since I don't want to cart them all the way to Rome. But you can keep the third, if you like, and if she turns out to have useful skills, as you say."

Selene resolved to teach the women Hellene and Latin,

at least a few words each, before they had to sell them. *It's the least I can do*, she thought, as they set out to the northwest now, heading back into Roman-Hellene territory.

She did try. Only one of the three seemed to have any aptitude for language, the same one who'd been owned by the weavers. She was a golden-haired girl with sea-green eyes, of about Selene's own age, who tapped her own sternum and articulated what Selene hoped was her name: *Arunia*. Arunia also seemed to like to sing, and frequently did so, just outside of their tent, where she slept with the other two slaves under an awning.

And so, as they toiled towards the shores of the Black Sea, Martius gave way to Aprilis. They found the city of Trapezus, with its double ring of walls. Let their carters go, dismissed their hired guards, and sold off the two other Scythian girls, keeping Arunia. Selene had just begun putting together bits and pieces of Arunia's story. She'd been Scythian-born, originally, of their warrior-caste, but she'd been captured during a raid by the Sarmatians, and enslaved. Or at least, that's what Selene *thought* the girl was saying. *Gods only know if I'll ever understand it all. But she likes music and sings along when I play — wordless tunes that more or less fit the melody. That's . . . the closest thing I've had to a friend in ages. Social status and language barriers aside.*

It wasn't much of a friendship, she had to admit. And while she'd finally come to enjoy at least a little of their time with the nomads—all she had to do to prove that to herself, was to take out that tiny rug the women had given her, and she'd feel a hint of a warm glow around her heart—the grinding reality of travel once again bore down on her.

Arunia and the two bowyers proved to be terrified of the sea and of the boats. They'd clearly never seen such things before, and spent the entire passage over the Black Sea praying in their own language, when they weren't retching. Which was precisely how Selene spent the passage, herself.

On being told that they'd have two more sea voyages ahead of them — one through Corinth to reach Rome, and then from Rome to Gaul, one of the men vanished in Megaran Hellene territory, disappearing into the night. Leaving Antyllus with exactly one bowyer and a load of irritation. Selene rather envied the bowyer who'd left, but she couldn't disappear the same way.

Finally, they reached Ostia on Aprilis eleventh. Selene had never been so glad to see a stretch of land in her entire life. However, she knew that this was just a stopover. While they were only two hours from Rome by carriage, they'd just be turning around and setting back out to sea again shortly. She wrote a polite letter to Alexander, and another note to Eurydice in Alexandria, informing both of her siblings that they'd arrived safely. She wasn't sure what else to put in the missives, so both read the same:

> *Arrived in Ostia today, after a journey of almost two months. Antyllus successfully purchased several hundred Scythian bows, and procured the services of one Sarmatian bowyer. My husband informs me that we will be departing for Britannia within the next two days.*
>
> *I hope that this letter finds you in good health. May the gods keep you.*

There wasn't much else to say. She could have rattled on about the smells of Antioch, but that seemed pointless. She could have mentioned the weavers of the Sarmatians, but that would surely have bored her busy siblings. Their eyes would skip over that sort of fluff.

She couldn't write any of the questions she ached to ask Eurydice. *At what point does love become the all-consuming fire I see between you and Caesarion? Does that only happen when the husband and the wife are . . . friends? More equal, like Father and Mother, or even Mother and Antony?* She sighed. *I admire Antyllus' strength and courage. I'm amazed by his ability to talk to and persuade <u>anyone</u>, even barbarians. I enjoy his ready humor. I feel safe with him.*

Listed, all the things that she liked about her husband certainly sounded like symptoms of love. Her uncertainty, however, was real, and cruel. *It's just. . . I expected more. I expected the feelings to grow. But they're . . . tepid. Whatever I feel is not a fire, and I thought it would be a blaze, after the first times he kissed me.* Selene swallowed, the pen still in her hand, dripping ink in a useless blotch on the parchment. *Still, this is probably more than other women in arranged marriages feel. He doesn't beat me or the servants. He lets me choose my own servants, gives me gifts, and . . . well, I doubt I'd have ever seen the weavers working, if he hadn't dragged me out of the tent. But on the other hand, I didn't want to be there to begin with.*

Tiredness rose up like a gray fog, and she pushed it down with an effort. *He's fond of me. He's faithful. He hasn't even been sleeping with any of the slaves — how could he, since he insists on me sharing his bed every night?* A tinge of resentment, even at that, however. Marital relations were nice enough, and Antyllus certainly seemed intent on pleasing her, but she spent every day in a haze of exhaustion that he didn't seem to feel. Sex was thus, something she hoped would be over with quickly, so that she could sleep, and not the joy it had been the first night on the ship, leaving Alexandria. Before the seasickness had set in, anyway.

And there was another component to that thought. Antyllus was *fond* of her. Nothing more. Oh he'd kiss her quite passionately when they were in bed. But the rest of the time? He'd stroke her hair sympathetically, rub her shoulders, and generally take care of her. But she was left with the impression that he'd have taken care of a child in exactly the same way. *Maybe what I feel isn't growing, because he doesn't feel much for me, either?* But that seemed unfair. *I could just as easily say that he doesn't feel more for me, because I don't feel more for him. Circular reasoning.*

Selene dropped the quill, sending a spray of ink over what she'd written, and not caring. Logic didn't seem to help her through the muddle in her own head. *I'm fortunate. I <u>know</u> I am. So why, when I'm throwing up over the side of yet another ship, do I wish that I'd never left the Julii villa? Why do I wish that I'd stayed a child forever? Why do I get so angry with him when he strokes my hair and tells me that the seasickness will pass, when he never seems stricken with it? How can I <u>resent</u> someone who treats me so well?* Selene sighed as she stared at the spattered, mostly-empty scroll in front of her. *I couldn't have stayed home forever. Things change, and I should be grateful to have so much.*

But . . . if she'd been able to pick up that pen again, and write her confession, it would have read, *I don't think I like adventure. No matter how much Antyllus enjoys it. I've been miserable since the moment I left Rome. Meeting the weavers was interesting. I liked that. But that was . . . five or six days out of eight horrible weeks of being dirty. Having to have Hebe wash my hair with yarrow and other oils to kill the fleas from that filthy inn. Getting horribly ill from strange food, or plain <u>bad</u> food. Shivering in a tent, terrified of Parthian patrols finding us. Wishing, every moment of almost every day, that I were <u>home</u>.*

She couldn't say that, though. Not to Eurydice, whom Selene knew had *hate* being cooped up in the palace in Alexandria. Who was far from Caesarion. Who actually seemed to *enjoy* living in a tent or a wooden *castra* building.

Who never seemed to get sick from bad food. Who'd gone with Caesarion on a trip to the Alps, just to see what the mountains looked like.

No, Eurydice would only tell Selene how *fortunate* she was, to have seen so much of the world—perhaps more than even Eurydice herself had, at this point. To have drunk sour, thick mare's milk—nevermind that she'd thrown most of it back up the next morning. To have seen golden Antioch and Trapezus, where Xenophon had retreated with ten thousand Hellene mercenaries, hired by Cyrus to help him try to take the throne of Persia.

I'm tired of traveling, but so are all the women married to officers who've made the crossing to Britannia by this point. Most women don't have any say in where they go. There's . . . nothing special about me. A brief thought crossed her mind, of what her life would have been like, if she'd married Tiberius instead. And she had to acknowledge, that it would be, in most ways, exactly the same. Oh, she wouldn't have been dragged through eastern Lydia, the steppes of Scythia, up to the Black Sea, and then across the Mediterranean. But right now? She'd probably be stuck in a *castra* in Britannia. *Or sitting alone in a villa in Rome, forced to hold political dinners and converse with people, because the military is politics and politics relies on the military.*

She'd never really thought about that reality when she'd been daydreaming about marriage when she was younger. Her own mother hadn't gone with Caesar on his wars since before Selene was born. Cleopatra had been too busy handling the political end of things, and ruling her own kingdom largely by correspondence. *So. This is my life now. If I had a choice, it would be between even more travel, and staying in Rome, equally miserable, and disappointing Antyllus into the bargain. At least by going with him, there's only one person unhappy, instead of both of us. That's the way to make a decision between two choices that will make me equally unhappy, isn't it? By determining how happy the choice makes the other people in my life?*

And there's no way out of it, short of the gods reaching down and transforming me into someone else. I wish it could all just stop. That I could stop being who I am.

She covered her face with her hands, trying to will the tears away. *I can't let Antyllus see this in me. He'd blame himself, or try to fix it, and there's nothing to fix. The problem is me. I wouldn't be happy alone in Rome, forced to hold political dinners and whatever else in his absence. I probably won't be happy in a* castra. *The only place I think I was really happy, was the Julii villa when my father was alive. And that's not my home anymore, and never will be again.* She swallowed. *As Antyllus' wife, I'm supposed to make* him *my home, and make a home for him. But the only home he* wants *is the road and the sea. And I just . . . can't. I can't feel that I'm home when I'm with him.*

And *that* thought made her head spin and her stomach curl with guilt. Because Antyllus *did* go out of his way, trying to make her happy. She knew that he did. His fondness showed in all the little things he did for her. But again, it was fondness. Not love, as far as she could comprehend it. Selene sighed, and reminded herself, yet again, *I need to appreciate the things that I have and stop whining, even in my thoughts. Fondness is better than nothing. And my own feelings . . . well, they're better than nothing, too, I suppose. Even if they're muffled and gray, and I can't understand* why, *when I know I was happy about it all, in Alexandria. But even that feels so distant, now.*

Selene stared at the bare words on the two scrolls, identical, but for the ink spatters on the one to Alexander. Signed them, exactly as they were. And asked Antyllus politely to put his seal on them, so that they could be passed to couriers and sent on their way.

Antyllus was surprised when Alexander showed up at Ostia the next morning, with an armed guard and a servant carrying a heavy chest as he knocked at their door. Antyllus could see weariness in the younger man's eyes—the strain of carrying the political weight of the Empire, while Caesarion was attending to the military half of the Roman equation. *It's only been a few months. He must have had to make some bad decisions, to look that tired already.*

Alexander clasped wrists with Antyllus politely, but didn't smile. "Congratulations on your marriage," the younger man said tersely, and accorded Selene, standing behind Antyllus, a brief nod and a single word: "Sister." No hug, no embrace for his youngest sibling.

Then he opened the chest, which was filled to bursting with coin, and told Antyllus, just as politely, "Caesarion sent a letter, asking me to ensure that you received Selene's dowry in full when you passed through."

"I wasn't going to charge you interest for keeping it for us," Antyllus replied, smiling. "And gods know, I don't want to keep a guard on my quarters at all times in a *castra*. You've wasted a trip here, Alexander. Take it back with you; I'll collect it later, when Selene needs it for the household accounts."

"No," Alexander replied calmly. "We need this off our books. I can send it to the Antonii villa instead, but I'd greatly prefer that it be signed for by your own hand."

Antyllus frowned at him. "So businesslike."

"We Julii have loaned money to three other major families at the moment. They're supposed to be repaying with interest, but I'm beginning to feel as if the word of a patrician isn't what it used to be. I'm debating sending thugs to their homes—the politest thugs I can find, mind you—and inquiring as to which of their knees they'd prefer to have broken."

Alexander's tone was sour, and Antyllus laughed. "I trust the word of *your* particular patrician family. But if you really want your accounts up to date, I can ride back with you, get it into my father's vault, update the books, and ride back." He made a face at the thought. "That'll delay our departure by a day, however. We're supposed to leave with the evening tide." He paused, gesturing to a seat. "Won't you have lunch with us, before you force me to ride to Rome and back?" He kept the humor in his voice.

"I'm not forcing you to do anything," Alexander said, shrugging.

Antyllus paused, frowning. He and Alexander had usually gotten along for the past four campaign seasons, always working together well. At the moment, however, Alexander's dark eyes were closed to him. "Is everything all right?" he asked Alexander directly, as he opened the door, asking Alexander's servant to go down to the kitchen and have them send up lunch.

A blink. "Nothing's wrong," Alexander returned mildly. "I simply have many, *many* pots boiling back in Rome at the moment. If you wouldn't mind? Please convey my sympathies to Tiberius and Drusus, when you catch up with them in Britannia. Their mother and several of her servants passed away some time ago, and while I already sent them a letter on the subject, I'd like a more personal touch on it. Also, you might tell Tiberius, in his ear, that it's being bruited about as the wrath of Asclepius—a sudden, terrible illness that occurred just after his mother supposedly profaned an item that carried the blessing of the healing god." Alexander's eyebrows went up. "Of course, I'm sure that's just superstition, casting blame on the victims of a terrible, swift disease."

Antyllus blinked several times. "I see," he said, finally, and heard the clatter of feet on the stairs as servants now returned, carrying platters of food. "I'll pass along your condolences," he added, as the servants began to lay out the meal on the room's small table, and then held Selene's chair for her, so she could sit down comfortably. "Sit," he told Alexander, genially, wanting to reach out to his brother-in-law, who seemed more distant than was his wont. "I'm sure you'll want to chat with Selene, after all. You haven't seen your sister in months."

Alexander glanced briefly at Selene, then back at Antyllus. "If you insist," he replied, taking a seat. "Though I can't think of anything I have to say that Selene might enjoy hearing," he added, looking at Selene for a moment. "I've been relieved of my betrothal to your old friend, Octavia, but that's hardly news at this point, as that ended two months ago." A little shrug. "Apparently, my offer to have you come and keep my house for me, so that you wouldn't have to get married with such haste, wouldn't have been quite the issue that our mother made it out to be, after all." Now Alexander looked directly at Antyllus. "But as I'm sure you're both overjoyed at how it all turned out, there's really not much else to discuss on that front, is there?" He raised his eyebrows, and directed his attention to the food in front of him. Not taking more than a thin slice of bread and dabbing it lightly in oil.

Antyllus felt his teeth snap shut as he took his own seat. The urge to smack Alexander at the moment was very strong, though the words and the tone weren't sarcastic— rather, they were uninflected. But they were a strong suggestion that some of Selene's siblings had been inclined to keep her from marrying in a rush. "Didn't feel like haste to me," Antyllus said, picking up a spinach-stuffed sardine in his fingers and popping it in his mouth. After a moment, he added, "My father requested the match for three years. There was no *haste* about it."

"Not for you," Alexander agreed, nodding.

And Antyllus looked at Selene . . . and saw absolutely nothing in his wife's face. Waited for her to respond. And when she said nothing, he sighed internally and prompted, "Selene, did it feel hasty to you?" A smile, trying to coax one from her, as well. *I have been trying to make her smile, and keep her smiling, for months now. I thought I'd convinced her that I wasn't a monster. And yet, every time I think I've made a step forward with her, I wind up two steps back again.*

Selene shook her head and looked at the table. "I made the decision, Alexander," she said quietly. "And Caesarion made it clear that I'd taken more than enough of everyone's time in so doing."

Antyllus grimaced with irritation. Caesarion *had* been abrupt about the whole thing. "In his defense, my lark, he was in the middle of dealing with an assassination attempt. I'd have been abrupt with us, too. If I'd been him, and not myself." He waved a finger, pretending to do sums in his head. "I think that one added up, in the end." He gave Alexander a glance, realizing abruptly, *He's still irked because his sister didn't wind up marrying his friend. All it was, was a* crush, Antyllus thought. *Yes, we put Tiberius out a bit, but* he *was the one offended, not Alexander. And Tiberius clasped my wrist and offered me the gift of time and space to help clear her head.*

He cleared his throat, still trying to mend ties. "Selene, why don't you tell your brother a little about our travels? I'm sure he'd enjoy hearing about what you thought of the Scythians and the Sarmatians. Maybe something about the music you heard played along our route?" *Stop punishing her,*

Alexander.

Antyllus watched Selene close her eyes. "The journey was very interesting," she replied, her voice thin.

The words hung there, unaccompanied by any of their kin. Antyllus cleared his throat. "The mountains of Cappadocia were really beautiful, weren't they?" he offered. "Still covered in snow in places, so we had to detour several times. One avalanche in a lifetime is enough for me." He paused, and prompted again, "And the Sarmatians, lark? You seemed to enjoy the time we spent among them."

"I found their weaving techniques very interesting."

She kept using the same word, *interesting*, but her voice remained dull. Antyllus couldn't decide if it was because Alexander's distant attitude had hurt her feelings, or if she genuinely didn't *care*. "Selene decided to keep one of the slaves they traded with us, mostly because the girl trained with their rug-makers."

Social conversation was the lifeblood of Roman politics; when Romans met, they *talked*. For hours, usually. Antyllus could handle almost any group, but at the moment, he felt as if he were drowning in an ocean of silence. "Has been teaching the girl Latin, too. The rest of the goods we wound up with, besides the bows, I already sent to my father's villa for storage. No sense, really, in dragging that all to Britannia."

Alexander nodded, and looked once more at Antyllus. "It all sounds fascinating. Perhaps one day, you'll write a book about your travels, Antyllus. Should be rather more accurate than Herodotus, so I'll look forward to reading it whenever you get around to it." He tossed his piece of bread, of which Antyllus didn't think he'd eaten a single crumb, down on the table. "I really must be going. If you want to accompany me and my sister's dowry back to Rome, we'll need to take horse shortly."

"And leave Selene here alone?" Antyllus returned, immediately. "I'll hire a *carruca* for her." He glanced across the table at his wife. "No need for a donkey so close to Rome." He paused, and offered, gently, taking her hand in his across the table, "Of course, if we're going so far as Rome anyway, perhaps you might just like to stay there for the campaign season? My youngest sister's staying with my uncle, Lucius, until my father sends for her to come to Alexandria . . . oh, wait. She might already have left. Antonia the Elder married Lepidus' son years ago. And Antonia Major, poor thing, was just married to Ahenobarbus."

"Poor thing, indeed," Alexander muttered. "Ahenobarbus is an ass."

Antyllus grimaced. He hadn't liked that particular match at all. "Ironically, my father only set that one up, because you were set to marry Octavia," he noted. "Otherwise, you could have been my brother-in-law twice over, Alexander." He turned back to Selene, ignoring Alexander's slight snort at his words. "I expect she's in Britannia herself by now. You must remember her." Antyllus paused, drawing a blank.

"I remember her," Selene confirmed dully. "I've lived in your father's house the past three campaign seasons." She paused. "She's very kind. Always cheerful." Another pause, as Selene clearly dredged up more words. "She had a garden of medicinal herbs in the *peristylium*."

Antyllus' mind churned, trying to take into account the need for a sudden change of plans. *Selene can't stay in the family villa all by herself. Father stripped it down to a skeleton staff, sold off the slaves he didn't want to take to Egypt, and all that. It's being maintained, but she'd rattle there, like a single pea in a very large pod, on her own.* "I'm sure my uncle would welcome you, Selene. He has daughters, after all."

"Your uncle Lucius?" Selene repeated, her tone dispirited.

"He's Tribune of the Plebs again this year. Lots of socializing, lots of dinner parties—" Antyllus paused. *Which she hates.* He glanced at Alexander, who stood by the door now, his eyebrows raised. "Alexander once offered to look after you in the absence of the rest of your family," he suggested slowly. *Though gods know, his tone hasn't been welcoming so far today.* "It's an option."

And to his shock, a tear trickled down her cheek. "I hate all the travel," Selene admitted, her voice dull, her eyes fixed on the table in front of her. "I hate the fleas, I hate the food. I hate being sick *from* the food, and from the movement of the ships. I hate being exhausted and hurting at the end of every day. I know it's all an adventure for you," she added quietly, "and that you enjoy every minute of it. But I hate it."

Antyllus' hand convulsed on hers, and he was acutely aware of Alexander's eyes on them. "Lark, why didn't you *say* something before now?" he asked, his voice gentle as he walked around the table to crouch beside her.

"There isn't any point in complaining when there's no place else to be but where you are." She scrubbed at her face for a moment. "Complaining wouldn't have magically brought me back to Rome."

"Fleas?" Alexander muttered, clearly stuck on a previous comment still.

"Happened in one inn in Syria," Antyllus shot back tersely. "I don't have a network of social contacts in the eastern provinces, so we couldn't stop over at various nobles' houses. I'd have gone over to sleeping just in our tents, but I didn't want Selene to miss the comforts of baths and such for too long." He reached up and touched Selene's face gently. "Lark, is it just the travel? Don't I treat you well?"

Her eyes flicked up from the table. "No, you're always very kind to me," Selene replied earnestly. "You're kind. Brave. Strong. Smart. You go out of your way to . . . show how fond you are of me. You're reasonable and rational. So much so that sometimes, I wish you'd just yell at me, because them I wouldn't have to feel so guilty at . . . being how I am." She closed her eyes. "I'm nothing that you'd have wanted if our parents hadn't made such a fuss. I'm not brave. I'm not . . . adventurous." The words, now that she'd finally started saying them, welled out of her. "You'll be disappointed in me if I don't go with you—"

"Most women *don't* go with their husbands into the field. I won't deny that I've always pictured my wife being with me, the way my mother went with my father, but if it makes you *this* unhappy, of course, you don't have to come with me." Antyllus shrugged a little helplessly. *What else can I possibly say?*

"See? You're so *reasonable*," she said, her voice catching. "Why don't you ever *yell*?"

"My mother and father yelled at each other all the time. Never seemed to solve anything, though my father looked as if he'd been kicked by a mule when she died." He picked up her cold hands in his, rubbing the palms gently with his thumbs. "I want you with me. But I'll survive if you don't come along. I'm not even one for camp followers, so you don't even need to worry about that. You can stay in Rome. We'll work something out."

She didn't look up. "I don't want to stay in Rome," she admitted, and *that* confused Antyllus to no end.

"But you just said—"

A snort from Alexander by the door reminded Antyllus that his brother-in-law remained in the room. But before he could ask for privacy, Selene said rapidly, as if trying to get the words out all at once, "I wouldn't be any happier in Rome, sitting in your uncle's house with strangers, or in the Julii villa that I know isn't my home anymore. I . . . do *like* being with you." Her voice faltered.

Well, that's at least something, Antyllus thought, only to have the thoughts erased by her next words. "You haven't done anything wrong, Antyllus. It's me. *I'm* wrong. And I can't seem to fix myself. I *have* tried. I just can't seem to be happy, no matter how I tell myself that this was the right decision. That I should be grateful for what I have. For your kindness. For the fact that you're . . . you're fond of me." She swallowed again. "And now I'm *pregnant* and I'm just going to be sick and tired even more of the time."

Antyllus stared at her, stunned by the depth of the unhappiness in her, as well as by her final words. This was *not* how he'd ever imagined hearing that particular piece of information, as tears slipped from his wife's eyes. "Pregnant?" he repeated, a little dazed. He was *elated* by the news, but he could see that she wasn't. "How long have you known?" he asked, wanting to wrap his arms around her, but not knowing if she'd even accept it at the moment. He settled for touching her hair, gently.

"A week or so. I've never been late before. Ever." She shook her head. "I feel like I should drag myself back to Egypt and shove the baby in my mother's arms and ask if she's finally happy with me, since nothing else I've ever done has pleased her." She swallowed, her throat working for a moment. "There are days that I wish I weren't who I am. Not a Julia. Some days, I wish I had never even been born."

"To Dis with your mother," Antyllus told her firmly, and gave up, standing to wrap his arms around her. Trying to warm her with touch. *She did say she liked being with me. That's . . . something. I've known something's been wrong for a while now, but this is the first she's actually* <u>talked</u> *about it.* "She gets about as much say in anything in your life now as the corner flower vendor. Look, it. . . " *Doesn't matter to me where you are, so long as you're happy,* didn't seem the right way to say what he needed her to understand. "The most important thing to me," he said, adjusting the phrasing with a diplomat's care, "is that you're happy. I have to go to Britannia. No choice in the matter. I will say that a *castra* is basically a walled city, love. I wouldn't be asking you to come into forward areas with me." He kissed the top of her head, his own mind churning. "Once we get there, you'd be staying in one place for weeks or months at a time. There will be other wives there, and their daughters. Even one of my sisters, as I said." He paused. "And sometimes, it feels like you can't get *away* from the sound of bawling infants in a *castra*, because between the wives and the, ah, sweethearts of the men, someone always has a new baby. Plenty of *medici* and midwives on hand, in other words." Now wasn't the time to mention how often the 'sweethearts' of the enlisted men tended to be natives of a given area. Who gravitated to the walls of the *castra* for both safety and food. "I'll leave it up to you, though. I'd definitely prefer to have you with me. But seeing the woman I love miserable isn't really what I want out of life." *I can't do better than that. I can't leave the military in the middle of the campaign season for no better reason than an unhappy wife. I need at least another three or four years before floating my name for* <u>quaestor</u>.

She'd looked up at that last. Not really a sparkle in her eyes, but the beginnings of relief, he thought. "So . . . only a few more weeks of travel?" Selene said, quietly.

"Shouldn't be more than that, no. Not for a bit."

"Then I'll go with you. And I promise that I'll try to be better." She swallowed. "I don't know why I can't just manage that on my own."

Antyllus kissed her hair again. "Some people are melancholic by nature. I don't think you are, though. But I'm not sure how many times I have to remind you that I'm not a monster. *Talk* to me before things build up in your head." He sighed, and then abruptly realized that Alexander had tactfully withdrawn from the room at some point. "Let me go deal with your brother. I'll be right back."

Outside, Alexander appeared to be getting ready to head back to Rome. Antyllus caught him just as he swung up into the saddle. "Leaving me here without getting my signature?" he asked the younger man dryly.

"I'll consider that you're a man of honor, and won't try to say that we never delivered the coin," Alexander said, turning his horse around to face east now. "You're doing a good job with Selene."

Antyllus blinked. The words of approval, given Alexander's clear antagonism towards the marriage, meant something. "I've never had to work so hard in my life to make someone smile," he admitted. "Besides Octavia, who didn't smile on principle. It's . . . draining. I don't suppose you know how it feels, though."

Alexander gave him a look. "Have you ever *met* Tiberius?" he asked, dryly. "He's a confirmed melancholic. With quite a bit more reason than Selene, given all the shit Octavian did to him. The weekly beatings with a stick, administered by one of the slaves, weren't even the half of it." Alexander's eyes met Antyllus' steadily.

"Octavia felt that *firm discipline* was necessary, too." Antyllus grimaced. "But Father usually backed me up. Hate to think what life would have been like if Father hadn't been there." *Of course, all I need to do is look at my brother Jullus, and I can see some of the results.*

"My point was, I'm used to dealing with his periodic

bouts of self-loathing and working him out of them. Most of which have to do with feeling he isn't living up to some impossible ideal of honor and duty. I haven't a clue what Selene's upset about, beyond the travel. Which is annoying, yes, but necessary if you want to get from one place to another."

Antyllus shook his head. "Honestly?" he said, with a flash of insight that surprised him. "You, Alexander, are angry at quite a bit of the world. You've said, in my hearing, that there are days that you hate Rome for what its people make you have to do. Imagine how much anger there must be, locked up in Selene. Three brilliant older siblings. And the only gifts she has, are ones that women of her social class can't express. She can't go on a stage to play her music—not that she has the temperament for public performance. She can't go into trade, though her weaving's good enough that she could have, if she'd just been born a plebeian, not a patrician. None of you have looked twice at her since your father died—and he was the only one who called her his lark." *A name I've picked up for use on her. Maybe I shouldn't use it. Maybe it impinges too much on the sacred memory of her father. I'll ask her.* "She's angry and resentful, and she has absolutely no way to express it." Antyllus paused, putting it all together in his head. It made perfect sense. "Gods, Eurydice used to comment that Selene resented her. Didn't give her the proper respect; Eurydice wouldn't tolerate it, so Selene stopped showing the resentment. Did everything in her power to please Eurydice since then. Striving to please others is the very definition of a *phlegmatic*, not a melancholic, I might add."

"This is just a fit of the sulks, then?" Alexander said, raising his eyebrows.

"No," Antyllus replied, wanting to shake Alexander for a moment. "You're angry at the world. But *you* can fight. You can send your agents across the known world to deal with people who irritate you. People call you Cerastes, and step out of your way. She said she wished I'd yell at her. So she wouldn't have to feel *guilty* about being . . . angry and resentful. And being a woman, she can't really grab a sword and ride off to battle. So all the anger she can't direct out at the world, she focuses on whoever she *can*. Me, but it makes her feel guilty. Or on herself. Till she wishes she's never been born."

Antyllus wondered if it was just his desire to be a diplomat talking, or if it had something to do with being several years older than either Alexander or Selene . . . and detached from the problem. "I don't yell. I don't particularly get angry, unless it's a matter of life or death." He shrugged. *Even when I kill in battle, it's a distant thing, most of the time. A bow in my hand, a hundred feet from my target. Usually, so many arrows in the air that I don't know if mine hit anything till I go out afterwards to retrieve them, and find my fletchings lodged in this body or that. There's nothing visceral in archery. There's just calmness.* "Seems to me, she needs my help to get rid of some of the anger. And that will, in turn, balance her body's humors, and the fits of melancholia should pass. Doubt we'll even need to talk to a *medicus* about leeches or black bile or whatever else." *None of which seem a good idea, given her pregnancy.*

Alexander just stared at him for a moment. "You're a *sanguine*," he accused, after a moment, but he shook his head and a smile escaped him.

Antyllus shrugged. "Takes one to know one. I'll pass your, ah, condolences on to Tiberius and Drusus, as you requested." He knew of the strained relationship between Livia and her sons, and thus, his words held a certain politely dubious tone. "Safe journey back to Rome."

"And the gods keep you in their hands in Britannia." Alexander shook his head. "You'll need them looking out for you." He paused. "Britannia's home to the druids, after all. Them and all their circles of stone, and their words of power in the earth."

"We make our own luck," Antyllus countered, smiling slightly. But his smile faded as he looked out to sea. "I'll take all the luck I can make, and any fortune the gods see fit to offer me," he finally added, and the two men clasped wrists. "The gods know, Caesarion couldn't let the druids' actions in Hispania pass unanswered. But I hope we can manage the war there this time better than the three times it's been attempted before."

End of Book II

Notes

Edda-Earth's history diverged from that of Real-Earth thousands of years ago, both in and around the time of Akhenaten, and, most notably, in and around the failed assassination of Julius Caesar. All dates in Edda are presented as AC, after the ascension of Caesar, and are thus offset 44 years from the BCE/CE system we use in our world today. All dates are thus given as "AC," or "after the Ascension of Caesar."

Glossary

Accipiter, Accipitra, Accipitris — Accipiter is the term for a hawk; Accipitris is the plural. The female ending of *Accipitra* is non-standard.

Aediles — Elected officials in charge of putting on games, festivals, and renovating public works.

Alaude — The Larks. Nickname for the Fifth Legion.

Annona — Measures of wheat and bread granted by the government to the poor of Rome. A dole, effectively.

Armilustrium — October 19; the end of the war season, and the day on which weapons are ceremonially cleaned, anointed, and put up for the year.

Aquilus — Eagle.

Atrium — One of the two open-air sections of a Roman villa. Where the atrium was the formal area, and more traditional, being officially the 'bedroom of the mother of the house,' (not that any woman slept there) the *peristylium* was seen by some as a Hellene affectation.

The atrium was generally located closer to the entrance, it's the more formal of the two areas. Think of it as an outdoor parlor with fountains, possibly open-air, possibly with only a small oculus open to the sky, and the peristylium was the outdoor living room, and you'll be close.

Ballistae – Siege weapons that hurled carefully-shaped stone bullets. Specialized siege weapons that could hurl arrows also existed, but *ballistae* far more commonly used stones.

Bona Dea — The "Good Goddess," whose secret name was never spoken to men. Her ritual, held in early December of each year, was the only day on which patrician women could leave their houses unattended, conduct blood sacrifices on their own, and drink unwatered wine. These observances were eyed with some anxiety by Roman men, who felt their wives and daughters required their constant supervision and control. Only one man every entered into their ceremonies, in disguise as a woman; at which point the ceremonies of that year were considered completely desecrated.

Bulla — hollow golden amulet worn by boys until adulthood; contains many small charms, including phallic images, meant to tie the boy to his household *lares* and ward off bad luck, jealousy, and magic. Set aside when the *toga virilis* is given, such amulets are kept in the house so that the amulet can be worn during adulthood during times of magical danger, or to ward off jealousy.

Caligae — Boots made up of dozens of straps of leather, with iron nails in the soles, worn by legionnaires. These boots were almost as much a symbol of citizenship as the toga, though not quite. Many men serving as auxiliaries affiliated with the legions, in order to *attain* citizenship and its rights and privileges (including immunity to torture) wore *caligae* in the course of normal duty before earning their togas.

Carruca — an early closed carriage used by Roman noblewomen, the invalids, and the infirm who could not ride, or who were prohibited from doing so by cultural reasons.

Circumvallation – a line of fortifications built around a besieged location, to block the defenders in, and protect a field camp against sorties from the defenders. Romans saw little point in pitched battles when they could let their engineering defeat the enemy for them.

Clementia — Clemency. Mercy, but in a sense that says "You live, but only because I, in my power, have permitted you to do so."

Collegia — Groups of colleagues, usually men of equivalent rank or profession, or those who lived in the same neighborhood. *Collegia* served a number of purposes, including, but not limited to: providing a social circle of drinking brothers/lodge brothers; providing a neighborhood watch; providing a place where money could be held in trust for religious observances; overseeing civic/religious duties on holidays.

Conditum paradoxum — Heavily sweetened and spiced wine, served at major events such as funerals, homecomings, welcomes, and holy days. Almost all wine was served watered, and was frequently flavored with condensed fruit syrups, effectively making the favorite beverage of ancient Rome a wine cooler. Unwatered wine was generally reserved for sacrifice to the gods, and men *could* drink it unwatered if they chose, but usually did not. Women could only drink wine unwatered on Bona Dea.

Compitalia — Festival beginning in early Ianuarius honoring the *lares* of each household with offerings of cakes at crossroads. And in every household, slaves and masters alike left representations of themselves outside the doors—small poppets, identical to the masters, hanging from nooses, and small balls of cotton or wool for the slaves—in a bid to keep Mania (the underworld goddess who *wasn't* Proserpina) from taking any of their lives in sacrifice. Any resemblance to Halloween *isn't* strictly in the eye of the beholder.

Cubicula — The small rooms of a Roman villa, including bedrooms. Singular: *cubiculum*.

Devotio — Root of the word devotion. This meant both the willingness of the ordinary soldier to die in battle, and was also a specialized term for a ritual in which a leader of a group of soldiers would pledge his life to Pluto, Proserpina, Jupiter, and Quirinus, offering himself in sacrifice in battle, for the lives of his men and the victory of his army. This sacrifice was almost inevitably accepted.

Divalia — Festival held on December 21 of each year, dedicated to Angerona and Voluptia, goddesses of peace, plenty, and joy.

Domina, dominus — Lady or lord.

Equestris — Horseman; nickname for the Tenth Legion, an infantry division, is a homage to some of them having mounted up to accompany Caesar as his bodyguards. Otherwise, used in mild irony for that legion.

Ferrata — Ironclad. *Nom de guerre* of the Sixth Legion

Frontem allargate — Form staggered formation!

Galli — Castrated priests of Cybele, who dressed as women after mutilating themselves in her rites. No Roman-born man was permitted to be castrated, or to join her cult.

Garum — Fish sauce.

Imperator — Technically, the leader of an army invested with *imperium* by the Senate. By this point in time, the dictator-for-life position taken by Caesar and by Caesarion has become solidly associated with this term.

Imperium — the legal authority of leadership invested in consuls or imperators by the Senate (in theory), which enabled them to recruit armies. Someone without sufficient imperium could not command armies.

Infamio — The condition of infamy. An *infamis* (male singular) or *infames* (plural) were people who had put themselves beyond the social pale, sunk themselves below the condition of slaves. A male on the receiving end of penetrative sexual relations was an *infamis*; a freeborn or noble-born male who became a gladiator — effectively willingly becoming a slave, giving someone else the right to order him to die — was an *infamis*. Actors, who by custom handled the masks of dead ancestors, and wore those masks in a bid to allow the ghosts, the *penates*, to enter into them, were also considered unclean — almost as unclean as, say, mortuary workers or Untouchables in the Indian caste system.

Infamio had serious social repercussions, including being stripped of citizenship and potentially even property. But with that in mind, gladiators enjoyed a certain amount of panache. And even *they* had their pride, and limits to what they considered acceptable behavior.

Accusations of behavior that was infamous was rife in the rhetoric of the Senate, with Senators almost constantly accusing one another of terrible misdeeds and peccadillos. And given that duels were not a thing in their culture, the only recourse for such accusations were libel lawsuits, or crushing the house of the accused in some fashion.

Landica — Obscene term for the clitoris.

Lares — House-spirits, or small gods.

Libra/librae — A Roman measure of weight, equivalent to .725 modern pounds, or 328.9 g

Lorica hamata — *Lorica* means *body armor*; the hamata was a chain shirt, commonly worn by many legionnaires and their Gallic adversaries.

Lorica plumata — The *plumata* was a type of scaled armor designed to look like bird feathers and often gilded. Due to the expense of crafting it, this armor was generally only owned by high-ranking officers.

Lorica segmentata — This is the prototypical Hollywood legionnaire armor, similar to a plate hauberk for the torso and shoulders. It would not be developed in Real-Earth until the mid-Augustan period, and only saw a couple of centuries of use.

Lorica squamata — armor of heavy, overlapping scales favored by legionnaires who didn't affect a flashy muscle cuirass. This is Caesarion's personal armor choice through the first several books.

Ludes/ludi — Games offered for ritual reasons or for purposes of public entertainment. Could include gladiatorial combat, horse or chariot races, or other activities.

Lunula — Amulet worn by girls before becoming women. Burned, along with all their other possessions, on becoming women/wives for the first time, and being permitted to wear a *stola*. Intended to bind them to their household *lares* and offer the protection of the spirits, the burning symbolically cuts their ties to their original family in the tradition of female exogamy common to Rome.

Lustration — Ritual in which an infant is made known to the spirits and people of the city to which it will belong as a resident; generally involves circling the city several times, and the child's name being made known after anointment.

Malleolus — A hammer, or maul.

Mappae — Napkins.

Matronalia — The day on which Mars was theoretically born to Juno, if you follow Roman mythology. If you follow Hellene myths, Ares is one of Hera's brothers. In any event, this is Mother's Day. On which sons and fathers recognize the efforts of their mothers and wives throughout the year with gifts. . . and on which day, the mother of the house must cook for and serve everyone, including the slaves. All women's hair must be unbound, and not a single knot in their garments.

Medicus — Physician

Munera — Games that included gladiatorial combat.

Munifex — A non-specialist soldier, or *milites*.

Novendialis — The ninth and final required day of official mourning for a dead family member. For the wealthy, this involved sacrifices, actors hired to wear the masks of dead ancestors, and the offering of games in honor of the chthonic gods.

Optimates — The "Best men," otherwise known as the *boni*, or "good men," these men were a political faction of traditionalists and conservatives in the late Roman Republic, who tried to limit the power of public assemblies and the Tribune of the Plebs.

Oppidum — A walled city or hill fort, particularly used to describe the fortified cities of non-Romans.

Panis — The round emmer-grain bread on which most of Rome lived.

Parazonium — Long, leaf-bladed dagger carried by senior officers as a symbol of rank. Also almost always carried by Roma in images of the city personified as a goddess.

Penates — The spirits of the dead.

Peristylium — One of the two open-air areas of a Roman villa, the other being the atrium. This section was added to Roman houses after an influx of Hellene culture, and was a more informal garden, equivalent to an outdoor living room.

Pes/pesi — A Roman foot, or .971 English feet/296 mm.

Pilum; pl. Pila — Long spear carried by legionnaires.

Proscription — Legal proceeding by which an otherwise sacrosanct, inviolate Roman citizen could be stripped of his citizenship and its protection from torture, etc., and could also be stripped of his lands and money. People who aided proscribed individuals who fled the state, could be proscribed themselves.

Pugio — A short, wide-bladed dagger carried by every legionnaire.

Quaestorium — The storehouse of a legion; it can double as a prison for slaves taken in battle, or important prisoners.

Salii — The leaping priests of Mars. Limited to twelve in number, they were a rare life-time appointment to their positions, and technically barred from pursuing political office, but if they were *appointed* to a higher office, that office superseded that of the *salii*. They were in charge of opening and closing the war-season in March and October, and theoretically protected the sacred and magical shield of Numa, the first king of Rome. So long as that shield remained in Roman hands, it ensured that their civilization would remain the preeminent one on Earth.

Sambucae — Shipboard siege ladders. Largely ineffective in combat in the pre-Imperial era.

Saturnalia — Festival beginning on December 23, honoring Saturn. Like Matronalia, social inversions rule the festival, with the servants in charge of the house, and the father of the house serving them. During the Punic Wars, after a crushing defeat by the Carthaginians, a prophecy suggested that if the Romans adopted Hellene observances on this day, Rome would appease both the Hellene gods, and potentially Baal Hamon of Carthage, and win victory. Thus, the holiday was Hellenized, and eventually extended out to three days instead of one. People exchanged gifts, ate and drank too much, and masters served the slaves. Any resemblance to modern observances of Christmas and Boxing Day are entirely accurate.

Subligaria — Loincloths worn by most men under their clothing, and by women on their menstrual flows, or by some male and female athletes.

Tablinium — Room in a Roman villa located between the *peristylium* and the atrium. Quite often, only a window, curtain, or some manner of wooden screen separated this roofed-over room from these two open areas, allowing air circulation. Caesarion uses the *tablinium* as his study.

Taraxacum — Dandelions

Testudo — "Tortoise." A slow-moving, defensive formation in which men of a legion move into a tight square and the men in the middle raise their shields overhead in an overlapping, scale-like pattern to hold off incoming missiles.

Testudinem formate — Turtle formation!

Tinnunculi — kestrels

Triclinium — This word refers both to the formal dining room of a Roman villa and to the couches that occupied it. Reclining to eat was originally a Hellene custom adopted by Romans; significantly, however, most Romans did not separate the genders at meals, unless absolute sticklers for Hellene manners.

Toga picta — The 'colored' or 'painted' toga, chiefly used by kings in ancient Roman history, now chiefly the purple-dyed one worn by Imperators.

Toga virilis — The white toga given to a young boy when he becomes a man, officially. The toga may be presented by his family any time after the age of fourteen. Delaying it until the age of eighteen would indicate that his family didn't think much of him.

Vallum — a wooden palisade, part of the more elaborate circumvallation.

Uncia — A "thumb." Unit of measure equivalent to .971 inches/24.6 mm

Via — by way of, through; also, highway or road.

www.ingramcontent.com/pod-product-compliance
Lightning Source LLC
Chambersburg PA
CBHW071634260626
47170CB00001B/95